Michele Tracy Berger

Samantha Bryant

Jay Caselberg

Eddie Generous

DeAnna Knippling

Gregory L. Norris

...and more !

volume two

SToRiES wE TeLL AFTEr MiDNIGhT

EDITED BY
RACHEL A. BRUNE

XeroGravity,
Don't stay up
too late!

STORIES WE TELL
AFTER MIDNIGHT
VOLUME 2

edited by Rachel A. Brune

CRONE
GIRLS
press

Seaside, CA

ISBN: 978-1-952388-02-6 (print)
978-1-952388-03-3 (ebook)

Cover Design by James, GoOnWrite.com

Published by
Crone Girls Press

Crone Girls Press Trade Paperback Edition October 2020
Printed in the USA

Table of Contents

BEDTIME TALES

Nicola Lombardi

Translated by J. Weintraub

By then, only the light from the lamp sitting on top of the old, worm-eaten dresser was left, forsaken even by the delicate touch of the sun that, up to only a moment before, had tinted the dusty windows of the attic with a red haze. Giacomo and Chiara were lying flat, blissfully, on their stomachs, their elbows well-anchored to the floor, their small faces sunk between the palms of their hands.

Now that the fateful words, "...and they lived happily ever after," were softly fading into their ears, the silence returned, cradling in its quiet the rhythmic creak of the rocking chair.

"That was great," mumbled Chiara, moving her head grotesquely since, given her position, it was impossible for her to lower her chin.

"Good, good..." remarked their grandmother, moistening her dry lips with her tongue and continuing to rock back and forth. "I'd say that it's now time to go to bed, don't you think?"

Chiara looked at her brother who, being a year older than she, probably had greater experience with delaying the retreat into the bedroom. And, in fact, Giacomo did not disappoint her.

"Just one more!" he exclaimed. "Come on, Granma, tell us just one more, and then we'll go to bed!"

Chiara nodded eagerly.

"Look, children, it's already dark, and if your Mom and Dad come back and find you still..."

"No, no, don't worry," Giacomo said, interrupting her, sure of himself. "They never come back before eleven. There's still time. Come on, just one more story!"

Their grandmother smiled wearily, passing her hand over her eyes.

"This is really the last, and then you'll go like good little children right to bed. Promise?"

"I promise!" the two children blurted out in a single voice.

The rocking shadow of the old woman continued to sway through the flickering yellow puddle cast by the lamp against the sloping beams of the attic, and the now invisible spider webs prepared to capture the words that were beginning to weave another story in the silence.

"So... once upon a time, there were two children, two wonderful children, brother and sister, who were named, just like you, Giacomo and Chiara." A tried-and-true technique, and always effective in drawing the audience directly into the tale being told. The eyes of the two children glimmered in the shadows.

"By now it was getting late, and yet still they did not want to get into bed. Their grandmother, with great patience, had already told them a wonderful tale, and yet still they were not happy. 'Another one! Tell us another one,' the two children repeated in chorus. And so the grandmother, although old and tired by then, began once more to tell a story. Evening had fallen all about the comfortable and quiet attic, and Giacomo and Chiara were listening in fascination. At a certain point, though, the grandmother, who was very, very old, let out a deep and profound sigh..."

And here, seasoned by years of dramatic storytelling, the woman stopped short and resoundingly sighed, as if to impart an even greater depth to her narrative; then she completed the sentence left hanging:

"...and then she died."

Both children shivered and exchanged glances, instinctively

consoling one another from the shock caused by that unwelcome and unexpected twist. Their grandmother, persistently rocking back and forth, continued:

"The two children, at first, did not realize what had happened, and so stayed quietly in place while their grandmother continued to tell her story. But before long, both Giacomo and Chiara noticed that their old grandma's voice had changed, that it had grown a bit deeper, as if it were coming from far away..."

The children lay there still, mouths wide open, almost frozen with fear. Their grandmother was play-acting brilliantly, and yet, was her voice now actually coming from the depths of a well dug into the night, into the black spaces around the attic? The effect, in any case, was chilling.

"The children were overcome with terror," the grandmother continued, and as she was speaking those words, her rocking chair—which already for some time had begun to slacken its tranquil roll—stopped with a sharp and sinister groan.

The woman did not make the slightest movement. She remained quietly seated there, with the circle of yellow light cutting across her face, leaving a portion of it at the mercy of the shadows.

The first to recognize what was happening was Giacomo, who, moving very slowly, brought his knees together, preparing to abandon the floor. The grandmother kept sitting there, her jaw hanging low enough to display, ominously, the arch of her teeth, and yet she continued to speak.

"Even though she was dead, the grandmother wanted to please her beloved grandchildren, and she continued to tell her story..."

As slowly as possible, Chiara followed her brother's example, curling up like a snail, ready to jump to her feet. The flickering light of panic began to gleam ever more intensely in their little eyes—wide open and riveted to those withered lips that framed the black crevice of her petrified mouth.

In the meantime, the grandmother went on, undeterred. "Giacomo and Chiara, horrified by this calamity, stood up from the floor and got ready to leave. By now they understood that this was not just some joke, and that their grandmother was really dead!"

It was in that same instant that Chiara stretched out a small trembling finger, silently directing her brother towards that stiffened mouth. A little spider, having emerged from behind the woman's neck, through her hair, was making its way across her wrinkled cheek; after a moment's hesitation, it decided that the cavern on the other side of those teeth, ought to furnish an exceptional den, and it went inside. This was the final straw.

Chiara cried out as if possessed, and Giacomo could do no less than copy her.

"Then the two children ran screaming into their bedroom, crawled under their blankets, and stayed there like good little angels until their parents came back from the theater."

The grandmother's dead voice continued echoing among the attic's beams as the children's shadows disrupted the calm that had been prevalent just a few moments before. Bumping awkwardly against the bureau, risking almost sending the lamp shattering to the floor, Giacomo and Chiara burst out from that infernal loft and rushed to hide themselves beneath the blankets in their room. But their grandmother's voice, deranged and cavernous, was not going to leave them, and it continued to reverberate throughout the house.

"Despite the fact her grandchildren had finally gone to bed, the grandmother, however, still had many tales to tell, yes, very, very many tales to tell."

Their parents, upon their return, found Giacomo and Chiara wrapped in their blankets, moist with sweat and tears, both in the grip of a nervous trauma that prevented them from forming coherent sentences.

"Your grandmother, where is she?" their mother asked in a low, murmuring voice.

Neither of the two managed to reply. But there was no need.

From the attic, the hoarse words simmering around the corpse, by now stiffening in its rocking chair, thundered mournfully like a curse from above.

"And the grandmother continued to tell her tales, tell her tales, tell her tales. No good carrying her away from the house and burying her. Her stories would be shadowing the nights of her beloved grandchildren for ever and ever."

About the Author

Nicola Lombardi (Italy, 1965) has been writing horror and weird fiction since the late '80s. He is author of various novels and collections, and has published two novelizations from the films of Dario Argento "Deep Red" and "Suspiria." He also works as a translator, essayist, and anthology editor. A full bibliography can be found on his website at: www.nicolalombardi.com.

About the Translator

A member of the Dramatists Guild, J. Weintraub has had one-act plays and staged readings produced throughout the world. He has published fiction, essays, and poetry in all sorts of literary places, from The Massachusetts Review to New Criterion, from Prairie Schooner to Modern Philology. As a translator he has introduced the Italian horror writer Nicola Lombardi to the English-speaking public and his annotated translation of Eugène Briffault's Paris à table: 1846 was published by Oxford University Press in 2018. More at https://jweintraub.weebly.com/

Baby Gray

Gregory L. Norris

"You fucking grave robber!" the man barked.

Jessup saw him from the cut of his eye, charging. One second, the man was ten feet tall, a Viking, all muscle, the embodiment of Tyler Jessup's death. Then Jessup blinked, and his killer shrank back to his actual size—somewhere around the five-eight, five-ten mark. His crown of Nordic blond hair evaporated. In its place, thinning mousy-brown locks. A mullet. The man's rage, however, was no illusion, and intensified as he knocked the cameraman aside. Jessup's second thought was for Harris Pastore's well-being; his first involved how fantastic this wrinkle would play out on the episode of *Storage Kings*. A gift, truly, from whatever dark gods had blessed him with this trashy but lucrative reality TV gig.

Nina screamed, "Oh my God—*Tyler, look out!*"

But at that pivotal moment, as the rest of the outbid looters on Storage Unit 217 parted, and the man whom he assumed was the former owner of its contents charged at him, Jessup made a decision: he could run or meet the enemy on his terms. One would play better for the camera, once more in Harris's steady hands.

Jessup dug in his boots and, at the last second, extended his meaty right arm, clotheslining the former Viking hard, right on his Adam's apple. A pitiful half-scream rose up, choked off before it could fully emerge. His attacker went down flailing. Even better, as the brief scream effectively ended, pissing himself.

Someone attempted to pull him back—the security guard, who hadn't done much in the way of his job description.

Jessup spat into the man's face. "Fucker came at me." He launched into a blue streak. Let them bleep over it in post-production. Ratings gold had dropped into his lap.

Jessup swung, growled, howled. Madness was money, and oh—what a moneymaker this day turned out to be!

* * *

The storage unit was filled with old furniture, boxes, and a filing cabinet. Jessup knew the backstory as soon as he and Nina began their inventory: Viking Mullet had lost a house to foreclosure, moved out everything he owned in haste. The filing cabinet's top drawers contained old family photos—unidentified faces and rooms, cats whose names had been forgotten. Nothing of value; he wouldn't make back the two grand the unit had cost him by selling off the furniture, which was all cheap particle board crap. Office furniture, especially used filing cabinets, was dead weight. He'd be lucky to sell the four-drawer beast for twenty bucks.

"Well, shit," Jessup grumbled.

A storm trooper, one of L.A.'s finest, strutted over. The day's heat put a sheen of sweat on the giant's face and dampened his armpits.

"Do you plan to file assault charges on Mister Dunlevy?" the officer asked.

Jessup slammed the open file drawer shut, the clang sharp on his ear. "Yes," he huffed. "No. I don't give a rat's ass as long as he stays the fuck away from me."

The policeman wiped his face. "That's big of you."

Jessup snorted and faced the other man directly. The cop had a full foot in height on him, easily. He couldn't tell if the camera was still recording, but Jessup assumed it was always on. "You tell Mister Dunlevy he can pick up his family photo albums in the dumpster."

He then turned back and, bending down, attempted to open the lowest of the filing cabinet's drawers. The rusting metal denied him access. Jessup pulled harder. The door rolled forward an inch before snapping back into place and ripping off the corner of his pointer finger's nail.

* * *

"It's all garbage," he sighed.

A beaut of a headache brewed at Jessup's temples. He popped a handful of aspirin, likely two or three too many, and washed them down with a gulp of cold beer. Jessup caught Nina's disapproval from the periphery as she gave up on another cardboard box full of the worthless. She wiped her hands on her jeans. It would take more than that, more than soap and water, to remove the oily residue he imagined now on them from touching the contents in the storage unit.

"Why anyone would pay to store this junk?" She sighed and kicked at something plastic on the concrete floor.

Jessup polished off the longneck in a single, deep pull and belched. "Silver lining possibilities, darling. The moment this episode airs, idiots'll be lining up to buy this crap online."

They'd potentially make more selling the relics of Dunlevy's unit than the network paid them per episode. Some fool might even float the mulleted fucker enough money to get it all back. Jessup could hope. In that vein, he reached for Nina. She sidestepped his arm. His hand brushed the length of her long mane of bottled platinum hair spilling down to her tiny ass.

"No?" Jessup asked.

"Try it again, Tyler, and I'll finish what that creep Dunlevy started," Nina said coolly. "I think I've had enough for one day."

She bid him goodnight until the cameras resumed taping in the morning and wandered out of the sad junkyard. Jessup pitched the empty bottle into the mess, heard it shatter, and locked up.

* * *

The house was your typical California ranch, earthquake-ready, surrounded by citrus trees that produced more bugs than edible fruit. The production had footed the bill to pretty it up for the camera crew, which normally meant only Harris, the line producer, and a handful of college dickheads dressed in basic black serving time until better gigs—and networks—came calling.

A warm breeze blew, and the leaves of the orange, lime, and lemon trees undulated, reminding him of some giant scaled horror wrapped around the house, ready to squeeze Jessup unconscious and then swallow him whole.

Jessup thumbed the electronic fob, securing his pickup. A sharp squawk chirped out. At least a full season of *Storage Kings* antics had paid off the truck. He still had fifteen years to go on the house and knew the show—which considered eight episodes a full season order—wouldn't last a third of the remaining mortgage. After it fizzled and passed into the ether, not likely to be remembered any more than the worst of the rest of reality TV, there'd only be auctions to fall back on. He wasn't there yet.

The motion sensor lights cast a rusty glow on the house and citrus trees. Jessup marched up to the front door, keys in hand. He punched in the security system's code—*JUNKMAN*—and turned on the kitchen light. Technically, Nina Westbridge was an employee as well as his right-hand sidekick on the show. She'd made it clear more than once that she had no interest beyond their working relationship. Jessup grumbled a curse and reached into the fridge for another beer. According to his fan mail, there were plenty of star fuckers out there aroused into frenzies over the character and role he'd been cast into by the show's producers, that of the Big Bad, the clear villain among younger, more attractive stars—the Giamboni brothers in particular. Apparently, numerous women—and more than a few male viewers— considered him ugly-sexy. Jessup could live with that. But it sucked spending the night alone.

Only, he soon discovered on his amble toward the bedroom, Jessup wasn't.

A light switched on at his right. The living room. Jessup whirled. The oldest man he'd ever encountered sat on the overstuffed sofa, looking as though the mushroom-colored microfiber cushions had engulfed him. Jessup barked another expletive and felt the bottle's sweaty neck slip from his fingers. He recovered, but not before slopping suds on the Persian carpet, a storage unit find he'd held onto.

"Who the fuck are you?" Jessup gasped.

In the second or so that followed, he absorbed additional details, like the man's blue velvet jacket and tailored pants, the rings on his bony fingers, one boasting a gigantic oxblood ruby, and the walking stick he balanced his hands atop, a twisting length of gnarled driftwood capped by an orb of smooth black stone. Jessup's imagination wondered if both rock and stick had tumbled through the waves together, fusing on the same stretch of beach.

"My name is Visoli Duran, Mister Jessup," the old man said. "And I am here in regard to my grandson. I believe you've met him. His name is Theodore Dunlevy."

Jessup's shock morphed into rage. "Dunlevy? That deadbeat prick?"

Bony fingers flexed on the walking stick's top. The old man's lips curled, forming a pale blue smile around the blackened nubs of his teeth. "My grandson's not the family's proudest moment, agreed, but you must understand his desperation regarding what's stored in the shadows inside that unit."

"I purchased that unit's contents fairly and by the law," Jessup spat. "What's in there's mine. So I suggest you shuffle your skeleton ass out of my house before you find yourself sharing a cell with your kin."

Duran held up a hand, gesturing for calm. "Mister Jessup, please. I'm here to make you a deal. I'll reimburse you whatever you paid, as well as a fee for your inconvenience."

"How the hell did you get into my house?"

"I'm an old man," Duran said. "I've been through many closed doors." He reached into his jacket pocket and produced a fat roll of Benjamins held together by a rubber band. "Would an additional ten percent be acceptable?"

Jessup's eyes narrowed. He watched, incensed, as the old man's shaking fingers counted out bills. "The trash in that unit isn't worth the price of a cup of coffee. Why would you be interested in shelling out a small fortune for Dunlevy's garbage?"

Duran's fingers ceased thumbing through bills. "Time is short, so I will be blunt, Mister Jessup. There is one object of interest among my grandson's garbage."

"Something valuable?"

Duran's eyes narrowed. Jessup's sudden grin evaporated as an icy chill tickled him unpleasantly behind the balls.

"Only to my family. An ancient curiosity of no interest to you or anyone else. You've seen the Gray Baby?"

Jessup shook his head. In the absence of conversation, the wind rippling through the citrus trees moaned with a disembodied voice. The sound crawled over Jessup's flesh. Duran's words made his pulse race and his mental wheels turn.

"I can guess what you're thinking, Jessup," the skeleton said. "It has no worth. Except to my bloodline."

"What's the Gray Baby?"

"Our legacy. It was a blessing at first—and a curse you won't want to inherit. When I was a young boy—"

"Five centuries ago?" Jessup chuckled. The joke went unappreciated.

"My father's sister, Carlotte, was an artist. She worked mostly in clay. Carlotte wanted nothing more than to be with child, but it wasn't to be. And so, she created one. A baby made of clay, which she carried with her everywhere she went. People ridiculed my Aunt Carlotte. Even I wasn't immune, though I pitied her."

Jessup exhaled through his nostrils. "Duran…"

"Until one night, I heard a child's hungry cries coming from Carlotte's room in the attic. I crept upstairs in my stocking feet, looked through the keyhole, and what did I see? The child, struggling in her arms. Not alive, no, for it was an abomination formed from my aunt's tears and sorrow, with a belly as empty as she who birthed it."

Jessup reached for his cell. "I'm calling the cops." He pulled the phone out of his pocket and started to dial.

"*Jessup*," Duran barked, and the intensity in the old man's voice sent ice through his arteries.

Jessup's finger stilled. His heart galloped.

"Hear my words. You are no better than any other tomb

robbers who've desecrated the sacred vaults of their victims throughout history."

"Victim?" Jessup parroted. "Fuck you, *Tutankhamun*."

He turned away from Duran and finished dialing. On the second ring, Duran said, "Don't wake up the Gray Baby, Jessup. He rises hungry. Hungry for—"

"911. What's your emergency?" a disinterested male voice asked from the other end of the phone call.

"—*blood!*"

Jessup turned back. Visoli Duran was gone.

"Hello?" the dispatcher pressed.

"Um," Jessup said. A shiver teased the fine hairs at the nape of his neck. He fought it, failed. The shiver tumbled. The only way out of the living room was past him or through the windows, both of which were still down and locked.

Thinking on his feet, Jessup said he'd made a mistake, was trying to dial 411. They sent a cruiser anyway, and Jessup signed an autograph on the policeman's warning form.

* * *

Jessup didn't sleep, even with most of the lights on and after checking every corner of the house, making sure Duran wasn't still lurking about the place. Maybe he should have taken the dusty old prick's money. But the memory of the rusty filing cabinet drawer in the storage unit lit a fire within his psyche. Additional conflagrations burned in his belly and at the back of his throat.

His mind kept returning to the old man's words. Slippery fucker—whatever was contained in that drawer *was* valuable. Family treasure, no doubt. If he opened it and found a gray ceramic baby, he knew that if he gave it a shake, the damn thing would jingle from all the gold coins and precious gemstones sealed within.

Soaked in sweat, he tore back the covers and pulled on the same clothes and boots shed at the side of the bed hours earlier. Not even 4 a.m., according to the clock. Stopping only long enough to relieve his bladder, Jessup headed out the door.

* * *

Paying so steep a price at auction for 217 gave him twenty-four-hour access to the unit. Jessup parked the truck across from the storage space, removed his padlock, and rolled up the gate. The sound struck his ears at so early an hour twice as loudly as it would have after sunrise. He returned to the truck for a flashlight and crowbar and used the former to locate the light switch. When he flipped it on, the bulb was dead. Jessup thumbed the flashlight. A cold white glare shot out, illuminating the desolate landscape whose musty stink burned in his breaths. Duran's accusations about tomb robbers rose fresh in his memory. For a terrifying second, Jessup wasn't standing at the mouth of a storage unit on Cedros Avenue in Sylmar, but deep beneath a pyramid, surrounded by vengeful spirits.

Jessup cursed himself and woke from his paralysis. He hurried over to the filing cabinet, kicking against boxes of things en route. Junk—all junk. He knelt down, reminded of his years in the pops of joints and tender muscles, and made another grab at the bottom drawer. When it resisted, he wedged the crowbar into the gap. The drawer rolled open an inch before freezing in place. Rust, he was sure. But for just an instant, in his imagination, the rust had hands with little gray fingers that pulled the drawer backwards, denying him access.

Rage replaced fear. Jessup dug in and yanked. The drawer screamed itself open. Wheels jumped tracks. Metal warped. He'd opened the damned thing, but it would never close properly again.

Inside, he found a strange assortment of objects, not the sort one would expect to store in the bottom drawer of a file cabinet: an old wool scarf dyed royal blue with a snowflake pattern woven throughout, an ancient book written in a foreign tongue with a golden circle embossed on the cover, and a lump of something gray wrapped in a baby's blanket.

Jessup reached into the drawer, hands shaking, and withdrew the cold, hideous object. It had no facial features. Its feet were chubby cubes, its hands only basic representations. It was posed in a fetal curl. The flashlight's beam added to its ugliness by illuminating the dark splotches of what he assumed were mold that covered part of its face where a mouth would be on a living child. Maybe Duran's crazy aunt had attempted to feed the thing.

He gave it a shake. The Gray Baby's insides didn't jingle with hidden wealth, though it was heavy even for an object the size of a doll.

Jessup walked it out of the storage unit, raised the statue over his head, and slammed it down on the pitted pavement. The Gray Baby shattered with a dull thudding sound. The thing was ceramic, with no secret treasure hidden inside. Jessup gathered up most of the pieces and tossed them into the nearest dumpster. He kicked at the rest of the dusty residue and mentally booted himself for not taking Duran's offer.

* * *

Nina examined the book. "It could be worth something. I'll check it out with our library guy."

"And the rest? We'll be lucky to break fifty bucks on this sad yard sale shit if we don't light a fire with the audience." Jessup sighed. "It's gonna cost more to dispose of it."

Harris Pastore gave the signal that let them know the camera was off. Jessup could imagine how the scene would play—a slow fade out, the sound of junk being dumped in the trash, the fade in back to the disgusted look on his and Nina's faces that telegraphed that some days you win, others you lose. The emotion felt like what the day tasted on his tongue—stale, sour.

"You want to go for a drink?" he asked Nina.

She shook her head. He asked Harris. Same deal. Another night alone loomed, and he was no richer as a result of their long, exhausting day.

* * *

The sound reached beyond the citrus trees and windows, past the hard sleep in possession of body and spirit, and posited him in a curious dream in which Visoli Duran was bouncing a sad little cherub upon his bony knee.

"I told you to not wake him up," the old man tisked.

The pink-skinned toddler was wrapped in a colorful blanket,

15

its back turned toward Jessup. It sobbed as it rode those skeletal bounces. The child's cries grew louder, more demanding. Nearer? Jessup turned his head away, toward the source of the wails. When he glanced back, Duran had degenerated into a withered effigy of scabrous skin stretched over bone dressed in time-eroded tatters, and the thing upon his knee was gray-skinned and swaddled in rags.

"The baby always wakes up hungry," the skeleton slurred in a voice spoken through what sounded like a filter of phlegm.

The thing on the dead man's knee spun its head Jessup's way. The gray-skinned abomination leered at him with black eyes. Its mouth was filled with jagged little pin teeth that chattered around its plaintive howls.

Jessup jolted awake, a scream lodged in his throat. He gulped it down, swallowing it and a nugget of snot hard. In the moment of shock that follows a nightmare, he imagined the scream lodging in the soft tissue of his stomach, where it would eventually turn cancerous.

Then the sobs drew his terrified eyes to the windows. Outside, the leaves of the citrus trees undulated in a dry breeze, producing a papery desert melody of desiccated corpses and old flesh. If death and dying had their own playlist, this would be one of the tracks, he thought.

He waited and listened, aware of his racing pulse and the slick sweat lying over his skin. The wail came again, nearer. It was only a cat, his mind tried to sell itself. A cat in heat, yowling to have its hormonal itches scratched. He'd once seen something on another of those low-tier cable channels owned by the same network that *Storage Kings* ran on, about how cats had evolved their human-baby sound so as to manipulate human sympathy. Crafty fuckers.

The cat was in the room with him. He heard its dragging footsteps, the scrabble of what he assumed was nails across the hardwood floors. He lay still, aware of the tic in his lower jaw, the pounding of his heart in his ears, and the slow, rolling sweat seeping down his forehead, closing on his eyes, which had forgotten how to blink. One of the fat beads spilled down. He wiped it away. And there, at the foot of the bed, stood a small form, its toddler-sized outline darker than the surrounding night. It extended its thin arms and tiny hands toward him and sobbed.

* * *

His phone rang. Jessup's guts attempted to tie themselves into knots. He answered without looking at the caller's identity.

"What?" Jessup snapped.

"Where the hell are you?" Nina demanded.

Jessup looked out the truck window. Panorama City? Damned if he knew.

"You're supposed to be here," Nina said before he could hazard a guess.

Here meant the storage facility in Sylmar. Not the Dunlevy Crypt of Cursed Antiquities, no—*Storage Kings* had moved on to other, better units to plunder. Unfortunately, he was still stuck in the fallout from the previous episode. Perhaps the producers could come up with some clever, clichéd title for the affair—*And Dead Baby Makes Three*; *Cardboard, Crap, and Cursed Clay*; or simply, *It Came From Storage Unit 217*.

"Can't talk," Jessup said and hung up. He shut off the phone and tossed it onto the empty passenger seat.

The place was one of your seedier dives, stinking of despair. He knocked on the metal bars of the security door. No one answered at first. Of course not. This was a section of the world where people slept in as late as possible in order to avoid facing the day's grim realities. Jessup pounded harder.

A face appeared in a window, and then the door opened. A boy Jessup guessed was ten or eleven going on middle age sized him up through the bars.

"Yeah?" the kid asked.

"I'm looking for a dude named Dunlevy. He your dad?"

The kid—a punk, Jessup thought—shook his head and sighed. "You're that dickhead. The one who stole our shit."

"Jessup," Dunlevy said.

He moved into the space occupied by the punk and coaxed the kid away. When the punk dug in his heels, Dunlevy shoved and issued a warning. The punk vanished out of view. The noxious stink of the cigarette dangling from Dunlevy's unshaved mouth mixed with something fruity—an air freshener clearly

17

overwhelmed by the pungent stew of odors trapped inside the hopeless apartment.

"Look," Jessup started. "I—"

"Let me guess. You found it." Dunlevy grinned around the butt in his mouth.

Jessup choked down a dry swallow. "I'll give you back everything."

"Good luck, asshole," Dunlevy replied.

"All of it. I'll pay you."

Dunlevy exhaled. A cloud of gray smoke formed a question mark over Jessup's face. "I'm sure you would, only it's too late if you woke it up. Tough titty, and all that. It's yours now, and if you want it to go back to sleep you'll have to feed it."

Jessup's bladder cramped. With very little coaxing, he imagined himself pissing his pants in front of Dunlevy, a fine payback, as he had in the bed when, thinking he had to still be asleep, he'd reached for the lamp. The Gray Baby was there, its hands outstretched, its voice shrieking for comfort. Its body had somehow reformed, but showed cracks where it had come apart on the pavement in Sylmar.

"It'll keep crying until you feed it," Dunlevy said in a slippery voice, a smug little grin on his stupid face. "Drive you mad. No one else will hear it, just you—because it's your problem now, fuck face. You woke it up, you have to put it back to sleep."

Jessup's mind raced. "Let me talk to your grandfather."

"My grandfather?" Dunlevy asked, his face screwing in confusion.

"That old fuck—Duran."

"Grandpa Duran? Good luck with that."

Jessup shrugged. "Why?"

"He's on a shelf at my cousin's place. In an urn, you dickweed."

Dunlevy slammed the door. Cigarette smoke and fake fruit gusted into Jessup's face as the metal bars rattled.

* * *

It followed him from room to room. The hollow scrape of its soles on the floor conjured images of tomb doors rolling shut on crypts being pilfered by grave robbers and archeologists. They were one and the same when you got down to it, and he was one of them, his hands stained in guilt.

The baby howled. He tried to appease it with milk, cereal, and even a bottle of beer, but it wanted none of those things. And as the Gray Baby's cries drove him steadily madder, he thought he saw eyes, black ones, from within the ceramic sockets. Those eyes bore into him. They were filled with anger. And hunger.

* * *

The doorbell gonged. The Gray Baby ceased its wails and retreated behind Jessup's recliner. He caught the ghost of its movements from the cut of his eye, a gray shimmer, barely visible, as it peered out from the arm.

He opened the door. Nina stood on the front stoop. She breezed into the house.

"What the hell's wrong with you?" she asked.

Jessup flashed what he imagined was quite the insane smile in response. What was wrong with him? Oh, where to begin. To start, he figured days of being incommunicado, enough that Nina would track him down at his home.

"Where have you been?" she pressed.

"About seven hundred miles up the coast," he said. "Little seaside motel right off the PCH. Hadn't even finished my first cold one and there it was, crying to be fed."

Nina studied him through slitted, judging eyes. "Are you drunk?"

"I wish."

"Coleman's threatening to cut us both from the cast. Bring in a new team, if you care. He's not screwing around."

Jessup turned and marched into the kitchen.

"Don't you walk away from me," Nina bellowed and pursued. "This is all your fault!"

Jessup reached the counter. He closed his eyes, inhaled, and then just as deeply released the breath. "Yeah, it is. I woke it up, and it's hungry."

He drew the knife from the block—another of the decent finds pilfered from a storage unit, one more tomb he'd robbed.

Jessup turned and slashed. Blood sprayed the front of the high-end, stainless steel fridge and a section of wall. Nina grabbed at her throat, gasping something that sounded nonsensical. She dropped to the floor, her wide eyes filled with equal parts surprise and hatred.

Blood flowed, and Jessup remembered Duran's final word to him before the old man's vanishing act. *Blood.*

He heard the baby's ceramic feet hastening across the floor, the most terrible sound he'd ever heard. But it only occupied that top spot for a matter of seconds. The abomination flopped down inelegantly and pressed its dirty mouth to Nina's severed throat. The Gray Baby's cries shorted out, replaced by a sickening, wet slurp. At long last, the Gray Baby fed.

Jessup prayed that after it had gorged itself, it would sleep.

About the Author

Gregory L. Norris writes full time from the outer limits of New Hampshire's North Country. His work appears in national magazines, fiction anthologies, novels, and the occasional episode for TV and film. Follow his literary adventures at www.gregorylnorris.blogspot.com.

IRON TEETH

Jude Reid

The apartment was empty when I woke, and frost had formed on the inside of the windows. The cold was nothing new, of course, but there should have been noise—Mama clattering empty pans in the kitchen as though she could conjure food out of thin air, Luda drooling and snoring beside me in the bed we shared, Grandmother shuffling and crooning and coughing in the other room. But Granny was gone, and so, it seemed, was everyone else.

That was how it went, that first winter of the siege. Everyone was leaving or dying, one after the other. The sick and the old went first, and then the very young. Those of us who remained took on a translucent quality, as if our flesh was transmuting into paper and glass, our shadows shrinking, bodies unable to hold back the thin, piercing rays of sunlight.

I had slept in my clothes, so there was no need to waste time dressing. I stuffed my feet into my boots—a size too small, now, but they would do another few months—and shuffled around the empty apartment, as if my family might be playing an unexpected game of hide and seek. My hand hovered over the door to Grandmother's room, then I turned away. We didn't open that door, not anymore.

"Mrs. Kukolnik?" I knocked on the front door of the

apartment opposite, and it opened a crack, as though she'd been waiting for me. The chain, I noticed, was on.

"Hello, Vasya," she said, and I thought she relaxed just a little as she recognised me. Her coat was on, hat pulled down over her golden curls, but the air inside her apartment seemed fractionally warmer than the corridor where I was standing, and there was a smell of cooking that made me salivate. She glanced over her shoulder, as if guilty to be caught with food when the rest of the city was starving.

"Did my mother leave a message when she went out?" I asked. Mrs. Kukolnik shook her head.

"I heard her on the steps," she said. "An hour ago, maybe. Gone for the ration queue, I think."

You never saw Mrs. Kukolnik in the ration queue.

"And Luda? With her?"

She shrugged with a half shake of her head. "I don't think so. How's your grandmother doing, Vasya?"

"Fine."

She took a step back from the door, and I wondered for a moment if she was going to fetch something for me to eat, but that was ridiculous, of course. If lovable little Luda-with-the-golden-hair had been there she would have brought out a morsel or two. Everyone always had something for Luda, even when they had nothing at all.

"If she comes back looking for me, tell her I'll be home soon, please?"

Mrs. Kukolnik nodded. "I'll tell her."

* * *

If you could eat stories, we would have been well-fed at the start of that winter. When Mama was still working—before the shops closed for want of things to sell and the factories for things to make—Luda and I spent our days curled up with Grandmother in the big bed. With my eyes half shut, I traced the knots and whorls in the wood of the bedstead like they were ripples in the river, while Granny conjured up *vilas* and *rusalkas* and *vodanoi* out of empty air. If I was lucky, as I often was, she would tell me the story of my namesake and Baba Yaga of the Iron Teeth, the way she had been taught it as a girl in *Gorodishche*. Vasilisa the Quick, the Wise, the Beautiful. I was none of the above.

The daily ration was cut again in November. It had hardly been sufficient before, but now an adult received only enough flour each day to bake a loaf hardly big enough for a child. The bread tasted of chalk and sawdust, but it filled a belly for an hour or two, even if it did nothing for the sour taste that we all carried in our mouths. Sometimes word would spread through the quarter that old Mrs. Tatarinova had been sent eggs from her daughter in the country, though how they had made it through the blockade no one knew, and there would be a flurry of women at her door, ready to barter furs and jewels and watches for a smooth and priceless treasure. We never had enough for even one.

There would be eggs again, Granny told me. When the siege was over. When Papa returned. After the winter.

* * *

Wrapped in Granny's old coat, I locked the door and hid the key beneath the loose board under the doormat. The stairs were dark for this time of day, and the light was obscured by a broad-shouldered man in a woolen greatcoat kicking the snow from his boots, ushanka pulled low over his eyes and a parcel wrapped in brown paper under one arm. He didn't look at me as I passed, but I recognised him as one of Mrs. Kukolnik's visitors. I'd asked Mama about her, once, when the smell of broth and the sound of the gramophone from across the hall had drifted into our room.

"We all do what we need to survive," she had said.

Outside, the cold bit like a dog. Tiny sharp flakes of snow blew in flurries, forcing their way into my hair, under my collar and my eyelids. The morning was still new enough that the footsteps in the snow were fresh, and alongside the heavy-treaded boots of Mrs. Kukolnik's visitor were the prints of my sister's five-year-old-sized shoes—too thin for this weather but all she had—heading in the opposite direction.

* * *

"Uncle Kolya sent us a letter," my mother said. "He says the ice road is almost finished. When it's ready, they'll start the evacuation. Over the lake. Away."

"When?" I asked, and she shrugged.

"Soon, I think. Before the thaw."

There was plenty of winter still to go, but the hope of leaving Leningrad kindled in me like a beacon.

"Is it dangerous?" Luda asked.

"A little. But the ice is thick, and the drivers are very fast."

"Will we have to pay?"

"What about Granny?"

I saw my mother flinch at Luda's question. She hid it with a shrug. "She'll meet us on the other side."

I wondered if my mother chose the words deliberately, hiding one comforting lie within the other. Luda's eyes were wide and full of faith as she nodded. At twelve, I understood the truth, but I knew from my mother's expression to stay silent.

* * *

The church bell struck the half hour as I hurried along in my sister's footprints, wondering what had possessed her to leave our apartment and head out into the streets alone. From the marks she had left in the snow, I guessed she was running, and I increased my pace to match. The ration queue never moved quickly even this early in the morning, but I didn't want to risk Mama coming home to an empty house. The footsteps turned left at the next junction, heading towards the river, and a lead weight settled in my belly as I realised where she must be going. I started to run, slithering through the hard-packed snow and the fresh dusting on top until her footsteps led me to a chained-up gate. I followed the fence along to the left, and could see where Luda had lain flat to wriggle through a narrow gap. I lowered myself to the ground and followed her in.

She had gone to the Leningrad Zoo.

* * *

"Do you think Granny will have a present for us when we see her?" Luda asked me.

We were tucked up in the box bed in the kitchen, Mama asleep under a woolen blanket on our last chair. There was enough of a moon through the window to make out shadow and light, but nothing more than that.

"No. I don't know. Maybe."

"Eggs. She'll have eggs for us. Will Papa be there too?"

"Papa's off with the army, remember?"

"I thought he might be there."

The crestfallen note in her voice irritated me. "Don't be stupid."

"How will he find us, if we're not at home?"

"Mama will write him a letter," I said, though truthfully I had no idea. "It's late, Luda. Time for sleep."

"I miss Papa. I miss Granny," she said, in a tiny voice.

"Go and find them then."

I turned my back on her and pretended to sleep, but I could hear sobbing in the darkness through the hours that followed.

* * *

Luda was standing by the tiger enclosure when I found her, leaning over the rail and looking down to the pit, and its occupant below. Before the war, the tiger had been the pride of the zoo, an eleven-foot Siberian monster of striped fur and lean muscle. The zoo had been shut for months, now, but it seemed that some of the workers still took their duty of care seriously. The tiger was crouched in the snow, tearing into the carcass of a deer so fresh it was still steaming. I wondered if it had been another of the zoo's animals until recently, the one sacrificed to keep the other alive.

Luda heard the crunch of my footsteps and turned. Her expression showed no surprise, only a dull sort of acceptance. "Are you cross?" she asked. I shook my head.

"Not really. Why did you run away?"

She turned back to the tiger. I watched it ripping at the chunks of red meat with its long white teeth.

"I thought Granny might be here. She always used to take us to the zoo. And you said—"

"You could have got lost. Or stolen." I shook my head, feeling a tight ball of resentment coiling in my chest. "If Mama knew you were missing, she'd worry herself to death. We should get home before she notices we're gone."

Luda nodded her head, eyes fixed on her feet. "I'm sorry."

"You should be."

"I hoped she might be here, that was all."

Luda's lower lip stuck out and started to tremble. I felt a hot flush cross my face, my hands balling into fists at this reminder once again that Luda was the baby, Luda was the one to be protected from the truth at all costs, Luda who was fed and watered with comforting lies while I was old enough to be told the poisonous truth.

"She's not here because she's dead."

Luda frowned, as if she hadn't heard me properly.

"Granny's dead." This time my voice cracked.

"You're lying."

"She's dead in her room, behind that locked door. Mama's kept it a secret. You've been eating her ration for a week."

"It's not true." Luda's face twisted in on itself. "You're lying."

"In a week or two you'll be eating her," I said, satisfied by the look of agonised revulsion crossing her face. "Like the cannibals they arrested down on Aleksandrovsky Prospekt. Mama will take the big carving knife and cut pieces off to put in the stewpot and stir it all up like Baba Yaga's cauldron, and you'll be next—"

"Stop it!" Luda screamed, and ran. I lunged to catch her, but my foot slipped on the snow and she darted away just ahead of my outstretched hand.

"Luda! Wait! I'm sorry!" She didn't stop. "It was just a story, I didn't mean it!" I started to run after her, my feet thick and stupid in the snow, the blizzard spinning around me. If I lost sight of her in this, I might not find her again, at least not in time for Mama's return. "Please, Luda, wait!"

I could just make out her shadow through the whirling flakes as I stamped and slithered across the snow. Her silhouette darted in and out of view, the ground sloping gradually downwards under my feet. I almost ran directly into the whitewashed wall of a building, then noticed the doorway that Luda must have gone through. This new part of the zoo was even more desolate than the rest—in another time it might have been a reptile house or an aquarium, but now the tanks were empty and the air ice cold. The roof was intact, and while it was a relief to be out of the falling snow, I could still see my breath pluming into motes of glittering ice as soon as it left my lungs. I drew a deep breath, and became aware of a faint, rich sweetness to the frozen air. Luda had stopped in front of me and was standing very still.

"We need to go home," I said, but she didn't turn. "I'm sorry, all right?" I stepped towards her and put a hand on her shoulder, meaning to move her to face me, but she was rigid. "What is it?"

She raised a small glove and pointed.

Directly ahead of us, swinging gently on metal hooks, were haunches of meat, skinned and headless, enough there to feed our entire building for a month. For a moment I thought it must be more of the zoo's animals—deer, or sheep, or pigs—but there was something wrong with the shape, and the limbs that dangled towards the concrete floor ended not in hooves, but in fingers. And in the corner of the room, carelessly discarded, was a pile of human heads, the frozen eyes glinting in the dim light.

We bolted, Luda and I, feet thudding over the concrete and back out into the snow beyond, as though the corpses were dragging themselves from their hooks and pursuing us with a hunger of their own. All the horror stories that the boys downstairs had told with such rapacious glee were true after all. Leningrad had become a city divided into butchers and sheep.

We were only just out of the building when I caught sight of the shadow blocking the light up ahead and heard its heavy tread. I shoved Luda to the ground and threw myself beside her, both of us cowering behind a snow-heaped bench, certain that an iron-toothed monster was approaching, ready to tear us to shreds or devour us whole. I held my breath and waited. Through the thick snowfall I could just make out a broad-shouldered silhouette topped with an ushanka; it was, I realised, Mrs. Kukolnik's visitor.

"Where are you?" he called, and my blood froze. Inches from my face, I saw Luda's wide eyes reflecting my own terror. I pressed my lips tightly shut, as if afraid they would answer of their own volition. But it wasn't my voice that spoke.

"I'm here, Vassily." It was a woman's voice, high and musical. Mrs. Kukolnik's. Luda's eyes widened even further.

"What is it you wanted to show me, then?" The man's voice was impatient. "God knows you've kept me waiting long enough."

Mrs. Kukolnik laughed. "You've been so patient," she said, one hand tracing down the side of his face as she leaned in, pressing her red lips to his.

"My patience has its limits," he said, when they separated, though something of the irritation had gone from his tone. She moved in close to him again, gloved hands fumbling with the buttons of his greatcoat, opening it and folding herself inside. I heard him let out a soft gasp, his posture softening, eyes half-closed—and then he stiffened again, his head jerking back.

"You—" he managed, and Mrs. Kukolnik brought out her hand from beneath his coat, holding a knife slick with blood. With deft, practiced ease, she brought the blade's edge around and across his throat, the cut deep enough that as his head fell back again the wound opened like a second mouth, a cloud of steam rising into the air as the blood soaked down his chest and he crumpled into the snow.

With no apparent urgency, Mrs. Kukolnik lifted the man by his ankles and began the laborious work of dragging him into her makeshift abattoir. His arms splayed behind him, angel wings in the snow, as she heaved him like a child with a sledge across the frozen ground. Luda and I lay in silence, too frightened even to shiver, listening to her soft, satisfied sounds as she stripped him of his clothing and worked on the cooling flesh underneath. At last we heard the heavy clank of a chain and what sounded like the turning of a ratchet, then the spark of a lighter. A bitter cloud of burning tobacco drifted past us, followed by Mrs. Kukolnik herself, so close I could smell her lavender cologne, which lingered long after her soft footsteps faded.

"We need to go," I whispered.

Luda shook her head. "What if she's waiting for us up ahead?"

"She didn't see us. She doesn't know we're here. If we stay, she might come back and find us." I spoke slowly, trying to reassure my sister—no easy task, given the ball of panic rising in my throat that threatened to emerge in the form of a scream at any moment. I tried to coax her to her feet, but she point-blank refused to move, and I started to worry that if I dragged her then she would scream.

"Fine," I said at last. "I'll go ahead, make sure she's gone. If I do that, will you come then?"

After a pause Luda nodded, and I piled snow on top of her until her red coat was completely covered. "Wait here," I said, and crept forward.

The crunch of snow underfoot was deafening as I crept up the slope. The heavy flakes had given way to slow, drifting specks which would do little to conceal me. I rounded the corner that led past the tiger enclosure, holding my breath as if that faint noise would be what betrayed me. My lips moved as I prayed silently to find our exit route empty, but God, it seemed, had other things on his mind.

Mrs. Kukolnik was standing by the parapet overlooking the tiger enclosure, a lit cigarette at her lips. Her golden curls were peeping out from below her hat, and she looked every bit the image of a beautiful saint, until you noticed the bloody knife in her hand.

Her eyes widened as she saw me, and a flicker of doubt that was almost fear crossed her face. Then her mouth split into a wide, red-lipped smile.

"Vasya," she said, her voice low and sweet. "Did you find your sister?"

I shook my head and took a hasty step back. "No. I found my mother. She knows I'm here, looking for Luda."

"Your mother's still in the ration queue." She stepped forward, her feet leaving dainty, pointed prints in the snow. "Are you hungry?" I shook my head again. My guts twisted at the thought of food. "Silly question. You're always hungry. Everyone in Leningrad is hungry."

"Except for you," I blurted.

She frowned. "Except for me?"

I looked for Luda out of the corner of my eye, desperately trying not to turn my head or give away any hint that she was there.

"What did you see, Vasya?"

"Nothing!" My voice was high, the syllables coming out too hastily. "Nothing at all."

"You could help me," Mrs. Kukolnik said. The wind stirred the fur collar of her coat where it sat close around her chin, tiny snowflakes settling in the sable like stars. "A clever girl like you, you'd never need to go hungry again."

I couldn't stop myself from glancing back towards the charnel house. She spotted the movement and let out a sweet, musical laugh.

"It's only food, Vasya. Would it help if I told you what they were planning to do to me? Use me to satisfy a hunger of a different kind, then spit me out and throw me away. The first one tried to kill me, strangle me in bed as soon as he'd finished. He was high up in the Party. No one would have dared question him, let alone arrest him for something as small as a murdered woman. But I had a knife under my pillow, and when he was dead, I could only think of one way to hide the body. I kept him by the open window and cooked a piece at a time, until he was gone. It took a fortnight, but the last bite of him tasted just as good as the first."

I watched the streaks of blood on her knife turn pale as the metal cooled. One drip hung like a stalactite, eternally poised just at the moment of its fall.

"Leningrad has been devouring itself since the siege began. The tiger eats the deer, the strong eat the weak. We do what we must to survive." The image of my mother and her clumsy compassion flashed across my mind's eye. "And you want to survive, don't you?"

I felt my head make an involuntary jerk.

"Of course you do. What a good girl you are." She offered me her free hand. "Come and help me with the butchering, and you can take a piece home for your mother."

I salivated so intensely that I felt it as pain in the roof of my mouth, and swallowed with a thick, wet gulp. I thought of the flour ration that was less flour and more chalk every day, of my grandmother's frozen corpse and her stolen ration book, of the expression on Mama's face the day I'd walked into the kitchen to find her sitting with a carving knife on the floor beside her, and our dog lying bloody and lifeless across her lap.

"I'm hungry," I whispered, and slipped my hand into the soft fur of Mrs. Kukolnik's glove. She smiled, and her teeth were very white.

"No!" A tiny shape hurtled out of the blizzard, red coat flapping as it struck Mrs. Kukolnik at waist height. The surprise more than the impact made her step back, almost losing her footing on the ice, but she recovered quickly, freeing her hand from mine to seize the small figure by the collar.

"Your sister?"

I nodded. "Luda, please stop—it's fine—"

Luda struggled furiously in the woman's grip. "You can't! She's a witch! She'll take you away—" She heaved a huge, sobbing breath, her face streaked with half-frozen tears. "She'll eat you up!"

Mrs. Kukolnik brought her other hand round, perhaps to try to constrain the frantic thrashing of Luda's limbs, but at the sight of the knife my sister started to scream. I tried to hush her, but she was beyond soothing, and I saw Mrs. Kukolnik glance uneasily over her shoulder. We were a good distance from the road, but noise like this might draw attention of a very unwelcome kind. She caught my eye, and in her cold blue gaze I saw what she intended. She raised the carving knife, pulling Luda in close by the collar of her red wool jacket. And I was so hungry, and there was enough meat here to see us safely through the siege and to buy our way down the ice road to freedom when the time came, and Luda had ruined everything again.

I grabbed Mrs. Kukolnik's arm—the one holding the knife— in both my hands, pulled it sharply towards my mouth, and bit.

Her scream was so loud that even Luda was shocked into silence. As I became aware of the salt taste of blood in my mouth,

Mrs. Kukolnik jerked her arm away, the knife falling with a muffled thud into the snow. "You little fool," she hissed, lunging for the weapon and locking her hand around its hilt despite the blood running into her glove, but this time I didn't hesitate. Like Luda a moment before, I slammed my shoulder into her waist with all the force at my disposal.

Hunger had made me insubstantial, but what I lacked in mass I made up for in desperation. Mrs. Kukolnik took a step back onto sheet ice, her eyes locked on mine with hunger, then she lost her footing, stumbled and struck the knee-high barrier behind her. Her arms pinwheeled, eyes widening—and she toppled backwards over the edge and into the enclosure below. I heard the tiger's low cough and the padding of huge and heavy paws, and then the screaming began, and continued long after we had turned away.

* * *

We found Mama at the entrance to the zoo, her weary face slackening with relief as she caught sight of us and broke into a run, her woolen hat tumbling into the snow, her grey-brown hair a wild crown around her.

"Where were you? What were you *thinking?*"

She dropped to her knees beside us, heedless of the snow, and threw her arms around first Luda and then me, pulling us into a jagged three-cornered embrace.

"The zoo—" I said.

"The witch—" said Luda.

"What happened to you?" Mama asked. She looked over her shoulder, a hasty, guilty gesture that reminded me, just for an instant, of Mrs. Kukolnik. "Let's go home. You can tell me when we're out of the cold."

"I'm hungry," I said.

Mama reached into her pocket and produced a piece of stale bread, tore it into two and offered us a piece each. Obediently, I took my half—the smaller half—chewed it and swallowed.

"Better?" she asked.

I nodded my lie.

The bread was bland as chalk, dry as sawdust, and all I could taste was the iron of my teeth.

About the Author

Jude Reid lives in Scotland and writes horror stories in the narrow gaps between full time work, wrangling two kids, and trying to wear out a border collie. She is a fan of Zombies, Run! and ITF Tae-Kwon Do, co-writes and co-stars in the podcast audiodrama Tales from the Aletheian Society, and drinks a powerful load of coffee. You can find her on twitter @squintywitch, or at www.hunterhoose.co.uk.

VICTORIA

Jay Caselberg

Jason swayed slightly with the movement of the carriage and then sneezed. With that sneeze came revelation. His dreams of omnipotence were gone. Gobbets of his past life sprayed across the space filled moments before with commuters. They hung glistening on the stained metal pole in the carriage's entryway.

He looked around nervously, checking to see if any of the remaining passengers had seen. He dug in his coat pocket for his handkerchief and rubbed at the moist edges of his fleshy nostrils. Crumpled, damp handkerchief, crumpled damp ambition—his almost-reached successes had deserted him at the last stop. District Line between Sloane Square and St. James Park.

He pressed his forehead against the glass, feeling the coolness against his skin. Where was the sense of it? His gaze flickered from face to face, scanning hollowed cheek and baggy eye. Attention buried in the papers or watching reflections surreptitiously in the windows opposite. Fifteen years he'd worked for the company. Fifteen years. Fifteen bloody years of traveling back and forth on this line, the litany of stops recited one after the other in his head.

Another sneeze was gathering, swelling in his head like a balloon.

How the hell was he going to tell Sarah?

Fifteen years.

He clutched the handkerchief to his face, forcing back the sneeze.

"We all make mistakes," a voice said from behind his shoulder, some other conversation.

Ain't that the truth, he thought. *Ain't that the stinkin' truth.*

The conversation continued behind him, but he'd lost focus again, and his attention had drifted away, the carriage's motion rocking his head against the glass partition, banging slightly against it with an uneven rhythm. What a life, hey? And what was it he was looking for anyway? Perhaps it was just a set of dreams to guard him against reality. Did you shape the goals merely as an effort to position yourself against a conception of reality that was nothing more than a dream in the first place? Well, so much for dreams.

The employment market out there was a nightmare. Always talk of the economy, of impending recession, the price of oil. Jobs were at a premium. Sure, he was too fat, too old, too nondescript. He was going to have a hell of a time. He knew that much with a certainty.

The train rattled to a stop, and a mother and child got on. Victoria. He checked the station with a little duck of his head, the blue lettering confirming where he was. The kid reached for the metal pole and started swinging on it, back and forth. Jason looked guiltily up the length of the pole, making sure that the glistening remains of his sneeze had disappeared from sight. The child seemed oblivious. Jason looked studiedly in some other direction, cleared his throat, blinked his watery eyes, and held his already damp handkerchief to his face.

He couldn't stand it anymore. He had to get some drugs, something to quell this sneezing, the ache within his head. Apologising, he forced his way past a man standing in the doorway and barged out onto the platform, just making it out before they rumbled shut. He had to be clear when he broke the news to Sarah. That would be better. He knew within that he was simply kidding himself, that this was merely another way of forestalling the inevitable. He searched for a way through the crowd. The platform was packed with commuters, basic blacks and greys, here and there a brighter slash of colour, but mostly that uniformity of non-colour that described the rush hour population. Coats and bags and the occasional umbrella did nothing to aid his passage along the platform. Face firmly covered, he shouldered his way through the crowd and headed towards one of the tunnel exits, craning to see the signs above and on the walls. He was sure there was a Boots up on the main station. Somewhere close anyway.

This was a particularly nasty little bug. Strangely, he didn't know of anyone else in the office—his former office more to the point—that had come down with it. These sorts of things usually ripped through an office population like a dose of salts. Not only was he leaking from everywhere, his head feeling like it was going to burst, but his entire body felt as if it had expanded, stretching within his clothing and making everything feel tight, stretched, as if he were wearing clothing one size too small. So far, praise the Almighty, his digestion was still intact. He even felt a little peckish. What was it they said? Starve a fever, feed a cold? Well this was more than a simple cold, that much was sure.

And still he struggled through the packed bodies, seeming to get no closer to the exit. Of course, the train had gone now. All the platform traffic was heading in completely the opposite direction. A young man barrelled into him, hooded sweatshirt, earbuds firmly in place, oblivious. Not even an apology. Finally, finally, he was through the worst of it. He took a moment to lean against the white, shiny tiles. So much humanity packing itself into this platform space and the tunnels. The wide, curved arc was full, and there, over the other side, was the same picture, heaving with commuters. He'd subjected himself to this for fifteen years, and for what? A desk, an expanding waistline, and a house in the suburbs. There was still the mortgage. The kids had already gone. And now, nothing. There were some savings, but lower middle management in an administrative function didn't really do that much to feather the nest. London was expensive. They'd have to eat. You always had to eat. It seemed like the South of France was going to be out this year as well. He felt a deep sigh welling up within him. He screwed up his face and shook his head. It was just so unfair.

Enough indulgence, he thought to himself. He simply had to get on with it.

His head was pounding again, the pressure inside coming and going in waves. His eyes were bleary with moisture, and he rubbed them clear, blinking a couple of times, and then gave a deep, wet sniff. He had to find the way out of this zoo. Hopefully they'd have some max-strength medication. Something fast-acting. One of those bright silver and orange boxes with something he could swallow. He simply couldn't abide syrups. They either tasted like honey or something you might clean the toilet with. He spied the entrance he needed to make for, pushed himself off from the wall, and started shoving towards it, head bowed, his handkerchief pressed firmly to his face.

He'd seen it coming, of course. Downsizing, rightsizing, putting talent where it was most effective, making use of cost efficiencies. He'd been naïve enough to think it might not happen to him, but then they'd opened the service centre in Eastern Europe. His job could be done from anywhere, and really, it was a purely administrative role. Certainly, it needed experience and training, but there would of course be knowledge transfer and the centre would grow to meet the challenge. Fine. But where did that leave him?

He had almost reached the platform entrance when another sneeze felt like it was blowing his head off. A thick spray of mucous exploded from his nose and mouth, spraying forward and earning disgusted and disapproving looks from those he was passing. There was a muttered comment, a woman sidestepped, and he feebly wiped at his face with the sodden and now virtually useless piece of cloth. He avoided the looks and shuffled forward and through the entry. God, despite everything, he was feeling hungry. Perhaps he could pick up something to eat once he had found his medication.

Jason managed to struggle against the human tide with an effort of will to reach the bottom of the escalators. It seemed that a sea of faces was peering at him from the descending stairs and above him lay serried ranks of humped dark shoulders. It made him feel constricted, more than the pressure he was feeling inside his too-tight suit, and with handkerchief clutched firmly to his nose, he closed his eyes to shut it out as the metallic stairway juddered and moaned beneath his feet. He let a long slow breath out of his mouth, swallowed back an accumulation of liquid, and then, having adjudged that he must be reaching close to the top, opened his eyes again.

"What?" he said out loud and looked around in confusion. The people had gone. The escalator was empty. The tunnel above was empty. The light, too, was somehow different, tinged with a yellow, brassy veil. He looked down at his feet. The escalator steps were no longer shiny, silver. They looked stained, and they were a different colour. Slowly, the stairway shuddered to a halt with a grind and clank of machinery that echoed through the arched space. Where in the hell was he? Again, he looked quickly around himself, glancing at all of the unfamiliar surrounds. This looked like some old, abandoned part of the station. He'd heard tales of ancient disused parts of the underground rail network, about empty tunnels and platforms, but how could he have wound up here?

Hesitantly he took one step, and then another and then another after that. The scent of old metal, brick and dust was heavy in the air. The brassy light was dim, providing scant enough illumination to cut through the shadows. He couldn't possibly have wandered here in some sort of illness-induced reverie. And yet, here he was. He stopped at the top of the escalator to take stock, see if he could see anything that would give a proper clue as to where he was. In front of him stood a tunnel, curved, cylindrical, made out of old bricks, their edges and the spaces between them blackened with age. Patches of lighter brick peppered the length, lime or something similar scumming the surface. A rounded stone entry arch, yellow and greying at the sides, led to another section of the tunnel which rapidly disappeared into the darkness around a corner. He stood still to listen but at that moment, a huge sneeze took him, exploding out from his mouth and echoing from the walls and passages. He caught his breath, waiting for the shock of the noise to subside, and then listened again, trying not to sniffle.

A faint stirring of the air came from around him, and then his breathing, seeming too loud in the empty space. Somewhere off in the darkness, he thought he heard something moving. There was a feeling of wetness about the sound, as if something large and damp was moving between the old stained walls.

"Hello," he called. "Can anybody hear me? Is there somebody there?"

Only the echoes of his voice came back. That other faint noise in the background seemed to go still.

"Hello? Are you there? I seem to have become lost. I could do with some assistance here."

Again, a great sneeze shook him, and spittle flew from his mouth, and thick clear mucous from his nose. He wiped futilely, clumsily at the strands of moisture.

"Seriously, if you are out there, I need some help here."

Nothing.

Jason peered back down the escalator to the way he had come, but that way lay a forbidding well of darkness. He didn't really very much feel like testing what might lie down there. He had the sudden thought of rats, and he swallowed back the revulsion that swelled up within him. No, not that way. He turned back to face the tunnel in front of him. Swallowing again, he stepped tentatively forward. There was nothing else for it. He couldn't see what was around that corner, and he couldn't really hear any sounds of life apart from those he'd probably wished into being. He dug around uselessly in his pockets, hoping that somewhere within multiple pockets lay another forgotten handkerchief.

"Hello?" he called again. He could hear the desperation growing in his voice now. It sounded positively plaintive.

It was cool in the tunnels, but he was sweating now. His clothes were even damp. It was the fever, no doubt.

Again, somewhere up ahead, around the corner and out of sight, came the sound of something big. Although he strained to hear, he couldn't make out what it was. He also realised then that there were no sounds of machinery, no escalators, no distant rumble of trains, no fans, just the noise of his own footfalls echoing from the walls and that vague distant movement. If he'd been in any other position, that noise might have filled him with dread, but for now, all he wanted to do was find his way out of here, pick up his drugs, and get home, probably to a night of nursing his misery with Sarah, but home all the same. He was beyond trying to work out how he'd come to be here. All he wanted was to get out.

He followed the tunnel 'round the corner to find more of the same, but he pressed ahead. There had to be some stairs or an entrance or something somewhere. He stopped a couple of times as sneezes wracked his body, trying to wipe some of the wetness from his face and neck with his sleeves, but it did little good. The handle of his briefcase was slick with moisture and felt soggy in his grip. Again he sneezed, and with it came a slight dizziness. That was not good. Not good at all. He was feeling miserable, and though he'd been miserable to start with before this unplanned trek through the mysterious underground, all thought of what had occurred earlier that afternoon had completely left him.

One intersection and then another passed Jason by, and still he plodded doggedly on, using the muffled noises as a beacon in the gloomy tunnel system. He knew that echoes could confuse direction, muddle things in underground spaces, but he was sure he was going the right way. If there was anything that would lead him out of here, he'd find it with the source of those noises.

Just when he thought he was irretrievably lost and he would be reconciled to spending a night huddled against an unforgiving brick wall, the noises seemed to be getting stronger. Hoping there was maybe someone there, or a sign to show the way, something, he turned the next corner. He stepped forward into still another tunnel, but this time, at last, he had found something.

At the end of the passage sat a figure on an old wooden chair. Beside him, on a small table, sat a brass lamp, shedding a yellow glow around the arched brick space.

"Hello! At last!" Jason said. "Hello! You there." He quickened his pace, walking rapidly towards the tunnel's end.

The man slowly turned his head. "Ahh, you must be the new one," he said. "Max's replacement. That's right."

There was something funny about the man's clothes. He clearly had something to do with the station. He had on a peaked flat cap, but his collar was too high, the jacket too short, with brass buttons running up the front. Big round-toed boots sat upon his feet. He sported a thick red beard which somehow also seemed out of place, but with today's fashions, Jason couldn't quite be sure. It did seem to fit with the general style of his garb. He wasn't going to question it though. Nor was he about to ask what the strange little man was doing down here, wherever here was.

"I'm sorry. Replacement? I don't understand."

"Aye, takes a bit of getting used to at first. You're the one all right, though. No mistake there." He got to his feet and brushed at his trousers and then thrust out a hand. "Oliver," he said. "But most just call me Ollie. Oliver's a bit formal if you know what I mean."

Jason looked at the proffered hand and said, "Jason. I'd rather not. You see…"

A giant sneeze emphasised the point for him.

The man called Ollie nodded, seemingly unperturbed. "Yes, you get that. It'll pass soon enough."

"Listen, okay. Perhaps you can point me to the way out. Maybe show me?"

"Oh, you'll not be needing a way out, Jason. At least not for a while yet."

"I don't follow."

"Well, you've got things to do. Things to take care of. Max here, you see, is getting too big now. Can't fit through the tunnels proper. Gives him all sorts of bother." Ollie gestured into a shadowed space behind him, but even though Jason peered forward with his bleary vision in the indicated direction, he could make nothing out. The lamp's glow didn't reach far enough into the gloom to pierce that darkness. Somewhere from that direction came the noise of something shifting, and then a wet slap. Jason got the impression of some huge bulk.

"Listen," Jason said, starting to become a little annoyed. "I think you must have me mixed up with someone else. I'm not quite sure what you're talking about, but if you'd be kind enough to simply point me to the exit, I'll be on my way."

He was wracked with another massive sneeze. This one seemed to be even more liquid than the last. He wiped at his cheek in distaste.

Ollie shook his head. "Oh, you're the one, right enough. You might as well come meet Max. There's nowhere else to go."

Perhaps he should humour him if he was going to find any way out of here back to what he was fast considering the real world. None of this was feeling real right now. He was stuck in some sort of delusion. If not his own, then definitely that of this Ollie character.

Ollie waved him forward, reaching for his lamp as he did so.

"Just down here a bit. It's a bit too tight for him here now. Doesn't matter. As soon as you're settled in, he'll be off. Out off to the ocean where he can have proper room to move."

With each sentence out of the man's mouth, things seemed to become stranger still. Holding down his growing reservations, Jason followed as they traipsed into the other darkened tunnel. Ollie chatted along amiably as they walked, making less and less sense.

"I would imagine you're getting hungry around about now. Don't worry. You'll soon have the chance to feed properly. I'm reckoning you just came from there, so there's plenty of them to pick and choose and to take your fill. Nobody minds, you know. A couple here, a couple there. Keeps down the population. There's too many of them these days. Hard work it is just to keep the numbers down. Herd that size, it puts a strain on the network. Infrastructure can't take it. That's where you lot come in. You, Max, others like him. But you'll meet them soon enough. You won't see each other too often, having assigned stations and all, but I'm sure you'll run into each other along the way. Bound to happen in the connectors. Friendly bunch on the whole. I'd tread carefully with Stevie, but that's another story. He's got King's Cross. You know."

Ollie stopped and held up his lamp. "Well, here we are," he said. "Jason, meet Max."

At first Jason could see nothing, just a wall of blackness, but then something shifted in that darkness, and his mouth fell open. It wasn't darkness standing before him, but a wall of green-black flesh. Again, the bulk shifted. Jason made out a huge mouth, and above, big round eyes, the size of dinner plates. They were bright blue and human. From the hill of pulsing flesh oozed sticky clear liquid, coating the tunnel walls and sliding down slowly to the floor. Struggling, his mind tried to make sense of what he was seeing.

It was nothing more than a giant, pulsing, green-black slug, but it was a slug with seemingly human features. It simply couldn't be.

"Hi," said the slug.

A chill swept through Jason, and then a sneeze that dwarfed any of the previous. Wet liquid flew from his face and dripped from his chin.

"Good," Ollie said. "It's almost done. Once you're through, we can see about starting up a bit of knowledge transfer."

The pressure inside him was almost unbearable now. The urge to sneeze was gone, but the throbbing in his head had increased manifold degrees. He felt himself stretching further. His trousers, his shirt, straining against his body. His jacket pulled tight against his shoulders. Sweat dripped down his forehead, down his face, down his neck, but no, it wasn't sweat. It was wet and thick and it kept on coming. There came the ripping of seams, the tearing of fabric. His buttons popped, his belt snapped, and then as he stretched further, feeling the expansion throughout his body, scraps of his clothing slapped wetly to the floor, one by one.

He could feel his bulk. The tunnel was smaller, and he could sense its edges.

Ollie held up his lantern and peered at him, no concern, merely interest on his face.

"How do you feel?" he asked.

"I'm hungry," Jason said.

There was not much more to say. It seemed he had a job after all.

About the Author

Jay Caselberg is an Australian author based in Germany via the UK. His work, poetry, short fiction, and novels, have appeared in many places worldwide and been translated into several languages. Sometimes he writes as other people.

FAMILY LINE

Michele Tracy Berger

You barely notice your mother's tears and your father's solemn hug, on the Amtrak platform, as they release you into the muggy night. You're the oldest cousin, and they say it's time for you to make this special trip. You overhear your mother say to your father, "Maybe it's been long enough now and everyone's forgotten," but you don't pay it any attention. You're looking good in black jeans wearing a gold belt that spells N-A-T-E. You're eager to get out of here; you've had one too many close calls with guys much tougher than you, even though your younger cousins Violetta, Corey, and Little Tate strike you as interesting as a drawer of socks. You've only met them once at a family reunion, their drawl and talk of porch sitting made little impression on you. You will call them "Bamas" as a matter of course. You're a sixteen-year-old Bronx boy about to visit your backwards cousins in North Carolina for the first time. A familiar twitchy feeling of restlessness runs through you like a racehorse that's been held at the gate too long.

* * *

You arrive, and they love your wavy hair, your swagger, and

your tales about spraying graffiti all over the city. But two weeks later, you've kissed all the hotties, rumbled with two guys, and seen all the snakes, raccoons, and trees that you can take. Just when you think you'll die of boredom sitting on their grand wraparound porch, Little Tate taps you on the shoulder. A year younger than you, but much taller and meatier—linebacker ready, there's nothing little about him. "We got a book—a special book."

"This book is how Edward, one of our ancestors, got his freedom," Violetta chimes in with a dimpled smile. You pegged her for slow because of her lisp, and although twelve, she's babyish, wearing her hair in a one-sided ponytail.

"Never heard of—" you begin to say.

"Yeah, he stole *Beasts and Spells from the Savage Lands* from his master's library and learned its secrets," Corey, Violetta's twin brother, interrupts, as he has been doing during your entire visit. A contrast to the steady mountain of Little Tate, Corey's jumpy, impatient, picking at scabs on his legs and arms when he's not running his mouth.

"Shut up, Corey," Violetta says.

"Edward was an OG, original gangster," Little Tate says, laughing.

You lean back in the chair and any lingering doubt about how stupid your cousins are vanishes. *Superstitious Bamas,* you think. "Don't they teach you anything down here? Will you believe every dumb story you hear? Nobody ever earned their freedom with a book."

"Nate'd be afraid to see the book," Corey goads.

He's in your face now, and you want to slap him. He's a bully even without Little Tate's girth and confidence.

"Cousin probably ain't never even been in the woods at night," Corey says. "That and the book make you run for the next train to New York."

"Me, scared of a book?" You howl with laughter and the pink Kool-Aid that you've been drinking snorts out your nose. "You crazy? Hell, I tag trains in the middle of the night. What's some old book to me? At home, I've got men who'll shoot me as soon as look at me." For a moment, you remember the train yards, the petty fights, and the effort it takes to stay out of trouble.

Your cousins nod in unison, and Little Tate looks satisfied as if he just scored a field goal.

* * *

And with the challenge in the air, the pack of cousins and you trudge through their woods to see the slave shack where this book lives. You've never been to a slave shack, or any shack. Although it's getting dark and pinpricks rise along the back of your neck, you say nothing. You're tough. And, besides they're just fucking with you, right?

The walk is short, and soon you spy a building roughly framed and fashioned of rough logs chinked with mud, roofed with tarred clapboards.

"Edward's shack was closest to the big house because he tended to the master," Little Tate says.

"Big house burned down long time ago," Violetta adds as she opens the door.

Your eyes adjust as she lights two blue candles. Pitiful place. Not even the size of the smallest bathroom in your house. No furniture, just a mud floor, one window, and musty rags moldering in crevices in the wall closest to you.

In the middle of the room an encyclopedia—large, gilded, blue book—sits open on a rotted log.

You're not surprised that a book is here, but you are impressed with its size. "So you put this book here?" you say. "Just for me, huh? Probably got this from some used bookstore before I got here."

"This is where the book stays," Corey says leaning down and brushing his fingertips across it.

"It's been in the family for*ever*," Violetta says, and she also bends down to touch the book. Her fingers glide across the width of it. Smoothing her skirt with care, she makes a place for herself on the log.

"Never heard about it… besides slaves down here weren't taught to read," you say.

"Edward's master collected rare books and some slaves here could read and our Edward could read some," Corey answers you, and gives a nod to his brother.

"Ever think about what you might do if you were a slave?" Little Tate asks.

For a moment, you finger your name belt and imagine everything about you stripped away and extinguished. A momentary panic shoots through like when you're running on the train tracks and it's dark and you have to make sure not to touch the third rail. One touch of the rail and you'd be gone. "I'd run, escape." That's what a racehorse would do, you think.

"Please," Little Tate says holding up a hand. "We all like to think we would've run. Some people did run, some people stayed—"

"Edward didn't do anything of those things!" Corey shouts. He is standing so close that some of his spit lands on your arm.

Violetta looks to the book and back to you as if she is waiting for something. You think what a good actress she is, because her mouth trembles some and she looks frightened.

Everybody pauses.

"Tell him," she says.

"Edward called a beast up and it did his bidding," Little Tate says.

"Oh, brother," you mutter. These Bamas are so dramatic, you think.

Still, you lean in closer to the book trying to imagine your ancestor moving his mouth slowly over the words, on the pages, that looked like "Ye Olde English"—*betimes, shew, drync*. It reminds you of a recent class on Shakespeare and Chaucer. A class you liked. *How did he do it?* you wonder. *How did he steal the book, and when did he read it?* Despite how ridiculous your cousins are being, a tiny bit of admiration for Edward snakes up inside you.

"At first the beast did," Violetta says, a nervous giggle and a belch escaping from her lips.

"What happened?" you ask. "Edward start getting greedy? Like the beast was some kind of genie?"

"No, he asked for small stuff—more cornmeal, a blanket, bowls." Little Tate bends down, just like his siblings did, and lingers on the pages of the book, turning some over. "He did *everything* Edward asked."

"Then Edward tried his hand at bigger things, like asking for the overseer to get sick," Corey adds. You notice Corey's chest puff out with pride as he talks.

At first you don't believe it... swirling blue mist rising from the pages of the book. For real. You squat down and place your hand on the stump. Feels real. You squint, looking around for the gizmos, wires, cables or machines that could produce this special effect. You were sweating when you walked in, and now the air feels cool in the shack. They are better at this hoodoo trick than you thought.

"It promised him things," Violetta says.

You flinch when Corey roars, "The beast said it would kill the master!"

"But, he wanted something in return," Violetta continues.

"A sacrifice," Little Tate says, rising.

"Poor Edward had a son, Nate. He was sixteen, too," Violetta whispers. She gets up and stands next to Corey. She no longer seems so young. Corey and Violetta look united, purposeful. You wonder how long they have rehearsed this moment.

"I get it... This is where you're trying to scare the city kid!"

"No, that beast wanted the son," Corey says. "Edward gave him his son for us... so that we could be free. Edward started over again, a new man, with money and land. He did it for us." Violetta reaches for his hand, and he takes it and gives it a little shake.

They all point at you, eyes big and wide.

Little Tate lowers his arms and takes a step forward. "The beast waits for one boy in every generation," Little Tate says. "One sacrifice."

What you see forming in the mist makes you doubt everything you know. A faint shape. Familiar... from field trips to museums. Dogs of Egypt. Anubis? Book of the Dead. Hermanubis. Half-man, half-jackal. It's the head of a large jackal, its muzzle a yellow and dull gray. Soon, its white torso appears. Its presence fills the room. You stare at its pointed, salmon-colored tongue, drooling saliva.

Violetta is the first to weep and shuts her eyes. She leans into Corey for a moment. "They never told us it was so big."

"Shut up!" Corey says through clenched teeth.

You rush headlong for the door and smack into the bulk of Little Tate.

With studied ease he turns you, holding you firmly under the neck and arm in a lock. Part of you wonders how many times he might have rehearsed this move. How long has he been preparing?

"You're going do this right, Nate. We have to do this, just like our parents did."

"And those before them," Corey says.

And, now you remember your mother's last embrace, holding on so tight like she was losing you forever. You remember the quiet stories at family gatherings of distant uncles and cousins, all dying young, drowning, car accidents, fires and disappearances—always in North Carolina.

"But... but, we've been free... are free," your dry mouth mumbles.

"Beast don't care," Corey says now with a self-assured laugh.

"Hey, hey... you can make a different choice," you say, straining against your cousin's grip hearing the pleading in every word you utter.

"Who knows what'll happen if we don't offer someone up?" Corey says with a shrug. "What we'll lose?"

Little Tate's lips brush against your ear. "He's family; just like you," he whispers.

In the struggle, you start to wonder—what had you done with all that freedom you had gathering up around you like endless cans of spray paint stacked across vast train yards.

Little Tate releases you back to the center of the room. As Corey's knife rams into the soft spot above your collarbone and you fall, you see no doubt in your cousin's eyes. You see a beast's shadow and madness.

The wound is deep and although your fingers grip the long knife and pull it out, you know it is over. You've seen this before on the streets, too many times.

Violetta yells, "We've got to get some of his blood, or they'll be mad. It's leaking out so fast."

"I know, I know," Corey says.

Little Tate bends down next to you and with trembling hands tries to unscrew the top of a small mason jar. The disc shaped lid rolls away from him and next to you. "Stupid!" Violetta shouts at him.

You turn your head away from your cousin's fumbling. You thought you might die along train tracks running from the police, or shot for your sneakers, or beaten by men who have nothing better to do. Lots of people die for stupid reasons. For less than this, you think. For less wisdom, for less freedom, for less than Edward's sacrifice. Your blood finds its way down your chest, to your stomach, and drips into the belt buckle. You clutch it. I am Nate. I am free now, and I will die free.

About the Author

Michele Tracy Berger is a professor, a creative writer, a creativity coach, and a pug-lover. Her short fiction, poetry and creative nonfiction has appeared, or is forthcoming in *100 Word Story, Glint, Thing, FIYAH: Magazine of Black Speculative Fiction, Flying South, Oracle: Fine Arts Review, Carolina Woman, Trivia: Voices of Feminism, Ms., The Feminist Wire, Western North Carolina Woman*, various zines and anthologies.

Her science fiction novella, "Reenu You" was recently published by Falstaff Books. Much of her work explores psychological horror, especially through issues of race and gender.

Come visit her award-winning blog, 'The Practice of Creativity' where she delves into what sustains creativity. You can also find her on Twitter @MicheleTBerger and through her Author Facebook Page: Michele T Berger.

Primary Manifestations

Laura E. Price

Someone came back.

The door opens. Closes. Someone has come back. Someone. Just one. Which one? It's been so long; I don't know what to do. I remember last time, I remember the little girls—one, two, three—creeping tumbling rough screech laughter tangles that broke into a thousand pieces that scattered from sun room to attic nursery, embedded in the bricks and mortar and seams and grains of the floors. Sinking in, becoming mine. Then gone. They never stay. Well, almost never.

They never come back.

Well, almost never.

* * *

The first thing that happened was Jeff lost his job. Which was scary. The next thing that happened was he started drinking. This was less scary than irritating, because Jeff drunk had two modes: self-pity and *weepy* self-pity, neither of which were much of a help when facing the crap-ass job market in front of us.

And the account balances went lower and lower, not that they were all that hot to begin with, so I started playing roulette with the bills, Jeff no goddamned help at all, *Pippa* telling both her sisters to leave Mom alone right now, she's got things to do, and *she's* worried, and *I'm* worried, and on top of that I am so, so tired. It's not like it was easy *before*.

Which, I guess, is what Cousin Lacey heard in my voice when I called and told her we were moving into the house, because all she said was, "Okay, Jessie. I'll send you the keys." In possibly the most dubious tone of voice, ever, but she didn't give me any of the shit I was expecting about whatever the fuck happened to her the year *her* family moved in when we were kids. She did not remind me of the week I spent with them that particular summer, and I *refused* to think about how I slept on the floor for three weeks after I got home.

Because what the fuck was I supposed to do? It was this or live in our fucking minivan—Lacey lives in a one-bedroom condo with a no-kids policy, and my parents are dead; her mom and dad are in assisted living. Jeff's mom lives across the country—I wasn't sure the van would make it across Florida to the house, let alone to Oregon and her tiny apartment. I had nowhere else to turn; I knew it; Lacey knew it when I asked—hell, it was why her parents did it when we were kids. Sometimes the only choice you have is horror.

The place really is a horror. It looks less like it was built and more like it grew up next to the bay, in the mangroves and the Australian pines. Like a mushroom among the pine needles, roots in the salt-stench muck.

* * *

PRIMARY MANIFESTATIONS
Nursery/2nd Floor Bedrooms ("Nanny")
Alcove by Main Stairs/2nd Floor Hallway/Bedroom 3 ("Creepy Old Man") (Prince Charming) *Are you kidding me, B?*
Shut up, he's kind of cute.
How in hell is that cute?
Have you looked at him?
What if we're not seeing the same thing? (Observer B. sees a young, handsome man. Observers M. and P. see an older man [maybe J. Collins' age] with too many teeth.)
Stairway to Third Floor Nursery ("The Boy")

* * *

I've never driven up the driveway before. Not myself.

I rode the first time in the back of the family minivan; since "Pippa never gets car sick," I always took the very back seat and then slept the entire way to wherever we went.

The trees drew back to reveal the house. The house. Our house.

"It's huge," Maisie said.

"It's ugly," Bess said.

"It's definitely odd," I said. I was trying to be positive. Help Mom keep us all together.

"Huge, ugly, and odd—but it's ours. Or your mom's." That was Dad. Worn down, sick with depression. You could hear his longing to be left the hell alone for a while in every word he said. But of course we couldn't. We had to unload the van, sort out who got what bedroom, argue—voices echoing through the house—over whether we had to all sleep on the same floor or not, and he had to tell us not to go out on the terrace until he got a chance to check it over ("Which means *never*," Maisie said, and she was right).

This time, though, I'm driving. Past the banyans, the oaks, over the pits in the gravel from all the rain this summer. The shocks on my car will never be the same.

The trees draw back to reveal the house. The house. Our house.

I can see the light sparking off the water as I climb out of the car. It's not horribly humid yet. The air smells briny, with a hint of red tide. And the house—terra cotta tiles and cracked mosaics, a Venetian adobe nightmare, huge, ugly, and odd. Still ours. Or we're still *its*. From the moment we tumbled out of the van.

The steps to the front door are gritty. The key turns easily in the lock. *Finally* runs through the walls and ceiling. Relief streams down the windows. Manic glee emanates from up the stairs. One of us is home.

* * *

This one. This one on the stairs. This one always writing, writing, looking and writing. She came back. She came home. The middle one. The one who made food, locked doors, got the grown people. The one who went out on the veranda alone, alone, alone. The other ones I could fathom, the other ones wanted playmate, lover, rest, but she wanted... what? Alone. She's grown now, but just the same, not mine not mine just inside me, just herself, she belongs to I don't know what, to her pens, to her notebooks, to the water, but she's the one who came home. She came home. Why is she the one who came home?

* * *

I told the girls. Well, I told Pippa while I was packing, which meant the other two would know about twenty minutes after I sent her to their room to pack her stuff. I did not tell Jeff. I mean, maybe I ought to've, but at that point I was so pissed at him that I figured he deserved whatever he got there.

"Look," I said to Pippa, shoving my clothes into garbage bags, "weird shit happens there, okay? It's scary, because it's not a great place, but none of it is going to *hurt* you." Not in any way anybody'd be able to see, anyway—but again, would it have been better to live in the van? Who knows? Not me.

So that's shelter taken care of, right? Far enough from town that Jeff couldn't just casually wander down to the 7-11 for beer, so all he could manage was a vague irritation at being depressed and sober at the same time. But that wasn't enough to get him off his ass, no, I was the one driving to the library to use the computer to print resumes and running around town filling out job applications.

But, wonder of wonders, I actually got an interview. And then I actually got a job. Night clerk at the local Traveler's Inn, which is a franchise, so it wasn't even that creepy. Part-time, but it bought us food and kept the lights on at the house, so long as we were careful. My boss at the Traveler's—not the owner, just the supervisor—was so nice I could have cried; she handed me the company Costco card so I could stock up on ramen noodles and soup and other bulk stuff for the girls to eat. Pippa made sure they had lunch and dinner. It was summer, so they weren't in school— god only knew how we would manage to get them there and back, because the bus didn't come down that far and Jeff wasn't going to fucking homeschool worth shit, but I shoved that off for Future Me to worry about.

* * *

SECONDARY PHENOMENA
(Are these their own hauntings? Part of the primary manifestations? The house settling?)
~~Phantom sobbing~~
Walls dripping (water? blood? hard to tell with the wallpaper)
Giggling in first floor bathroom
Fireplaces rattling
~~Thumping from master bedroom~~ - *just Dad stumbling around --P.*
House is usually cold, including Sun Room, but dining room is always hot
Nursery shutters close at night, even when blocked open
Cracked windows that mend themselves
~~Bad dreams.~~ *No, shut up, P.* BAD DREAMS.

* * *

Under the attic stairs.
Legs. Always legs and feet. Shoes. Socks. Never see faces. Nobody looks, not between, not into the dark space. So I crouch. One little goblin under the stairs, lone troll in the dark. Trip trap. Thunk thud. Step. Step. Step. Step.
Skinny girl legs. Long thick rope of tendon from knee to heel. Skin. Soft hair. Ankle, hollowed on either side, bone points. Could a goblin wrap a hand all the way around?
Shriek, thud, clang. Eyes looking into the dark space. Eyes on a goblin, littlest girl sees the troll. Littlest girl want to play?

* * *

[1] ENCOUNTER: 5/2/95
Observer P. was awake, heard muffled ~~screaming~~ noises from

Observer M.'s room and ~~ran to help~~ investigated. The manifestation dubbed "The Nanny" had wrapped a blanket around M.'s head, such that the pillow was tied to her face, preventing her from breathing. P. climbed onto the bed and attempted to remove the bedding from M.'s face. "The Nanny" did not visually manifest at this time, but did not let go easily. Upon arrival of J. Collins the encounter abruptly ended. M. was freed from the bedding.

No long-term physical harm was discerned. M. and P. decided to share a room ~~for safety reasons~~ in the hope of saving time in future observations.

* * *

It's not bad inside. Dusty. It smells like nobody's lived here in years. But no smell of rot—no dead squirrels or rats in the walls—no whiffs of mildew or mold. No kids have broken the windows. No one's forced the door.

The little bit of mess here is familiar—scattered things on the staircase. A stuffed rabbit. A blanket. Bess's left sneaker. Mom's old purse tossed to the side, its contents—makeup, a paperback book, some paper clips, gum, her work name tag, opened mail—in a scrambled pile at the bottom of the stairs. I thought, a couple of times, that I should pick it all up, put it back in the bag, but I just... couldn't. Maybe Bess or Maisie can.

If I walk up those stairs and turn left, I will find our old rooms. If I turn right, I will pass the stain on the carpet on my way to the master suite.

Through the solarium are the French doors that lead to the patio. It wouldn't take much to clean this place up to sell or live in. Bess and Maisie and Maisie's kids could fit in here easily. I told them this, during one of the interminable family three-way phone calls.

But. "How could we do that to someone else's family?" Bess asked. She sounds more and more like Dad every time I talk to her. Drifting, slipping down and down.

"I'm not doing that to my kids, no," Maisie said. She sounds sure, like Mom. But Maisie isn't an anchor, like Mom. Maisie just sinks; she doesn't catch hold.

So, as usual, it's up to me.

* * *

[2] ENCOUNTER: 5/3/95

Observers P. and M. woke up ~~with a weird feeling about Bess~~ with a hunch to investigate Observer B.'s room. Upon entering B.'s room, they found "The Old Man/Prince Charming" at the side of her bed, staring at B., who was awake ~~but frozen and whimpering~~ and staring ~~straight~~ back ~~like she was under a spell~~. Encounter ended when Observer P. spoke to "The Old Man/Prince Charming" to ask what he was doing in the room, at which point she and Observer M. noticed that the manifestation was floating approximately six inches above the floor. The manifestation left the room via the outside-facing wall.

No physical harm was discerned. B. decided to stay with M. and P. to continue to save time in future observations.

~~It was like something out of Twilight.   B. That doesn't make it less creepy.   P.~~

* * *

The oldest wears a long sweatshirt with letters on the front. It comes almost to her knobby knees. Bare legs. Bare feet.

She piles her hair on top of her head. Princess, going to a ball. Fairy queen, looking for a flower crown. Girl, dreaming of a prince.

The nape of her neck, soft-furred, tendrils falling across it. My finger across it—she jumps, screams—leaves a mark.

* * *

But.

Of course there's a but.

There is always, always a but.

Even in the utter shitstorm that was my life, even then… there was a but. Somewhere to go, even further into the dank, fungal mire beneath our foundations.

Because Maisie sprained her ankle on the nursery stairs and bruises ringed it like jewelry. Because Bess went all dreamy-eyed and strange, and there was a burn across the back of her neck like frostbite. Because Pippa sat on the veranda alone as soon as I got home, filled notebook after notebook with observations of things she saw, of things they all saw, and she didn't sleep unless both her sisters were in bed with her, one wrapped in each arm. Even then she slept so light that I woke her whenever I came in of a morning and peeked at them to make sure they were all still breathing.

* * *

THEORIES - Observer P.

There are stories about ghosts/spirits/demons being unable to cross running water. [Research at library?] Maybe the water is why the veranda is the only place in the house (so far as I can ascertain) that has no manifestations? Is the house protecting the manifestations from the water? Is the veranda a safe place, if needed?

* * *

She finds the blood, the middle girl. She touches it. Whose blood? Hers? Her mother's? Her father's? My blood, now, stained on my floors. My blood, my mother, my father. Not my middle girl. Blood on the stairs, in the carpets, in the sheets. Fingertip oils in the doorways, shrieks lodged in the walls. Tears in the nursery, the kitchen, the baths. Soaked in it all am I, sticky with it; whoever's it was before, now it's all mine.

* * *

The veranda was, once, the crown jewel of the house, a mosaic masterpiece that glittered in the sun while beautiful people gathered on it to watch the sunset, waving at boats passing on the water. The house's facade framed everyone perfectly, like a painting; every person gathered there knew that, reveled in it, added to the scene.

Or so I imagine; I've not researched the house past Bess finding out for sure that Mom was on its deed. To be honest, I never cared much who built it; it wouldn't surprise any of us, I don't think, if the house sprung up fully formed in the Florida pine groves. Maisie may have asked around about who lived here and who died here, but I never asked her what she found. It's enough for me that they're here.

The large French doors leading to the patio are filled with glass pooled thicker at the bottom; the world outside blurs into smears of blue, pink, orange, white, brown. The doors scrape open with a good shove from my shoulder, and then I'm back, staring out over the choppy bay with the house behind me, wind that hadn't blown at the front filling my ears, pulling my hair sideways across my face, the smell of salt and a bit of red tide in my nose.

This is where I came when Mom was home, when I could stop being responsible Pippa. I could just breathe. Just write. Nobody else came out here; not my parents, not my sisters, not the ghosts.

This is mine. I've never forgiven any of them for taking it from me.

* * *

She was always on the veranda. Staring at the water. Water eats at my roots, seeps into cracks way, way down under the ground. I can't stop it, can't keep it out, it seeps seeps in anyway, to where I live. I live. Me.

Nobody knows it, nobody thinks of it, of things like me as alive. Are there other things like me? Alive and alone and mute and echoing and lost and forgotten?

Or not forgotten, because she's roaming my halls.

The middle girl is on the veranda, where I can't reach. I could never reach. Could never know what she wanted, what I could give her. Seeping. Seeking.

* * *

Because Jeff started, guilty as sin, whenever I walked into the bedroom. He stopped showering. Stopped shaving. The bedroom smelled like sex and his sour-ass sweat. I wondered what the actual fuck he got up to during the day, but then realized I really, really did not care because I was so, so, so tired. The bed, dirty sheets and never made, looked like heaven. Every day. I fell into it and sank into dreams I wished I could live in, dreams of the girls and me at amusement parks I couldn't afford, living in beautiful apartments, living with gorgeous actors who smiled and laughed and played with my hair.

The night I realized that whatever Jeff was seeing, my version of it was my fucking bed… I ended up crying in the break room. My boss saw me. Asked what was going on.

I couldn't say to her, *I brought my family to a haunted house because I couldn't think of anything else to do; I'm trying my best but I think it's going to eat all of us in the end.* So I said… something. About my girls, and me, and their father unemployed and drinking too much. I think I said the house was full of mold.

She listened. Gave me tissues. The next night she told me about a full-time desk clerk job at the Sweet Sleep Inn, farther out toward the highway, where she knew the manager. I applied; she put in a reference. I got the job; she handed me eight hundred bucks to get my girls out of the mold. I cried, again, huge wracking sobs.

Then I went back to the house. I told the girls to pack their things. I went to our bedroom, stood in front of Jeff, and said, "Therapy," and he actually said nothing because he was stoned to fuck on ghost pheromones or whatever, so for a long few minutes I debated just leaving his ass right there.

But.

"Okay," he said. "Yeah. Okay, Jessie. Let me… you know what? Fuck it all. I'll meet you at the van."

I watched him, up the hall and down the main stairs, out the front door.

I turned back and started to climb the smaller stairs to the nursery floor. At the top was a kid. Not my kid, just a kid. A kid with big, sad eyes.

"Why are you leaving?" it asked me. "Why won't you stay?"

I thought, *Oh. Oh, now I see.*

The kid reached out. Pushed me hard, in the chest.

And down I fell.

And here I am.

That's my blood, right there in the carpet.

* * *

It's crumbling now; it was crumbling then. The railing looks the same: thick cement, cracked plaster, worn paint, missing sections where the concrete beneath it has fallen into the water. Huge cracks snake through the floor; I step over them now like I did then. To the edge, where I kneel to see what I can see.

Then: a shadow. Just beneath the surface. My face, clouded with water so it looks like my face, then. Rounder cheeks. Longer hair. Past me, baby Pippa, so tired, so scared, trying so hard and so angry about it. I'm still angry. The water rushes in and out, hollow liquid roar and ripple and splash against the foundations. Empty echoes. Like the house, empty and echoing. Like me, I think, with a grimace. I've watched them, Bess and Maisie, pulling away. Maisie, divorced, retreating to her kids, not talking to me. Bess, no kids, no husband, no idea how to be alone. I know how to be alone, but not her. Their lives are crumbling; they're falling through my fingers, and I was the one who held onto them the first time. Caregiver, was baby Pippa. Protector.

Without my sisters, what's me? Dead-end job. No lovers. No kids. Apartment, car. Notebooks full of words, amounting to not much. Words I can't keep hold of, like I can't keep hold of anything.

Without Mom, what were we? Lost. Mom always knew what to do. Mom always had a plan. And maybe it wasn't a good plan, but she had it. Dad was lost, with or without her. Surfacing enough to take us away, off to Gran's, but then sinking again.

Maybe it's a family curse, our lives dissolving like sugar into water, leading us back over and over.

So it's up to me. To find some kind of answer, some kind of

plan, even if it's cracked or imperfect or only half right. Problem solver, is grown Pippa.

Without people, what's a house? That's the question I'll ask, when this is over, when it's begun. I'll ask them all—the old man, the nanny, the boy under the stairs. Without people, what are you all?

I will take care of you, and of them. We'll protect them, this time. I will make this house a haven for my sisters, for the kids.

I take off my shoes, shift onto my knees. The cracked plaster fractures under them as I stand up.

* * *

One thing rattling around inside me. One thing shouting her story over and over like a dream she's stuck in. I'm not sure I dream unless there are people here, children here. "I had a dream," they say. Children. Grown ones. "Such a strange dream," they say. Maybe I don't dream because I'm not. A child. A grown one. But I am grown. I have grown. A dream. Maybe.

The middle girl goes into the water.

* * *

The next thing I know, not a fucking thing is different except I'm *dead*; my idiot husband finds my corpse and proceeds to forget he needs to get our girls away—once the cops come and the coroner hauls my earthly remains out, he's back to doing goddamned nothing while my girls huddle in the nursery and cry; Pippa trying to take care of them while the house is just happy they're all here, staying.

So I stand in the middle of the foyer, stare up at the chandelier, and I say, "You've got me. I'm going *nowhere*. You let the rest of them go or I will figure out a way to burn it all down."

I still don't know what Jeff thinks he's fucking, what the house makes him see, but boy does me swirling into being in front of him in the middle of it make him stop real quick.

Haunting Jeff is kind of fun, I'm not going to lie. I can unhinge my jaw because it's not real; I can scream but also *not* scream, do this raspy horror show thing with my voice; there's a whole *Beetlejuice* collection of vignettes to choose from. He's got the girls out the front door when I realize I forgot something; I pop up behind him and have to tell him, "There's eight hundred dollars in the glove box of the van. *Get out.*"

So they did. They got out. Just me and the house, now. I dunno if it likes me much; I dunno if I'm what it wanted. But here I am. A deal's a deal. It makes playmates and distractions, its imaginary friends, but I'm the only one here.

Except... except. Is that Pippa? Coming up the stairs?

* * *

I suppose I will always be wet.

You would think that it would be easier to climb out of the water once you're dead, but I haul myself out just as awkwardly as I would have before. And yet. My hands don't get scraped, nor my knees. I bang my shins painlessly on the broken rock foundations.

I trail streams of water behind me when I walk. The world has grown darker; I can see myself in the pooled-glass windows, distorted, soaking, gray and brown and deep-set eyes full of shadow and water. I smell salt and red tide as the French doors open to let me in the house. My house.

I feel it take a breath. It cowers under the stairs. It pauses in the upstairs hallway. It cries because the babies are gone. It waits. To see. All those manifestations, I thought they were ghosts, but I was wrong. It's alone.

No, wait. Still wrong.

Someone is here.

I start up the broad, main staircase. One step, then the next. Water drips down the steps, runs down the bannister where I trail my fingers.

At the top of the stairs, bloody head and broken spine, my mother stands.

"Pippa?" she asks, she croaks.

"Mom?" I ask, my voice full of water.

"Pippa, baby, what did you do?"

"I drowned myself, Mom, what do you think I did?"

"Bloody fucking Jesus, Pippa."

"Mom," I say, and I'm drowned dead, I can't tell if I'm crying. I don't know the rules.

* * *

They climb out of the car, they trudge up the drive. The boy picks up one of his sisters as one of the grown girls—the oldest—says to the other, "There's her car, just like she said."

The boy takes the hand of the other sister while the other grown one, the youngest girl, says, "I mean, we said it—if anyone could talk to me in a dream, it would be Pippa."

"I hope she was right about everything else. Because I don't know what else to do."

The girl in the boy's arms—baby, baby, how long has it been since there's been a baby—says, sleepy, "Auntie Pip?"

The boy is looking at the rusting car as they pass. "No, not Aunt Pip, Aunt Pip's dead," but the baby girl isn't looking at the car, the baby girl is looking at the windows, the baby girl is waving at the wet middle girl in the window.

* * *

The water from my hair drips, drips, drips. Maisie frowns in her sleep, waves her hand irritably to brush me away, then bolts straight up in bed, scaring Bess awake, too.

"Pip... Pippa?" she asks, eyes wide, voice tiny.

"Hey, May. Hey Bess." My voice is still full of water. My feet don't touch the ground. "It's okay," I tell them. "It's going to be okay."

"Fucking hell, Pip, you're *dead*," Bess says. Her voice is wet, too.

"Yeah," I tell her. "That's how I know."

* * *

I have grandchildren.

They yell and run through the house. They find wet footprints. They find the bloodstain and the boy ushers them away from it. (Bess, when she sees it, runs to the bathroom to puke. Maisie just sighs and pokes at the—what the fuck is that, a PDA?—computer thing in her hand.) I hide because Pippa and I agreed we would, to start out.

The house is practically vibrating. It's excited. Kid voices echo off the walls, shatter the silence of the place like my shouted storytelling never could.

I have grandkids. I have grandbabies.

I have all my girls.

I have them all and none of them is going to be bruised, or burned, or scared this time. There will be no But. This time, I know.

* * *

They came home.

Finally, finally, someone remembered. Someone came home.

And this time, this time, this time I know what to do. This time, I have a mother and a sister to tell me what to do. To keep them happy. To keep them safe. To keep them here. At home.

About the Author

Laura E. Price lives with her family in Florida in a house that is most definitely not haunted. Really. Nothing to see there. The lights just… do that, sometimes. Her work has appeared in Strange Horizons, Beneath Ceaseless Skies, GigaNotoSaurus, Curiosities, Broad Knowledge: 35 Women Up to No Good, as well as other venues—you can find her full bibliography at her blog, https://seldnei.wordpress.com.

CAMERAMAN

Joe Scipione

Acamera operator on the set of a big budget major motion picture made a lot more than one working on a small independent film. Victor had spent enough time as a camera operator making next to nothing; this was his chance to do what he loved and actually make a decent living. But he had to do a good job. One screwup, and this would be his first and last big budget film.

He turned the beat-up Honda right in the middle of the desert and drove east somewhere between California and Arizona. He didn't know exactly where he was, though the coordinates he'd been given by the cinematographer said the shoot was in Arizona. He hadn't seen a sign letting him know he'd left California and entered Arizona, but his phone said he was less than five miles from his destination.

In every direction, there was nothing, save the vast openness of a barren desert. Everything was flat, sand. The only evidence of civilization was the road he drove on. A wavy haze of heat lifted off the pavement as he sped through desolation. The Honda's A/C had long since stopped being able to keep up with the rising temperatures. Less than a mile from his destination, he saw a light flash through the heated air, rising up to the cloudless sky. The glint of sunlight reflected off something ahead on the left. A windshield or a car window. Something. A glance down at the phone in Victor's lap told him this had to be the spot. An atmospheric setting for a scene to say the least. It was a mob movie, and one of the opening scenes of the film was a stand-off in the desert. It also happened to be the first scene they were filming. This stretch of remote desert would make for some great shots.

Victor slowed then stopped the Honda when he approached the small group of cars and two massive buses that were still running. The cars were the crew, he knew that. The buses for actors, director, writers, and cinematographer most likely.

Sweat caused his shirt to stick to the seat when he got out of the car. He shut the door, exhaled, and used his ball cap to wipe the sweat from his forehead.

"Victor," the cinematographer said. Victor turned and shook the man's hand.

"This is the spot?"

"Yeah." He ran a hand through the wavy grey mop of hair that sat atop his head. His eyes shifted back and forth behind wire-rimmed glasses, never focusing on one point for too long. "The director drove through here once a few years ago and knew that this had to be the spot to film a scene for a movie. He just had to wait for the right movie to come along."

"It looks like the last fifty miles to me," Victor said.

"I tend to agree." The cinematographer took a step back toward the bus and leaned his shoulder against it.

All the equipment Victor needed was there. He didn't have much to do other than operate the camera. He was told where to point it and how to move it. This was a dual camera scene, so there were two camera dollies set up. Victor would operate one; a woman he didn't know would operate the other. Once they'd finished filming for the day, they'd be on their way.

"We're just waiting now for the director to tell us we're ready to go," the cinematographer said. He opened the door to the air-conditioned bus and got in, closing it behind him.

Victor stood in silence. He looked out across the desert and back down the road in the direction he'd come from, trying to figure out what was so special about this particular spot.

The sun rose higher in the sky, and no one came out of the bus. Victor, the other camera operator, and a few others stood out in the sun and waited. They made small talk, but Victor wasn't especially good at small talk, so kept to himself. He sipped a bottle of water and waited, knowing he still had to make a good impression with everyone here to keep his job and earn more money.

Finally, with the sun directly overhead and the day at its hottest, the cinematographer exited the bus, his face dripping sweat, wet spots under each arm.

"Are we ready?" he said.

Victor and the other nodded. Victor noticed the sweat, but didn't mention it, hoping it would be explained in short order.

"Alright, they were waiting for the hottest part of the day for a reason, they need the actors to look sweaty and hot. They turned the A/C off in there about half an hour ago, so they are certainly warm."

Victor looked skyward, wiped his forehead again.

The actors stepped off the bus followed by the director. He recognized all of them from movies and award shows, but he'd never been this close to big name movie stars before. He was glad he wasn't the type of person to get star struck.

"Set up the shots," the director said.

The cinematographer told Victor and the other where to set up and the direction of the shots. He told them the actors would do their parts, and when the acting was done for the day, they were going to get some setting shots. Victor nodded.

The actors moved into position; Victor adjusted his camera to them.

"Action," the director said.

The scene ran smoothly. Victor continued to film, tracking the actor he was supposed to follow. They reset and did the scene again, but one actor kept going off script.

"Do you want to keep ad-libbing?" the director asked the actor. "I like some of this stuff." The actor nodded.

The director looked at Victor and the other camera operator. "They are going to ad-lib some stuff in the scene so we're going off script. Don't turn the cameras off—just keep rolling and we'll edit it all together later. Understood?"

Victor and the other nodded.

The day wore on Victor. Everyone on set was sweating; the more takes they had, the worse everyone looked, but in the end, he thought, that would be better for the film. There were water breaks, but they were not frequent enough. Victor felt dizzy a few times, but he remained on his camera, doing his best to get the exact shots the director wanted. This was one of the most well-known directors in Hollywood. The cinematographer had won an Oscar. If he failed, he'd be relegated to low budget films the rest of his career. Still, whenever the cinematographer and director looked over his shoulder to check the frame, each time they said it was perfect. In spite of the weariness brought on by the heat and sun, Victor was succeeding.

They took a break, waiting for the sun to drop lower in the sky. They had one more short scene to shoot, and they needed it to be later in the afternoon. The crew and cast ate and had water. The director refused to let anyone into the air-conditioned bus until the scene was completed. The cast moved off to the side, away from the rest of the crew; Victor noticed but didn't give it much thought, it's what he expected. Among the rest of the crew, Victor stayed off by himself, content to stand and wait to resume his job.

After about an hour the director declared that the sun was low enough in the sky to begin shooting the final sequence. Magic hour meant they didn't have a lot of time to get all the shots they needed. If they didn't get the right shots, they'd be back out in the desert the next day to finish. Victor did not want that. No one did. He had to be perfect.

The first shot was a pan shot, a difficult one for Victor. He would film the barren desert, the clear sky, then pan over to the sweating, exhausted actor. He had to line everything up perfectly from the beginning to get the shot just right.

He set up the camera, and the director and cinematographer watched as he practiced the pan to the right with a stand-in.

"Perfect," the director said. "Let's do it for real."

Victor nodded.

The actors got into position; Victor reset to get the same perfect shot again. He started out on the desert, barren and empty, and waited for the action call.

There was something on the viewer that should not have been there. Victor leaned in, not bothering to look over the camera to see what was actually there, but trying to figure out what was wrong with the lens.

He leaned in to get a closer look at the object on his viewer. It was long, dark, and moved from the center of the screen to the right side. But it also appeared to be coming out of the ground. It took up a quarter of his screen, meaning if it were actually there, it would be huge, and someone would have mentioned something that large by now. But no one had.

Victor reached out and wiped his screen. But the screen was smooth; there was nothing there.

"Action," he heard a voice call from over his shoulder.

Victor froze. He forgot about the pan shot for a moment and stared at the thing that must have been in front of the camera. He turned to look at the rest of the crew behind him.

"Victor, let's go," the cinematographer said.

He said nothing at first, just paused and waited, then realized he needed to say *something*.

"Sorry, there's a bug on the lens, I've got to clear it off before the shot."

"Alright, cut," the director said. "Stand by. Back to one. Action in five." Victor got out of his position behind the camera and grabbed the rag he always kept in his back pocket when shooting. He looked out at the empty desert in front of the camera, saw the rock sticking up and angled to the right that would have been right next to the thing he saw on the viewer. There was nothing there. No sign that what he'd seen on the screen was actually there. The only explanation was exactly what he'd told everyone, a bug on the lens.

Victor turned to clean off the lens, but there was nothing there either. He felt a look of shock cross his face, but he quickly hid it, not wanting anyone to know what was going on. He pretended to wipe a bug off the lens, then gave the lens a wipe all over to make sure there was no dust or sand in the shot. He slid back behind the camera expecting the thing he saw to be gone.

It wasn't. What looked like a massive worm or snake had pushed more of itself out of the sand and slid across his screen, stretching now from one side almost all the way to the other. Victor stood up and looked over the camera at the desert—there was nothing there. He shook his head. Was it a mirage? He'd been out in the sun all day. Little water. It was possible. Maybe. He moved the camera into position to film the pan shot. He was just going to pretend he didn't see the thing on his screen.

"Are we ready?" the director asked.

"A—all set," Victor replied. "Rolling."

"Very good," he said. "Action!"

Victor watched the large snake-like creature slide across his screen as he panned from the not-so-empty desert toward the actor. The actor, standing in the middle of the screen, blocked one end of the snake. While the snake slithered across the left side of Victor's screen, the side to the right of the actor showed only barren desert. He held the camera in place while the actors went through their lines. The snake continued to slide across one half of the screen. Victor could not take his eyes off it.

Just as the actors finished their lines, the snake-thing, no longer hidden by the actor, appeared on the other side of the actor. It was the head of the thing. Victor's eyes widened. The snake was bigger than he'd thought, the head of the monster almost as big as Victor's Honda. It moved slowly along the sand, massive tongue flitting out and back in, crossing the rest of his screen and then out of the shot.

The scene ended; Victor glanced at the director who made a circular motion with his finger, reminding Victor to get the ad-libs. Victor kept the camera rolling as instructed, but used the opportunity to lean to the side, to see if he could see the snake monster slithering across the desert. Obviously, he couldn't. Anything that size would have been seen by someone other than him.

He was losing his mind. He couldn't let them know anything was wrong.

The actors kept talking for a while then stopped once the cut call was given. Victor moved the camera back to its original position. He stared at the huge snake still pushing its way out of the sand.

"Ready again," the director said. "Two more times I think, and we can wrap up the desert stuff. We can get the setting shots real quick after and call it a day. If the shots are clean, we won't need to come back."

Some part of Victor's brain registered that the comment was being made toward him and he responded.

"Everything looked good for me," Victor said, eyes glued to the screen in front of him.

"Great," came the reply.

A few minutes later they did another take. The snake thing had completely emerged from the sand, but Victor could still see it moving away in the distance. By the third take, the screen was empty, everything was the way it should be. Victor was glad to be rid of that monster, and by the time they had most of the equipment packed up, he'd almost convinced himself it had been a hallucination or mirage of some sort.

As he drove back across the desert toward home, Victor couldn't get the snake out of his head. If he wasn't losing his mind, the snake must have changed his brain somehow. He couldn't think straight. It had looked huge on the screen. It could have swallowed his car and probably the buses the actors had taken as well. If he'd stood next to it, it would have been at least as tall as his waist, maybe higher.

The sun dropped lower in the sky as he drove west, off into the sunset. But once the sun went down and darkness took over, fear overcame him. Twice he thought he saw movement behind him. Both times he jerked the car over to the side of the road and got out, expecting to see that massive snake behind his car, its gaping mouth ready to devour him. But when he pulled over, there was nothing there. After the second time, he checked his phone—he had about four hours of driving left. He was hot and tired and hungry, he told himself. It was those things that made him anxious. There wasn't a real monster snake out there. But he'd seen it. Or did he? He couldn't be sure what he saw. His mind reeled. Thoughts spun; some clear, others unclear thoughts or visions of things that may or may not have happened.

He left the desert behind and civilization sprang up around

him, He welcomed the gas stations and fast food restaurants on the side of the road. But he didn't dare stop. He was hungry, but the desert wasn't far enough away. He hoped once he got home, that the distance would be enough to make him feel safe.

Victor pulled into the parking garage of his complex, his vision blurred, unsure of exactly how he came to be there. He stumbled up to his apartment, managed to order a pizza, then drank two bottles of water before cracking open two bottles of beer and collapsing on the couch. Both beers were gone by the time the pizza arrived, so he had two more, trying his best to forget the day. To forget the monster.

With the pizza half eaten and the second pair of beers drained, Victor found himself drifting off in a hazy combination of hallucinations and fitful sleep.

His sleep was haunted by visions. Not dreams, because in a part of his mind, he knew he was asleep. He knew the images he saw weren't real, but he could do nothing to wake himself up or to stop the visions from being pushed to the fore of his mind. He saw the snake. This time it was coming after him. It was faster and more agile then he imagined. When he tried to outrun the monster, he failed. Victor tripped and fell to the ground, and the monster was on him, its mouth opening wide, its jaw extending and then closing down around him.

Victor woke with a shout.

He sat up on the couch as light streamed in his window, making his head ache and his eyes burn. He'd been there all night, but now felt compelled to leave. There was something pulling at him, forcing him out the door, but he didn't know why. Something from the dream he couldn't quite remember told him he had to get out of his apartment and back to the desert. Victor knew what it was. It was calling him. He composed himself and felt for his car keys in the front pocket of his pants. They were there, along with his wallet and phone, which he hadn't charged all night. The apartment closed in around him. The walls were closer together, his shoulders touching both walls when he sat on the couch. The ceiling was lower than it had been when he got home the day before. Something was not right. This wasn't really his apartment.

It was the monster. The monster changed it. The monster called him.

It had tricked him into thinking this was his apartment. It had done something to his brain. It had to be; it was the only thing that made sense. He had to get back to the desert. Had to get back to the same place he first saw the thing. He couldn't live in this fake apartment. He had to see the monster again.

He was thirsty, but wary of what drinking some of the fake water might do to him. Victor couldn't focus on anything for very long. His eyes shifted in his head, back and forth, up and down; somehow, he was still able to focus his thoughts. He decided the water had been safe the day before, so it was probably safe again. He twisted the plastic cap off and downed an entire bottle, then looked in the fridge and saw three more bottles of water and two more beer bottles. He collected all five bottles in a plastic bag and left the apartment, leaving the door open behind him.

The drive back out to the desert felt shorter than it had the day before. But there were stretches of the drive he had no memory of. His phone, now less than fifty percent charged, called out the rights and lefts as he drove through the city, then called out the mileage until his destination as he crossed the barren world toward the spot of the shoot the day before. The charging cord for his phone hung lifeless and unused from the charging port, unimportant to Victor in his need to get back to the desert.

Victor remembered most of the turns and even some of the landmarks. The desert looked different in the daylight than it had at night on his way home. It looked safer. Less inhospitable. Though he knew if he stayed in the desert without food or drink for more than a few days, he'd never make it out.

"Your destination is ahead on the right in one mile," the female voice on his phone announced.

Victor slowed the Honda. It had been an hour since he'd seen any cars; he didn't expect any to drive by. The previous day, he'd seen only a handful of cars in the desert, and he'd spent more than twelve hours there. Civilization was the exception, not the rule.

He pulled onto the same sand he had the day before. The tire marks from his car and the others were still there, marking the side of the road. Victor sat and looked out the windshield at the desert. Out to where the monster had been. Out where the monster still was. Somewhere in that world, hidden behind the lens of a camera.

He didn't get out of the car. Not yet. The battery of his phone read twenty percent. There was at least some battery. He should be able to make it back home from memory, it wasn't that difficult of a drive. Just a long one.

It was mid-day; about the same time they'd started shooting the day before. The sun was hot, and the heat radiated up off the pavement behind him and the sand in front of him. Again, just like the day before. The snake was there. It had to be there.

Victor reached into the back seat and groped around, finding the plastic water bottles and ignoring them, then feeling the now-warm glass of the beer bottles. He grabbed them and brought them up front with him. He twisted the cap off and downed the entire first bottle, then opened the second and did the same. Victor exited the car and dropped both glass bottles in the sand. Not bothering to shut his car door, he exhaled and looked out at the desert. Everything was the same as the day before, but somehow, the desert looked different. It was not the same desert as the one he'd captured on film. This desert was more. This desert was alive.

Warm wind whipped across his face. Small bits of sand stung his skin and eyes. Victor squinted, held a hand up to his forehead to block the glare of the sun and the bite of sand against his face. He didn't know what he was looking for—something told him he would know when he found it. The monster had to be found to return him to his real place, the real world.

Victor walked.

The sun beat down, but the wind was strong. His sweat cooled him, the gusts drying it as soon as it formed.

He ventured further into the desert, looking back occasionally to see how far he'd gone. His car, a mere speck in the distance behind him, nothing but flat, hot sand and sun in front of him.

Victor pressed on, exhausted and a little full from the warm beers, his trek slow, but with a purpose. He stopped again to look behind, his car no longer visible. There was nothing to see in any direction. He started forward again, not wanting to get himself turned around. If that happened, he'd die in the desert before he found his car.

Another step forward, but just one. The ground trembled beneath his feet. It was soft, and slow, but he was certain he'd felt it. Victor stood still. The wind still blew hard enough that it made listening for anything else impossible, but he listened anyway. He crouched down, first resting his arms on his bent knees, then reached down and pressed his palm flat against the hot sand.

It burned, reminding him of the time he burned his feet at the beach in Mexico, but he didn't stop walking on the beach then and he didn't pull his hand back now. He waited. Waited. Waited. And the ground trembled again, harder than before, or perhaps he just noticed it more.

Victor stood up, his hand trembling, but did not hesitate. He reached into his pocket and pulled out his phone as he stared at the ground. Somehow, he knew it was the right thing to do. He took a small step back then, just to be safe, one more. He opened up his phone and switched on the camera app, but closed his eyes. One long hard breath in, then he opened his eyes and looked at the screen of his camera. It was pointed right at the area where he'd felt the trembling.

The screen didn't show anything except his foot in the frame. Victor waited, but there was no change. Then he switched the phone from picture mode to video mode. There was still no change. An alert popped up telling him he had only ten percent battery remaining. He ignored the alert and watched the ground through the video viewer. Still nothing. Defeated and discouraged Victor hit the record button. He didn't expect to see anything but jumped back when the snake materialized less than a yard away from his foot.

"Shit!" Victor shouted.

The monster was not yet out of the ground. He could see the

massive head of the thing forcing its way up through the sand. Its dark snout appeared in the shot on his phone next to his foot. The head moved back and forth, forcing the sand one way, then the other. Its probing tongue flitted in and out of its mouth as it emerged from the depths.

Victor was glued to the screen in front of him, entranced by the monster snake being birthed from the desolate landscape.

Its gigantic head crested and slid out on the sand feet from where he stood. Victor looked past the screen at the sand in front of him. Without the camera there was no sign of the monster. The sand was the same as it had been. He could even see his footprint still there underneath where the monster should have been.

Back to the phone screen—the snake, as it had the previous day, moved to Victor's right. He filmed as it moved, at first getting the massive, chest-high body as it silently pulled itself out of the sand, then deciding to stay with its head as it travelled across the desert.

Victor lost track of time. The monster hypnotized him, or put a spell on him, or something. He couldn't pull himself away as he walked along next to it. The head filled the screen; Victor stayed what he hoped was a safe distance away. He couldn't feel the heat of the desert anymore. Couldn't feel the aches and soreness of his muscles. He was pulled along with it.

The time on the video said forty-five minutes. And he'd long since ignored the five percent battery life warning.

The snake kept going, and so did Victor, following the ebony head of the thing poking and prodding then continuing at a leisurely pace. Then it would stop, flick its tongue, let its bright red eyes scan the surroundings, though it never looked at Victor, before carrying on again. It repeated this process every twenty or thirty steps. Then, with no warning, it stopped and pressed its snout down against the sand. This was something new.

Victor wanted to take a step forward to get a better view of, what he assumed, would be the monster's descent back down below the sand. He glanced at his battery life, there couldn't be much left, but he continued recording.

It forced its head against the sand and writhed back and forth, its mouth and nose disappearing below. Victor took a step forward, then another; he couldn't control his body, he had to get a closer look. Had to get as close to the monster as he could. When he did, he tripped, his tired legs couldn't lift his foot up high enough, and the toes of his shoes dragged against the sand. It was only a stumble. He regained his balance, then shuffled back a step to avoid getting too close. But the monster stopped submerging itself. Its head turned. The tongue flitted one way then the other, back and forth, up and down. Its bright red eyes narrowed.

Then its gaze settled on Victor, as if they no longer lived in two separate worlds. He took another step back, then another. The snake moved toward him at a pace much faster than the rest of its journey. Victor back-pedaled, but his weary legs failed him once more.

He went down. His phone tumbled out of his hand. He looked around. There was nothing but desert. Victor scrambled to grab his phone and get to his feet, trying to move away from the predator he could no longer see.

At last he was able to close his hand around the phone, his window into that other world. He pointed the camera in front of him, but there was nothing there. Had he got turned around? He scanned right with the camera and found it. It still came at him, its movement no longer slow and plodding but fast and violent. Its massive maw gaping as it rushed toward Victor who was unable to stop the monster's approach. He scrambled back faster as the monster snake barreled toward him, its tongue tucked in its mouth, sand flying up in the air on either side of it. Victor turned to run. As he sprinted, he kept turning back with his phone to see if he was putting any distance between himself and the snake. He didn't think he was. The heat and sun sucked the energy from him, he felt himself slowing down. He pulled air into his lungs, but he couldn't get enough. He turned back toward the monster and lifted his phone. It was right behind him, its mouth wide, jaw unhinged and ready to eat.

Victor screamed, his eyes locked on the screen as he collapsed and awaited the inevitable.

The phone battery died, and the screen went blank.

About the Author

Joe Scipione lives in Illinois with his wife and two children. His stories have appeared in a number of anthologies, including "Satan is Your Friend Anthology," "Forgotten Ones," and "Throw Down Your Dead: An Anthology of Western Horror." He is also a book reviewer and senior contributor at horrorbound.net.

Seek, Don't Hide

Liam Hogan

The outcome is different every time they play.

As Rupert counts between sobs, children find new hiding places. Five- and six-year-olds fit into clothes hampers, under beds, behind curtains. Even, on occasion, the under-the-stairs cupboard, folded between the tightly sealed crates of Christmas decorations and the vacuum cleaner. Though in such cramped, upright positions they rarely stay still or quiet very long.

However hard he looks, he can never find them all.

And so, he has to watch as flashing lights gather outside and emergency services drag limp, blue bodies from whatever crevasse they wedged themselves into, party frocks torn and dirtied. He has to suffer the looks of pity, of contempt.

Of blame.

Then the game starts anew.

He refused to play, once. Just once. Thirteen bodies pulled from thirteen different hiding places, all bedraggled, all dead.

All his fault, or perhaps his wife's, busy in the kitchen decorating a baker's dozen cupcakes that will never be eaten. Fiddling with the central heating because, although it is a mild October, the doors have been opened so many times to so many parents, delivering their precious children into his and her care. None of the parents stay; that is the age the children are. Old enough to be left on their own, young enough that the parents are thankful for a couple of hours unencumbered to rush through weekend chores.

He's tried to convince the kids *not* to play. That play time is, in fact, over. Soft little hands cover his eyes when his won't. The countdown begins again and again until, heart breaking, he takes it up.

And he searches, and he searches. In the belief—the desperate hope—that if he finds them all the punishment will end.

But he never can. Never can find the most important of them. Little Amy, their pride and joy, the birthday girl. The one it started with. The one, he prays, it will end with.

Assuming his damnation is not eternal.

How can a father *not* know his child's favourite hiding place? The crawl space behind the built-in wardrobe where only Amy could fit. Was it the first time she'd hidden there, or merely the first time she'd done so when the central heating was on? The boiler not even in the same room, but sharing a wall. A wall through which carbon monoxide seeps.

Is that why their darling daughter never answers their calls, long after the game should have been over? The frantic, nightmarish search, the other kids more and more distressed, tears replacing joy, wails replacing laughter.

It took a sniffer dog to find Amy. A firecrew to rip apart the sturdily-built wardrobe. A single medic to carry her limp body to the ambulance, which didn't bother to sound its siren, to flash its lights, didn't bother to *pretend*.

The wardrobe is always the first place Rupert looks. She's not there, and nor are any of the other kids.

Something else lurks in the darkness but never comes out, never answers his calls.

Something the shape and size of his guilt.

Is he to blame? Any more so than his wife? Or the heating engineer who, only a month earlier, inspected the boiler? The previous owner who fitted the wardrobe and left such an inviting gap?

Or even Amy herself, for choosing to hide there?

All trying to work out who might be responsible proves is that it doesn't matter which god you pray to, how comfortably well off you are, how damned *careful* you are. Fate is always waiting in the wings. Waiting to crush you into the dirt on a whim. You, or your loved ones; and what, really, is the difference? How can you remain a family when the heart has been torn from it?

So maybe he *is* a coward. Maybe he shouldn't have sat in the garage as the car filled with fumes the day after the double funeral. But is that any worse than the vodka and paracetamol route his wife chose?

Is that why they're being punished? Is it their failure, their neglect? Or their subsequent weakness?

He can put the desperate hunt off no longer. "100," his voice creaks. He blinks the veil of tears from his reddened eyes.

The game begins again.

About the Author

Liam Hogan is an award-winning short story writer, with stories in Best of British Science Fiction 2016, and Best of British Fantasy 2018 (NewCon Press). He's been published by Analog, Daily Science Fiction, Nosleep Podcast, and Flametree Press, among others. He helps host Liars' League London, volunteers at the creative writing charity Ministry of Stories, and lives and avoids work in London.

Hey Diddle Diddle

By Jeff Samson

I should have known it would end like this. Should have seen the whole thing coming a mile away. Should have. But I didn't. Because how could I have?

But some things you can't see unless you're looking for them. Which I wasn't. Nor was anyone else. And you're a liar if you try to tell me otherwise. As if anyone in their right mind—and I won't pretend to be someone in their right mind—but as if anyone in their right mind could have known it wasn't just a rhyme. As if anyone in their right mind could have known that little old Mother Goose was a regular fucking Nostradamus.

* * *

"Daniel!"

I swiveled around in my chair. Luna slouched in the doorway of our lab. The makeup around her eyes was running. The hair she usually kept drawn into a tight little knot at the back of her head was coming undone. A few jet-black wisps were matted to her forehead with sweat. She was panting hard.

"You have to... have to come with me," she said.

"Is everything—" I said and started to get up.

"I can't..." she said and caught her breath. "I mean yes but... oh, Daniel, just come!"

I followed her out into the corridor and was almost run over by Tom McGinty, a big Irish fellow from Scranton who worked in Receiving and ran Texas Hold'em games out of East Wing's retired mess hall twice a month.

"Whoa, Danny Boy," he bellowed as he maneuvered around me with a gracefulness that belied his size.

I watched him lope down the corridor and quickly realized he was only one of countless more bodies bounding after one another as if they were running for their lives. And I would have thought they were doing just that had I not registered the exhilaration in their faces.

"Daniel!" Luna said.

And the next thing I knew my hand was in hers, and she was nearly dragging me down the hall. Towards what I had no idea. But I followed along like a heat-seeking missile as we wound through the wing. Banking around the reflexively locked-in-place bodies of those who'd stepped out of their offices and into a stampede. Snaking through knots of administrators too stubborn to break from their "all of the conference rooms are booked so let's just regroup in the hallway" meetings. Blowing past fellow lab rats whose healthy skepticism outpaced their curiosity enough to halt their steps, which, in light of a few recent mishaps, was completely understandable. And, to be honest, had Luna not been dragging me along, I probably would have counted myself among that last group. I might even have been running in the opposite direction.

We spilled out into a large, horseshoe-shaped clearing. The crowd gathered around the half-circle of windows at the center of the room was at least five white coats deep and expanding fast. At six foot three, I didn't have a problem seeing over the crowd. I did, however, have a problem making sense of what I was seeing.

"Boost!"

I looked down at Luna looking up at me imploringly.

"Daniel, I can't see!" she said and motioned under her arms, ape-like. "I need a boost!"

I placed my hands under her arms and lifted her off the ground, resting her back against my chest. And while I was sure our HR department would have had plenty to say about that—despite half the lab knowing we were something more than colleagues—I was also sure there wasn't a soul among us paying us any mind. Not with what was happening on the other side of the glass.

She whipped her head around. "Can you see?" Her mouth was close enough to kiss. And I must have nodded, because she said, "Good," and whipped it back around. Still, she cocked her head to the right to give me a better view.

Of the cat.

A Chinchilla Silver Persian, to be precise.

Sitting on a pedestal in the center of the room.

With a bow in its paw.

And a violin tucked under its chin.

Drawing the bow back and forth across the strings.

And fretting the notes with its little, snowy-white digits.

I can't remember everything that swept through my head in that instant. My first thought might have been that I was simply dreaming. And realizing I was not, I might have then questioned whether or not I'd slipped into a tangential reality around my third cup of morning coffee. And my next notion was very likely that we'd all been duped. That this was some elaborate prank on us all. Or on me alone. Which meant everyone else was in on it. Including Luna. Was that why she'd dragged me along? And what poor taste to pull a joke like this given what had happened with—

"Is that...?"

My eyes shifted to where the voice came from and found a young woman in the front row with her hands pressed up against the glass, her head turned away from the spectacle. Her wide-set eyes were darting back and forth at the faces around her, searching for an answer to the question she never finished, either because she was second guessing herself, or, I wondered, because she'd decided it was too absurd a thing to ask.

"I think I recognize the fingering," she said mostly to herself.

She turned back around and rapped three times on the window, trying to get the attention of any one of the twenty or so scientists and technicians and administrators inside the room observing, monitoring readouts, and furiously tapping and swiping away at tablets. After another round of rapping, a short, bearded man with coke bottle thick glasses looked up from his tablet. He jolted some, clearly unaware that such an audience had amassed in the viewing room. Then the woman up front motioned to her ear. And he jolted again, realizing we couldn't hear what he was hearing. He rushed to a nearby console and gave the screen a definitive tap.

The notes leapt from the speakers mounted above the viewing windows and into the air overhead. There were eight in total. Five in sequence from low to high. The last three of the sequence repeated. Their tone was sweet and floating. Their pitch precise. Their timing thoughtful. Playful. Sure.

The music stopped. The Persian lowered her instrument. Then reached out and twisted one of the tuning keys almost imperceptibly. She readjusted the placement of the violin under her chin and wiped a bit of resin off the low string.

Again, the viewing room was filled with music. And not just any music. But a singular piece of music. And it dawned on me what the woman in the front had meant to say. The question that should have been too absurd to ask.

Is that Bach's *Prelude*?

And the answer that should have been impossible to give.

Yes.

Luna shifted again, making me suddenly aware of the awful burn in my arms and lower back, and whipped her head around to face me. Her almond eyes were wide as aspen leaves and shimmering like they were lit from the inside. Her smile was full of wonder. The smooth skin around and between it all was pulled taut and mask-like. It was a look that seemed to me like the kind she might make if she fingered the killer in a whodunnit a chapter ahead of the reveal.

"Hey, Diddle Diddle," she said, barely suppressing a whisper.

We both heard a chuckle to our left and turned to find Tom McGinty beside us, shaking his head in disbelief.

"The cat and the fiddle," he said.

Luna must have seen something in my face that told her I wasn't sharing in her Eureka moment. Because she slid her hands over mine. She gave them a reassuring squeeze. And god, her hands were soft and warm.

I didn't want to take anything away from her. So I forced an easy smile. Pushed down the burn in my biceps. And laughed a little laugh.

But as she turned away to look at the cat with the fiddle, I felt my smile fall.

It was clear that, to Luna, we were witnessing some kind of kismet. Some kind of strange and silly cosmic work. For me? I couldn't shake the feeling that it was something else. Something strange indeed. But not silly. No.

Not silly at all.

* * *

That cat really did play beautifully. So beautifully, in fact, that we replicated the composition and regimen of serum MG102B across our whole vast suite of subjects, hoping to level up the progress that had, up to that point, been lacking within every single other species at our disposal.

And the results? Well...

* * *

"This is big, Daniel."

Luna was staring up at the waxing moon through the skylight set deep into the ceiling of my quarters. The moonlight bathed her bare skin in breathless blue, sculpting her pale body in polished agate.

Her eyes were narrowed from almonds to canoes, the way they always set when she was feeling pensive. And she always felt pensive after we made love. She propped herself up on an elbow, her pose mirroring mine, and reached behind her for the glass of whiskey on the nightstand. She rolled the last few sips of the last bottle of rye she'd been able to smuggle in around in her glass.

"Think about it," she said and took a sip. "We've essentially cheated a cool million years of cognitive evolution in the span of what... six months?"

"If Zander's models are correct," I nodded, still running a hand up and over the gentle curve of her hip and back down by way of her full, freckled butt.

"Models, schmodels," she said. "We don't need a computer model to tell us what we can see clear as day with our own two eyes."

I couldn't argue the point. Not in light of the progress we'd made in the last six months. And especially not in light of the last two weeks, where our progress was turning line graphs from gentle slopes into sheer cliffs rising—always rising—well above where the charts' upper limits had initially been set. And yes, charts and models aside, the things Luna and I had seen...

"I heard from Maria. You know, the Dominican data cruncher with the aquatics division. And don't give me that look like you don't know exactly who I'm talking about, Mister I-can't-stop-staring-at-her-*pompas.*"

I cleared my throat to protest, but she cut me off.

"It's fine, really. And I don't blame you. I can barely look away myself. I mean, when that gal walks down the hall it's an event.

"Anyhow, Maria said that yesterday they had a whole pod of Belugas watching *Young Frankenstein.*" She leaned in closer to me, flashing that big wonder-filled smile she seemed to wear more and more each day. "And they were laughing, Daniel. The fucking whales were laughing!"

I so badly wanted to say that what she was relaying was impossible. But that word—impossible—had taken a serious hit in terms of application of late. And at the rate we were going, improbable was very probably next in line for demotion.

"And not just at the slapstick stuff like Gene Wilder getting caught in the spinning bookcase or Peter Boyle dancing," she continued. "They got all the jokes. And you can't dismiss it as some kind of strange collective behavior, because they all laughed differently. Some guffawed, some chuckled, some snickered here and there. Maria said one was laughing so hard, she literally forgot to breathe. Three trainers had to dive in and practically drag her to the surface. Those whales might as well have been a bunch of humans in a movie theater."

I felt a chill run up my back at the word "humans." She must have seen me shiver because she set her glass on the nightstand and drew her soft, blue body up against mine. She cupped my face in her hand. Her long, delicate fingers were cool from the glass.

"Wanna hear the best part?"

"Sure," I said, fairly sure I did not.

"Maria said each whale had its own distinct laugh. One with a big, hearty belly laugh. Another with a high-pitched cackle. She said if she closed her eyes, this one chummy pair was a dead ringer for Burt Reynolds and Dom Deluise in the *Cannonball Run* outtakes. I can't even..."

She trailed off, lost for words and looking amazed. And I wanted to tell her I found it amazing, too. Because I did. I really did. But what came out was—

"What about the sheep?"

She cocked her head, and a solitary crinkle formed above her nose.

"The sheep?" she said with a breathy little laugh. "What—"

"The sheep," I said. I held her eyes as she searched mine.

"The sheep..." she said and gently shook her head. "Daniel, I don't think we're ever gonna know exactly why that happened. Or even exactly what happened. It's been what—six? Seven months? And it seems like the story's grown a dozen wrinkles since I first heard it."

"But doesn't that bother you? I mean, as a scientist, doesn't it bother you not knowing exactly what happened? Exactly why it happened?"

She dropped her head and rolled onto her back. She sighed a long time. Then reached over and took another sip of rye. This time she set the glass down on her stomach.

I followed her tongue as she tossed something around in her mouth without saying it out loud. I watched it tap-tap-tap her palate and come to rest against the back of her top two front teeth again and again. I watched her lips twitch and thin. When I looked in her eyes, they seemed fixed on some unseeable thing a thousand light years away.

"I don't know," she said at last. "Of course I'd like to understand it. But when I try to wrap my head around it all... Cats playing Bach. Roosters piloting flight simulators. Grizzlies writing out the complete works of Shakespeare in perfect cursive like a bunch of medieval monks trying to save civilization. And now...

belugas laughing at Mel Brooks. As a scientist, I don't have a fucking clue what's going on. I don't think any of us do. And I'm not sure science is gonna get us any closer to figuring this mystery out."

Then it was my turn to be lost for words. Because what was there to say? She was right. And I knew it.

She giggled.

"Igor, could you help me with the bags?" she said.

And I reacted without hesitation, as if she'd triggered a conditioned response.

"Sure. You take the blonde. I'll take the one in the turban."

And for the first time in my life, I found no joy in that classic exchange.

We laid there together, looking up at the stars softly twinkling in the square of sky above my bed. She was laughing her big, bright, leveling laugh. Real and free and peppered with snorts. The kind of laugh that could get a whole room laughing along. Or make a person fall in love. Or end a war.

I so badly wanted to revel in that laugh. And had I known then that her laughs were numbered I would have pushed aside what was gnawing at my head and savored it as lovingly and completely as Luna did her last few sips of rye. But I couldn't have known that. And I couldn't stop thinking.

About what possible reason there could be. For a sheep. To charge a technician. A technician who'd been working with it every day for the better part of two years. To knock him down. To ram its head into his face as he lay half propped up against the observation window. Over and over and over again. Until there was nothing left of the man's head but an unrecognizable mess of flesh and blood and brain and bone.

What reason there could be for a sheep—the skin at the top of its head split clear to the skull—to keep on charging until it punched through the plated glass. To poke its ruined head through the hole. To take a slow scan of the five security officers with tranquilizer guns drawn and cocked and aimed at its gory face. And proceed to draw its head back and forth across the razor edge of glass at its throat. Over and over and over again. Until its blood stopped spurting. Its frenzied bleating fell silent. And it moved no more.

"*Toy-bin,*" she laughed. "How the hell did he think to pronounce it *toy-bin?*"

And when it hurt to think anymore, it was her laughter, and the way her pale body quivered in the moonlight, and the subtle tremors that echoed through our bed, that lulled me to sleep.

* * *

When I was very young—I don't remember exactly how young—my grandfather passed away in the guest bedroom of our house after a long and painful battle with congestive heart failure. My mother had been by his side when he passed, cradling his wrist as she held his hand, and telling him that if it was time for him to go, then that would be all right. That everything would be all right. She'd stayed with him for hours, repeating those words until she no longer felt his breath on her cheek or his pulse at his wrist.

She'd told me it was an honor to be in the presence of someone when they passed. That it was a kind of bearing witness to one of the two most important stories in a person's life. And, just as with their birth, it was a story they themselves would never be able to tell. So the telling of that story fell to those who were with them in their final moments.

What I do remember, quite clearly, is what I asked her.

"What about when people die alone?"

And her answer.

"Then it is a loss doubly so. Which makes it all the more an honor to be with them."

And I remember the awful regret that fell over me like a heavy blanket. For not being there beside him, holding his hand as he passed. For not being the one who could tell his untellable story for him.

I felt none of that the night Luna died in my arms.

* * *

I found her in the long corridor that ran between the East and North Wings. The corridor we'd walked many times together and discovered held some rather remarkable acoustic properties, allowing two people to stand at opposite ends, and despite the hundred-meter distance between, carry on a crystal clear conversation at a whisper. We'd taken to doing just that. Even made a ritual out of it. She at one end. Me at the other. Whispering back and forth all the things we were aching to do to each other.

This time, she was halfway between those two points. She was on her back. One of her legs was bent in a way a leg shouldn't bend. Same with one of her arms. Jagged bones poked through her sleeve and pant leg. And her right hand was blown up to the size of a softball.

Her face...

Had I not known it so intimately, I would have had to check the ID on the lanyard around her neck. The lanyard that was looped around her left breast. The left breast that lay flopped over beside the right, a mere finger's width of skin connecting it to her body. The body that was framed in a pool of blood spreading out over the polished concrete floor.

I dropped to my knees beside her, certain she was gone. But she was breathing. It was slow and shallow and ragged and wet. And I don't know how. But she was breathing.

"Lu," I said, "Lu, I'm gonna get you help." But in fact, I had no idea how I might go about doing that. I knew if I called for help that no one would answer. And I knew if I tried to move her, I'd probably kill her. I took her by the hand that wasn't showing its bones. "I just need you to hold on."

Her right eye was nearly swollen shut. The white of her left was all but blotted out by deep-red florets. Blood pooled in her tear duct and spilled down the side of her nose and cheek in a thin, dark line.

Still she looked up at me with something like recognition.

"Ow..." she whispered.

A dam broke behind my eyes.

"I know it hurts, Lu. I—"

"No." She coughed hard, sending a shudder through her body and spraying a mist of blood on her lips. She took a few breaths. "The cow..."

I felt her hand shift in mine. "Lu, don't try to move," I said. But she slipped free of my grasp, and with agonizing slowness, lifted a finger.

"The cow..." she said.

I followed her finger, taking in the scene in the corridor as I looked down its length, the walls pocked with bullet holes and spattered with blood. The floors scuffed, cracked and chipped, littered with phones and tablets and scattered shell casings, some still smoking thin white wisps. Loose papers strewn all about. A pair of glasses. An overturned custodial cart, a slick of gray mop water running beneath one lifeless body. And another. And two more turned and twisted around each other to where I couldn't tell which limbs belonged to whom.

My eyes came to rest on a huge form beneath a row of flickering overhead lights. Black and white and bleeding out from what looked like half a dozen holes in its chest and neck and head. Its long tongue spilled from its maw like an oversized slug.

Beyond it lay five more like it. Every bit as massive. Every bit as riddled with rough, gaping wounds. The one farthest away lay half hidden by the emergency door, which had nearly cut it in two.

"The cow," she whispered.

I turned back to find her flashing a smile. A smile that still managed to shine with wonder, despite most of her teeth being broken off at the gum line. I suddenly remembered where I'd seen that smile before. I suddenly understood. And it wasn't Luna that finished the line, but me.

"Jumped over the moon," I whispered back.

Her smile lingered for a breath. Then slipped away. And took all of her wonder with it.

* * *

I don't know how long I sat there beside her. Only that at some point I was too spent to sob anymore. The world around me stormed back into existence. The world of distant screams. And muffled shots. And great, big concussions. And wailing klaxons. And smoke. Pouring black and oily into the corridor from the doorway behind me.

The next thing I knew I was running. Pounding down the corridor. Squeezing under the jammed emergency door. Bursting out the emergency exit. Sprinting across the grounds. Scuttling down the cliffside. Stumbling over the sand. And plunging into the icy sea. The sea I couldn't possibly have crossed. Not if I were an Olympic swimmer. Not a sea as rough as this. As cold as this.

Sensation quickly left my hands and feet as blood fled my extremities to warm my core. My strokes grew sloppy and weak. My body floated lower and lower in the waves. My presence of mind ebbed away.

I heard what sounded like yelling from somewhere on the beach behind me. I glanced over my shoulder to see a flurry of dark shapes emerging from the shadowy cliffs and clambering across the sand.

I swam harder. Or at least I tried to. If my arms and legs were still attached to my body, I couldn't be sure. Each cutting breath seemed shallower than the one before.

I heard the sound of something sloshing into the water. Then heavy, panting breath. Growing louder.

When I sensed that whatever it was in the water was right behind me, I spun around and raised my dead hands. As if they could have done me any good.

A huge head forged through the waves. A big, fat, blunted diamond, shimmering the dark and wet blue-black of ink, darker even than the sea that hid the rest of its body. Its eyes smoldered with cold yellow moonlight. A pair of powerful looking canines popped stark white against the empty black of its maw.

The last thing I remember was my head sinking beneath the waves, but not before the great, big, shaggy Newfoundland paddled up to me, its face so close to mine it could have licked my nose. And snarled.

"The fuck you think you're going?"

* * *

I can't be sure of what happened next. Or for how long it

happened. And I wish it wasn't all so hazy. But being confined to an eight-by-eight-by-eight-foot cell without any natural light tends to give your clock a fairly serious cleaning.

At first, I lost track of day and night. It wasn't long before my whole grasp of time came loose. That concept that had always been a fixed and rigid thing started to soften. Had five seconds passed? Or barely one? A handful of minutes or a handful of hours? Days? Weeks? Certainly not a month? But I couldn't be certain of any of it.

The only sense I could somewhat rely on to gauge the passage of time was touch. The blackness was too complete for my eyes to ever adjust. I couldn't smell anything beyond the blood in my nose and my own waste. What little I could hear was distant and underwater. And they'd made me an enemy of taste.

But touch? That was as acute as ever.

I could feel my body screaming with pain when the chimps would pay me a visit and whale on me with truncheons. Could feel my body performing its healing process and sense that it was always at the same point in that process when they would return to blacken my bruises and open my cuts. But as to how many visits they paid me, or how often, I couldn't say for sure.

I could feel the hunger pangs tugging at my guts and tying them in knots. And it was always when the pain got to the point where I was whimpering and begging for whatever it was still inside me to claw itself the fuck out already so I could die, that I'd hear the cell's Judas gate scrape open. And I'd reach into the tray to find a pocked and pitted dish with a rusty spoon inside containing something that might or might not have been soup with small chunks of what might or might not have been meat, but that I devoured without a thought or care, and devoured again and again no matter how many times it came back up. Based on what I knew about starvation symptoms, that might have been every four or five days. But again, I couldn't be certain.

And I could feel the drugs the pigs pumped into my veins spreading through me like molten lead, my skin turning to fire when the fevers spiked, the sweat sloughing off me when they broke. Could feel my mind engorged with strange pictures and phantasmagoric scenes, racing like a time-lapse movie, whether I was awake or in a dream. And it was always when the fevers lost their edge and the hallucinations were at their fuzziest that they would return and pump me full of whatever concoctions their needles held. But duration? Frequency? I couldn't possibly know.

* * *

They let me out once. Or dragged me out, I should say. Two hulking silverbacks, one on each arm, walked me through the darkened halls, still rank with the smell of carnage, towards the main auditorium and lecture hall. I could see the flicker of torches through the large double doors, hear a babble of shrieks and hoots, barks and bleats. Tense. Excited. Expectant.

The lecture hall harkened back to old school universities, with tiers of seats arranged in a horseshoe, surrounding the stage on three sides, the fourth wall being for blackboards, projection screens, and diagrams. Every seat was filled, and the crowd roared when I was brought in and dragged down the wide carpeted stairs to the stage. A public execution, I thought.

But I was stunned to see another person already there. I hadn't seen nor heard another human in... however long it had been. The poor guy was so beaten and bloodied and bruised that I didn't recognize him at first.

"Hey!" I tried to shout. But all that came out was a weak croak. And if the man heard me, he didn't show it. He just stood there, wavering between another pair of silverbacks holding him by his arms. Or rather, holding him up. He looked like he could barely stand. And his eyes were little more than lumps of swollen eyelid.

It was the sheer size of him that jogged my memory. He was, despite it all, still the biggest man I had ever seen.

"Tom?" I said. "Tom! Tom, are you okay?"

Nothing. No reaction.

"It's me, Tom. It's Danny!"

His lips parted at the sound of my name, revealing a jagged row of smashed teeth. And the sound—I couldn't call it a word—

that slushed out from between them was low and pained and oddly like the rustle of dead leaves.

The four gorillas released their steel grips on our arms and lumbered off and up into the audience. Tom tottered, wavered, but kept his legs under him. I ran up to him. Grabbed him by the shoulders. Then lost myself and hugged him. It never felt so good to touch another human being. Even one as broken as Tom.

But he didn't react. He just slumped against me.

"Jesus, Tom," I said, spilling tears onto his barrel chest. "What the fuck did they do to you?"

The crowd was getting louder. More barking and bleating, hooting and squealing. Then a chant began. Indistinct at first. Like a song heard softly under the roar of the tide. Growing louder. And louder. And louder. Until it was all I could hear.

Two men enter. One man leaves.

* * *

They didn't release me afterwards. Not that I really expected them to. But I had hoped they might. A slim hope. Though not so slim as to keep me from nearly...

As for why they kept me alive at all, that remained a mystery.

Was it in the name of science? To experiment upon and observe? To learn? Or was it simply to inflict pain upon me?

I asked as much of the Jack Russell Terrier who would come to my cell when my fevers were at their worst and place a chess board between us and arrange his pieces before him and mine before me.

"Why are you doing this?" I would ask him. "What do you want from me? What are you hoping to accomplish?"

But he wouldn't answer my questions. He'd simply make his move. And say things that hurt.

"Maria." He'd lick his chops. "Would you believe that sweet, round ass of hers fed us for a whole week? A whole. Fucking. Week. She was a long time dying."

And I'd make my move.

"Is that what this is?" I'd ask. "Revenge?"

And he'd ignore me.

"Your big friend from Scranton?" he'd say. "We chained him to a rock and had an eagle peck his liver out. Spoiler alert: it didn't grow back."

He'd look thoughtfully towards the ceiling in the silence that followed. And it was a long time that passed before he'd say, "You should have killed him, you know. Would have been better that way. We might have even let you go." He'd bark a laughing bark. "I'm kidding, of course. But you. *You.* Those words you spoke all dramatic-like when you took your hands off his throat? When you stood up and addressed the crowd? What was it you said again?"

I'd be silent. He'd wait. He'd always wait. And I knew he'd wait as long as it took. So I'd say them.

"I am not an animal," I'd mutter.

"That was it," he'd say. And he'd cock his head, look me in the eye, point a furry paw towards my face. Then he'd grin a doggy grin and say, "You." Like we were old friends who'd just shared a secret.

Then he'd make his final move and beat me. Always with his knight finding my king.

"Checkmate, lab rat," he'd say. And he'd laugh and laugh and laugh. So hard that he'd fall off his stool and roll around on the floor. Wheezing like Muttley from *Wacky Races.*

* * *

It's been a long time—or at least what feels like a long time— since I've had any visitors. Or since I've heard the paddings and murmurs of my captors beyond my cell. Or the washed-out sounds of pain and death in the distance. The wounds from my beatings have healed well past the point of when they'd usually come and work me over again. I haven't felt the awful work of their drugs in my system. And the pain that both gnawed at my insides and portended my meals has given up trying to alert me to that most basic of needs, and has instead given way to a numbed acceptance of the inevitable.

I sit at the edge of my cell, staring at my Judas gate, what little saliva I have left oozing into my parched mouth. I imagine hearing the awful scrape of it sliding open. Drawing myself up to the dish and the spoon inside. Feasting on whatever vileness my masters were kind enough to bring me.

But I know my last meal has come and gone. Like I knew it would. Like I've known all along.

Because I know this rhyme.

I know how it goes.

And I know how it ends.

About the Author

Jeff Samson makes a living as a creative director in the advertising industry. Like Don Draper, you ask? Yes, just like Don Draper... with brain damage. He brews beer when he's not writing and occasionally drinks it when he is. His work can be found in numerous publications, including Nature, Lore, Cast of Wonders and Perihelion. Jeff lives in New Jersey with his wife and two children, and no cats. You can find him at jeffsamsonwrites.com.

THE CLEANING LADY

Samantha Bryant

Margarita groaned when she opened the door. Blood spattered the walls in streaks and drips. The sink was clogged with gore. Stiffly-dried rags that had probably been bonds for the sacrifices littered the floor, and a wave of putrid air nearly made her gag. The reel-to-reel still spun, though the film had run out hours ago.

Sighing, she propped the door open with the trash can and spilled a single drop of lavender essential oil into her face mask before she donned it. This was going to be a hard day's work. If she wanted to finish before nightfall, she'd better get to it. She clicked the off button, and the projector came to a shuddering halt. She bumped her foot against the canister. Another cheesy old vampire movie. Junior thought it funny to feed while fictional accounts of his kind ran in the background.

When the Old Master had been alive, it had never been like this. Sure, there had been bloody messes to clean up, but he had at least made an effort. He'd comported himself with elegance and grace. A simple slicing of the throat and the capture of the blood into a spotless golden ewer so it could be consumed from crystal goblets. Sophisticated. Debonair. Sometimes you could even believe the girls were only sleeping, they looked so untouched when she arrived to clean up after him. They'd died with words of love in their ears and ecstasy on their minds.

None of this evisceration nonsense, leaving the room saturated and stinking. Junior was little better than an animal.

Leaving chunks of flesh in the sink and long bones scattered across the floor. Disgusting. The stench of fear saturated the walls. If she found this young woman's head, the face would be paralyzed mid-scream, eyes wide and unblinking.

Manuel probably appreciated that there were no longer bodies to dispose of, but Margarita thought a corpse was preferable. The family owned plenty of land and the bones could rest alongside the generations of others that had fed the family fortunes. Investigators who wouldn't be deterred by money could always be mesmerized into misdirection. At worst, they too could fertilize the land.

She wiped her sponge across the ridiculous illuminati eye first. It looked like Junior had painted it on the wall with the blood of his victim. What was he, four years old? Playing with his food? Spoiled, nasty cretin. He deserved to be staked. She half wanted to do it herself, but Manuel still felt they owed the family loyalty for their wealth and longevity.

She wondered if he'd been half in love with the Old Master himself. She could understand that. She still dreamed about the one time he had touched her, the shiver that had caressed her spine. If he had ever asked it of her, she'd have bared her throat to him, but he'd always told her that she was family, not food. And now, the Old Master was no more. He'd taken the walk into the dawn from which none of his kind can return. He'd said, he'd had all the life he wanted.

How could Junior be his legacy? The Young Master was a disgrace, an abomination. She imagined wiping him off the earth as easily as she cleaned the entrails from the sink.

Catching a glimpse of herself reflected in the window, she unbuttoned the top two buttons of her work dress and posed suggestively. She still had it. Nearly two hundred years in the Master's employ, and she hadn't aged more than ten years.

Manuel could be persuaded if she played her cards right. It was time they washed their hands of the degraded remnants of this once-great family and took their own walk into the dawn together, hand in hand, just as they'd begun. Some jobs weren't worth it.

About the Author

Samantha Bryant teaches Spanish to middle schoolers. Clearly, she's tougher than she looks. She writes The Menopausal Superhero series of novels, and other feminist leaning speculative fiction. When she's not writing or teaching, Samantha enjoys family time, watching old movies, baking, reading, gaming, walking in the woods with her rescue dog, and going places. Her favorite gift is tickets (to just about anything). You can find her on Twitter and Instagram @samanthabwriter or at: http://samanthabryant.com.

WHISPER WOODS

Eddie Generous

They acted like Darren didn't understand what "five years and eligible for parole in three" meant. They said Darren's dad just happened to win the fight, and it was the system that was flawed. Assault was only what they called it when a poor man beat a rich man.

In the living room, floral patterned couches and off-white doilies under dusty vases of plastic flowers, Darren's half-drunk grandfather, Leroy—legal guardian until Dad got out because Mom was in the wind—told him all about the good fights he'd been in. How fighting was noble and righteous, and how the law just had to stick their noses in and protect one of their own.

"That doctor man should've watched his mouth 'round your dad. If he wasn't rich and didn't have all them connections with politicians and judges, your dad would be out and you'd back at home, normal. And I'd be retired again instead of playing house. Like, ain't I had enough? Sixty-six, ain't I had enough?"

The ways of the world weren't news, and Darren didn't need to hear it to know they didn't want him there. He didn't want to be there either. It might've been better if he was somewhere cool, a town where everybody didn't call his mom a slut for taking off, and everyone didn't know his dad was in jail, and everyone didn't know his grandmother had to get a job at the tennis club—she'd been saving to become a member, before—because the budget went out of whack with Darren's existence.

Darren got up and took a step away from the loveseat he'd

been sitting on because the sun glare hitting the TV was too much and listening to his grandfather get drunker made him mad.

"Take your glass out and see if Nancy's got any Vachon's in the cupboard."

Darren turned and took the glass from the table, bumping the strange stone sculpture his grandmother placed on the coffee table as a centerpiece to the room. It was ugly and dark green, polished soft smooth. Its overlong arms and legs coiled around its slender body. The head was oblong and faceless.

"Watch that, Nancy'd have your ass if you broke it."

"Stupid looking."

"Don't matter, she likes it."

Darren grumbled non-words as he shuffled to the kitchen, dragging his socked feet. Even lifting to walk seemed like work. The cup went into the sink, and Darren checked the cupboard next to the stove. It smelled funny in there, spices and fruit stink from the compost bin. There was a wicker cradle full of dried flowers hanging from the ceiling next to the lightbulb, but it hardly helped the scent, and more than anything, it was in the way. He ducked it; something about it made him feel off, but his grandmother hung it and it was her pantry. "…and Nancy'd have your ass," he said in a whiny mockery. He reached into the box of Ah Caramel! cakes and took out two packs.

"Hey, gonna make me spill," his grandfather said, barely catching the cake package Darren tossed onto his chest. "Maybe I teach you some manners? You're not too big to go over my knee."

Darren *was* too big to go over his grandfather's knee, and he grumbled something to that effect as he made for *his* bedroom. The old man had pins in his legs and a fake hip, had arthritis in his hands from working at Ford for forty-seven years. The old man was all talk. Now his grandmother, she might try, might succeed even. She was only sixty and strong like a farm hog. She didn't get drunk, and she didn't threaten him, but that didn't mean she liked Darren living there. She talked about him without really talking about him—the money, the free time gone, the changes in lifestyle she hadn't anticipated, ones that went against the lifestyle she'd come to expect from retirement—despite rarely having anything golden about her golden years, so far. She said it all without saying how come so much was different, as if his being twelve meant he was dumb.

The spare room where he slept was stiff, with a musty smell, and had flower wallpaper and an ugly wooden bureau. His grandmother said he had to make the bed every day; he'd never made his bed living with his dad. Most times, he'd slept on a bare mattress with a pillow and blanket. All the extra was just trouble.

The whole scene made him sick, like it was him who got the sentence when his dad whooped that dude's ass. "Bullshit," he said.

He sat on the made bed and opened the second cake package. As he chewed, he thought about the future. Three to five years living like a prisoner, under their roof, playing by their rules. No thanks.

It hit him then. The answer. Butterflies set free in his heart. Everything he needed was out in the garage where they'd put all of his dad's stuff when his dad went away.

* * *

Richie lived in the apartment three over from where Darren lived before the arrest. His parents both worked, and his five siblings hung out, unattended to, most weekends. Richie answered the text from Darren's grandfather's cell, coming into *the kids'* shared smartphone, with the simple statement: *10 min.*

Darren had a backpack of food and was in the garage digging out the little tent and all the other camping stuff when Richie came through the door. He had a cigarette between his lips, unlit.

"You got to help me carry all this," Darren said without looking up as he tied a cord around the tent bag and a tarp. He'd been kicking the tarp flat and dust rode the atmosphere like fog.

"Where to?"

"Whisper Woods."

Richie took a lighter from his pocket and lit the tip of the cigarette. He exhaled heavy after inhaling heavy. "You gonna live in Whisper Woods?"

Darren shouldered his backpack and stood straight. "Yeah." He wiped cobwebs onto his pant leg. "Why not? Not like any of that stuff's true."

111

Richie shrugged and grabbed the handles of the tent bag. "Got T.P.?"

Darren's eyes flashed, and he dropped his bag before hurrying inside to steal toilet paper.

* * *

Sweaty hot, the boys got to the trailhead, hiked into the forest about fifty yards, and then hooked a right, toward the creek. They pushed through a wall of cedars and found a small clearing. Rough but enough. They dropped their bags, and Darren unzipped one to grab the two cans of Lucky Lager he'd stolen from his grandfather's beer fridge. Richie handed over a cigarette when he accepted a cool can.

"How long you gonna stay out here?"

"Three to five," Darren said. "You could stay, too. No school. No sisters. No bullshit."

Richie shook his head. "I ain't home by eight, my mom got my face on milk cartons and telephone poles."

"Pussy."

"Whatever, just 'cause your mom took off. Not my fault my mom gets real worried."

Darren spat onto the brown forest floor. "You just like looking at your sisters in the shower."

"Bitch, you like looking at my sisters in the shower."

Darren sucked hard on the cigarette and spoke around a cloudy exhale, "They like me looking at them in the shower."

"Yeah, right."

The tent reached about four feet high. It was red and grey, cheap. Where they'd settled, it had only a couple roots poking up, nothing Darren couldn't deal with. His fishing pole leaned against a balsa right by where Richie had set up a circle of rocks for a fire pit. They'd gathered twigs and made a teepee in the center of the pit for when it was time to light the thing. Darren sat in the dirt to carve into a felled cedar branch, peeling away smaller offshoots and brown needles.

"Look man, I'm going."

Darren huffed. "What, you scared of the whispering pervert?"

"Nah, ain't no pervert. Pervert's just what they call him nowadays. I ain't being in here after dark, hell, not even when the sun starts going down. You know what they say. They say everybody knows but won't nobody do shit."

"Pussy. Who's everybody?"

"Yeah, whatever. Rich people, I guess. I'll come back tomorrow, check out your corpse."

"Tell Bernice I said hey."

"Fuck you, man," Richie said as he pushed through the cedar wall, headed back for the trail.

* * *

The fire crackled as the sun went down. Darren had a marshmallow speared, dangling six inches above the peak of the flames. All was quiet aside from the fire's crackle until he heard the soft, helpless voice floating on the warm, evening air. It was feminine, old, and familiar... somehow.

"Help me.

"I am hurt.

"I cannot move."

Darren looked around, fear digging in deep, but also something else. A part of him needed to help that voice. He stood, his aged and weathered Nikes brown with freshly-turned soil. "Hello?" he said. "Who's there?"

* * *

Richie sniffled back tears and snot as he led three police officers and Darren's grandparents to the place where he'd last seen Darren. The tent had blown into the wall of cedars and the fishing pole leaned into a shrubby bush, but the site appeared otherwise undisturbed. The backpack was there. The beer cans and the empty wrapper from a pack of marshmallows were there.

"And when did you last see him?" one of the cops asked.

"Like two days ago. Maybe like six o'clock. I got home in time for supper." Richie swiped his wrist beneath his nose. "You think the woods got him?"

One of the cops scoffed, but nobody said anything for a few seconds.

"The whispering tongue and the blood begun run."

The cops and Richie turned to Darren's grandfather.

"Mr., uh, Leroy?" The cop leaned forward as he spoke, as if to give the man a better angle to hear by.

Darren's grandfather ignored him, staring blankly into the shadows cast by the trees and the sun peeking through the flora umbrella overhead. "Mothers do weep, and fathers do rage. Death and sadness many a hearts do cage."

"Chaisson, we have a leg and a Devils T-shirt." The voice crackled from one of the cops' radios.

Nancy put her hand over her mouth. The cop keyed the mic. "Copy."

Leroy continued. "Dry be the flesh, the flesh of the once supple young."

When he finished, everyone remained silent while the birds chirped and the chipmunks chattered, leaves and needles crunched gently. Leroy kept his eyes trained hard on the deeper woods.

* * *

In the basement of the hospital, Richie, alongside Darren's grandparents, identified the faded New Jersey Devils Stanley Cup Champions shirt Darren had been wearing.

"So, you got a foot, what about the rest of him?" Leroy asked.

The doctor scrunched his face tight and said, "The rest is almost certainly in bits or somewhere down river. The river's running fast, and the dam's doing its part. I'm sorry, but…"

"Almost certainly, huh?" Leroy said. "You in on it too? The secret? Try to keep anyone from knowing the truth? Why you all do it?"

The doctor lifted his left eyebrow and clicked his tongue, said nothing, but shook his head like Leroy had a case of lost marbles.

* * *

The funeral was somber. Kids from Darren's school showed up in stuffy, ill-fitting suits and dresses. They stood, bored, while the adults shook hands and offered empty platitudes. The mayor and the chief of police, and a whole host of recognizable, unnameable faces stood around Nancy, shaking her hand and giving her hugs. A few kissed her cheeks.

"Those guys smoothing her over. Make it so she don't ask questions," Gerald Thompson said, leaning in close to Leroy's ear. "They know like I know, like you know. Even more, my bet."

Leroy licked his teeth beneath his lips. He never trusted the upper crust, and he knew things. Strange things. Things about Whisper Woods. But most of that was so long ago, and mythical. It was the kind of thing ingrained in him, like buying that Jesus walked on water.

"I don't doubt it," Leroy said, and the line progressed. The mayor took Leroy's hand in a surprisingly sandpaper-rough grasp. "Mayor."

"We're all real broke up about this one. Wish it could've been different." The mayor pumped the hold twice and then moved on.

Leroy looked at Nancy. Tears dampened the makeup on her cheeks, her eyes glared at nothing, unfocussed, while her fingers fidgeted with the leather charm bracelet she wore.

"I bet you're real broke up," Leroy hissed to himself.

* * *

Nancy said he was crazy, his son refused to speak to him, and more than four hundred townsfolk had already shook his hand at the memorial service three days after the boy had gone missing— they'd cremated the leg. Nancy was wild with grief, but went into work anyway—to keep her mind elsewhere. Leroy went through the motions, but ached to re-pitch the tent Darren had pitched, in Darren's campsite, knew that *almost certainly* he'd hear something.

People didn't talk about the stories much anymore, but when he was a boy, Leroy knew all about Whisper Woods; everybody knew when Janine Teirny went missing from the woods, only to be found a day later, burned beyond recognition in an abandoned shack, that she was still out there, being used up. People talked indirectly and pointed fingers and demanded there be a search of the woods, despite finding what the medical examiner claimed was her body.

But there was no search, never even got to that point.

"It's Dracula that's out there," Chad Hunwick told Leroy back in the third grade.

"My gramma says there's a hole that goes all the way to hell, that's how come nobody ever cut the forest down even though it's in the middle of town," Beatrice Shea told Leroy in fifth grade.

"Maybe it's like aliens," Leroy told Adrian Runner between coughs in the tenth grade as they passed back and forth a pinner of the scratchiest marijuana either would ever smoke.

The only thing that never changed was that the voice was there, and that everybody knew it was there, but nobody did anything about it. Once, in the sixties, the local daily printed a story of outrage and demands—a mother had lost her daughters to Whisper Woods. The mayor was quoted the next day, promising that they took missing children seriously, but also pointed out that the woman's daughters had been seen—according to three eyewitness accounts—getting into an all-black van a block from the trail entry into the forest, and that van was seen heading southbound toward the highway. Then nothing, not a peep.

* * *

The tent was up, and Leroy wore a sheen of Deep Woods Off, though hardly any sanguivorous insects frequented Whisper Woods. He lit a fire a few minutes before full sundown and waited, twelve-pack of Lucky Lager by the front right foot of his canvas pop-chair. He tapped the scuffed toe of his sneaker now and then, as if to remind himself the beer was all there still.

The moon was up, but hardly dented the blackness of the forest. The air had chilled, but was still a fine fit for short sleeves. So, comfortable.

Dozing, eight beers deep, a sound roused Leroy enough to focus him. The sound drifted to him again and he knew it immediately.

His eyes remained closed when he heard Darren's voice. "Help, Grandpa.

"I'm hurtin'.

"I can't move nothin'."

Leroy popped to his feet, knocking the dregs of a warm can of Lucky onto the smoldering fire pit. The foam hissed, and Leroy shouted, "Darren?"

Nothing.

Nothing.

Nothing.

"Darren, where are you, boy?"

The silence was total. No animals hooting or screeching. No forest sounds of cracking or breaking detritus. Only quiet and his quickening breath.

"Darren?"

Nothing.

Nothing.

Noth—

The voice, seemingly further away, said, "Help me."

Leroy ducked into the tent, feeling around the darkness. He came up with the Maglite he'd borrowed from Reba Lechance—a widow from up the block with a dead cop husband and a thing for Leroy Stewart. The light shined a powerful beam, and Leroy called out, "Darren, where are ya?"

"This way," Darren said, and Leroy took off in an ambling jog down the trail.

Immediately his knees and hip ached, his chest burned, and his throat became full with chunky mucous. He spat and coughed. But he kept on.

Twigs snapped beneath his feet. Tree limbs brushed his arms. Needles and sticks raked at his neck and face. But he kept on.

"Help me."

That voice was closer, but Leroy had no wind left in him to respond.

"Come get me!"

Closer yet and Leroy pushed, walking, but quickly as he dared, wishing he was sober, or maybe a little more drunk. The light bounced, playing off the wild browns and greens of the season. He was hundreds of yards from the trail and moving deeper into the thick of the woods.

"I'm hurtin' all over!"

The voice seemed right there, right next to him.

Ahead, the trees thickened into a wall, and the light cast only a foot in front of him. The branches and limbs pressed against his arms and face, and then his legs. But he kept on, pushing through, the gnarly twigs and limbs driving bloody divots into his flesh.

He began to emerge, as if being birthed by the trees.

"I'm stuck in here!"

The voice came with an echo and once Leroy's face was through the wall of brush—blood bubbling and running down his cheeks and neck—he saw why. There was an old mine shaft with a wooden frame entry. He stumbled and leaned against his knees, shining the light into the mouth of the tunnel. The wood inside had been replaced and kept up, as if the mine were live. The stone of the walls shined with black symbols painted thereon.

Leroy gasped a breath and then exhaled, "Dare-en!"

"Help me!"

The pain and terror in those words rejuvenated the old man's well-worn frame, and he barrelled down the slope of the tunnel, ignoring the paintings, ignoring the fresh beams buttressing the ceiling, ignoring all but the rocky floor and the sound of his grandson's pleas.

"Get me!"

The floor began to level some, but Leroy's momentum had him running still. His toe bumped an up-risen stone and sent the man into a plunge. His arms shot out, and the snap of his right wrist echoed from the walls before the reports of his groaning drowned all else. The Maglite rolled until it lit above a chasm. Leroy grabbed his right arm with his left hand and tried to squeeze off the pain. He attempted to rise then, but different pain sliced into his bones from his prosthetic hip down. He groaned again.

"Grandpa?"

The voice was so close the pain melted and dripped into the periphery. Leroy kicked with his good leg and reached for the flashlight. His breathing was ragged and anguished, he tasted copper and snot. Painful tendrils reached from his lungs into his biceps.

He got to the lip of the chasm and shined the light down.

It wasn't so deep.

Leroy saw only two shapes, at first. One was an emaciated, pale, shirtless, one-legged version of Darren. A map of red and blue veins and arteries coursed his frame. The other was a slender form, too tall to be a man, too skinny to exist in a world of gravity. The thing had legs and feet. It had a torso and shoulders. It had arms, arms that reached up through a jagged tear in Darren's stomach. Its head was oblong and bulbous at the bottom. It had no eyes, but it had a mouth, and a tongue. The tongue was long and deep red. It plunged into a vein jutting from Darren's neck.

It looked strangely familiar, but he couldn't place it.

"Help me," Darren's mouth said, his eyes teary and blinking up at his grandfather. Despite it all, the boy was alive.

Leroy began shaking and the Maglite's beam played over a wider swathe of the darkness. Bones. Thousands upon thousands of human bones—the skulls the determinant factor—lined the floor of the chasm.

The thing turned its attention into the shine of the light and withdrew its long arms from the slit gash in Darren's abdomen. Its smooth, eyeless face seemed to peer into Leroy, and then those impossibly long arms reached for him.

Leroy's breaths came and left in tiny pants. Darren began moaning words of his own accord, "Make it stop. Make it stop. Make it stop."

"I... I'll... get... just... a—" Leroy squeezed the Maglite and swung at the thing, nailing its reaching arms. It jerked away from the pain and opened its mouth, letting its tongue dance. "Fuck... you," he said and took another swipe.

Darren began breathing heavier and lifted his hands no more than a foot before exhaustion forced them to drop. The thing slithered a leg around Darren's waist. Leroy threw the flashlight and the thing balled into itself and he recognized it as the statue from the coffee table.

"Up... up," he said, leaning in deep, grasping his grandson's naked thigh, and tugging. Darren cried out and flopped his upper half onto Leroy's arm. Pain tremored, and the old man went rigid.

Darren whined into his grandfather's ear, "There's three of them."

The thing in the pit lashed out and laid Darren flat. Terrified, self-preservation instinct activated, Leroy used all the strength he had left to whip backward. He panted and gasped, stretching out beyond the edge of the pit, blowing dust with each exhale. "I... I'll... get... hel—"

Footfalls chasing down the tunnel silenced Leroy's hapless promise before it could be made, and he waited, knowing they'd come to help him, knowing they'd rescue Darren, knowing they'd destroy the abomination. He turned onto his spine, felt the long spindly fingers of the thing brush the back of his head.

Firelight ignited from copper fixtures perched high on the walls. The footfalls drew closer, and Leroy looked up at Nancy. She wore a tennis skirt, sneakers, a pink polo tee, and her charm bracelet. She touched at the little silver charm.

"Oh, Leroy," she said, rushing to his side.

"It's... Dare... en," Leroy managed between gasps.

"Shh, it's all over now." She patted his head and looked anywhere but in the pit. "It's all over."

"Dare..." Leroy trailed off taking in a whooping inhale. "A... live."

More footfalls approached, quicker. Heavier. Two cops, the mayor, and three garbagemen. The light of the chamber fixtures played yellow off their pale faces.

"I... found... him," Leroy tried again, his eyes wild with wonder and desperation.

The mayor frowned and patted Nancy on the back. She stood and the man said over his shoulder, "Feed the Lords what they want, if they want him, and then put the body out at the campsite."

"You want'm burned?" one of the garbage men asked.

The mayor and Nancy backed away a few steps. "Probably won't make a difference. He looks a hundred years old as it is, sapping him won't change much," the mayor said. "Plus, the widow won't question if he looks a little off."

Nancy shook her head, tears budding.

"Nan... see?" Leroy locked his gaze with his wife's.

Nancy looked away, brought the charm to her lips.

"Go on now," the mayor said, nodding to the garbagemen. Two of them grabbed Leroy's feet. Pain rocketed up his legs, and he wailed. Nancy's breath hitched, but she did not move.

"What if they want'm all the way?" one of the garbagemen asked as they pitched Leroy down into the embrace of their gods.

Leroy tumbled, which lessened the pain in his legs, letting him focus. He felt the strange grasping limbs tighten around him, and the thing's tongue break the skin of his throat. Beneath him, Darren moaned and began panting for air.

"That's a good thing," the mayor said. "To feed our Lords is a good thing."

Darren's gasps drew short and reedy, then ceased.

The mayor leaned over to look into the shadowy pit. Leroy struggled to rise, but it was hopeless, his arm broken and the strength sapped out of him by the pain and effort.

"Pull the kid out," the mayor said before he bowed his head and closed his eyes. "Please accept this offering, our Lords. Please bless us, you of knowledge and light and flesh."

In unison, the garbagemen and cops said, "Amen."

Nancy whispered, "Amen."

Leroy felt his blood reversing course and those unhuman hands and legs pressing into him, peeling his clothing. The other two abominations, identical to the first, slithered from beneath the bone pile and began running cool, clammy appendages against his bare flesh. He tried to scream but managed only a whisper. "Nancy... please."

About the Author

Eddie Generous is the author of numerous books, including Savage Beasts of the Arctic Circle, Rawr, Plantation Pan, and many more. He is the founder/editor/publisher/artist behind Unnerving and Unnerving Magazine, and the host of the Unnerving Podcast. He lives on the Pacific Coast of Canada with his wife and their cat overlords.
www.jiffypopandhorror.com

Last Shot

Tim Jeffreys

His phone rang. It was Vinny from the agency.

"Great news," Vinny said. "Coleman's dead."

Russell took the phone from his ear and looked at it for a few moments before putting it to his ear again.

"Did you say *dead?*"

"Yes, dead, you lucky bastard. Dead."

"Lucky? What are you talking about?"

"That photo. You got the last shot of him before he died. It's going to make us—I mean, *you*—a fortune. All the newspapers are going to want to run it, probably front page. Turns out he was on his way to hospital. He'd been getting chest pains. They tried to do a bypass, but he died on the operating table. Great, huh?"

On a hunch, Russell had spent the previous evening standing in the cold outside the Bexley Building whilst spats of snow twisted down out of the sky. When he'd arrived, there'd been a small huddle of photographers at the foot of the building's steps, all, like him, hoping to get a shot of pop singer Valeria Lopez who was rumoured to be in London and was supposed to have an apartment at the Bexley. It had turned into a battle of endurance, them against the freezing temperatures. One by one, the other photographers had surrendered until only Russell remained. It had gone eleven o'clock, he could no longer feel his feet, and he'd almost waved his own metaphorical white flag, when a limo pulled up alongside the front steps. But instead of Lopez, it was the actor Yale Coleman who emerged from the building's entrance.

Though he'd had his camera poised for a shot, Russell didn't start snapping straight away. He didn't think anyone would be interested in pictures of an elderly TV star who hadn't done any notable work for years. Coleman was accompanied by his wife, who was supporting him, and a bodyguard. The bodyguard, an intimidating presence, gave Russell a warning glace as they passed: another reason he hadn't started firing off his camera. It was only when Coleman was seated in the limo with the window half wound down that Russell decided to grab a shot of him, if only so his evening wouldn't be a total waste. He doubted the agency would buy the pics. But he'd captured something: Coleman, pale and grey, looking out through the half-closed window at something to the right of the photographer and an odd expression of anticipation on his face, as if he'd seen something that both delighted and terrified him. Russell could see how the picture would be something the press would be clamouring for now that the man was dead.

"It's a shame," Russell said into the phone. "He was great in his time."

"Oh yeah, he was a *legend*. And now he's dead, everyone's going to be talking about him again. You did well, Russell. You did brilliantly. Be in touch, yeah?"

And with that, Vinny ended the call.

* * *

It didn't feel good. If Coleman was ill and on his way to hospital, the last thing he would've wanted was someone flashing a camera in his face. Russell could only hope that when he got home and told Natalie the news, she would find a way to make him feel better about it. Perhaps she'd say that it was all part of the fame game. "If you chose to be in the public eye," he imagined her saying, "you had to expect to have people shoving a camera in your face, and you couldn't decide when and where it would happen.

"I know," she'd say, "because I've been there, remember? I've tasted it. You put yourself in the limelight, you have to accept everything that goes along with that.

"And anyway," she might add, "God knows we need the money, right?"

Something along those lines was what he wanted to hear from her, but when he arrived at their apartment, she had news of her own.

"Don's managed to set up a European tour."

"What?"

He found her at the dressing table in the bedroom wearing only her kimono. Her hair was bunched on top of her head, and her face was slathered with a green face mask. Just recently, she'd given up on her beauty regime—something of a relief to Russell—but this news must have spurred her on again.

He watched as she fussed with items on her dressing table, got up and crossed to the wardrobe, then sat down again. "God, I need some new outfits." She spoke rapidly. He recognised the signs of mania. "And I'll have to get my hair done. And my nails. I can't go out on tour looking like this." She let her eyes flit around the room. He knew she was avoiding meeting his.

He took a deep breath. "Do you really think that's a good idea, Nat?"

"Why wouldn't it be? This could be my last shot."

"But you know how when you're on tour... that's when the problems start."

She drew in a deep breath and pursed her lips. "I can't believe you'd bring that up."

"You were three months in rehab. You almost..."

She stopped him with a hard glance. "I'm over all that now. I'm not going to ruin things again. I won't get another chance after this. From now on, it's just about the music, okay?"

He bowed his head and nodded. "Right."

"You going to get dinner ready?"

"There was something I wanted to tell you actually. Yesterday I was hanging around outside the Bexley and I got a shot of Yale Coleman—you know the actor. Anyway, turns out he was on his way to hospital and now he's dead. I got the last shot of him. Vinny says I should make quite a bit of money off of it."

Natalie had twisted around on her stool to face him, and for a long moment she looked at him in silence. Her face couldn't show any expression under the mask, but her eyes were bright with thought.

"What?" he said. "What is it?"

"Nothing." She shivered. "Just... it's almost—I dunno—like you're the angel of death or something."

He gasped in disbelief. "What?"

"Didn't you shoot someone else just before they died? That rocker—Jules Starr. Wasn't that his name?"

Russell laughed. "That doesn't make me the angel of death. He overdosed on heroin."

"Oh, and there was that model. You snapped her right before her car crashed."

"You can't blame me for that."

"I'm not blaming you. I'm just saying. It's a coincidence, that's all." She stood up and twirled towards him. The face mask she wore should have made it comical, but Russell couldn't laugh. "Hey, look at me. I'm going up on stage again."

"It's wonderful," he said. To hide his concern, he put his back to her and started for the kitchen. "I'll start dinner. What do you fancy?"

* * *

The next day, Russell's snap of Coleman was front-page on all the dailies, just as Vinny promised. When he saw it, Russell was surprised to see the face of a girl about nine or ten years old reflected in the limo's front passenger side window. Russell couldn't remember seeing any girl at the time. It had been getting on for midnight when Coleman emerged from the Bexley, and the temperature had to have been around zero. What would a little girl be doing out at that time, in those conditions?

He examined the picture closely. The girl's face appeared slightly out of focus, but there was no mistake. She would have been running towards the limo from Russell's right, and it was she that Coleman appeared to be looking at with that odd expression of delight and terror.

"That's weird."

* * *

Around six, Russell received a text from Natalie asking him to pick her up. She'd spent the day in some Hackney rehearsal room running through songs with a new band her manager had put together. Russell was happy to fetch her as he wanted to meet the band members and see what kind of people they were. Unfortunately, he didn't get a chance as Natalie waited for him by the doors of the rehearsal room and hopped into the car the moment he pulled up at the curb.

"How'd it go?"

"Wonderful. Just wonderful." Natalie seemed jittery. She took a pack of cigarettes from her handbag, slid one out, and put it in her mouth.

"You're smoking again?"

"I need something to calm my nerves. I'm all over the place."

"How're the new band?"

She lowered the window a crack, and for some reason he thought of Yale Coleman; how he'd half-lowered the window of his limo that evening outside the Bexley despite the cold. Why had he done that? Had he needed fresh air, or was he expecting someone?

"Oh brilliant," Natalie said. "Just brilliant. I love them, and they know my songs already. Don says there could be a new album if the tour goes well. He says Island might be interested."

"Really. That is… wow… Island Records? That's amazing."

He glanced across at her as she blew smoke through the gap in the side window. He wanted with all his heart to be happy for her, but all he felt was concern. As he steered the car through the congested streets, she looked at him and said: "What're you thinking?"

He smiled at her. "Nothing. Nothing. I was just thinking about the day we met."

"That magazine shoot. You remember that?"

"I remember it well. A call from Vinny saying some culture mag I'd never heard of needed a photographer for a photoshoot as their man had gone sick. A dash across London. The subject of the photoshoot was an upcoming singer who'd just been signed to Mute Records. I never heard of her either."

"You bastard," she said, and laughed. "And what was your

first impression of her? This upcoming singer?"

Russell took a moment to recall his first impressions of Natalie. She was self-effacing and shy, her personality seemingly at odds with the glamorous clothes and makeup she'd been decked out in for the shoot. It was this aspect that had struck him most about her during the session; she didn't seem cut out for stardom. She had something compelling though, a surety about her, determination. She wouldn't smile on cue like so many of the eager-to-please wannabes he'd photographed over the years.

"I left that shoot a little in love with you. And that was before I'd listened to your album."

She laughed. "I can remember you babbling on about how talented you thought I was when we met up again to go through the proofs. Sweet."

He nodded then fixed his eyes on the road ahead. He remembered how she'd smiled coyly when he told her how much he'd loved her album, as if no one had ever told her that before. Somehow their relationship had developed from there. Later, he got to discover the real Natalie Voeman. Her struggles with depression. Her occasional bouts of mania. How humble she was despite her incredible talent. It only made him fall for her more, and now he couldn't imagine life without her. One day, five years ago, he'd asked her to marry him, and as he stood at the altar watching her step down the aisle, all he could remember thinking was: *How the hell did this happen?*

After the second album flopped, and she was dropped from her label, she spiraled into depression. They argued all the time. In a last-ditch attempt to save the relationship, Russell suggested that they try for a child. Natalie had seemed keen on the idea. So for two years, they'd been trying, and for two years—nothing.

"You know," he said as he steered the car towards home, "I never understood why you married me."

She looked sideways at him. "Fishing for compliments?"

He laughed. "No, I'm serious. You could have had anyone you wanted, and you chose me."

"Anyone who?" she said, wrinkling her brow.

"Well, you know—you're gorgeous and talented. What am I?"

"You're gorgeous and talented, too."

He felt a flush rising in his cheeks. He shook his head. "I'm not talented. I'm not an artist like you. I'm a hack. I just point and shoot."

"That's not true. You have a very good eye."

He smiled at her. "For people who're about to croak you mean?"

She ignored this. "I think you are an artist. Those photographs you take just for the love of it are brilliant. You should do more of those. Try and get a gallery interested. All the other stuff you do is just to make a living. And besides that, you're my rock. I wouldn't have got through that last tour without you. I think I'd be dead."

His smile fell away, and he felt the unease surface in him again. "Don't say that."

"It's true. You know it is. I think Don was even counting on some increased sales if I OD'd. He once told me they were stocking *In Utero* in Woolworths after Kurt Cobain shot himself. Before that, all they had on the shelves was Simply Red and Diana Ross. He said it with this funny little smile on his face. Kind of a greedy smile. I was so out of it at the time, I didn't even know what he was talking about."

"That bastard."

Natalie sighed. "He's okay. He knows the business, that's all. He knows how things work."

"Encouraging you to kill yourself so your album can go to number one?"

"I never said he encouraged me. He's always looked after me. And he hasn't been looking good lately. Kind of tired and pale. I think the stress is getting to him."

"My heart bleeds."

"Come on, he's not that bad. Hey, guess what. The tour starts in two weeks."

"Two weeks? So soon?"

"That's good, isn't it?"

Before he could answer, she began frantically waving her hands as if she were trying to tell him something.

"What is it?" he said, alarmed.

"Pull over. Rus—pull over."

He pulled the car up to the curb. At once she popped the door open, leaned out, and vomited into the gutter.

"Jesus Christ, are you okay?"

Natalie drew herself back into the car and closed the door. She looked pale and tired herself now, suddenly old. "I'm okay. It's just nerves, that's all."

"Nerves?" He heard the suspicion in his own voice, too late.

"Yes, *nerves*," she said, her voice sharp. She gave him a dark look. "I haven't been taking anything, if that's what you're thinking."

"I wasn't... maybe you should see a doctor."

"I'm fine. Honestly. It's all just been a bit sudden." She looked sideways at him again, tried a smile. "You know?"

* * *

Something made Russell dig out his proofs from the Jules Starr photoshoot. Starr had wanted the shoot to take place on the South London council estate where he'd grown up, so the two of them had wandered the estate looking for locations which Starr thought suitably 'real' enough to pose in. He was a millionaire rock star living in L.A., but he wanted to make it look as if he still had some connection to the tower blocks and tenements of South London. For the duration of the shoot, two bodyguards had followed at a distance, as had a growing gang of inquisitive children.

In one of the pictures, Starr leant against the wall of a house, framed by a window behind him. The glass in one of the lower panes was broken. As he studied the picture, Russell noticed a girl looking out through the broken pane, a small pale face floating in the gloom inside the house. The child rolled her eyes upwards to look at Starr. Her face should have been sharply in focus, as she occupied the same depth of field as Starr, but instead it was slightly blurred.

"Weird."

He remembered how, when he woke the day after the shoot, he'd already had fourteen missed calls from the agency. Vinny had been frantic when he finally got through. He wanted the shots from the Starr shoot sent over to him straight away. It turned out Starr had gone back to his hotel after the session with Russell, shot himself full of heroin, and died.

A black feeling welling inside him, Russell next searched through his archives for the picture he'd taken of Fabrizia Sousa, the Brazilian supermodel, as she strolled through the crowds at Heathrow airport. Less than half an hour later, her limo had crashed after being pursued by photographers through the London streets. The driver had been speeding as he tried to outrun them. There had been fresh calls for control of the paparazzi. Russell's picture turned out to be the last one taken of Sousa.

It's almost like you're the angel of death or something.

Funny. Very funny. But the thought made him go cold.

He got a deeper chill when he noticed something in the picture he'd never seen before. There, trailing in Fabrizia's wake, was a lone little girl, maybe ten years old. It could almost have been the same girl from the Jules Starr photo. Russell compared the two. They did look alike. Certainly there was something similar in the way they looked at the picture's subject; a fixed gaze, an upward roll of the eyes. In the Heathrow picture, it looked as if the girl had just picked Sousa out of the crowd and decided to follow her. Russell pulled up the Coleman shot for comparison. That, too, could have been the same girl, though there was the added difficulty of her only being a reflection in the Coleman shot. For some reason Russell couldn't work out, the girl was slightly out of focus in all three pictures whilst everything surrounding her was sharp.

Coincidence, that's all. Just coincidence.

* * *

Within what seemed like no time at all, Natalie was gone. And though she promised to call Russell every day, she didn't. During the first week of the tour, he only spoke to her once.

"It's just so hectic," she said, when he finally got through to her mobile. "There's so much press. Don has set up interviews all over the place. And we're travelling every day. It's a whirlwind."

She sounded tired but happy. In the background, Russell detected sounds of revelry. He listened for a drawl in Natalie's voice but didn't detect any. He hated himself for his lack of trust.

"The best thing is, we're selling out every concert," she said. "I thought people would have forgotten me, but it looks like they haven't. Not at all."

"That's wonderful."

"How're you doing?"

"Me? I'm fine."

"Good. I'm glad you're bearing up. This might be something you have to get used to now, Rus. Me being away for long spells. I hate leaving you, but it's great you can be so understanding about it."

"Can't keep someone with your talent cooped up, Nat. Gotta share you with the world. And I'm okay with that. Honestly. I'm fine. Keeping busy, you know?"

It wasn't strictly true. He missed her. He worried. And with her gone, he was bored. He called the agency every day, but they had no work for him so he took himself out into the streets to see if he could find subjects to photograph. He ended up at Highgate Cemetery photographing the statues erected amongst the gravestones: Virgin Marys with eroded faces, angels with missing heads, weatherworn lions. Hidden amongst a spinney of cedars, he discovered a small statue of a cherub. It clutched a handful of flowers to its chest and had lost its head, which lay in the grass beside it. Upon its neck, someone had placed a human skull. At first he thought it was a real skull, but when he looked closer, he saw that it was made from resin. He laughed at himself for thinking it was real. It was the kind of thing you could buy in a shop which also sold bongs. Nevertheless, the effect was chilling. Russell photographed the statue a number of times from various angles. Later, riding the tube home, he deleted all the cemetery pictures.

Clichéd nonsense. The kind of pictures some college kid might take. I'm no artist. Anyway, it's just morbid.

The cherub statue with its resin skull haunted him, though. For days afterward, the image would spring unbidden into his mind's eye.

He received no call from Natalie during the second week of the tour, just a few hastily-written texts. In order to feel close to her, he took to watching her Twitter feed with all her other fans. Towards the end of that week, she posted a photograph of a soundcheck in Rome. Seeing her onstage with the band behind her, he recalled her last tour—four years ago—and his thoughts darkened. He scanned the picture. There was a blonde girl sitting on the lip of the stage, turning her head to watch Natalie as she sang.

Child.

What the hell is that child doing there?

He spent the next two hours frantically trying to get Natalie on the phone, but there was no answer. Rooting around in her bedside drawer, he found one of her old mobiles. It took him a while, hunting frantically through the house, to find a charger that would fit it. When he finally got it working, he was relieved to see that it still had a number for Don programmed into it. He tried the number on his own phone. After a few rings, Don answered.

"I need to speak to Nat," Russell said. "It's urgent."

"I can't put her on right now," Don said. "She's with a journalist."

"Are you telling me the truth, Don?"

For a moment, Don was overcome with a fit of coughing. "Isn't it time you had a bit of faith in that girl of yours, Russell?"

"I worry, that's all. And I sure as fuck can't trust *you* to take care of her."

"What? What does that mean?"

"You just want whatever sells more records."

"That's not fair." Don broke into a coughing fit again. Russell wondered if it was some kind of delaying tactic.

"Well, whatever. Let me speak to her. It's urgent, Don. I'm worried about her."

"I'll ask her to call you, Russell. As soon as she's done."

Russell took a deep breath to keep his growing anger in check. "Who was the child at the soundcheck, Don?"

"Child?"

"The photo Natalie posted to Twitter this morning. The one at the soundcheck. There's a little girl on the stage—"

"Listen, Russell," Don said. "I'll ask your wife to call you once she's done with the interview, okay? I gotta go, I—"

"No, wait! Don! Wait! Tell me the truth. Is Natalie doing drugs again?"

A long silence. "Russell, man, she's clean. That's not who she is anymore."

"What about the players? Are any of those guys doing anything?"

"Man, what has got into you?"

"I'm worried. That child. It's... I'm worried."

"Worried about what?"

"That Natalie's going to wind up dead."

* * *

Waiting for Natalie to call, he put on some music to distract himself. He was surprised when he heard Jules Starr's final album coming out of the hi-fi speakers. Natalie must have been playing it before she left. Why, though? He hadn't been aware that she even owned the album. Sitting on the sofa, he waited for the phone to ring, but jerked to his feet again when he heard Jules Starr sing a lyric which sounded like: *The night you died, that little girl was at your side.*

"What?"

He crossed the room, and started the current song over. Eventually the line came again. He picked up the CD case and scanned the titles. "Why Are Your Eyes So Black?" was the name of the song that currently played. Other songs had names like: "Here She Comes" and "Girl in the Corner of My Eye." Russell skipped to "Here She Comes." *Here she comes,* Starr sang, *with her list of the lost. Making them fall. Coming closer towards the one she wants the most.* There followed a nerve-shredding scream from Starr, which Russell wasn't expecting, and which sent a bolt of shock through him. He switched the music off.

Either he was going mad, or Starr had been seeing this little girl as well.

What did it mean?

And why the fuck hadn't Natalie called?

* * *

It was another couple of hours before the phone rang. There

was a croak in Natalie's voice. She said it was from all the singing and talking she'd been doing.

"What's the matter, babes?" she asked. "Don said you sounded frantic."

"That photo you put on Twitter. There's a child on the stage."

"Child...?"

"A girl. It's just that I was looking back on my pictures of Coleman, and Starr, and Fabrizia Sousa, and their last shots all had this child in them. And Starr was singing about her. Starr saw her too, just before he died. I think... listen, I'm not crazy, Nat. That child was there right before they died. All of them. It's the same child that's in your picture."

"You mean Chloe?"

"Chloe?"

"Little blonde-haired girl?"

"Yes, that's right. That's her."

"Rus, that's Chloe. Andy's kid."

"Eh? Andy? Who...?"

"The bassist. That's his daughter. His girlfriend brought her over for the weekend so she could see her dad. She was sitting on stage with him all through soundcheck. She loved it."

"Wha...? You mean...? You...?"

"What was all that about Coleman and Starr?"

"Uh... nothing. It doesn't matter. Listen, I want to see you, Nat. I want to fly out. Where're you headed next?"

"The next gig is in Milan the day after tomorrow. But I'm not sure it's worth it for you to come out, Rus. I'm pretty busy. I'm not sure how much time I'll be able to spend with you. And I know you hate flying. Listen, there was something I wanted to talk to you about. Don't get mad."

A hole opened up in his chest. What was it this time? Smack again, or coke, or crystal meth? "Mad? What is it?"

"I wanted to tell you before, but I was worried you'd make me cancel the tour."

"What is it, Nat?"

"I'm..." A pause. "I'm pregnant."

His head felt suddenly light. He staggered backwards a few steps. "I'm coming to Milan," he said in a daze. "I'll be okay with the flight. I'll take a couple of Valium. I'll…"

"Russell, are you sure?"

* * *

The two days he spent in Milan with his wife sped by. He watched her perform on stage and thought about the new life she was carrying. What better reason for staying clean and avoiding temptation? He knew she wouldn't risk harming their baby. She wouldn't. His anxieties melted away.

He managed to grab a couple of hours with her before soundcheck on the day he was due to fly back to London. Natalie insisted that they had to see Leonardo Da Vinci's *The Last Supper*, which hung in a convent just outside the city centre. Afterwards, she treated him to lunch at a nearby restaurant which was quiet and had a romantic vibe. They giggled like newlyweds and talked about baby names.

"It's like we're starting over," Natalie said. "Don't you feel that? Like we've been given another chance to make a go of things."

"A last shot," he said.

Soon they were saying goodbye over coffee at the Milan airport. Don lingered in the background, keen to whisk Natalie away to a festival appearance in Munich. Natalie had been right when she said he looked ill. His face looked ghastly white, and there were bags under his eyes. He was also so prone to coughing fits that Russell became concerned and suggested Don see a doctor as soon as possible. Don said he was fine.

At the airport café, Natalie called Don over to the table, handed him her phone and asked him to take a picture of her and Russell together. Don hurriedly did as instructed then checked his watch.

"We gotta go, Natalie."

Natalie put her phone away and stood. "Well, I suppose this is it."

"Take care," Russell said, when she released him from her embrace. He placed a hand on her belly. "And take care of my little man in there."

"It might be a girl."

"Well, just take good care of it, whatever it is."

"You bet I will. I can't believe everything's suddenly going so well. Can you?"

"Shush," he said, putting his fingers to her lips now. "Don't jinx it."

Don said: "Break it up, lovebirds, we gotta move."

* * *

Russell was on the plane waiting for takeoff when his phone buzzed. Natalie had texted him the picture from her phone that Don had taken of the two of them. WE LOOK SO HAPPY, she'd written in her text. It was true. They both wore wide grins. He began writing a reply to her, but before he finished, stopped and looked at the picture again. He jerked upright so that the young couple in the adjacent seats looked at him fretfully. Standing behind himself and Natalie, in the background of the picture, was a blonde girl of about ten years old. She was in such sharp focus that he wondered why his eyes had not gone to her straight away.

He returned to his text message.

THAT GIRL IN THE BACKGROUND LOOKING AT U. CHLOE AGAIN?

He watched the cabin crew checking seatbelts along the aisle as he waited for a reply. When his phone buzzed, he almost jumped out of his seat.

NOT CHLOE. GONE HOME.

One of the cabin crew stopped by his row of seats and asked him to turn off his mobile phone.

"Just one second," he said, waving him away.

"Sir—"

Another text from Natalie.

AND SHE'S NOT LOOKING AT ME, HON. LOOKING AT U. LOOKS BESOTTED. THINK SHE'S IN LOVE. CAN'T BLAME HER.

She finished her message with two rows of kisses.

"Sir—?"

Russell felt the roar of the plane's engines beneath his seat, and a sudden jolt of terror went through him. He looked up, past the flight attendant who was still asking him to put his mobile phone away, and caught his breath. There she was, further along the aisle, towards the front of the plane but moving closer. A blonde-haired girl of perhaps ten, the same girl from the picture on his phone, the same girl who'd run towards Coleman's limo, the same girl looking through the window at Jules Starr, the girl who'd stalked Fabrizia Sousa at the airport, the girl Starr had been singing about on his final album. There was no mistake. She skipped down the aisle of the plane. Skipped as if they were all going on a jolly outing together, all the people on the plane, and it was she who would be deciding their destination. In one hand, pressed against her chest, she held a small bunch of pink flowers. They might have been carnations.

"Who's that?" Russell asked the flight attendant.

The man glanced behind himself. "Sir?"

"That girl. Who is she?"

"Sir, I'm going to have to ask you to stay in your seat. The pilot's getting ready for takeoff."

"Don't you see her? That girl? There! Behind you!"

"Sir, you need to sit down and remain calm during takeoff, okay?"

No, Russell thought, sinking down into his seat. Tears stung his eyes. *No. I want to see my child.*

I can't believe everything's suddenly going so well. Can you?

Shush. Don't jinx it.

Natalie—

Here she comes.

Coming closer towards the one she wants the most.

As the girl neared, he caught her eye. They weren't blue as he'd imagined—no, they were black, little black abysses. *Why are your eyes so black?* She tilted her head at Russell and gave a tight little smile, as if to say: *Ready?*

About the Author

Tim Jeffreys' short fiction has appeared in Weirdbook, Not One of Us, The Alchemy Press Book of Horrors 2, and Nightscript, among various other publications, and his latest collection of horror stories and strange tales 'You Will Never Lose Me' is available now. He lives in Bristol, England, with his partner and two children. Follow his progress at www.timjeffreys.blogspot.co.uk.

FALSE CONFESSION

Joseph Rubas

The old drifter sat alone in his cell, the last light of the dying day falling meekly through the window and casting bar-shaped shadows across his dirty face. He was a small man with curly gray hair and a week's growth of stubble. His lips were thin, and his left eye stared blankly out, unseeing and made of glass. When he was a kid, he fell in a woodpile and a sliver the size of a pencil skewered the orb, destroying it. His mother was drunk and whoring around when it happened. She told him, "Man up." Two weeks later it got infected and he nearly died.

He grinned as he remembered cutting her throat. Her blood was hot and spurted onto his face, into his mouth. He was nineteen. Two weeks before, they'd discharged him from the army on a Section 8. Mental reasons.

When they found out what he did to his mother, they stuck him in prison and forgot about him. Twenty years later, they needed space for new inmates, so they deemed him reformed and let him go. That was two years ago. In that time, he killed two women. One was an eighty-year-old socialite who hired him to fix her roof, and the other was a twelve-year-old he took from a gas station in Myrtle Beach.

The cops didn't know that, though. They came from across the country with binders full of cold cases, and he cleared as many as he thought he could get away with. Not too many, though. He didn't want to look like he was confessing to everything now. If they figured out he was lying, the jig was up, and he didn't plan on coming clean until they sent him to court. It was his way of getting back at the system. The same system that kicked him out of the army and sent him back to his mother; the same system that locked him up and threw away the key when she finally got what she had coming; the same system that turned him out onto the street with fifty dollars and a bus ticket to Wilmington, where he wouldn't be their problem anymore. If he couldn't kill them, he figured he'd at least throw a wrench in their machine, fuck things up for a little while. Plus, it was a good deal. They took him to crime scenes and got him fast food. In six months, he'd spent maybe a full week in a cell.

Today, he was in a dusty no-name town in the west Texas panhandle. The case the local authorities were interested in involved a fifteen-year-old girl someone raped, strangled, and threw from a moving car. They found her carcass rotting in a roadside ditch, naked except for white socks with pink stripes. The pictures of her body, crumpled and twisted in tall grass, excited him, and he sincerely wished he had done the crime.

He didn't get the girl, but he'd get the credit, by God!

He smiled.

Presently, the single guard on duty came around with a can of Coke and handed it to him through the bars. "Thank you," the drifter said with a nod.

Being the star of the show and all, he got special treatment. They even let him smoke cigarettes.

The guard nodded curtly and went to his desk, out of sight around a corner. The drifter popped the tab and drank deeply, relishing the cold liquid. The light went from bright orange, to blood red, to soft purple. The only sound was the occasional squeak of the guard's chair as he shifted his weight and the occasional cry of a crow outside. Maybe he was funny, but the drifter liked the peace. In here, he didn't have a thing to worry about. No bills, no traffic; all you gotta do is play by their rules, and things aren't half bad. Except not having women, hooch, and meth.

Finishing his Coke, he sat the empty can on the bare concrete floor and took a glossy color photo from under his pillow.

It was the girl with the socks. Her breasts were exposed,

nipples puffy and pink, and so was her bare privates, the area around it red and bruised. The killer did a number on her, that was for sure. The report said she was raped both front and back, and that when they opened her up, they found things inside of her, things that had been shoved in through either hole.

While she was alive.

Yep, he told the investigators earlier that day, a stick, a rock, a knife...

There was no knife, the lead investigator, a bald man with a mustache, said.

No? Maybe that was someone else then. I did that to a few people.

There was a pen...

Yeah. I remember that.

Like a thousand investigators before them, they looked at each other but didn't say anything. Even if they had their misgivings, they wouldn't voice them. They wanted these cases off their books, and if the guy who did it was a roving alcoholic who didn't always remember the details, hey, who cares?

"I care."

The drifter jerked, the photograph falling from his hands.

The woman from the photo was standing before his cell, her auburn hair matted around her soft, bloodless face. She was nude, as she was when they found her, the socks pulled halfway up her thick thighs. Blood crusted her pink lips. Her eyes were white and glazed.

The drifter blinked.

"You didn't kill me," she said again in that dead, hollow voice.

He blinked again, but she stayed where she was, head slightly lowered, watching him sternly, like he did something wrong and she was sore at him because of it.

"You didn't kill me."

"Go away," he muttered.

"You're not my killer..."

"Go away, bitch."

"You're not my killer, either."

Startling, the drifter turned. A black woman with a rope tied around her neck stood in the shadows of the cell. She was wearing panties and nothing else. He cleared her case three months ago in Florida.

"Or mine."

Another girl was standing at the foot of his bed. She wore a thin, ratty white dress on her skeletal frame. Her face was a skull dotted with bits of brown, rotting flesh. He let out a strangled cry and fell to the side, catching himself on one shaking arm.

"G-Guard! Guard!"

More of them were at the cell door looking in. Some were pale and covered in blood, others were in various states of decay.

"Guard!"

"Tell the truth... tell the truth..."

"Make them go away!"

They reached through the bars. The ones in the cell shuffled to him, their feet dragging on the concrete. He looked left, right, a dozen, two dozen. He pressed himself against the wall and waved his hand as if to ward them off.

"Go away! Go away!"

"Tell the truth... tell the truth..."

Hands reaching.

He screamed and blacked out.

When he woke up, he told the truth.

About the Author

Joseph Rubas is the author of over 300 short stories and several novels. His work has been collected in Pocketful of Fear (2012), After Midnight (2014), and Shades (2017). He is also the editor of the 3rd Spectral Book of Horror Stories. He currently resides in Albany, New York. He can be found on Facebook at Joseph Rubas: Horror Writer.

THE CURSE OF THE CUCUY

Pedro Iniguez

As the bus hissed to a stop, Richard Mercado rubbed his eyes and cleared away the thin layers of film that had covered them as he slept.

Outside the windows, the sun began its slow crawl over the western horizon, painting the cobblestone streets of Fortaleza, Mexico, in an orange wash.

Richard grabbed his bag from the overhead compartment and shuffled down the empty aisle. The driver scanned the streets nervously, one hand on the wheel, the other on the door release lever.

"*Gracias*," Richard told the driver as he stepped out.

The driver nodded, keeping his eyes fixed on the road as if expecting something nefarious skulking around the corner. Before Richard hopped off of the last step, the bus driver turned to him. "Maybe you watch a movie when you are in town?"

"Huh?" Richard said, taking off his sunglasses.

The bus driver pulled a ticket out of his jacket and handed it to him with a trembling hand. "Free movie, courtesy of the Fortaleza Department of Tourism."

Richard grabbed the ticket. "Oh. Thank you, *amigo*."

The bus pulled away as soon as Richard's feet touched the ground, jerking into a hard U-turn before rolling back toward Puebla.

Richard fanned a cloud of dust from his face and looked about Fortaleza in awe. Worn cobblestone streets intersected the town where he pictured cars rolling jerkily across as they weaved through traffic. In the nooks of the alleyways, the walls of sloping buildings nearly nuzzled each other like lovers. Above his head, a string of gas lamps swayed gently over the arched entrances of old storefronts. It was as if the place remained untouched by the progress of time, nestled secretly under the shadow of the mountain. Even now the old, red church in the town square stood above all as its bell rang and echoed across the pueblo. Six o'clock. He would need a place to stay for the night.

He hoisted his backpack over his shoulder and strolled down the boulevard. It was as his father had described to him when he was a child. All around him the buildings stood proud, painted in warm, cheery colors. Their walls had chipped and faded and been left undisturbed, adding to their ageless charm. His father would be proud that the wave of commercialization from Puebla or Mexico City had spared his hometown.

The thoughts of his father brought back the sinking feeling deep in his chest again. Then came the knots twirling in his stomach. *I miss you, Dad.*

He stopped and inhaled a deep breath of Fortaleza's crisp, clean air and pictured his father doing the same as a boy. The thought of the very same air molecules filling his lungs as his father had breathed brought him a deep joy he couldn't explain. Maybe Los Angeles did him in. Maybe the pristine air of Fortaleza wouldn't have brought about the cancer.

Richard shook the thought and regarded the town once more. It really was a gem. *Why did you ever leave this place, Dad?*

Until two days ago, he'd never visited the homeland of his parents. Now he had the chance to finally connect with the spirit of his father, and maybe even find himself along the way.

Across the street, a man in a faded baseball cap placed a hand on his son's shoulders and gently ushered him through the doorway of an old apartment building.

Richard smiled as tears began to collect under his eyes. How many of his father's birthdays had he missed while he was away? How many *I Love You*'s did he not get to hear in person? Sometimes, the year he'd spent overseas felt like a decade. The guilt took on life as a fire burning in his chest, so that the very act of breathing, living, had been torture. He wiped his tears and moved on.

Suddenly, there came a loud hiss and then the soft clink of a dented bottle cap landing at his feet. He jumped back, startled. Above, two men chatted quietly on a balcony, leaning on thin iron railings as they smoked cigarettes and drank from their glass soda bottles. They watched him amble past through tired, sleepless eyes.

Through the open window of a shop, antiquated *talavera* pottery neatly lined the windowsills, beautiful jars and vases painted in white and cobalt blue. Little handmade treasures tucked away from the rest of the world. He looked up and saw the old woman inside the shop regarding him with pity in her eyes. She mumbled under her breath and twirled the beads of her rosary in between her thumb and index finger until he walked away.

As he ambled past the rest of the shops, he found no signs of a hotel. The bus driver had mentioned a Department of Tourism. There had to be one. Only he hadn't spotted any tourists meandering about. Hell, there weren't even many locals to be found.

It was late, though, and maybe the townsfolk had turned in early for the evening.

Richard came upon an old Spanish fort toward the end of the main street, the entrance a large terracotta archway sheltering a small box office smattered in dust. A rusty cannon on two large wooden wheels sat bolted to the floor, and a large marquee jutted out over the roof of the fort. The words THE CURSE OF THE CUCUY, NOW PLAYING, were spelled out in bold, red letters.

It seemed that the fort had been converted into a movie theater. His father had never mentioned that part. Maybe it was a new addition, a way to entertain the locals.

Something stirred inside the glass of the box office. Richard wasn't sure if it was his reflection or someone else.

"Can I help you?" a muffled voice said from inside.

Richard approached the box office. A young man in his early twenties stared at him tiredly, as if his job had sucked the soul out of him some time ago.

"Yes," Richard said, "actually I'm looking for a place to stay for the night. I just came in from the United States and I don't know my way around here."

"All the hotels are booked for the night," the young man said, shaking his head.

"I see," Richard said, running a hand through his hair in frustration. "Maybe I can come back tomorrow morning. Are there any buses running back to Puebla?"

"Nothing runs here at this time, I'm afraid."

Richard bit his lip and nodded. The sun had completed its descent over the western hills as the air grew chill and the sky turned purple. He'd have to find a cozy spot by a back alley and curl up for the night. He'd roughed worse before in the Army. Him and his pal Sal had spent a few nights out in the cold, open air of Afghanistan. How bad could it be?

"But for you," the man said in his best English, "we have a special opportunity. Do you have your movie ticket?"

Richard reached for his shirt pocket. "This thing?" he said retrieving the ticket the bus driver had handed him. "Yeah, but I don't wanna watch a movie right now. I need a place to sleep."

The man said nothing, simply jabbed his index finger on the counter of the box office.

Richard slid the ticket through the slot at the bottom of the window.

"We have a special focus group screening tonight, *Señor*. The director of *The Curse of the Cucuy* is here from Hollywood. All participants receive a free shuttle ride and accommodations to the Estrella Hotel in Puebla. Very nice hotel."

"Well, hell yes," Richard said, just as the night's breeze began to sting his hands like little razors.

"Proceed through the entrance," the young man said, tearing the ticket in half and sliding Richard the other piece. "Enjoy your viewing." It didn't make sense, but the knots began twisting in his stomach again. He slung his bag over his shoulder and made his way into the movie theater.

* * *

He stepped into a spacious, dimly-lit room of stucco walls and about fifty seats, nearly all of them occupied by men and women in floral sundresses, loose Hawaiian shirts, and khaki shorts. This is where Fortaleza's tourists had come to venture for the night. They'd already settled in as they stared at their cellphones, twisted chunks off their pretzels, and reached for their tubs of popcorn.

A wave of warmth from the insulated heat bounced off the old walls. Sweat began to drip down his temples. As he wiped his face, two men in dress shirts and black slacks directed a few of the tourists toward their seats, handing out clipboards and pens.

One of the men approached Richard with a warm smile.

"Hi, amigo, here for the focus group?"

"I, yeah, I suppose I am," Richard said.

"Allow me to introduce myself. My name is Michael Richter, and I'm a producer on this movie. And don't worry, we'll take care of you for the night. We just need your help answering a few questions after the film ends. Your feedback is crucial."

"Yeah, alright," Richard said. "And you'll offer lodging if I do this, right?"

"Like I said, you'll be well taken care of. Here, let me guide you to your seat."

The man led him toward the back row, the darkest space in the theater.

"If you need anything before the film starts, please let me know."

"Thanks, I'm good."

Michael handed him a sheet of paper and a pen and ambled off. Richard set his bag on the floor and took up his aisle seat beside an old man in flip-flops who smelled of potent tequila. The man eyed Richard and leaned in to whisper something to his other drunken friend. They howled in laughter, slapping their thighs like there'd been spiders crawling on them. A young man sitting in front of him wearing an Arizona State baseball cap reached an arm over his girlfriend's shoulder and drew her in for a kiss. Even from his seat in the back, he could hear the wet, slurping sounds emanating from their mouths.

Richard scanned the audience. Retirees and raucous party-going college kids shifted impatiently in their seats. Some of the men cackled boisterously while they snapped selfies and chattered about their sexual conquests with the Mexican locals. Everyone in the room looked like they'd been out tanning and slurping down margaritas before arriving. He wondered why none of the locals had attended the screening and thought better of it. This group was enough to scare anyone off from coming here.

A tall man sporting a blazer and thick-rimmed glasses strode into the room and stood beside the producers near a pair of large, red drapes.

"Hello, and welcome," the man said, projecting his voice across the theater. "My name is Eddie Void and I am the director of the picture you are about to see."

The audience stirred and murmured. Richard perked up in his chair and exhaled a long, deep breath. He'd been familiar with Eddie Void's work as a horror director on account of Sal. Back at base, on those slow, hot days, Sal would entertain the guys by popping in a bootleg DVD of whatever schlock he could find at the local markets. Sometimes he'd score some local warlord's private snuff films. Sometimes there'd be worse, like on the days he'd snag a Void movie. Even though everyone gave Sal shit for it, no one could ever look away. It was like seeing your first dead body all over again.

Void looked over the audience, smiling, taking delight in the people squirming in their chairs. The man was infamous for his gory, guerilla-style horror films. Nothing was sacred to him. He'd produced some of the most disturbing images known to man. And yet, audiences flocked to his every release.

Void had even run into trouble with the law on account that the lead actress from his last flick had been decapitated when the villain's buzz-saw accidentally sliced through her neck. Before the public found out, he'd snuck actual footage of her death into the final cut.

Last he'd heard, Void took to filming his movies outside of the States where labor laws were a little more lax: Cambodia, Sudan, now some tucked away little town in Mexico.

Richard grabbed his bag and thought about leaving right then and there. He wasn't sure he could put himself through a Void picture again. He rubbed his stubbly cheek and settled back into his chair. He thought about Sal and allowed himself to smile. *Screw it*, he thought. *It's just a movie. Just a movie.*

"As you know," Void continued, "you are all about to watch *The Curse of the Cucuy*, my latest horror film set right here in beautiful Fortaleza. As we did research for this movie we actually stumbled on a gem. Now I won't spoil it for you, but I'll say we drew heavily from local folklore and superstition, and we can't wait to show you the authenticity we put into this one. The locals have been more than accommodating with their knowledge of the supernatural.

"We are quite pleased with the film but some of my cohorts here," he swept a hand toward his producers, "are not quite satisfied with the ending. They think I need to tone down the violence. Hollywood execs, am I right?"

The crowd laughed and hollered. Richard swallowed a lump of saliva, wishing they'd play the movie and get it over with.

Void clasped his hands together, smiling. "I say more, they say less. That's where you come in, folks. I'm hoping to prove a point tonight, and you guys will determine how this movie will end. So I'd appreciate any feedback, however appalling this may all seem. And if I hear you screaming, I'll know it's good. Without further ado, I present you with *The Curse of the Cucuy*."

The audience cheered and threw up their arms while the lights dimmed and the red curtains drew back, revealing the white screen. The three Hollywood men took their seats in the front row.

The light from the projector blasted the screen and, as the opening credits rolled, the applause died down and the crowd settled in.

The movie began with its standard fare of reckless, vacationing teens from Florida touching down in Mexico City. At the airport they get word from some dazed college kid that he'd just come from a small town called Amistad, where he had partied so hard they wouldn't believe it. After a little deliberation, they decide to take the first bus there.

The town's name was different but there was no mistaking Fortaleza's charming streets.

Not long into the story, the kids wind up partying at a local club when one of the meatheads strangles a young woman who had spurned his advances. Twist—she just so happens to be the town *curandera's* daughter.

As the movie rolled, the Hollywood executives stood, silhouetted briefly against the screen, and silently stalked out of the front row, past the entrance doors, exiting the theater.

When the doors shut behind them, the outside light reflected off of something for an instant. It was that small glint up near the top left corner of the room just behind the screen that caught Richard's attention. His eyes had trouble adjusting, but it looked like a small camera mounted on the wall. He frowned. It would have been polite if they had mentioned they were taping the focus group. Last thing he wanted was his screaming face plastered in commercials worldwide.

He pushed the thought from his mind and returned his attention to the screen. The movie continued and more revelations came to light. The *curandera*, in revenge for her daughter's murder, makes a pact with dark forces beyond her understanding and summons the story's titular evil: *The Cucuy*. The old woman wishes harm upon all outsiders who have come to desecrate their peaceful little town and sets loose the Mexican boogeyman on them.

Soon, the kids start to succumb to the shadow man and his reign of slaughter. One kid for instance, breaks his neck after getting pushed down a dark well. Another gets heaved into the path of an oncoming tour bus.

Richard let out a sigh of relief and let his heart rate stabilize. For a Void picture, it was playing like a tame, by-the-numbers sort of affair. He had seen the same watered-down story done a million times before. Maybe Void's financiers were trying to reach a wider market.

Richard yawned and tapped his fingers on his chair's armrest. He wanted nothing more than to lie down on a soft bed and call it a night. He considered closing his eyes for a moment to catch a spell. They'd never know.

Then the film took a hard turn.

One actress screamed in pain as the Cucuy ran a sharp fingernail over her belly, splitting it down the middle. A wealth of viscera spilled out, and the actress's screams alone, Richard thought, were worthy of an Academy Award.

Another partygoer had his lower jaw wrenched apart as his tongue waggled like an earthworm in the mud.

The practical effects were too on the money. He'd only ever seen anything that realistic in Afghanistan.

One woman in the audience jolted from her seat, placing a hand over her mouth while she ran for the entrance. Her boyfriend chased after her, spilling his popcorn on the floor.

Suddenly, a slight distortion cut into the picture. Richard turned to see three obscured shadows in the projection room peering out over the small window and into the audience below.

As Richard spun his head, he caught another glimmer on the opposite side of the wall. A second camera.

Then the woman at the entrance bent over and vomited. Her boyfriend shoved the latches on the double doors. A resounding *click* reverberated throughout the room. "It's locked," he yelled.

On the screen, the violence reached a fevered frenzy. During their death throes, the actors looked like they were in the thralls of excruciating pain. Their cheeks flushed with coursing blood, and the veins on their heads throbbed to the pulse of a pounding heart.

Richard squirmed in his seat. It was coming back in torrents. Friends, villagers, limbs, hanging skin. The screams.

The special effects were so convincing that the movie played more like a snuff film than a Hollywood production. Was this real?

The carnage on the screen unfolded like a lucid nightmare.

The old man beside him shot out of his seat and retched over the blonde girl in front of him. She cried out and toppled over the seats in front of her.

Richard rose from his chair and clasped the old man's shoulder. "Sir, are you—"

Scattered screams filled the cinema as the moviegoers flocked for the exit where they pounded and kicked the doors.

One man pulled the emergency lever. The fire alarm blared jarringly throughout the room.

On screen, the film abruptly froze on a sputtering frame of

the Cucuy facing the audience. The wraith's features were obscured by dim lighting and carefully placed shadows, but its form was akin to the Grim Reaper, covered in a hood and dressed in long, dark rags. The projector flickered like a strobe light as something bumped against the screen. It pounded against the fabric over and over. The jutting shape writhed and thrashed until the screen finally spat it out, giving birth to something abominable.

Richard couldn't make out its features too clearly, but the shape took on the form of the grainy, flickering frame of the Cucuy, as if the film had now come alive inside the theater.

The specter sprang on the nearest person, a young woman in a white tank top. Before she could react, it raked a long-nailed hand across her throat and snuffed her scream.

Dropping her, it flew toward the cornered mob by the entrance. Richard watched as their limbs flew and their bodily fluids sprayed the walls.

He slid a shaky hand down his thigh, his fingers probing for a holster. There was no gun. He wasn't in combat.

His legs trembled until they buckled, and he collapsed into his seat.

He bit down on his lip and clutched the armrests until his fingers burned. He scoured the theater for another exit but there was none. The three shadows lurked behind the glass, observing quietly the terror that swept across the theater.

"It's not real, it's not real," he said, gasping for breath.

And it came to him at once. His eyes darted back and forth across the pandemonium, capturing every detail of the scene. The robed terror hacking away at the horrified partygoers, the wailing alarm, the locked doors, the cameras hidden on the wall. "We're not just watching the damn movie," he said. "We're *in* the movie."

No one heard him. Their screams drowned out his voice. It wouldn't make a difference, anyway, as the Cucuy slashed its way across the sacks of crying, pleading flesh.

And at last, as the Cucuy came for him with gnarled, outstretched hands, Richard began to cry. Though the distortion of his tears, the black figure suddenly appeared as his father. He managed to form a smile as the Cucuy's nails penetrated his heart. It was strange, he thought, but the fire in his chest began to subside, and one last, consoling thought entered his mind.

Dad, he thought, *I'll see you soon.*

Then, the scene faded to black.

About the Author

Pedro Iniguez lives in Eagle Rock, California, a quiet community in Northeast Los Angeles. Since childhood he has been fascinated with science-fiction, horror, and comic books. His work can be found in various magazines and anthologies such as: Space and Time Magazine, Crossed Genres, Writers of Mystery and Imagination, Deserts of Fire, and Altered States II. He can be found online at: https://pedroiniguezauthor.com/.

THE CUT-MOUTH WOMAN AND ME

Elizabeth Davis

Stop me if you heard this one before...

She looks like a woman you might see on the train or down the street—but you won't see her in bright sunlight or even under good fluorescent lights. She shrinks to the shadows, forgotten corners, all the more easier to ambush passing kids without an adult noticing.

Everyone argues about what she looks like, but they agree on three things: her long, black hair, never tied, nearly wild; that she wears a hospital mask over her face; and she came from Japan.

She will approach you on an empty street. If you look down, you can see the razor she holds in her hands, and she will ask, "Am I pretty?" You should answer yes—it is only polite. She will take off her mask and show you her mouth—cut at the corners, all the way to her ears, giving you a gory smile. And then she will ask again, "Am I pretty?" Say no, and she will kill you on the spot, with the sharp razor that mutilated her face. Say yes, and she will follow you home, killing you that night, or maybe in a week or a month—that isn't important. The important thing is that she will come, and no adult will stop her. But if you say, "You are so-so," or some nonsense phrase, then she will slide the mask back on and walk away.

We call her the Cut-Mouth Woman. *Kuchisake-Onna.*

When I met her, I was not surprised by the mask-wearing woman lurking in the shadows of an abandoned apartment complex near my bus stop. Other kids at school had been talking about her since the start of the new school year.

She was dressed in a white sundress, her pale skin somehow not sweating in the burning heat raising from the sidewalk. Her wild hair was tossed by the wind, obscuring her mask as she approached. Her eyes darted this way and that before latching on to mine.

"Yes," I said before she even asked her first question. I thought I could see her face wrinkle in frustration, but she asked her question all the same.

"Do you think I am—"

"Yes."

She ripped her face mask off, tearing the paper as her red grin came into view. "What do you think now?"

"Do you want a soda?" Talking about a different subject confuses her—at least that is what is claimed on Instagram stories and whispers over lunch.

"What?"

This was my chance, to run as fast as I could with my heavy backpack. To get lost on the twisty streets, having to figure my way back home. To a scolding from my mother for being home late that would eventually escalate into a litany about grades, my chores, and anything else she could think of, before I slammed the door to my bedroom, before climbing into the endless pit of homework.

I was too tired to run, so I just ended up repeating slowly, "Do you want a soda or anything like that?"

"Oh, um, sure." Her mask still dangled, her words slurred thanks to her cut face—only then did I realize how hard it must be for her to talk.

She was loitering in the shadows, mask back on her face when I returned from a street bodega. Her eyes, lost in the distance, jerked back in surprise as I stepped into the shadow shielding her, our cold plastic drinks in my hands. I handed her one drink before sliding off my backpack and leaning against the wall.

She fumbled with her drink, as if it was her first time holding a soda. "You weren't just saying that as an excuse to run away?"

"I guess not."

I watched her twist open the top, and then start the messy and comedic process of trying to drink from the plastic bottle. I hid my laughter as she wiped the trickles of soda from the sides of her face.

"Why didn't you run away? Do you have a death wish?"

"Maybe." I tried to imagine what a death wish would feel like. "I don't think so."

"Then why did you stay?" She tried to take another gulp, with the same comedic effect.

"You looked lonely." The answer surprised me.

"Ghost don't get lonely." She fiddled with her razor, holding it against her soda.

I shrugged and took another gulp.

She looked down at her bottle and jerked her head, clearing her throat. I wondered why a ghost would clear her throat.

"What's your name?"

"Linus," I answered, even though I didn't like it. My parents had named me Linus, thinking I was a boy. "You?"

"I am what I am." Silence as we stared past each other. "So, how are you?" I had all the awkwardness of a relative that you only saw once a year.

"Good. I'm fine."

She didn't say anything else, just stared at me with her strange gaze. She didn't jump in like all the other adults, asking more questions, or telling me, "that's good" to whatever I said, how I should enjoy my school years, before turning away to find another adult to chat with. As the silence stretched, my words started to spill out.

Perhaps it was because she wasn't an adult—not really. Adults didn't know about her, or if they did, dismissed her with a laugh. But she also wasn't a kid. Not just in the way she towered over me, but because I knew that none of them had talked to her, just bragged about how close they had gotten to her red smile, how they could feel her footsteps behind them as they ran down the street. She stood outside the ever-shifting alliances and friendships—nothing I told her would be turned against me.

So, I talked and talked, and she listened and listened, as I finished my soda, and she discarded hers, apparently deciding it wasn't worth the effort. Then she walked alongside me, as I made my way back home, not thinking about it until I saw several older kids spill out of a store in front of us. I instinctively tensed; older kids should be treated as natural disasters, never know when they might turn into a storm on you.

But they only looked at us once, saw her and then pretended to walk nonchalantly around the corner, looking back too often for it to be fully natural. The Cut-Mouth Woman looked smug, despite most of her expression being covered under her mask.

"What are you doing?" I asked, tightening the grip on my backpack.

"Walking you home."

"Does that mean you are going to kill me?"

"No, I just figured," she waved with her empty hand at the empty sidewalk, "that people who think others are lonely might be lonely themselves. Take risks that are dangerous just not to feel lonely."

"I'm not lonely," I claimed, even while wondering what loneliness was. Was loneliness being small for your age, constantly at the mercy of shifting friends and bullies, feeling like you didn't fit, a piece from a different puzzle? Maybe that was being lonely— if the comfort of walking with someone like this was not loneliness.

The Cut-Mouth Woman smiled beneath her mask, I could tell from the way the muscles twitched on her face. If nothing else, at least I would have the best story that no one would believe at school.

* * *

There are many stories about the origin of the Cut-Mouth Woman. At least if you ask the internet. Some of my friends claimed that she was an escaped or former patient of a mental asylum. A YouTube video traced her to a coroner's report from 1970s Japan, from a woman who was chasing little children and hit by a car doing so. Her mouth was ripped from ear to ear by the impact of the car.

But the smarter sounding people, whose videos aren't all jump scares, or creepypastas found on forums, claim she is older, born in the Heian period, that she has haunted Japan for centuries originally using a fan or festive mask to hide her face, much more colorful then her surgical mask. She used to wear bright layered, kimonos, though the top was always burial white. I wondered how a ghost so fancy became so plain.

A question that I could've asked her, but it seemed rude to tell her that I was research/stalking her on the internet, especially when she walked with me to school every day. Especially when I was worried that one question would lead to another, and I wouldn't stop myself until too late. My mother had always told me that I shouldn't ask questions I didn't want answers to.

* * *

A few years later, this time walking home, me nervous in my long skirt. It was my first day being out—fully out—drawing raised eyebrows from teachers, who tried to ignore me and pretend that nothing had changed, letting their annoyance slip when I insisted that I be called Selene—a name taken from a beautiful and vanishing butterfly—and correcting them whenever they called me Linus. Teasing from some of my classmates, calling me Linus, and telling me, "You are beautiful, hun." The protective circle of my friends, which bloomed with hormones, as they glared at the others, loudly whispering that I shouldn't listen to "people who couldn't figure out the difference between their asshole and their mouth."

But that was earlier today. I had said goodbye to my friends on the bus, stepping off to walk home. I was nervous that someone might see me, might see me as just a pretender, and might do something to me. The Cut-Mouth Woman glided up to me, silent underneath the sound of traffic, with me not noticing her until she spoke.

"Why are you dressed like a girl?" Her directly asking a question beyond how my day went was strange. While she was a good listener, she didn't usually talk much. I always chalked it up to how hard it actually was to talk with a cut smile that never healed.

"Because I'm a girl."

"You were a boy yesterday."

I let my frustration out as thin stream of air out of the mouth. I should've known that gender as a concept might be hard for a centuries-old ghost to understand. Still, she chased the fears of greater damage away. Others wouldn't come close as long as she walked next to me.

"I've always been a girl. I just was born in a male body."

"I don't know why you would want to be a girl. I'm worried for you—it's much better to be a boy than a girl, a man than a woman. It can be dangerous being girl." Her words hit me in the gut, where all my fears swam.

"I heard about your husband," I said, and she stiffened up, eye darting across the street to a man that wasn't there. Today she carried scissors, clenching the blades tightly in her fist.

I knew why. I knew her story from the same people who had lectured on her kimono, and her older origins.

She had been a beautiful woman in a rural village and every day she would ask, "Am I pretty?" The villagers would always reply, "Yes," and she grew quite confident. She married well, a high-class samurai, but that didn't satisfy her. So she started an affair with one of the soldiers that served under her lord. When her husband found out, he approached the soldier and demanded, "Why her? Why my wife compared to all the other woman in the village."

The soldier replied, "She is the most beautiful woman in the village. I couldn't pass up such a chance." The samurai admired the honesty of the soldier and acknowledged that he had the right response and reason. The soldier was just a poor soldier after all, and had not had many positive things in his life. Like his wife was a nice steak in front of a hungry man, and he couldn't be at fault for eating it. So, the samurai blamed his wife.

He decided, if she didn't have her beauty, she would have nothing. So, taking his sword, he slit her mouth from ear to ear. Afterwards, she killed herself and was cursed to be a ghost terrorizing others.

And that's the end. Nothing happens to the husband.

No wonder she worried about me being a girl. Deep down, she was still a woman who had been judged by society for her pride and mutilated by her husband.

"It's different nowadays—it's safer," I said. "I will be fine." I gripped the straps of my backpack, hoping that her mind wasn't going down memory lane. "Women are treated better nowadays."

The Cut-Mouth Woman's eyes returned to me. "Women

aren't always safe. Here." She rummaged in the pockets of her ghost dress and pulled out a straight razor, flipping the square blade out of its wooden holster, examining it for a moment, then folding it closed. She handed it to me. "In case you have trouble."

I looked down in disbelief at the razor in my hands. Before I could ask what I was supposed to do with a razor, why she couldn't just give me a taser, pepper spray, or even a gun, we turned the corner, bumping into a group of middle schoolers.

Their chattering and shoving stopped as soon as they looked up the Cut-Mouth Woman, and I remembered how it felt the first time I saw her, how she loomed over me, how she was now shorter than me.

"Am I beautiful?" she asked, swirling her scissors on one finger. The brave one—a girl with pigtails, her backpack covered in bright cartoon characters, piped up with, "Yes." The rest nodded their agreement. My own heart started beating out of my chest. With our long relationship, I had been able to dismiss the stories, but now I was faced with what to do if she attacked these children.

Could I fight a ghost?

She unlooped the mask from her ears, letting the moment hang before she showed her full smile. "Am I beautiful now?" she said, her voice barely rising higher than a whisper, as she crouched down to their eye level.

"We have an appointment!" the brave one screamed. The rest just screamed, "Appointment!" before turning and running. She stood up, putting her mask back on with a snap, chuckling.

"Appointment?" I asked, watching her. Was she going to follow the running children?

"It's a new thing. Apparently, if you tell me that you have an appointment, I'm supposed to apologize and let you go. Though they didn't give me a chance."

My heart still in my throat, I asked a question that I had refused to ask for years. "Have you ever killed anyone?"

"Like this?" She gestured at the whole of her, not just the mask. "No. Everyone who meets me knows how to deal with me."

"You really aren't that scary of a ghost, are you?"

She shrugged, looking away from me. "No. Not compared to the ones back home. Are we going to get sodas? I want to try drinking one again."

* * *

A few years pass, not as many years as I would've liked. A summer night spent clubbing with high school friends, ones I had not seen since I left for college. Leaving behind the usual friendly bars, where drag queen nights are celebrated monthly events for a friend's birthday, with her picking the places. Exchanging them for men flirting, me with my face red, turning them away, not wanting anyone close who I couldn't trust, who wouldn't call me a trap. Them refusing to accept my "No," pressing harder and harder. My old friends, too drunk to pay attention as I grow more and more uncomfortable. Me trying to lose the most persistent one, the one that boasted of his high school ring, and years spent on the football team there, me trying to slip out into the crowd, and leaving through the back. Me wanting to breathe in the cold night air, to climb into the ride that should've been waiting for me. Looking back to see him climbing through the back door, out to the less popular road. A door I thought he would overlook. Me, trying to run in high heels. His friends following through the same door as his hand reaches out and grabs my dress, hands digging into padding, needed until everything was ready for my body to change. His face, set in the neon lights, transitioning from lust to anger.

Now, the Cut-Mouth Woman was standing over me, as I felt my face, numb from the pain and swelling, barely feeling my broken fingers, feeling the cuts that his class ring had left. Her scissors were bloody, and I wondered what police would see when they pulled down the security camera footage, whether they would see the Cut-Mouth Woman living up to her legend, her shrieks of "Am I beautiful?" intermixing with the screams of the men, the same men who now lay limp around us.

"I'm sorry that I wasn't here earlier."

"It's okay," I mumbled, words bloody as I felt my mouth, feeling for what was broken and what wasn't broken. "I wasn't expecting you to be here."

"I can't stay—not after, not after."

"You killed those men?" I asked, even though I had seen it through my own swelling eyes.

"Yes, I'm going to go back to what, to what…"

"What you should've always been," I said, trying to project confidence despite my shaking body.

An onryō. A grudge ghost. A child of Oiwa.

I don't know how the Cut-Mouth Woman became the way she did. Maybe her husband hired a monk or magician of great power, great enough power to reduce her grudge. To protect himself from what he had done. A ghost that only children would believe in. Or maybe the Cut-Mouth Woman is herself an echo of a grudge, an echo of Oiwa, reduced by repetition of the ripples of the grudge.

No one is sure. Not even me. Not even as she changed, her white summer dress turning into a layered kimono, its pale silk turning into something that sucked out the light from the surrounding neon signs. Her hair, blowing in a wind that did not exist on this summer night, a storm wind that lifted her up. Her scissors were now a wakizashi—a short blade, much shorter than a katana, a blade of a samurai. I wondered if it would always drip with blood.

"You are beautiful," I told her.

"You are foolish," she told me, her voice now booming and grand. "I should've never taken your soda. I should've never believed that you would be safe. This, this…" her voice dropped to a harsh whisper, like the howl of a wind heard through a thick window and muffled blanket, "…this may even have happened because of what I am. For you coming close. For you being beautiful."

I thought about my childhood, spent hiding in fear, waiting to grow big and strong. I thought of the constant words thrown against me, penetrating my walls even with the friends standing around me. My constant fear when dating, waiting to disclose who I was through the safety of internet messages, receiving vitriol. Not being able to see a cute boy and not think of danger when approaching him.

This night was just the final culmination of a prophecy given to me when I was born. "No, it was never you. It never was you."

She looked down at me, her black eyes endless in her pale face. "I am sorry, but this is the last time that we will meet. I don't know what I will do to you."

"No." I pushed myself up, stumbling on bruised legs. I thought of the long recovery, the scars I would be left with, the pity they would bring. Forever knowing that my fear was real whenever I looked in the mirror. To be a cautionary tale told in circles of people thinking they were being careful enough. I looked at the shadowed faces of the dead men around me, and saw the faces of everyone else that came before them. "Make me like you."

"No, Selene..."

"Make me powerful," I said as I walked up to her, her billowing mass touching my skin, her hair burning like frostbite. I grabbed the edge of the slippery blade, not caring as it slid in my swollen hands, cutting me. "Make me beautiful."

The Cut-Mouth Woman looked at me, and nodded understanding.

The blade was sharp—I barely felt it, when it cut my face. All I could see were the faces of those I would soon be meeting, as the grudge curse filled my body.

About the Author

Elizabeth Davis is a second-generation writer living in Dayton, Ohio. She lives there with her spouse and two cats—neither of which have been lost to ravenous corn mazes or sleeping serpent gods. She can be found at https://www.facebook.com/ElizabethDavisWritesSillyStories, and Deadfishbooks.com when she isn't busy creating beautiful nightmares and bizarre adventures. Her work can be found in, Monsters We Forgot: Volume III, The Black Room Manuscripts Volume IIII, and Tavistock Galleria: Stories from America's Retail Wasteland.

(AND I FEEL FINE)

EJ Sidle

"Oh *fuck* me! Learn to aim, arsehat!"

"I've got a cricket bat! You've got the pistol, how about you learn to aim?"

"I know how to aim! I'm not the one who nearly missed the goddamn head shot, am I?"

"You were perfectly safe, Princess, don't freak."

"Dude, there's blood on me! If it was close enough to fucking leak on me, it was close enough to—*hey!*"

"Aw, did the monster drool on you a little?"

"I'm going to fucking *wreck* you, douchebag."

"Yeah, yeah, I'm such a dick. You love it."

"...Logan. We've got incoming."

"Again? Jesus, what the hell is it today? Try not to shoot me in the back."

"If I shoot you, it'd be deliberate."

"You're just pissy I've killed more of them than you."

"Okay, first to twenty?"

"Deal."

* * *

Survivor Jack Conner is nineteen, a juvenile delinquent and an orphan. Once, before it all went wrong, he used to wear his handful of arrests like a badge of honour. They had been for boosting cars, mostly, and a handful of citations for underage drinking, plus the one for public urination that he was less proud of—the greatest hits of a kid in the system.

None of that matters now. What matters is that Jack Conner may have considered himself a shit-heel of a human being, but he was a shit-heel who had fooled around with a paramedic once or twice. So, when a woman collapsed in the middle of the street, he'd tried to resuscitate her. It was before everything, before the news started reporting transmission statistics, before blood in his mouth and her teeth scraping on his skin had meant anything to Jack other than that she was alive.

So Jack Conner is still nineteen, an ex-delinquent and an orphan. He still likes coffee and ice cream, hates between-shave stubble, and still has an enthusiastically-won reputation for kissing his arresting officers. But, now he also knows what a bite feels like, knows the steady horror of disease checkpoints and people morphing into something far more terrible.

Now, Jack Conner knows that when the whole world is losing itself, the last thing you want to be is immune.

* * *

They meet in a service station bathroom. Jack's got his gun balanced on the sink, trying unsuccessfully to pop one of his shoulders back into place when the door swings open. Logan grunts in surprise and takes a moment to give Jack a long look over before stalking across to the urinal.

"Dislocated shoulder and bruised ribs," he observes roughly. He can feel Jack's eyes on him in the mirror, red-rimmed and over-bright. "What the fuck happened to you?"

"You... you're serious, aren't you?"

"It was a question, yes."

"Fuck *me*, it's the end of the fucking world and you're the first human I've seen since Darwin went under and you say, '*dislocated shoulder*'? Jesus fucking Christ!"

"Well then, Princess," Logan snarls, "how was your day? Blow the brains out of some poor bastard? Kill any monsters? Oh, or maybe you thought you were the last one left and you just weren't smart enough to give your pistol a blow job?" He zips himself up and turns, meeting Jack's eyes in the mirror. "Sorry to disappoint, but I'm here too."

"Disappointed?" Jack laughs, quick and desperate. "Shit, this is the happiest fucking day of my life. You're just a dick. Could have opened with 'Hi', or 'Are you alright', or... or... Jesus, *fuck*, something! Wanker."

Logan sighs. "I can fix the shoulder. Not the ribs, you'll just have to go easy on them."

"Because easy is such an option," Jack counters, shoving his gun into his pants. "Jack."

"Logan. Put the safety on that thing before you blow your dick off."

* * *

Jack had actually jumped from the second-storey balcony. He'd bounced off a pool-side umbrella and dropped unceremoniously into an overgrown garden bed. The bathroom had seemed like a safe place to assess the damage.

Logan had just really needed to take a piss.

* * *

Caleb Logan is in his early forties, and he feels every decade like gravel under his skin. He was a soldier once, before he was discharged, a man made for foreign soil and no permanent address. As a mercenary, he found work in semi-reputable locations, and sometimes in places with reputations best not to consider at all. Not a good man, not even by Logan's own standards, but not an entirely bad one, either.

He landed in Darwin one week before the outbreak, a week and a half before the flights were grounded. A holiday, his first in more than a decade where he hadn't needed to bring guns. An irony that wasn't as amusing as it should have been.

Once the looting started, Logan found himself some riot batons and a cricket bat—blunt weapons, quiet weapons that would never run out of bullets or jam up at the worst moment. A lesson hard won on the other side of the world. After meeting Jack, he added a pistol and a sawn-off shotgun to his pack.

Logan knows about survival, knows about killing and living and the line in between. He knows about Jack, too, the way he rubs at the skin of his mouth like he can sandpaper off the teeth marks, knows about the way his eyes stay a little too long on the line of Logan's biceps. He figures the kid can have his secrets, even if he's doing a piss-poor job of hiding them. It's amusing, in a way that's so fucking sad it makes Logan's temples ache.

Then again, it's fucking sad for everyone still breathing, and there's nothing anyone can do about it.

* * *

Logan watches as Jack hotwires a car. He's slouched in the driver's seat, humming softly while he strips insulation off of wires, Logan's hand gripping his shoulder.

"We should be wiring the Patrol. *This* is a fucking joke."

"This is a *Ferrari*." Jack looks up at him, eyes wild and wide with excitement. "A red Ferrari. Jesus, this is probably the best car I've ever been in, let alone stolen..."

"Less mouth, more wiring," Logan snaps.

"Piss off," Jack hisses back. "Fuck me, I swear this used to be easier."

"Move your arse and let me, then." Logan gives his shoulder a rough squeeze and Jack yelps, pulling away from the contact. "Break a nail?"

"Dick." The engine starts with a stuttering hum and Jack's grin turns feral. "Yeah, I still got magic hands!" He wriggles his fingers in the air, and Logan grunts a vague acknowledgement. Jack laughs, reaching for the radio. "Oh, Bluetooth! And this fucker has a phone and car charger, so hello tunes! You look like an old-school Bowie fan."

"Just because you have a thing for tight pants," Logan starts, tossing their gear into the back seat and sliding into the car.

"Hey, hey—the Cranberries."

"Kid? Shut up and let's go," Logan orders. Jack snickers.

"What now?"

"Y'know," he says, revving the engine with a blissful smile. "They never actually gave me my licence." Logan swears, but Jack already has his foot down, and the car leaps into the street.

* * *

Jane Clearly is thirty-three and a schoolteacher from a town outside Cairns. When the end of the world started, she hacked the heads off two students before they could tear her apart. Then she dumped her work heels and ran, through the wreckage and the panic and the confusion.

Trevor is twenty-one and from a mining settlement somewhere North. He didn't realise anything was wrong until the place ran out of bourbon and some kid was eating the woman who ran the corner store. Next thing he knew, Jane came running into his life and nothing made as much sense as she did with her bare feet and her ruined mascara and the giant axe she swung like a saving grace.

She's the most beautiful woman Trevor thinks he's ever laid eyes on, so wrong and so *right* and sobbing in the street.

* * *

Somewhere near Cairns they collide with each other. Logan's driving, Jack's fiddling with the radio, then suddenly there are people on the road. The car clips an abandoned trailer and spins. It hits a pole with a thud that makes Logan's ears ring. And Jack is *laughing*, hysterical little whimpers that have Logan fumbling blindly with the seat belt. Jack's not hurt, he just knows that dying in a car accident would be too *easy* when everything else is so very wrong.

* * *

Logan spreads his map over the hood as the others crowd around him.

"We should follow the infection south," Jane suggests.

"Maybe find an evac point. Darwin went under fast, these guys had time. Melbourne might be our best bet."

"We could steal a boat?" Jack says, shrugging. "I can probably wire one. Get the fuck outta here."

"The world knows," Logan reminds him. "If it was up to me, I'd have the navy out there waiting to bomb the shit out of anyone who breaks quarantine."

* * *

When Trevor makes a head shot from the passenger side window of the moving car, Logan gives him a long look. "You're good with that rifle."

"...it's like pig hunting," Trevor says softly. "I mean, it's *not*, but it is."

"It's not but it is," Logan echoes, shaking his head. "I know the feeling."

* * *

The highways are littered with the corpses of cars, abandoned when the roads clogged and the infected came for the living. Outside Sydney there are crumbling barricades. The word 'help' is carved in big, desperate letters. Trevor makes a sound in the back seat, but Logan drives straight past without stopping.

* * *

Jack stands on the roof rack of an old land cruiser, forearm held up to shade his eyes. There's dirt blowing across the highway, abandoned vehicles groaning and shifting in the wind.

"Can you still see them?" Trevor asks.

"Yeah, Logan's siphoning fuel..." Jack snorts. "Trying to, anyway. Hope he chokes on it."

"Jane?" Trevor asks again.

"She's okay, dude," Jack promises, looking back over his shoulder. "Just looting. Looks like she has some bottled water."

"I don't like trading cars," Trevor says, shaking his head. "We're so spread out."

"It's alright, we'll be ready to go soon." Jack grins down at him. "Want to learn how to hotwire?"

"I... yes?"

"Good," Jack says. "You never know when it might come in handy."

* * *

Sydney is cold. They huddle together, eating food straight from the can.

"Do you think it got out of Australia?" Jack asks suddenly.

"They locked it down fast," Logan tells him seriously. "No one out and no one in."

"We might be the last ones left, I reckon," Trevor guesses. "At least in the built-up areas and outside of safe zones."

"Now that's a depressing thought," Jane mumbles. "Come visit Australia, where it's not just the wildlife that wants to eat you!" Logan barks out a surprised laugh, and Trevor smiles fondly. Jack blinks at her and she shrugs. "What? Too soon?"

"...what if you get pregnant?" he asks. Jane chokes on a mouthful of beans, and Logan hisses through his teeth. Jack gives him the finger. "What? I've got eyes, not like they're being secret about it!"

And Jane is laughing, long and clear and loud. Too loud, even, but no one wants to stop her, not until Trevor reaches over and squeezes her knee.

"Sorry." She's not apologetic, still grinning and shaking her head. "Don't worry about it, Jacky."

"What, did you stock up on condoms or something?" Jack asks, snorting. Trevor winces, and Logan reaches over to smack at the back of Jack's head. "Jesus, Logan, let up!"

"I can't get pregnant," Jane interrupts, patting Trevor's hand where it still sits on her leg. "I tried, beforehand. Followed all the rules, ate the proper diets, went to the best doctors I could find. I tried so hard. But I couldn't, I *can't.*"

"...oh fuck," Jack manages, soft and low. "Fucking *shit.* Sorry.

I'm sorry."

"So was I," Jane admits, sitting her empty can down in the dirt at her feet. "But now? The world is ending, Jacky, there's no future for anyone anymore." She shrugs. "Hell of a thing, hey?" Trevor wraps an arm around her waist, but she doesn't stop laughing for a long time.

* * *

Jane shoots two of them from the sunroof as they weave between the wreckage on the highway. Trevor takes aim and realises too late it's a child, skull half rotted and eyes falling out of her head, but still a *child*. He makes a sound when his bullet hits her, and Jane leans over to kiss the back of his neck.

"She was already gone, love," she promises softly. Trevor nods numbly, taking aim again when Logan barks a warning. His hands shake, and he isn't quite sure if he even hits the next one.

* * *

They get pissed in an old school bus. The booze comes from a highway bottle shop; the bus is just a lucky break.

Trevor doesn't drink, but Jane does. Half a bottle of rum in, and they're all over each other in the back seat. Logan laughs and passes Jack the whiskey.

"If we die shitfaced in a fucking bus I'm going to *kill* you," Jack slurs, drinking.

"Not forcing you, Princess."

Jack tries to flip him off but ends up giggling. "Y'know, I got bit by one. Right at the start. Still got her teeth marks."

"You've told me," Logan reminds him. Jack takes a swig from the bottle and pulls a face, handing it back over. Logan drinks.

"Did I tell you about Mark? He's immune, too," Jack continues. "Met him in Darwin, in quarantine. Whole fucking place went under, infected everywhere, and then Mark'n I... we were the only ones. Only humans, y'know? We're armed and fucking terrified, and then he's laughing 'cause he can see where I got ripped into."

"Mm?" Logan offers the bottle and Jack holds it in his lap, fingers absently rubbing over the glass.

"And I was thrilled, Logan. 'Cause there was two of us and I wasn't the only human left and I wouldn't be alone for the end of the world. You know what he did? He *laughed*, said he was so pleased it wasn't just him, that we had each other. Then he popped the end of the gun in his mouth and blew his fucking brains out. Just like that."

"You never said."

"I know why he did it." Jack takes another swig before passing the bottle back to Logan. "Didn't wanna be the last, y'know? Didn't want to wake up the only one left. I can feel 'em, the infected, how they *think*. It's lonely and hungry and it fucking *aches*, dude. He didn't want to die alone with that shit in his head, so he waited until he wasn't the only one, then BANG. How could he *do* that to me? *Coward.* I thought I... I th-thought... then... Oh fuck, I'm leaking."

"Crying," Logan corrects. "C'mere." Jack does, inching closer on the seat until he's sniffling into Logan's shirt. Logan drops an arm around his shoulders, finishing the bottle in one long mouthful.

* * *

The next morning Jack trips over Logan's feet as he races off the bus. Logan finds him puking by the side of the road and rubs his back until he's done. That's as close as they ever get to talking about it.

* * *

Trevor sleeps through the Victorian border. Jack wakes him when they find the first fire burning outside a pub, stuttering and dying in the darkness.

Inside, the beer cellar is a fortified bunker. The door is propped open, bullet casings scattered behind the bar. There are no bodies, and Trevor shares a nervous look with Logan.

"...is that a good sign?" he asks.

"Honestly?" Logan says. "No idea."

"Guys?" Jane calls, voice tight. Trevor blinks as she flicks the torchlight their way, turning to follow the beam onto the wall behind them.

"Please tell me that isn't blood," Jack hisses, but Trevor has already taken a step forwards to touch his fingers to the red numbers.

"What's it mean?" he asks.

"Not sure," Logan says slowly, moving in beside him. "But some of this gear looks army issue. Maybe an evac point?"

"Evacuation?" Jack spits. "There's no one left anymore."

* * *

Towns slide into each other. Jack likes it better when he drives, when it's about avoiding the wrecks and the roadblocks, following the white lines into nothing. When he's supposed to be sleeping, he counts the road signs, running the unfamiliar names over his tongue, feeling the aching hunger in the back of his mind.

It's getting harder to block out.

* * *

The hotel is quiet. Outside the room, Trevor sits guarding the door. Inside, Jack lies on his stomach next to Logan, snoring softly. Jane tenderly wipes down the blade of her axe, running a finger along the edge. Logan lays out his weapons.

"Never seen you use the gun," Jane comments, reaching for a small handgun. He doesn't stop her. "One bullet." It's not a question. Her eyes flicker down to Logan's hand resting on Jack's shoulder.

"Don't tell him," Logan asks. Jane nods, pulling a pistol from somewhere and handing it over. Logan checks the chamber. "One bullet."

"How about neither of us tells?" She weighs the gun in her palm before tucking it away. Logan never sees it again.

* * *

Trevor drives with one hand on the wheel, the other on the gear stick. Jane rubs her palm along his forearm, curled up in the passenger seat with her forehead resting on the side window.

"I've never been this far south," she says. "It's so cold."

"Blanket?" Logan offers, passing one forward. "There's an exit ramp coming up, maybe we should call it a day."

"Yeah."

"*Fuck!*" Jack sits upright in the back seat, lunging forward over the centre console. Trevor flinches, jerking the wheel to one side, and the car wobbles on the road.

"The hell?" Jane demands, but Jack grabs for Trevor's arm. "Jacky!"

"Stop!" he orders, and Trevor puts his foot on the brake.

"What?" Logan barks, gun in his hand as he checks over his shoulder. Jane's got her seatbelt off, swivelling around as Jack shakes his head. "What the fuck, Jack?"

"Just... just *hang on* for a second," Jack mutters, closing his eyes. "...they're hungry. I can feel it. They're hungry, really hungry... and they're close."

"Keep driving," Logan orders softly from the back seat. "Keep driving. We don't stop until we need to refuel."

Trevor puts his foot down as Jack slumps back into his seat. No one asks how he knew.

* * *

Victoria *fought*. Everywhere there are signs of resistance, barricades and blockades funnelling down to barbed wire traps. Logan feels a brief twist of hope, then the emptiness of the place hits him anew, and he realises it doesn't matter. They still lost.

Trevor finds words carved into walls. Information, names of the missing and sometimes the lost, plans to create new safe zones and escape. Sometimes, just *words*, nonsensical and gloriously human.

There's more of the infected, too. Jack starts cutting lines in his forearm. Logan knows, catches him at it one day. He pours vodka over the wounds, holding Jack's wrist still when he hisses and squirms, but there's nothing he can say to make it any better.

* * *

When they stop to sleep, it's in shifts. They hole up in the second floor of town houses or highway motels, sharing space and beds and couches. It's not the worst way Logan has ever moved across country, not even close.

There's a safe zone half a day to the south. Or, there's a rumour of a safe zone, anyway, scrawled on walls and bathroom doors at every place they stopped.

Logan takes first watch, slouching on the remnants of a patio set with his ankle resting on his knee. It's a dark night, the stars covered by clouds, and the silence from the streets around them a blessing.

"Want company?" Jack asks, sliding in next to him.

"Shouldn't you be taking advantage of the soft bed?" Logan counters. "It's been a lot of hard floors recently."

"Not tired," Jack says, shrugging. "Or can't sleep, I guess. Don't want to be alone."

"Alright then." Logan shifts, letting Jack lean against his side. "You wanting to talk, Princess, or just sit?"

"What do you think's going to happen?" Jack asks softly, and Logan sighs. "To us, I mean."

"Everyone dies, Jacky," Logan offers gently. "Guess we do, too."

"No, I mean what if we find people?" Jack chews on his bottom lip, not meeting Logan's eyes.

"A safe zone?" Logan asks, and Jack nods. "Well, we settle in and help them hold out. We watch each other's backs, keep each other alive. And, if the place is going under, the four of us bail out and move on."

"I like that," Jack mumbles, heavy against Logan's side. "I think... I think they might just shoot me in the head, though."

"You think any of us would let that happen?" Logan demands. "You're one of us, Jack."

"Yeah? I think I might be one of *them*," Jack counters, low and soft. "Or, maybe I will be, if enough time passes. They're in my head, what if I'm in theirs, too? Maybe they can feel me." He shifts, pressing closer. "I don't... I don't think I'm safe to be around."

"You're not," Logan agrees, settling an arm around Jack's shoulders before he can move away. "I've seen you drive, Princess, and you're definitely not safe to be around."

"That's not what I meant, fucker!" Jack spits.

"I know that!" Logan snaps. "And I know you're as human as the rest of us, too."

"...if I'm not, you'll kill me." Logan flinches, but Jack grabs at his arm. "Logan, if I'm not, you're going to kill me. Okay?"

"We won't have to worry about it," Logan argues. "It's not a problem we need a solution for, Jacky."

"I don't want it to be a random dude in a safe zone," Jack continues, ignoring him. "They'll figure it out, Logan, you know they will. I don't want them to kill me, I want..."

"Alright, Princess, I got you," Logan sighs. "I got it."

"Promise?" Jack demands.

"...yeah, I promise."

* * *

Trevor finds them on the balcony the next morning, Jack drooling on Logan's shoulder, and Logan staring steely eyed at the horizon.

"Long night?" Trevor guesses. Logan only grunts.

* * *

When they stop again, Jack settles on the roof of the car as lookout. Logan and Jane spread out, bundled up in jackets with their weapons in their hands. Trevor waits until they're out of earshot, then glances up at Jack.

"Do you really think other people would kill you?" Trevor asks. Jack twitches but doesn't look at him. "You don't talk quietly."

"Says the guy I hear getting laid every other day," Jack says.

"I would apologise, but..." Trevor grins and shrugs.

"Yeah, well, fuck you!" Jack laughs, shaking his head. "And, yeah... yes. I think they would. Kill me," he adds.

"Oh… oh." Trevor sighs. "I guess we try to avoid that?"

"If we can," Jack mutters, eyes already back on the road around them.

* * *

"Fuck me, this place sucks balls!" Jack moans as they clamber through an abandoned tram, dead on the tracks. "Tell me we can drive soon."

"Roads are clogged," Trevor reminds him, helping Jane step from the tram across to a car roof. Jack sighs, jumps across after them and lands awkwardly. He latches onto the tram window to save himself and hisses in pain.

"What?" Logan demands.

"Cut myself." There's blood oozing from his palm. "Bandages?"

"Let me look," Jane instructs.

"No!" Jack recoils, yanking his hand away from her.

"Damn it, Jacky," she sighs, reaching out again. "Show me."

"She bit me!" Jack forces out. "Okay? Understand? It's fucking fluid and blood and shit, Jane, and she *bit* me. So just… don't."

"Jacky," Jane breathes but Logan touches her shoulder, shaking his head as he hands over the bandages.

* * *

Trevor punches Logan in the jaw somewhere off a cobbled laneway. Logan stumbles backwards and gives him a terse nod, rubbing a hand over the side of his face.

"Why'd you do it?" Jane asks softly when they dig in for the night.

"Because Jack wouldn't," he says. "He's a little in love and a lot infected. Logan knows, but he still has us running for one of these rumoured safe zones."

"What, you think Logan'll let them separate us?" she says. Trevor shrugs. "…you do. Love, he's not going to let anyone hurt Jacky. Hell, none of us will let anyone hurt Jacky."

"And if we're the ones hurting him?" Trevor asks. "If we're

the ones that have to…" He sighs. "Babe. He got bitten."

"Right back at the start!" Jane snaps. "He's not one of them, Trevor! He's still one of us."

"I know," Trevor says. "I know. And I don't want to see him turn."

"So what would you have us do?" Jane demands. "You think we should leave him behind?"

"I think…" Trevor offers slowly, watching as Jack passes Logan an open can of cold beans. "Safe zones aren't going to be safe for all of us. I don't know what that means for the long term."

Jane doesn't know either, but she never brings it up again.

* * *

There is no safe zone, not anymore. Jane drives on, silent tears rolling down her face. They don't stop driving until the car is out of fuel, and no one says a word.

* * *

The State Library in Melbourne is a former army bunker. They miss the evacuation by four days, but not the air strike. Logan finds correspondence from the US military, Air Force documents ordering bombing runs on all major cities. According to the date on Jane's watch, they have two days. It's everything they could hope for, but none of them know how to say it.

* * *

"He's leaving," Jane says. It's pre-dusk and they're sitting side by side, Jane cleaning her axe and Logan chewing on a piece of leathered jerky.

"Why?"

"Says he only just started living."

"He'll get himself turned out there alone," Logan dismisses.

"Won't be alone," she corrects gently.

"Wandering off, just the two of you—it's suicide."

"No, it's *life*," Jane tells him, turning in the semi-darkness to meet his eyes. "You know, he got sober a few weeks before everything went to shit. First time since he was a kid. He's the most beautiful thing I've ever seen, and we should have never even met."

"So you run off to die together?" Logan asks. "Poetic."

"He's not ready to die like this," Jane says, shrugging. "If he wants to live, then I'll go with him. I'll protect him, love him, and god help me if it comes down to it, I'll make sure he dies human."

"Never took you for an executioner."

"I'm not the only one with a last option tucked into my waistband," Jane counters. "Would you leave Jacky here to die alone?"

"...no," he admits softly.

"From here it's all death, Logan. I choose him, for as long as I can have him."

"Fucking romantics," he mocks. She laughs, loud and honest, head back and staring up at the stars. He sighs. "When?"

"As soon as we're done talking."

"We are."

"I know."

"Jane? Good luck."

She stands and waits, her axe across her shoulders, calloused feet bare and long hair tangled. "Yeah. See you on the other side."

* * *

Jane uses her bullet in Alice Springs. It happens pretty much like she guessed it would.

* * *

The last night is dark, but the stars are beautiful. Jack perches on the edge of the roof, swinging his legs and watching the sky.

"What do you think it'll feel like?" he asks eventually. "Dying?"

"Fast," Logan promises. "You won't feel anything at all."

"Huh." Jack rubs a hand across his forearm. "Might have liked it to hurt. Would have felt like it all meant something."

"Yeah," he agrees. "I know."

* * *

The sky is perfectly quiet. They sit together, legs dangling towards the ground and Jack's hand restless on Logan's knee.

"What does it mean?" Jack asks softly, not really needing an answer. "This has to be it, they have to come, I can't..."

There's movement on the street below and silence above. Jack's warm, loose-limbed and pliant, hand moving to fist in Logan's shirt.

"Don't," Logan warns gently, and Jack doesn't, except that he already has.

About the Author

EJ Sidle is an Australian who currently finds herself living in Scotland. She has a day job that takes up too many hours, and likes to spend her free time with her dog, Bullet. EJ also enjoys travelling, playing video games, and drinking ludicrous volumes of coffee. Come say hi on Twitter @sidle_by.

MOUTHS TO FEED

Solange Hommel

You want to leave work early after that asshole, Jeff, spouts off about the state of your cubicle, but you know better. You may have Jeff beat in terms of seniority, experience, and brains, but Jeff's dad owns the company. Clamping your lips against a torrent of profanity, you push papers around your station until quitting time. You can't afford to lose this job.

You have mouths to feed.

You want to unload on the idiot cashier at the bus station when he rolls his eyes at your handful of change, as if coins aren't money. Instead, you lower your eyes and wait for him to count it up. His lips move with the effort. You thank him when he finally hands you a fresh pass, although your voice trembles with the effort of restraining yourself. You'd quit riding this dirty, stinking piece of shit, but it's too far to walk, and it's going to be a while before you can pay for those car repairs.

You don't read on the bus anymore. The crowded jumble in your mind makes it too hard to concentrate on the words. Instead, you stare down the snot-nosed kid hanging backwards over his seat three rows up until he turns, crying, to his mother. He's still sniveling when the bus reaches your stop.

You're sure the butcher has better cuts of meat in the back. You contemplate demanding he find you something nicer, a little less silvery gray around the edges, but you only have five dollars in your purse. Besides, if you challenge him, he might refuse to sell you even these scraps. You must not come home empty-handed.

You have mouths to feed.

You pass the same public works night crew meathead as always on the walk between the butcher and your apartment. Tonight, he fixates on your ass, telling you all the things he'd do to it if you'd just give him a smile. You imagine all the things we'd do to him, should you get him back to your bedroom, and then you *do* smile. Something about it makes him step back, look around for his buddies. It's just as well. Someone would probably come looking for him. You don't have time for that.

You have mouths to feed.

You drop your purse and kick off your shoes in the tiny hallway of your apartment. "I'm home, babies!" We hear you in the hall and in our collective mind. You carry the black foam tray of near-rancid meat toward the bedroom, unwrapping as you go. We skitter with excitement on the other side of the door. You break into your first real smile of the day.

You turn the knob. As you slide into the cool darkness of the room, light from the hall glistens along the wet ivory of teeth, the ebony slash of talons. You close the door behind you. Last week, you brought us a homeless man, too drunk to question your offer of a hot meal and a shower. The room still smells coppery and damp. You consider the tainted meat in your hand a poor substitute, but we're not picky. And maybe tomorrow that asshole, Jeff, will spout off one time too many.

You have mouths to feed.

About the Author

Solange Hommel is a former elementary school teacher turned author. She and her husband split their time between Texas and Minnesota, depending on the season. She most enjoys creating very short horror, but will ultimately write whatever her characters demand. When not agonizing over comma placement, Solange plays board games or works on one of her many unfinished craft projects. She is @SolHom on Twitter.

RED ROVER, RED ROVER

Larina Warnock

The second hardest decision I ever made was taking custody of my little sister, Bianca, when our folks died. I was only nineteen and she was fifteen and I didn't know nothing about being a man, much less a father. Weren't like we had much of example from Pa, and truth be told, I was downright scared to do it. But she was my little sister and the only person in the world who loved me despite me not always thinking as fast as everyone else. So I jumped through the hoops, and the social worker people let me, probably more 'cause there just weren't any foster homes in Reedy, Montana than 'cause they thought I'd be good at it. For two years, though, I turned out to be pretty good at it after all. I got a job at Meats & Eats grocery, paid the rent and electric on time, and got Bianca to school every single day so she could make something of herself. If one of us got out, I figured I'd done all I needed to do.

Then one day Sunrise showed up at the store with that basket of puppies. I was working, and there was a big ass shipment of flour and cooking oil that come in on the truck. The battery on the driver's pallet jack was dead, and the hydraulics busted on mine, so the driver and I were packing that whole order off by hand.

Ernie, my boss, had a strict "no sales or giveaways of any kind outside the store" rule, but he didn't notice Sunrise or them puppies on account of getting handsy with one of the seventeen-year old checkers, or begging her not to tell her folks and promising her a raise, or just standing creepy-like in front of the security camera screen. I didn't know Sunrise too well. She graduated a year ahead of me and quit Meats & Eats before I started there, but there weren't too many real lookers in Reedy, so like everyone else, I knew who she was. Rumor had it she spray-painted every wall in Ernie's office 'fore she left, but nobody could ever prove it was her. I figured it was just a rumor on account she still bought her groceries at Meats & Eats.

I didn't want her getting in any trouble, but I was sweating, and I mean *really* sweating, and there wasn't a chance in hell I was gonna get close enough for her to know how much. So I didn't say nothing when she sat down with her back against the wall near the door, that basket of whimpering cuteness set on the ground between her feet.

I clocked out thirty-seven minutes late, knowing Ernie was gonna be pissed to beat the band that I hit overtime, but not seeing much choice in it since he'd be just as pissed or more if I'd left without putting all that flour and cooking oil away. I walked out the side door with my jean jacket flung over my shoulder, not paying any mind to much of anything until I heard loud voices at the front of the store. A surge of guilt twisted my stomach in knots as I remembered Sunrise and the puppies and how I didn't say nothing when I saw her. I bolted around the corner ready to be some kind of hero.

I stopped real sudden-like, though, because things at the front of the store were downright weird. Sunrise was standing facing Ernie, and me behind Ernie, and that basket was sitting on the ground behind her legs. It looked like there was one pup left, some kind of hunting dog maybe, now that I was close enough to see, and it was staring up at Ernie with the saddest eyes.

"See?" Sunrise said, her voice quivering a little. "These puppies are special. You wouldn't do anything to that face, would you? I even saved this one for you. Don't you wanna take him home?"

The pup whined, a pathetic little whine that was likely to be a helluva lot louder in the middle of the night, and Ernie, all six-foot-four of him, squatted down and picked it up. Now, I can't say I've never been twitterpated by a baby animal before, but Ernie was, well, Ernie. Only thing he ever cared about was chasing high school girls and not getting caught. And here he was, holding this puppy face to face, and then he leaned forward and licked it right on its wet, little nose!

"I think I will take him," Ernie said. "Thank you." He strutted to his Chevy Nova, puppy cuddled under his chin. Ernie's graying hair wisped against the top of the door well as he climbed in, and instead of watching his own hard head, he put a hand over that pup's ears as if it was the one about to get a concussion. Then he closed the door, revved the engine, and sped off.

Sunrise smiled at me and for a minute, I thought that must be what had got to Ernie. I was jealous something awful right then, never being much of the guy anybody wanted, but I got all those emotions under control before my mouth could ruin my chance at talking to Sunrise alone.

"That was weird," I said.

Sunrise cocked her head to one side and raised an eyebrow. Her light brown hair dipped low on one side, and I could swear I saw an actual twinkle in her hazel eyes, probably on account of the sun moving down the horizon behind me. "Was it?" she asked, like maybe I saw something she didn't.

I replayed the whole scene in my head real quick-like and decided Ernie really *did* lick that pup. But the way she asked fed this little ball of doubt in my stomach. "Ernie don't let nobody sell stuff or give things away outside the store. He don't even let the Santa people ring bells at Christmas," I told her, not sure if I was trying to convince her or myself that something strange just happened.

"Is that right, Phillip?" she asked.

"That's right," I said, and nodded for emphasis. "It's like you hypnotized him or something." I didn't mean for it to sound all blamey and such, but it did, and I regretted it right away. I licked my lips to get the taste of my foot off my tongue.

Funny thing, though, Sunrise just nodded a little and strolled toward me like Taylor Swift in that crazy-girl video. "Not me," she said, "Rover. He's a Sin Hound. He transforms people's worst behaviors."

What she said sorta registered, but truth to tell, she smiled a little more and showed this tiny dimple at the corner of her mouth. Then the strap of her blue tank top fell off her shoulder and all of a sudden I remembered how bad I'd been sweating unloading all that flour and cooking oil. The closer she came, the more I could smell my own body odor. I backed up real slow at first, making my apologies in some sort of babbling idiot fashion, and then just to make sure I'd fucked it all up perfect-like, I turned around and ran to my car. I could hear Sunrise laughing, or thought I could hear her laughing, and that laugh struck me in the gut like dynamite.

* * *

Me messing things up with a pretty girl wasn't exactly an abnormal occurrence, so I did the only thing I knew how to do and went on with my life. When I got home, Bianca was sitting on the couch with a textbook plopped open over her knees and a notebook on the armchair. She looked up at me for just a second, and I could swear I saw my Ma back from the dead.

"Hey," Bianca said and went back to writing in her notebook, probably working on some hard-ass problem usually saved for college rockstars. "Did you know that flour is explosive?" She was smart like that, way smarter than me. She was seventeen and never touched no meth or nothing. I was proud of her.

"It is? Weird. I unloaded mountains of flour today and nothin' blew up," I said back. "You hungry? I can make some pancakes and eggs."

"Because there wasn't any fire, Big Brother Dear. And you always make pancakes and eggs." I did make pancakes and eggs a lot.

"How about—" I paused for a long minute. I couldn't think of nothing but pancakes and eggs, so I went into the kitchen and started looking through the cupboards. "Mac and cheese?" I hollered to the living room.

"You always make mac and cheese," Bianca hollered back.

I stomped back into the living room. "Wait a minute. I can't *always* make pancakes and eggs *and* always make mac and cheese!" I wasn't mad. Bianca was just a kid, after all. But I was annoyed for like thirty seconds until I saw her laughing.

"Gotcha," she said and tossed her pencil at me. I let it bounce off my chest and onto the beige carpet near an old stain, wine or blood, hard to tell.

I smiled at Bianca. I couldn't help it. Bianca always, or almost always, made me smile, except when she was flirting with some boy down at school.

She set her textbook on the rickety stand beside the couch and stood up. "You make the pancakes. I'll make the eggs. You never cook them all the way."

"I don't like 'em cooked all the way."

"It's all about *you*, isn't it?" Bianca elbowed me as she passed by. I followed her into the kitchen, going to the cabinet to get the stuff for pancakes. She pulled the carton of eggs out of the mostly empty refrigerator. "I think I'm going to apply to Meats & Eats. Can you help me with the application?"

I stopped breathing for a minute, my arm stretched out into the top cupboard and my hand on the plastic container we put our flour in. Visions of Ernie hanging around the checkers and watching the security screen made my face go hot. "I don't think that's a good idea," I said.

"Why not?" Bianca asked. "You got a job there, so you obviously know how to fill out an application."

I fumbled around in my head trying to figure out how to tell her I didn't want her to work there without telling her the owner was some creepy fuck and without her thinking I just didn't want her around. I could maybe not help her, but she was a smart kid and she'd figure out that application with or without my help. She was only asking for my help so I'd feel parental and needed and all that. Plus, it'd give her something to talk to the social worker about when the foster inspection came around again.

I pulled the flour and a mixing bowl out of the cupboard and walked to the tiny counter beside the oven where Bianca cracked the eggs into a pan like some chick on Hell's Kitchen. I tried and tried to think of a way out, but all I could think to do was distract her. "Maybe apply at that new expresso stand," I said.

"*Espresso*," she corrected. "And I don't want to work at the coffee shop or fast food. Hungry people are assholes. I know because I'm an asshole when I'm hungry."

I mixed the pancake batter. "Tips would be good. You'd probably make more than I do even working part time." I stopped stirring and looked at her. My heart started pounding in my chest real hard. "You aren't thinking about quitting school, are you?"

Bianca laughed. "No, I'm not quitting school, Phillip. But I *am* getting hungry."

"Oh. Good." I poured the batter into two small pancakes and one big one. Making a face outta pancakes was something Ma used to do for us when we were kids, and the only thing I could do like she did. Some days I even wished she was still around to do it, but then I'd remember how raging mad Pa would get at seeing childish stuff like that on our plates, and I'd know we was better off and she was better off. Sometimes bad things happen for good reasons.

* * *

Next day, Bianca showed up at the store after school and picked up a job application from Myra, one of the seventeen-year-old checkers. I stood behind the swinging doors to the back where I could just see the two of them talking at the register. I looked around for Ernie, ready to get all fired up and physical if I needed to, but he wasn't nowhere to be seen. I headed toward the back to make sure he wasn't creeping around the parking lot when Bianca headed home and found him in the breakroom with Rover.

Rover sat right on the crack in the Formica of the breakroom table, panting like he hadn't had nothing to drink all day. Ernie sat in one of the '70s-style, neon green-backed chairs, his huge torso sticking up over that chair back like a yeti. He was facing Rover and away from me, so I just watched for a couple of minutes. Ernie patted Rover's head, then took to petting him real slow, and I thought for sure I saw Rover's fur changing from creamy brown to fiery red. "Good dog," Ernie said, and his voice was so soft and calm I didn't even recognize it.

"Woof," Rover said, and it looked a little like Rover was looking at me instead of Ernie.

I backed out the door. Ernie wasn't paying no mind to Bianca, so I got back to my job stocking the cereal aisle. But that whole damn day I kept seeing images in my head of Ernie staring down Bianca's shirt or gaping at her ass. I heard him creepy-sweet talking about her legs and how he could help her learn how to run a business if she stayed just a bit late. Ernie hadn't done nothing, but anger swelled up in me, and I knew I couldn't let Bianca work there.

I checked the calendar in the breakroom every day, expecting to see Bianca's name on the interview list. Every day I saw Ernie and Rover sitting at the breakroom table. Ernie would pet Rover. Rover would drool on the table and his fur would fade and shimmer: brown, red, brown, red. I started to wonder when Ernie was ordering inventory or sending time cards to the payroll people he contracted or doing any of the stuff he usually did, but I was happy. Bianca's name wasn't on the calendar.

That Friday, Kylene walked into the breakroom behind me. She skirted around the table, holding her shoulder and arm inward, close to her, like Rover might bite if she accidentally touched Ernie. She opened her locker, put on her cashier vest with the bright red slogan *"Meet the Meat You Need"* sewn on the left breast pocket, and walked back out without saying a word.

I looked at Ernie and Rover. "Guess she don't like dogs," I said. Truth to tell, Ernie was weirding me out something awful, my stomach twisting like it used to right after Ma and Pa's accident—like something done went real wrong and wasn't done fucking with me yet. I thought if he said something, maybe it would stop.

Ernie turned and looked at me. His unshaven, graying beard stood out against a red polo he might not have washed in a couple days. "Will you take Rover for a walk?" he asked.

It wasn't my job, and I technically wasn't even on the clock yet, but he was my boss, and I never saw a cooler dog than Rover. Plus, there wasn't nothing to unload or organize in the storage room. So I walked over and took Rover's leash.

Ernie stood up and walked toward his office in the back.

I looked down at Rover. "Well, come on," I said.

Rover hopped onto Ernie's chair, then down to the floor, tail wagging a mile a minute. "Woof," he said.

We went out the side door. I looked around, not sure which way to take him. He started tugging on the leash, heading down the road toward the dog park, so I just followed along, moseying. I figured Ernie wouldn't get too pissed if I was late because I was walking his dog like he asked. Rover lifted his leg on somebody's car tire and a fire hydrant and a couple of bushes. When we got to the dog park and got through the gate, I looked down at him. "Does Ernie let you off-leash?"

"Woof," he said.

It was good enough for me. I leaned down and unhooked his leash before I went and sat on an old bench.

Rover followed me. He jumped up on the bench beside me, and we watched the other dogs racing and chasing around. I pet him while I tried to figure out how to fill my eight-hour shift with nothing new delivered, the storage room organized and reorganized three times in two days, and not being able to start stocking shelves until closing. I don't know how long we sat there like that, watching the other dogs that weren't paying us no mind, but I finally got off my ass and decided we should get back to the store. There wasn't no sense giving Ernie a good reason to be pissed off, and I was getting a little worried about Rover. I'd gotten used to that fade and shimmer pattern of his fur, but the longer we sat there, the redder his fur got and stayed.

We walked back, through the side door, and into the breakroom. Ernie came around the corner from his office and looked down at Rover. For a minute, his face got as red as Rover's fur. Rover jumped up on the table, looking Ernie right in the eyes. As Ernie moved closer and sat down in front of his pup, Rover's fur faded back to that pulsing cream, red, cream, red.

"Uh," I said, "what do you want me to do today, Ernie? There's not much stock left and no new deliveries."

"Doesn't matter," Ernie said, his voice low. "Take the day off, Phillip."

"Thanks anyway, but I really need the hours," I told him. "Rent's due next week and all."

"Paid time off," he said.

Now I know I probably should've known something was up right then, but Ernie hadn't never given anyone but the girls paid time off before, and I just couldn't see the point of arguing with him about it. "Alright," I said. "See you tomorrow, then."

"Good dog," Ernie said to Rover.

Rover woofed, and I headed out the side door.

When I got out to my car, I found Myra standing awkward-like by the driver's side door. Before I could ask her what was up, she said, all in a rush, "You can't let Bianca work here, Phillip. You can't."

"What are you talking about?"

Myra took a deep breath. I noticed her hands shaking, and my stomach started twisting in knots. Myra said, "When she came out of her interview today, she looked shaken up. You don't know what Ernie's like, Phillip. It only gets worse for the girls. Don't let her work here."

My chest tightened up like someone dropped a boulder on it. "Bianca interviewed today?"

"Yeah," Myra said. "While you were out doing whatever it was Ernie sent you to do."

"Walking his dog," I said.

"Ernie has a dog?" Myra asked.

I couldn't figure how Myra hadn't noticed Rover this past week, but those images I'd had before of Ernie looking down Bianca's shirt came straight to my mind and gut-punched me. "I need to go," I said. "I need to talk to Bianca."

* * *

I was damned lucky there weren't no cops between Meats & Eats and my house. I skidded to a stop in front of the house, the passenger side tire of my old Malibu up on the curb, and launched out the car and through the front door of the house.

One of Bianca's tennis shoes hit me in the chest as I came into the living room.

"What the fuck?" I said and saw the other one just in time to duck away from it.

I could tell Bianca'd been crying for a while by how swelled up her eyes were, but I couldn't get close to her on account of her throwing her binder and her math book and her science book and some other stuff at me. "How could you not *do* something?" she shouted. "I mean, the girls at school talk about how creepy he is, but I thought they must be exaggerating, or you would've DONE something! How can you work for him?"

"What did he say to you, Bianca?" I tried to skirt the living room to get close to her, thinking if I could get her into a hug, she'd calm down some.

She skirted the other direction, not throwing nothing anymore, but not letting me close to her, neither. "He has a list of things girls can do to get extra money," she said. "He says he doesn't usually show it to girls right off, but he's *under duress*. Those were his exact words. *Under duress* and couldn't do things that made him happy for most of the day. He said you *helped* him not be watched for *my interview!*" Her voice got louder and louder until everyone in town probably heard those last two words.

I closed my eyes real tight, thinking about how long I took on that walk with Rover. "I fucked up," I said, calm as I could. "I didn't know. I'm sorry." I didn't want to cry, but I couldn't help it. I could feel the tears burning my eyes and my cheeks, and even my ears felt red hot.

Bianca stopped moving and looked at me the same way a teacher looks at you when they're disappointed in what you turned in. "It isn't about me," she said. "He didn't do anything to me except show me the list. But Myra and Kylene and all the other girls that work there." She took a deep breath and her voice shook as she finished talking. "How could you not know?"

"He's a creeper, yeah, but it's not like he'd actually *do* anything," I said and knew right away it was the wrongest thing to say because Bianca walked over and slugged me in the chest hard as she could. Some other day, it might've been funny because hard as she could wasn't very hard at all and it barely made a thump, but it wasn't funny because Bianca was the only person in the world I cared about.

"He has a *list*," she said. "Blow jobs. Hand jobs. Missionary sex. Anal sex."

Her words came out clipped and fast and hearing them out of her mouth made me cringe over and over again. All of a sudden, I got it. Ernie *had* been doing something to those girls, and Bianca was right. I hadn't done nothing about it.

"I needed a job," I said. "I needed to be able to take care of you. I guess I didn't want to see what was going on." I stepped closer to her, sorta ready for her to hit me again. I wouldn't've blamed her if she did.

Bianca rested her head against my chest. "Big Brother Dear, you have to make this right."

I kissed her on top of the head and put my arms around her. I told myself I was comforting her, but when I think about it now, I know better. I was trying to convince myself I was a brother worth loving. "If I lose my job, I lose you," I said.

"You'll find a way," she said, and it sounded like she believed it.

* * *

When I pulled into the parking lot of Meats & Eats the next day, I knew right away something was off. As I stepped out of my car, this huge ass banner flapped against the front of the store announcing: "Closed Indefinitely." First, the sound startled me, like somebody's Pa done had enough and snapped an enormous leather belt. Then it hit me what that sign meant. My feet hit the pavement, and I all but ran into the store.

Rover met me at the automatic doors, a long line of drool dangling from the left side of his mouth. Still a puppy, Rover hadn't grown much bigger than a skunk or raccoon, but he *seemed* bigger somehow, and his eyes were downright spooky—one gold, one blue, both ringed with a solid black outline like one of those anime cartoons.

"Hi, Rover," I said.

"Woof," Rover said.

I leaned down and patted Rover on the head as I passed. "I gotta talk to Ernie," I said.

Rover licked my hand and I took that as permission. Just as I stood up, Myra rushed through the door and damn near bowled me over. I spun and grabbed her by the shoulders to keep her upright. Soon as I touched her, her muscles tightened up under my grasp like a rubber band going taut the third time around a roll of packing lists. Her brown eyes went so wide it's a wonder they didn't pop right out. I let her go as soon as she was steady.

She took a quick step backward and mumbled, "Thanks. Sorry. I just—"

"Wanted to know what the hell's going on here?" I finished.

Myra nodded. "Did you know?" she asked.

For a split second, I thought she was asking about Ernie and his list. Then I realized she just meant the store closing. I shook my head. "I just came to pick up my paycheck."

"Woof," Rover barked, and then he sat down and thumped his tail against the tile.

"We should go see what's up," I said.

Myra didn't say nothing, but she followed me down the produce aisle and through the swinging doors to the breakroom. Kylene sat at the table laughing and sobbing at the same time. Myra rushed over to her and put one arm around her. "Did he—?" she asked, her voice gone so cold I all but shivered to hear it.

Kylene dragged her paycheck along the table with one hand and pushed it toward Myra. Myra picked it up, and her eyes went all wide again. "Don't tell me he fucked up, sorry, I mean screwed up the paychecks again," I said, and I could hear the fire in my own voice. *First, he closes up all sudden, don't even give us notice, and then he messes up the paychecks.* Myra handed Kylene's check to me and I stared at the $15,000.00 on the payment line without saying one word. I imagine my eyes were big as Myra's right then.

"Woof," Rover barked. I didn't know he'd followed me in, but there he was, tail wagging, drool trailing along the floor. Neither of the girls even glanced his way.

I set Kylene's check back on the table and slid it over to her. Then me and Myra bolted for the filing cabinet where Ernie put the paychecks. Myra got there first. She jerked the drawer open, rifled through the files, and handed the envelope with my name on it to me before pulling her own out. I should've said thank you or something, but instead, I tore the end off my envelope and pulled out my check: $10,000.

Myra's hands shook as she tore hers open. She pulled out the check, and her shoulders started to shake, real slow at first, and then they shook hard. Tears spilled out of her eyes like she'd been holding a whole storm inside her for a long, long time.

I stood there all awkward, remembering what Bianca said the night before about the list.

A few minutes later, Myra took a deep breath, wiped her eyes with her sleeve, and set her check on the table. She sat down. "We can't take this, Kylene," she said.

"I know," Kylene replied.

"What the fuck do you mean we can't take this?" I shouted. I regretted shouting soon as I did it and lowered my voice. "Sorry. What do you mean?"

"What do they call it when somebody pays you to keep quiet?" Myra asked, pretty much to herself. "Oh yeah, hush money. This is hush money."

"We should take the money," I said. Bianca wanted me to do something about Ernie. Myra and Kylene needed me to do something. The money made it okay to lose the job.

Myra looked at me funny-like. I imagine the calm in my voice was pretty strange after I'd just been shouting. The calm in my gut felt pretty strange, too. "Is that what you'd tell Bianca to do? You think money can fix what Ernie done to us?" Myra asked.

I looked Myra straight in the eyes. "I'd say it like this, 'Bianca, you take that money and you make yourself a life. Let Big Brother take care of Ernie.'" I flipped the check over, grabbed a pen from the top of the filing cabinet, and wrote on the back of it, "Pay to Bianca Simms." I scribbled my name and slid the check across the table to Myra.

Myra picked it up and looked at what I'd written. Then she picked up her check and stood up. "I'll give it to her," she said. "I promise. Kylene, take yours."

"What's going on?" Kylene asked.

"Just take it, Kylene," Myra said.

"You get those checks cashed today, okay?"

They nodded, and the two girls walked right past Rover on their way out the door.

I looked in the filing cabinet and saw the paycheck file empty. Everybody else had already picked theirs up. I walked toward Ernie's office and saw him with his head down, napping on his desk it looked like. I checked the security cameras to make sure there weren't nobody left in the store and then I went out to the storage area, ducked behind the pallets of flour, and sat until I knew the banks were closed.

Rover sat next to me, tail thumping against the flour.

"Stop it," I told him. "We don't want Ernie to know we're here."

Rover stopped wagging and nuzzled my hand. I pet him absentmindedly while I thought about what I was going to do. I looked around and saw the last three cases of cooking oil sitting in the far corner.

I always knew I had a little of my Pa in me, and I always tried to be more like my Ma when she wasn't high, more like Bianca. But my Pa wasn't all bad and wasn't all wrong, neither. That night he and Ma went off the bridge, he'd dragged her away from a meth house, and he'd beaten the holy hell outta three dudes to do it. He even stabbed one with his own fucking knife. Everybody saw it and everybody agreed: sometimes bad men did good things.

This seemed one of those times to me. I stood up and opened every bottle of cooking oil. I tipped the open bottles upside down on the concrete around the flour.

All of a sudden, I heard Ernie call out, "Rover! You in here, Rover?" He sounded sad, somehow, lonely. I almost lost my nerve right then, but then I remembered what Bianca said. I rephrased it in my own brain: Everybody knew what my Ma was, and everybody knew what my Pa was, and nobody did nothing. Things were better when they died. Better for Bianca.

I looked down at Rover, sitting at my feet. His one gold eye was glowing, and his fur didn't look like fur no more. It looked like fire.

I snuck around the pallet over to the hardware section of the storage area. The box I chose made a scraping sound as I opened it, and I froze.

"Rover," Ernie called again, his voice a little closer than it had been.

I pulled a box of matches out and struck a flame right quick. If my plan was gonna work, I didn't have much time. I flung the lit match at the cooking oil. It sputtered out on its way through the air. I lit another match and flung it, too. The air smothered it before it hit the ground. I opened the box next to the case of matches and pulled out one of them click lighter things you use on a barbecue.

Ernie appeared at the doorway of the breakroom. "There you are, Rover!" he said, a smooth and eerie jubilance shading his tone. He didn't seem to see me.

I stepped over to the flour, squatted, and *click, click, clicked* until the oil lit. Then I stood up and grabbed one of them bags of flour. I ripped open the top as I backed toward the side exit. The fire spread around the pallet of flour like some kind of religious symbol, odd little twists and turns and curly cues.

"Rover, come," I said. I didn't want to hurt no pup.

Ernie looked up. "Phillip?"

I tossed the bag of flour hard as I could toward the flaming oil, opened the back door, and ran. The explosion didn't make much noise, but it ignited that whole pallet of flour and probably the stack of paper products beside it, and then the whole fucking store went up all grand-like. In the parking lot, I tripped over my own big feet and fell flat on my face. I rolled over and stared up at the sky where smoke billowed all spooky-like.

Rover came over and licked me across the nose. I sat up and he sat down next to me and wagged his tail. "Good boy," I told him.

"Woof," he said.

We sat there watching the fire and listening to the oncoming sirens, Rover wagging his tail and me petting him like I was hypnotized even though I wasn't. I supposed I'd have to pay some consequences for what I done. I needed to set a good example for Bianca, and that meant owning up to my actions. They'd put her in a foster home, and that made me sad, but she'd have $10,000 sitting around to pay for college and get the hell out of Reedy. She was too good for a place where everybody knew everything and almost nobody did nothing about what they knew. I did, though. I did something, not just for Bianca, but for those other girls she went to school with, and it felt right good.

When the fire department got done putting out the flames, I told them exactly what I done and why. While Deputy Michaels clapped handcuffs on me, I watched Rover run off down the street toward Sunrise standing at the end of the block. Rover stopped, turned and looked at me, and for a second, he looked like a normal hunting dog. Sunrise squatted down and put one arm around his neck, watching me and the cops and the firemen. All I could hear over the *whoosh* of fire hoses putting out hotspots and the voices of the gathering looky-loos was Sunrise saying, "He's a Sin Hound. He transforms people's worst behaviors."

I never did ask her what he transformed them behaviors to. As I ducked into the back of Deputy Michaels' cruiser, I remembered the one time, just before their accident, that I asked my Pa why he was the way he was, and why he did the things he did to Ma and to me, and if he was gonna do them things to Bianca when she got old enough. "Boy," he said in his gravelly voice, the smell of whiskey thick in the air between us as he drew back his hand for one more punch, "there's some things in life you just don't need to know."

And I guessed what Rover was and what he did was just another one of them things.

About the Author

A one-time teen mother and high school dropout, Larina Warnock holds a doctorate and teaches high school in rural Oregon. She has been a TEDx speaker, cofounder of an online literary journal, and an activist for underrepresented youth. Larina's fiction and poetry have appeared in Space & Time Magazine, All Worlds Wayfarer, Rattle, and others.

CELL PHONE LIGHTS

T. M. Starnes

Eric Rostrum sighed as he sank deeper into his subway car seat.

Tuesday night regulars lined the car. Always a slow night on Tuesday. There was the bag lady, the hipster, the tired janitorial mom with her kid, three teen girls coming back from dinner, two college guys hitting on them, a young black man with sagging pants and a Rastafarian cap, a construction worker wearing a reflective vest, two office workers—a Sikh male and the other an Indian female—and Eric, the graphic artist.

Some were on their cell phones already searching social media. The teen girls were taking selfies. The college guys tried to get into the pics. The bag lady mumbled to herself. The construction worker reclined, manspreading across his seat. The mom asked her little girl what she did at school today. The office workers spoke in their own language. The hipster slowly bounced his bearded head to the overly loud music on his headphones. The Rastafarian nodded at Eric when Eric looked at him and smiled.

Eric pushed up his glasses and rubbed his tired eyes as the train began to move; his stop was all the way to the end of the line, and he often took a short nap before walking home. He made himself more comfortable, shoving his backpack with his work up under his seat, crossed his arms and shut his eyes.

* * *

The subway train slowed to a halt and Eric woke.

Three more people had gotten on as he slept, an older Hispanic man who smelled of cooking grease, soap, and his chest and beard dappled with flour, a large black woman in a hoodie with a nose piercing, and an older man with gray hair and tattoos.

At first, no one said anything. The train had not stopped at a station. After a few moments and no announcements from the conductor, some of the passengers began trying to peer through the reflections of the windows on either side of the train.

Passengers began complaining their calls, their online connections, and their texts weren't getting through.

They asked others if they had any bars on their phone.

None did.

No emergency lights blinked, and no one could see far enough ahead in the other cars to see if something was obstructing the track. Eric shrugged and closed his eyes.

A startled gasp made him open them again.

The train car sat in darkness.

Cell phone screens lit the area until the teen girls and the office workers turned on the flashlights on their phones. All along the train, more cell phone lights were beginning to come on.

"What's going on?"

"What happened to the lights?"

"It'll be okay, baby; they'll be back on in a second."

"Man, I'm going to be late, my wife is going to kill me."

"Oh, c'mon."

"The darkness consumes us all."

The last raspy comment came from the bag lady at the far end of the car.

Several laughed in the darkness at her comment. Others moved to listen to the other cars on either end.

"No light that way either, can't even see the tracks," the Rastafarian said, turning on his cell phone light.

"Let's give it a few more minutes," the mom interjected. "The operator will tell us what's going on as soon as he can."

"Might as well get some sleep," the construction worker added, positioning himself in the dark.

The hipster continued to listen to his music, not saying a word.

Eric stood and stretched his legs. They had to be near his stop, but he couldn't remember the last station they passed.

A scream echoed from the front section of cars.

"Heh, somebody got groped in the dark," one of the college boys said, making the girls giggle.

"Not funny, man," the Rastafarian said.

"Chill, bro, it's just a joke."

"Assault is never a joke," the large black woman beside Eric replied.

"Oooo," the other college boy said, making the teens giggle.

Murmurs carried from the front of the train.

Another scream, cut off, echoed back to them.

Eric glanced down the train; other cell phone flashlights lit toward the front. Reflections were everywhere. Looking back, lights aimed toward their car and toward the front of the train.

"Where's the lights, Mommy?" the little girl asked, and her mom shushed her, but pulled her close.

The Rastafarian stepped toward the section between the trains and pulled up his sagging pants. "Something's not right."

"Terrorists?" the older tattooed man asked, his light directed and illuminating the Sikh and his lady friend. Other lights followed.

"Seriously?" the Sikh asked them all. "I'm a corporate lawyer. She's a financial lawyer."

"That don't mean you can't be some suicide bomber," someone said in the dark.

Irritated, the Sikh man puffed up his chest. "I'm Sikh, not Muslim, two completely different things. We don't—" His companion stopped him and shook her head.

Another scream came from the front of the train, startling everyone.

"Yo, someone needs to go check on people," the Rastafarian said. "Anyone want to come with?"

Someone made a heavy sigh. "Yeah, I'll come with you. Hold on." The construction worker stood and stomped his feet.

"Me too," the black woman said. "Look out behind you." She pointed behind him.

The Rastafarian stepped quickly to the side. Three older women had entered from the front of the car, hurrying toward the back of the train.

"What's going on?" the mother asked as they passed. "What's happening up there?"

The last woman answered her, "Don't know, don't care," and she kept moving.

"Anyone else?" the Rastafarian asked as the trio gathered together.

Eric thought about joining them, but decided it would be best to just sit and wait. It was probably just some idiots like the college boys messing with people toward the front.

"All right, we'll be back." The Rastafarian led the way, the construction worker coming up last in line.

"They won't come back."

Flashlights turned to the bag lady who was rocking back and forth, gnawing on her shirt collar.

"Hey, shut up," one of the college guys demanded.

"Crazy old woman," the teen girls giggled.

"Smelly, too," the other college guy added, making them giggle again.

The hipster continued bobbing to his music.

Eric felt a hand lightly tap his shoulder.

The large cook was leaning over him, holding onto the overhead bar. "I don't speak English good. What is going on?" He spoke with a heavy accent.

Eric shrugged. "You got me, I don't know anything either."

He nodded. "We stay here? Or go?" He pointed back toward the rear of the train.

"Better to just stay here for now," the Sikh lawyer responded as two more people hurried past. "It's just people playing jokes in the dark."

"Jokes?" the cook asked.

"Sure, just jokes," the mother confirmed to him, herself, and her child.

Another scream rang out from the front, a man's scream.

Several people in the car in front of them got up and hurried through their car to the back of the subway.

"Screw this," the older tattooed man said, standing, and following the other passengers as they moved toward the rear.

The Indian lady moved behind the Sikh man who took a protective stance in front of her, peering down the train.

"The darkness," the bag lady whispered. "The darkness. They're all in the darkness."

"Shut up, you old bitch!" one of the teen girls shouted.

The college boys were standing, facing the front, the three girls clinging to them as more people made their way back. In the illumination from the cell phones the college boys were smiling at each other as they wrapped their arms around the young women.

The hipster continued bobbing, his music piercing through the car.

Another scream, longer, louder, echoed from the front and several more people, their pace faster than previous passengers, fled from the sound.

The mother stood and clutched her girl in her arms. Eric stood as well, stepping up onto the cushioned seats to allow the fearful passengers by. Far along the cars ahead, he could just make out the crocheted cap of the Rastafarian caught occasionally in the bouncing cell phone lights.

A light illuminated Eric as he finally pulled out his own cellphone and turned on the flashlight function.

The mother was aiming hers at him. "Can you see anything?"

Eric shook his head. "I see the Rasta guy, but can't really tell what's happening. A lot of people are heading back this way."

The Sikh spoke rapidly to his female companion in their language; they argued for a moment quietly as he motioned to the back of the train. She shook her head in denial, he nodded reluctantly, and they both set their briefcases down on the floor. He remained protectively in front of her, but she gave him room to move.

"They're coming," the bag lady whispered. "They're coming."

"Lady!" one of the college boys yelled. "I'm about to punch you if you don't shut up!"

She began quietly murmuring.

Another scream echoed along the train.

This time from the rear.

All the flashlights turned toward that direction.

A scream came from the front. The lights twisted that way.

Another from the rear and the lights twisted that way.

Eric could see farther along toward the rear; the lights were bouncing to the floor, ceiling, front and back to the rear. Lights began to move back toward them.

The hipster continued bobbing to his music.

Eric shined his lights directly into the bearded hipster's closed eyes.

The hipster opened his eyes, squinted, flipped out a pair of shades and put them on, continuing to bounce to the beat.

"Asshole," Eric muttered.

"The darkness has them," the bag lady said as she rocked. "The darkness needs them."

"Damn it, lady!" one of the girls screamed and slapped her.

"Hey!" Eric yelled. "Leave her alone! She's crazy!"

The bag lady rubbed her face where the girl hit her but didn't react otherwise.

"Well, she should shut up!" the girl screamed back at him.

Several shouts and the sound of fighting rang out from the front. Eric and the others tried to see past the fleeing passengers who stopped to look back at the commotion. The Rasta cap moved back and forth in the light, the reflective jacket of the construction worker moving in jerks, too.

"Mommy, I saw something in the window."

The lights turned to the little girl in her mom's arms who was pointing at the window to her left, across from Eric's position.

"What? What did you see?" the Sikh man asked, aiming his light, trying to see through the reflective glass.

"What did you see, baby?" her mother asked.

The little girl shivered and buried her face in her mother's neck and chest.

"What did you see?" everyone began asking.

"Stop it!" the mother yelled. "Can't you see she's scared?"

Another scream came from the rear.

"We all are!" one of the girls yelled. "What the hell did she see?" The teen girl grabbed the little girl's shirt and pulled.

"Hey!" The cook jumped forward. "No!" He pulled the teen girl's hand off the girl.

More people hurried toward the rear.

"What's happening up there?" Eric shouted as a group ran past.

"You can't see anything," someone cried as they passed, "People are fighting or something, people just keep screaming!"

"They're needed," the bag lady said. "They're needed."

Screams broke out in both directions.

Eric happened to be looking toward the front and saw the reflective vest of the construction worker and the Rasta cap beside it.

The flashlights aimed away from them and when they came back to illuminate both, the reflective vest wasn't anywhere in sight and the Rasta cap was rapidly coming back toward their car.

Eric suddenly realized that there were no flashlights or reflections past where the Rastafarian and the construction worker had been standing.

Eric's fellow passengers climbed up on their seats like he had, as screaming passengers ran past. Screams echoed everywhere now as chaos took hold.

In the flashing darkness, the hipster lifted his feet out of the way but never stopped bouncing to his music. The bag lady began to cackle and two of the girls and one of the college boys attempted to slap her, but the cook kept interceding his bulk between the bag lady, the mother and child, and the angry, panicking teens and immature boys.

More, louder, shriller screams echoed from the rear of the train; the flow of the fleeing tide turned and began coming back toward them.

The large, hooded, black woman who had been sitting beside Eric dragged the Rastafarian back into the car, their arms over each other's shoulder. The Rastafarian looked hurt, the woman's hoodie was ripped and torn. The man's Rasta cap sat askew on the forest of dreadlocks the man sported.

"Hey, dude! Dude! What happened?" Eric shouted at them over the cacophony. "Where's the guy who went with you?"

As his fellow passengers' lights swung to their returning companions, Eric finally saw the blood covering not only the random fleeing passengers' clothing but the Rastafarian's and the hooded woman's as well.

The Rastafarian appeared to be in shock, dazed, cradling his right arm.

"Something in the dark got him!" the hooded woman yelled. "Something in the dark! One second he was there and then he wasn't!"

Eric directed his light behind them, over their heads, toward the front. Without lights to fill the darkness and less and less people aiming their lights behind them, anything, anything at all, could be hiding in the dark.

The Sikh pushed against the crowd coming toward him, ripping open the emergency door release to their car. He began trying to pull the door apart.

"What are you doing?" someone yelled from the crowd.

"To die here! Or to try to live out there!" He gestured at Eric to come help him as the Indian woman moved to help him too. "It comes from the front; it comes from the back! I want to meet it on my own terms!"

Eric glanced at the cook; they gave each other a mutual nod and crawled over seats in order to help the Sikh. The teenaged girls tried to run toward the rear, joined by the college boys, but the fleeing crowd from the back pushed them back to their own car.

Eric handed his phone to the large black woman and she turned it back toward the front of the train, shouting at others to do the same. The bag lady was standing and jumping in her seat laughing maniacally at the top of her lungs. People were screaming and pushing in both directions, cell phone lights bouncing everywhere.

The door cracked open slightly, and the men began prying their fingers through the gap to pull them apart.

"Which way?" Eric shouted over the din.

The Indian woman screamed at him, "To the left, to the rear of the train! We passed a station just before we lost power! Go that way!"

With a surge of strength, both sides of the door flew open.

The hipster, squeezing quickly through the people around the door, jumped down to the tracks, fast walking toward the rear of the train, his cell phone lighting the way. Its beam reflected off the close walls of the tunnel.

Stunned at the man's exit, Eric and the Sikh glanced at each other and then began helping others down.

Like a flooded drainpipe bursting, the panicked passengers shoved each other off the train. Several fell and were trampled or crushed by those leaping off the train. Passengers ran left and right. Screaming. Cell phone lights bouncing in all directions.

Into the darkness.

The bag lady continued to cackle as the Spanish cook helped the mother and child down, then jumped down and held up his hands to help first the Indian woman, then the Rastafarian.

The teenagers and college boys shoved Eric, the Sikh and the black woman out of the way, landing on crushed, moaning people, and fled toward the rear of the train.

Several people, slower ones, were still coming from the rear, and Eric decided it was time to leave. He helped a petite woman down into the arms of the cook, nodded at the Sikh's waiting companion supporting the Rastafarian. He held up his arms to help the black woman down.

A sliding whispering sound penetrated the chaos of the crowd, a noise that came from within the train, from both directions. The sound rose in volume and proximity.

"Do you hear that?" he asked the black woman as she came down.

"Hell yes! Let's get out of here!"

The Spanish cook screamed and glanced down at the tracks at his feet.

Eric looked down just as the cook fell backward. Something pulled him under the train.

Eric screamed and began to run toward the rear of the train in utter panic, grabbing a fallen cell phone to light his way. He felt no shame that he was running faster than the others, even passing other passengers in the dark tunnel.

Escape was the only thing on Eric's mind.

Ahead of him, lights from cellphones bounced, some fell, some flew to the other side of the tunnel.

That made him pause.

In sheer self-preservation, he dropped to the dirty, rat-pissed-stained, smelly ground, rolling against the tunnel wall. He lay still, covering the cell phone light.

Screams echoed from in front and behind him.

He could hear the Sikh and his lady companion whispering in the dark, but he was too afraid to look out or call for them. The Indian woman nearly on top of him, screamed, the Sikh screamed out her name, there was a wet thump, and the man didn't make another sound.

"Mommy! Mommy!" The little girl staggered through debris on the tunnel floor. "Where are you? Mommy! Mommy!"

There was a whoosh of air, and the girl stopped yelling for her mommy.

Someone kicked him in the back as they passed; he opened his eyes to look. Rigid with fear, he watched the disembodied figure's flashlight moving further along the tracks. There was a gasp, and the cell phone clattered to the ground.

Eric slowly, carefully, looked back the way they had come. Cell phone lights littered the tunnel, casting shadows in every direction, illuminating nothing. He glanced toward the way everyone had fled; lights lit the tunnel the same way. He noticed, though, that as the tunnel turned slightly to the right, there was brighter light.

The previous station.

He tried to steady his breathing. Control his panic. Search the darkness for aberrant movement. Minutes might have passed. Or hours. No other train rumbled past, no signs of help, no signs of danger. The cell phones continued to illuminate the darkness.

The light on his cell phone dimmed and died. As the light winked out, he stood, and ran toward the station, following the discarded cell phone path.

Any second, something was going to grab him.

Any minute.

It was behind him.

He felt it.

It was so close.

Eric entered a long stretch of light in the tunnel where the cell phones were not discarded; the station platform was just ahead.

Ignoring caution in his panic, he never slowed, sprinting toward his escape.

He knew the things in the dark would get him any second.

Maybe as he ran up the stairs from the tunnel floor to the platform.

Maybe now as he shouted for help running across the deserted platform.

Maybe now as he ran toward the exit stairs.

Maybe now as he jumped the deserted turnstiles.

Eric slowed, realization dawning on him, that he stood in a lit but currently closed platform. No one was around. No subway workers. No police.

A rumbling in the tunnel began, and wind blasted out of the darkness.

Eric recoiled and scuttled toward the nearest wall, expecting a gigantic worm monster at any moment roaring out of the train tunnel and hurrying up the stairs to eat him.

It was only a train making its way to another station.

Eric sighed.

Then he heard the music.

That hipster's music he had blaring in his ear while the rest of them dealt with the horror around them.

Eric hurried up the stairs to the street exit to confront the hipster and kick his ass just for good measure.

He came out of the stairs and rounded the corner to find another, shorter flight of stairs beyond that blocked by a closed chain-link barricade.

Laying on the floor was the hipster's cell phone, the earbuds still blasting his music.

Eric was going to shove his cell phone up his bearded ass as soon as he found that... pretentious... self-absorbed... idiot.

Eric reached down to pick up the phone. When he stood up, something sticky fell from the back of the phone, attached to the earbud.

It took a second to realize to what he was looking at.

An unattached ear, the black earbud stuck through the earlobe, the earpiece still in the ear.

The lights went out.

About the Author

When not practicing or teaching kung fu, T. M. Starnes is reading or watching horror, thrillers, or sci-fi movies. T. M.'s favorite authors include Clive Barker, Patricia Briggs, Dean Koontz, and Edgar Rice Burroughs. T. M. prefers writing in those genres or in post-apocalyptic and, occasionally, the romance genre. T. M.'s post-apocalyptic series "The Unchanged," the science fiction survival series "Aurora Skies," and other novels are currently available on the author's Amazon author page. Upcoming news of other short story anthologies he has participated in may be found on T. M. Starnes' Facebook page, https://www.facebook.com/tmstarnesauthor/.

LAMINA

Eliza Master

Now

Johnny's gone. Tyana texts from the windowsill. Her legs dangle outside. She won't tell Max where Johnny went. An updraft blows her skirt over her face. She wobbles. Could this be the moment? But it isn't.

She flips her legs inside the apartment and strides to the door, pulling it ajar. Passing the mirror, she sees blood on her face. Hastily, she washes it off.

Tyana throws a clean towel over the spots on the bed. Let Max figure out what he caused. She opens the window and looks down the thirteen floors. In the corner of her mind, she thinks he might save her, even though she knows what is done can't be undone. Then she climbs back on the sill and swings her legs outside.

The door flies open, and Max is there. "Tyana!" he calls, sprinting towards the window. His dark eyes shine at her. "Don't!" he shouts.

"Goodbye forever," she replies, summoning up bravery. Tyana slips off the ledge like she is easing into a swimming pool. And she flutters down, the wind flooding her nostrils. There is a single thud as she hits the pavement.

* * *

One hour earlier

Her sneakers bounce along the pavement as Tyana walks baby

Johnny home from the hospital and lays him on her bed. The infant has the same dark eyes as his father. His cheeks are rosy, and his mouth is like a black cherry, sweet and fresh. She takes a picture and texts it to Max. She kisses baby Johnny. There is an itch deep inside her skull.

Johnny screeches like only a newborn can, when Tyana bites through his lower lip. He is tender, and the flesh is better than anything she has ever eaten. The baby keens but it is too little to make much noise, as his mother gobbles a tiny hand. The finger bones remind her of eggshells. With eyes open, Tyana chews up Johnny's pudgy arm. Blood spouts from the shoulder. She opens wide and sucks voraciously, like it is breastmilk. One finger twitches on Johnny's remaining hand. Then it stops. The baby is dead. Tyana goes for the organs and eats the legs like drumsticks. Soon, only a mish-mosh of sinew and bones remain. She throws the grizzle in the kitchen sink.

Tyana is satiated. She hates herself.

* * *

Seven months earlier

She pisses on the pregnancy stick, hating that she is single. Max had pulled out every time, but now her period is late. It's just two days, but that never happens. Tyana decides she's definitely going to keep the baby, even without Max.

While she waits for the results, she thinks over names. She picks John after her grandfather, if it's a boy.

For a girl, she could do Maxine after Max. But she hasn't talked to him in weeks. Tyana wonders if he really loved her. She brushes away angry tears. Just because she came out only ninety-eight percent human doesn't mean he is better than her. That jerk!

She examines the pregnancy stick. It reads positive. Impulsively, she texts Max a photo of it and writes: *it's yours!*

Tossing the phone on her pillow, she wanders around her bedroom. Would a bassinet fit in the corner? Should she find out if it's a boy or girl?

Her phone whistles from the bed. It's Max. *Thanks for telling me. Are you sure it's mine?*

Yes! Tyana responds.

Of course, I want to be its dad, writes Max. Tyana sends him a red heart emoji. Max doesn't respond.

* * *

Eight months earlier

Tyana smiles at Max as he walks into the coffee shop. He doesn't respond. In his hand is an envelope. Maybe it is a gift?

Hey, hi," he says, joining her. Tyana wants to plant a kiss on his neck, but he lays the envelope on the table between them.

"I miss you," she gushes.

"Um oh, that's sweet, but…" he says.

"But what?"

"Well, I don't think we are good together."

"Why?"

Hesitantly, Max opens the envelope and pulls out the paper inside. He slides it across the table. The heading says, Origins Inc. Her name is on top. There is a line in red print, drawing Tyana's attention. It says the test detected a Lamia chromosome. Next to it is a warning also in red, it says, *Beware, Laminea have violent tendencies and are not suited for parenting.*

"What the heck does that mean? I'm not violent," Tyana says too loudly. Her cheeks redden. A woman from another table looks over, then looks away.

"Show me your results," she demands. Max pulls out a sheet from his lapel pocket. She can see right away that there is nothing in red print.

"I'm really sorry," he says, moving toward the door.

"It's two fucking percent!" Tyana shouts.

* * *

Nine months earlier

They say only two percent of men are completely honest when online dating. All the guys Tyana's chatted with are dweebs or creepy, except for Max. From his profile, he seems normal. She puts on her little black dress that fits perfectly. Then she rubs lotion all over. Her legs are dry as snakeskin.

Max makes reservations at an Italian place. There are white tablecloths, and jazz is playing in the background. Tyana has never met anyone as smart and handsome as Max. They get along perfectly. He asks her for a second date over the bruschetta.

"Are you free tomorrow? Go for Thai?"

Tyana says yes immediately. Everything moves like a dream. He's the real thing. Before dessert, Max pulls out a tiny scissors and cuts a piece of his hair, putting it in a small plastic tube marked "Origins." He hands her the scissors, saying, "It's for ancestry testing. I wonder what our babies would look like?" She cuts a lock, and he helps her put it in a different tube. Tyana feels like he has proposed.

They go back to his place and she wraps her legs around him. She says, "I love you forever, baby."

"I love you too, forever," he says back.

About the Author

Eliza Master began writing with crayons stored in an old cookie tin. Since then, many magazines have published her stories. Eliza's three novellas, The Scarlet Cord, The Twisted Rope, and The Shibari Knot are soon to be released. She attempts to make each day better than the previous one. When Eliza isn't writing, you can find her amongst brightly colored clay pots dreaming of her next adventure.

You can find her facebook page @elizawrites1.

THE TERRIBLE TEDDIES

Priya Sridhar

It wasn't my idea to take my little sister along to a Terrible Teddies run. Rona is sweet enough, but sometimes she can be both too tired and too awake at the same time. Not to mention it's easy to lose sight of her because she's into camouflage now. She once hid in her room for several hours because she did a great impression of laundry in the closet. You would not believe it.

"Take Rona with you or stay home," Mom said as I was leaving and changing from my soccer uniform to better running clothes. "The babysitter said that she couldn't make it, and we can't cancel this meeting."

"I have the night off!" I protested. "She's too little!"

"I'm sorry, Deryn, but you have to," Mom said. "The other option is you can stay home and do homework and watch movies with Rona. I promise you'll have time off for trick-or-treating."

I made a face at that. Trick-or-treating was one thing I *didn't* want to miss with my little sister. Plus, there wouldn't be a Teddies run on Halloween.

After Mom and Dad left, and I made sure Rona changed out of her blue pajamas into jeans and a colored sweatshirt. Meanwhile, I explained to her what the run was. *Terrible Teddies* was a whole series about toy store bears that came to life and started hunting people. They were tiny little bastards with fast feet. The Teddies runs were based on the movie; people dressed up like bears chased you, and if they caught you, you were out. It was a lot like a cross between tag and football, only you were the ball.

"Stay on the path, or we can watch," I said, wondering how I would have liked being chased by bears when I was her age. "Watching may be more fun."

"Are they cute bears?" she asked as she grabbed her kiddie phone. Mom was always stressing that we had to be in contact.

"No," I said cheerfully. "Try not to get scared."

* * *

The main reason I didn't want Rona to come was that I had to carpool with my friend Jill's older brother. The guy roared up in a black Jeep. It rattled on our driveway and made the loose cobblestones jostle.

"What's up, man!" Jett shouted at us. Then he paused on seeing my sister's braids. She took in his infected nose ring and how he stunk like burning grass.

The run was at a park nearby, about a five-minute drive. I'd have walked, except that part of the road is busy and has no sidewalks. And with Rona? There's no way I'd walk with her that far. She'd blend in with the trees and their hanging roots that looked like vines.

The car was filthy; ants ran around crushed soda cups, and there were sticky red stains. The inside smelled like stale caramel.

"You can't tell Mom about this," I told Rona as we climbed into the backseat.

"About what?" she asked, looking around. One side compartment held cigarettes, moldering in a pile. Another held what looked like sewing needles.

A dot of mischief entered each of her eyes. We both had brown eyes, but hers were a shade lighter.

"Here; I got a candy for you." I produced the offering, and she started unwrapping each piece. I always carried candy on me in case I needed to bribe Rona into silence. There had been many emergency babysitter situations. Sour lemon rounds were her favorite.

"Hey, Deryn," Jill said wearily. She slumped in the front.

"Hey." I leaned forward to talk over the noise of the Jeep. "You look like the living dead."

"I hope this run kills me." Her pink shorts were fraying at the hem. She was wearing a running shirt with star-sequin patterns.

"So are you excited?" Jett asked over the car music. "This is your first Teddy run?"

"Yeah." I shrugged.

I knew Jill from back in sixth-grade science class. We didn't hang—I didn't like anyone enough at school to hang with them, but we had sometimes talked about the movies. We had gone to a sleepover where someone had shown the bears, and then Jill and I had discovered a website where people enjoyed talking about them. So, we talked on online forums but didn't sit together for lunch.

Her older brother Jett was giving us a ride, but he was obnoxious. I kept reminding myself that it was nice that Jett was even driving us at all, and that he was not doing anything stupid. On this stretch of road, a drunk high school student had missed the curve and rammed into a tree.

We passed the memorial. Most of the balloons had withered into plastic lumps, and the stuffed animals had vanished. I didn't even know the driver's name. Perhaps she would have been with us, chased by bears in the dark.

"Poor girl," Jill said.

"Mom says that's why we can't walk out here." Rona sucked on a lemon round.

* * *

"Good evening!" A bear wearing a utility belt and overalls waved at us. Their fake marble eyes rolled around in their black fur mask. The teeth were huge and rubbery. "Have you all signed up?"

"Yes, we have!" Jett said.

"She hasn't." I gestured to Rona. "Is there a place where I can sign her up?"

"Children are free!" the bear sang. That trill in her throat—I assumed "her" because of the high voice—made my ears ring.

"Good, good," I said hurriedly.

"How old are you, young lady?" The bear bent at the knees so that the Rona could meet the mask's marble eyes.

"I'm six," she said, refusing to blink. Rona enjoyed staring contests, even though she couldn't win against someone with a fake plastic gaze.

"You should be careful when running," the bear said. "You never know when a bear may come and gobble you up!"

She lifted her claws. Rona jumped back. Then she laughed. The bear reached behind her ear and produced a lollipop. The wrapper glowed in the dark.

Jett shook his head.

"Save the candy for Halloween," he said. "Or you'll be too fat for the run."

"She'll never be too fat," I said defensively. "Besides, if it's too much of a run, we'll watch. It'll be great to see a bear tear you down."

"Ha!" He crossed his eyes. "You wish!"

"Just ignore him," Jill told us in a low tone. "Last night he didn't get in till like four in the morning. Dad was threatening to call the police until he showed up."

"It was nice of him to drive us," I whispered back.

"He's not doing it for us, trust me. It's the prize money. Jett used to be a track champion in high school. He thinks he can do it."

"Do you think he has a chance?" I asked.

Jill shook her head. As if to stress her point, a few runners were waiting for the race to start. They were taking off sweatsuits to reveal glowstick bracelets, reflector necklaces and pristine running shorts. Also, it looked like they hadn't stayed out all night until 4 a.m.

"Yeah, none of us are winning anything." I shook my head. "My only goal is to not be bear food."

"Are they really going to eat us?" Rona asked.

"Nah. More likely they'll tag us and say we're out," I said. "Trust me, the bears here won't want a lawsuit."

There was a path set up with bleachers, where volunteer bears were assembling metal barriers and lights. They all had the same mask: large furry ears, marble eyes, and rubber teeth. It was like a discount version of Disney World. They covered the path with glowing mulch, making it look like someone had painted it with phosphorus.

"Ooh, movie three," Jill whispered. "*Night in the Glowing Forest.*"

"I thought that was the bad sequel," I whispered back.

"Says you. It was awesome."

"Right, runners line up at the starting point!" A bear shouted through a microphone. "This track covers one mile and there are breaks in the barriers for if you want to drop out. If a bear catches you, go to the bleachers. We are watching so if you leave the path, you aren't allowed to return."

The lights got dimmer, and the runners set up. In the shadows, the path looked grimy and not very magical. A bear's ear fell off; they let it sit in the grass.

Rona studied the track. She scratched her neck and then her back. The bears passed out glow sticks to the runners.

"I don't like this," she said.

"I agree," I replied. "We should sit this one out."

"What?" Jill turned to us. "Okay, it's not *Derringer Don't Forest*, but it's no fun if you just watch."

"Hey, it means I get to see a bunch of people tackled by bears."

She wrinkled her nose at me. The runners were stretching and warming up.

"You have fun." I took Rona toward the bleachers. "Who knows? You might beat your brother."

"Nah." Jill snorted. "I just want to be in a movie for once."

She walked to the starting line, shoulders slumped. I guess it was a jerk thing to let her do it on her own, but with my sister I had to think about what would be fun and safe for her.

Rona and I reached the bleachers, which were painted green. Another bear handed out candy to us, more gummy bears and lollipops.

"You're not going to run?" he asked.

"I think it's too dark outside." I pocketed the lollipops.

"Don't get eaten!" he advised.

No one else was in the bleachers. We slid into the front and settled down. From this view, we could see a third of the track; even with lights, it would be hard to follow Jill once she went around the bend.

Rona took out her phone and turned it on. She pulled up a game that involved koi farming.

"Don't forget to cheer on Jill," I reminded her.

"Yeah, yeah," she said, taking out a lemon round from my purse.

"You aren't going to have a gummy?" I asked jokingly.

"I like these better," she said. "You can have them."

"Runners, you got ten seconds before the bears come!" the bear announcer shouted. "Ready…"

He took out a tiny pink water pistol and pressed the trigger. Steam came out, whistling loudly.

"Run! Run for your lives!"

The runners took off. Some stumbled on the path, while others got ahead.

"How did the steam not burn him?" Rona asked. She had burned her hand getting hot water when Dad had a cold.

"Trick gun," I reassured her.

After ten seconds, the bears sprinted down the path. A few got into character and brandished carving knives while roaring. Despite the Teddies being weighed down by obvious fake fur suits, they were fast.

"Are those real knives?" Rona nearly bit her lemon candy in half.

"Also fake. You can see the blades jiggling."

Jill was running with caution, moving to avoid attention. Some runners went down quickly. The Teddies rammed into them so hard, most of them stayed down. They could have played football with their flying tackles.

The runners that were tagged out early shuffled to the other side of the barrier. They trudged and limped, some with twisted ankles. Then the bears tackled them, like they were furry quarterbacks.

"Oof!" I winced. "That's gotta hurt."

The bears were relentless, batting at the runners with their paws. As the runners struggled, some groaning in pain, the bears dragged them back onto the track.

"Okay, now I'm glad that we sat this out," I said. If Rona hadn't come, then I would be out there, getting the air knocked out of me and facing the humiliation.

"I wonder why none of them are joining us," Rona said. She took another candy from her pocket. I breathed a sigh of relief that the bears had given us some extra to last the night. My stomach rumbled.

"Maybe they're just getting some water." I unwrapped one of the gummy bears and started sucking on it. Then I spat it out. It had a bitter flavor.

The gummy fell in front of the bleachers. It lay there under the dim lights like a red mini-bearskin rug.

"That's littering," Rona said.

"I'll get it." I reached out. One of my fingernails speared the bear. I jumped back.

"Um, Deryn?" Rona asked.

I stared. The bear lay suspended and pierced on what was formerly my nail. Candy dangled on a curved claw.

"That's weird," I said. "It's like in the third movie"

"What?"

"It's the bad sequel where the people who ate the candy mutated into bear hybrids. But that can't be right…"

My other hand still had regular fingernails. I stroked the bear claws. They were sharp and thick, like old-fashioned pencil tips. A sense of unrealness came over me. This wasn't happening.

Rona carefully touched the tip of the claw. No one had approached us, not even the Teddies.

"It's a real claw," I said with wonder. "But that means…" Rona and I locked gazes. Then we cupped our hands against our mouths.

"JILL!" we both shouted. "Get off the track!"

By then, Jill had vanished around the bend. I stood and turned frantically, trying to locate her. No luck.

"You stay here," I told Rona. "I'll get her."

I hopped off the bleachers. My feet clattered and made the metal rattle. Thank goodness I had put on running shoes.

"Hey, you can't enter!" the bear guarding the barrier said. "It's too late to join the run!"

A roar escaped my mouth. It was loud and guttural. The bear leaped back, and I ducked under their arms.

The barrier seemed to vanish when I went past it. All the metal turned into grass. Tall grasses sprouted, and they twisted and turned to block the lights from the park. My sneakers padded, like bear paws. I could hear a howling wind.

"Jill!" I called. "*Jill!* Where are you?"

Behind me, bears panted. They lumbered along, giant beasts—not the tiny menaces from the film. They stood tall, like grizzlies with motionless plastic eyes. Some rammed straight into the runners, making them tumble onto the dirt. Others were gnawing on the caught runners' shoulders; even if it was rubber teeth, the screams were very real. One bear stood to the side and chewed on a piece of bloodied nylon. I didn't want to think about where the nylon came from, and why rubber teeth were tearing it apart.

I kept running, a stitch in my side. If they caught me, it was game over, whatever they did with the other people would happen to me. One tackle, and my ribs would crack.

My nose twitched. The smell of sweaty despair, and a desire to run. That was Jill. I lumbered forward. There she was, with the three bears closing in on her. She hadn't seemed to have spotted the chaos.

"Hey, Mama Bear!" I shouted, swiping my claws at their backs. "Go find some colder porridge!"

Not the best line but in all honesty, I could barely put thoughts together.

I realized this was a bad idea when all the bears turned to face me. Their marble eyes rolled as their nostrils twitched. I lifted my sole, clawed hand.

"Deryn?" Jill panted, turning.

"Get off the track!" I shouted. "It's not an ordinary run! They're real Teddies!"

The bears were blocking the path. I couldn't get ahead of them to Jill. But I couldn't trust that I would cross the grasses and make it to the barrier.

"Deryn!" A bright orange sweatshirt flashed, outside the path. "Jill! Here!"

I turned and followed the orange. So did Jill. The grasses shrank and became metal; I know because I banged my knee against one.

Rona stopped waving her sweatshirt. The bears stopped short of the barrier. I lifted my claws, unsure if swiping would do it. Then another runner went past them. It hesitated, nose twitching.

"Come on, let's go!" Jill said. "Run!"

And we did, running across the park to the lot. We heard paws thudding, but not many. Once we made it through the trees, we heard no more growls. Since Jett had the keys, we had to wait for him.

"What the heck?!" Jill panted. "We were running and there were bears? What's going on?!"

"I have no idea," I gasped. My claws were still there, stuck to my fingers. They weren't retracting or fading away.

"Look who dropped in!" Jett waved at us. "You slowpokes missed me at the finish line! Guess who got first place?"

"We almost died," Rona said. She stared at Jett with disgust. "And your face looks funny."

"That's what happens when you run, kid." He ran a hand through his sweaty hair, pushing it back. We recoiled. His human ears had changed.

"Um, Jett," Jill started.

"I can't wait to show this to Dad!" Jett brandished the check, oblivious to the round, bristly ears sticking out of his hair. "This will get him off my back!"

I tugged Jill's arm. She gave us a bewildered look. I didn't blame her. My breathing was slowing down. Jett wasn't roaring or chasing us though. Plus, he was our ride home.

We filed into the car. I checked Rona had her seatbelt on, and Jill sat in silence in the front. She hugged herself amid the debris. Jett opened his driver's mirror to admire his medallion.

My bear claws were retracting, slowly; a tip snagged on the seatbelt. I poked them, feeling like pencil leads were entering my skin. I had only taken a small bite of a gummy bear. Maybe it would wear off by morning, or I'd have to get a heavy-duty nail file.

"We should probably get rid of the candy," I whispered to Rona. "It nearly turned me into a bear."

"Yeah." Rona pulled out the lollipop that the bear had given her. She handed it to me, and I put it with the remains of the gummy and the lollipop I had received. Altogether, it was three pieces.

"It's probably going to be police evidence," Jill said. "We can't eat any of it."

"Says you." Jett reached back and grabbed a gummy.

"NO!" we all shouted.

"Too late!" Jett popped the gummy into his mouth. He swallowed it in one gulp.

"Oh Jett," Jill said in a weak voice.

"What's with you guys?" he asked, scratching his head. Jett's fingertips already had black tips.

I should have said that we would walk or call our parents. But then we'd be in the park, as the other Teddies would emerge from their chase. They wouldn't let us escape a second time.

"Drive," I said. "Just drive."

Jett put the key in the ignition. We waited for the car to start, and could only hope he wouldn't turn around and roar, another Terrible Teddy to outrun. His growling already matched the sound of the motor.

About the Author

A 2016 MBA graduate and published author, Priya Sridhar has been writing fantasy and science fiction for fifteen years and counting. Capstone published the Powered series, and Alban Lake published her works Carousel and Neo-Mecha Mayhem. Priya lives in Miami, Florida, with her family. Visit her at her website http://priyajsridhar.com.

THE THING THESE RELATIONSHIPS ALL HAVE IN COMMON IS YOU

DeAnna Knippling

So it's 10 p.m., and the foodies are going home for the night. They come, they eat the pork belly banh mis, the shishito poppers, and the crispy chicken and sweet potato waffles with chili-infused honey, they drink their hipster cocktails and lovingly crafted beers, they take their loud, braying, performative laughter, and they go home again. But we love foodies, hipsters, and casual partiers here at Lavinia's Tragic & Magic Brewpub. Bring on the girls' nights out, the bachelor parties, the weddings, the wakes—the daytime people pay for everything else we do.

Soon the only people left will be my people, the creatures of the night. Some of them, sure, will be vampires and werewolves, but that's not the important part. The important part is the blessed hush that will fall over the brewpub. No acts are playing tonight; Saturday was Americana and blues, and Friday will be a solo electric guitar and a wailer to go with it, a charity benefit for something, I can't remember what.

But in between, there will be those divine weeknights where we turn down the sound system to a whisper and play Siouxsie and Bauhaus and Lacrimosa: dark, depressing, and just loud enough to provide ambience for the conversation. The overhead lights are put out, and the ten thousand LED yard-and-garden lights sprinkled around the high black ceiling are dimmed. The lights behind the bar become the brightest lights in the house, turning the denizens of the three sides of the bar into romantic, *Nighthawks*-style silhouettes, lonely souls who are marked by the absence of light. The absinthe comes out. The red velvet curtain is closed for the night, and the spotlight projects old black-and-white movies silently onto the blood-colored fabric. Two-dimensional women dressed mostly in feathers dance across the velvet without a sound.

We lock the front doors, and the night people move downstairs, to the pit in front of the stage.

Tables are pushed together. Old friends slip in through the back doors of the stage, trailing smoke. Feather boas... silver combat boots... eye makeup sharp enough to slice... leather jackets... teeth.

No killing or hunting until you get ten blocks away from Lavinia's Tragic & Magic Brewpub, and *never* anyone you met there. No politics (although some days, that rule gets broken). No running someone else's life for them; saying *should* three times can get you booted for the night. And everybody—*everybody*—gets a chance to be heard.

Simple things. The basics. But some folks disinvite themselves because of them. I try to keep things civil. Civility is in short supply these days, even among the night people.

Lavinia's is our refuge. Away from the normal, daylight people.

But that night, at ten o'clock, there are two people still sitting at a table along the wall near the upstairs bar. They came in at nine-forty and just got their food. They're going to hang around for a while, I can just smell it. A real pair of lovebirds. A couple of people at the bar, too, lonely souls.

I send Marisco, who has been having a shit week, downstairs to run the other bar, which is opposite the stage and covered with black lights that throw an eerie glow underneath the bartender's face. Lights up your teeth. I stay at the bar upstairs to take care of that couple: a cabernet sauvignon (a pretty blonde wearing heavy makeup, but not in a bad way) and a pinot noir that isn't really a pinot noir type, but a cheap whiskey putting on airs for the sake of the lady. Earlier, Miss Foodie Cabernet ordered a mushroom duxelle flatbread; Mister Covert Whiskey ordered the grilled hangar steak but is now pushing his trumpet mushrooms and fava beans to the side like a cretin.

The conversation is sparkling. She smiles a lot and looks to the side. He smiles a lot and forces her to make eye contact, again and again. Once, he even reaches across the table to take her chin in his hand when she turns her face away from him.

I like her; him, not so much. Back when I was still hunting, I would have marked him for the kill, just to improve the general lot of mankind. I know *all* about his type. He's the kind of guy who would treat a woman like a queen for eighteen months. Then he would try to start collecting on his investment; he made *her* feel good, now she owed *him* the same. The fact that he was so screwed up that nothing would ever be able to make him feel good was irrelevant.

When she couldn't produce, he would hurt her.

The fact that she was easy to please, and he couldn't be pleased at all, wouldn't make a bit of difference. Investment, return. He wasn't seducing her; he was farming her for a later harvest.

It told me two things about her, too. One, she had been broken a long time ago for someone else's convenience. Two, she craved the high of being wined and dined, even as she knew the crash was coming.

I'm not saying she deserved it. I'm just saying she'd never had better.

They keep talking. They're finishing up their plates. Mister Whiskey has already pushed his plate aside; he's eaten all his meat. He looks at me, then looks at me again.

He gestures me a *come here*. I come over.

"We're done eating. Take the plates."

I take his plate. The lady pushes her half-finished plate away from her. "Would you like a box?"

"We're good," Mister Whiskey says.

I wait until she answers. She says, "Yes, a box. I'll eat the rest for lunch tomorrow."

"Bring the check," Mister Covert Whiskey says. He's not happy. What he *wants* is meek compliance. He's already seeing signs that this one isn't going to cooperate, isn't going to be able to produce the milk of loving human kindness that he's been seeking for so long and can never seem to find.

It's a mystery, bub.

I bring back the box, then say, "Right, the check," before he can growl at me to bring it.

I wait until she has tomorrow's lunch packed up. Then I bring the check.

He thrusts a credit card into my hand without reviewing the bill. I ring it up, add a twenty-percent tip that he didn't authorize, and bring his card and the receipt back to the table. He snatches the card without looking at the receipt. *That*, I think, *is for Marisco.*

He stands up, takes two steps, and looks back at the lady. His face softens—scratch that. He suddenly realizes how this all looks, and he puts on a softer mask.

She gives me a helpless look. I shrug.

They leave.

The two drinkers are still at the bar. One of them finishes up and leaves, probably not understanding why she suddenly feels like getting some fresh air. The other one I invite downstairs. He lights up when he sees us.

I forget about Miss Foodie Cabernet and Mister Covert Whiskey for the night.

* * *

I don't see her again for a while, and then I do.

It's another weeknight, another menu, another Mister Covert Whiskey pretending to be something he isn't, this time a Fat Tire. Same table, though, along the brick wall near the window. I'm not surprised to see Miss Foodie Cabernet again, and I'm not surprised that she's not with Mister Covert Whiskey Number One, but has moved on to Number Two. What's a little surprising is that it's only a month or two after Mister Covert Whiskey Number One. Usually these patterns take longer to play themselves out.

Miss Foodie Cabernet orders crispy pig ears with an extra egg and a side salad with an aged sherry vinaigrette; Mister Covert Whiskey orders a bison burger and picks off the poblanos and most of the mushrooms.

They come in late, and once again I send Marisco downstairs to tend the other bar. I catch Miss Foodie Cabernet look up briefly at the faint but unmistakable sound of Siouxsie Sioux wailing about a city lying in dust. I wonder what's under her mask of heavy makeup. Probably just bad acne scars. She doesn't seem like the type to have much to hide. She dresses like a magazine article on how to go from daywear to an evening out by changing your accessories: a conservative silk blouse and a dark pencil skirt, livened up for the evening with gold bangles on one wrist and gold hoop earrings in her ears.

The evening plays out. She crunches away at the pigs' ears, dunking them in the egg and the red pepper jelly. Mister Covert Whiskey Number Two drinks four beers and starts running back and forth to the men's room. He's not as angry as Number One. I get the impression that he's a jellyfish kind of guy, helpless and hard to hold, but underneath everything you'll find not a heart but a painful stinger.

The upstairs clears out pretty quickly, except for the two of them.

When they *do* leave, they split the check, and I wonder if I miscalled it. Are they even dating?

But, on the way out, him holding his arm behind her in a courtly gesture, she gives me that same, helpless look. I shrug.

They leave.

I go downstairs and join the party. Marisco is getting good at this. No fights, no arguments, just a lively discussion that currently involves a pair of duelists at the end of the stage, fighting energetically with a couple of willow branches decorated with sparkling strips of cloth wound around the 'hilts.'

Once again, I forget about Miss Foodie Cabernet and Mister Covert Whiskey (both Number One and Number Two) for the night.

* * *

Lavinia's Tragic & Magic Brewpub lurches along like some kind of undead bride back from the grave, covered in black gauze and wearing a crown of blue-flame roses. I won't call her a well-oiled machine. I tried to run her that way back when I first bought her in 2010. It took me five years to get over that attitude. Now I let her run herself. Whenever I change the menu, or hire wait staff, or plan what acts to book, I leave the plans on the bar overnight next to a bookie's pencil and a Boulevardier over a single cube, which is a Negroni with rye instead of gin. If she doesn't like it, in the morning it'll be covered with a big X—and God help me if I make a typo, because she'll mark it up for me.

Before I got Lavinia's, people said the place was cursed. The location had gone through five owners in eight years. Now they just say the place is haunted.

A word, and a world, of difference.

"Bela." Marisco's pulling on my sleeve. I'm downstairs and enjoying the company at the tables in front of the stage. It's a Wednesday. The air smells like cherry blossoms, good weed, diesel exhaust, smoke, and Lagavulin. "Bela. Trouble upstairs."

I excuse myself and take the back stairs behind the downstairs bar, which is a rickety spiral staircase that comes up inside the upstairs bar through a trap door in the floor. I open the trap and climb out, closing it softly behind me. I'm behind the upstairs bar now.

As for the trouble, it's Miss Foodie Cabernet again. I don't know how I missed her coming in, but there she is. Same table near the bar and everything.

She and Mister Covert Whiskey Number Three are arguing. He's wearing skin-tight red corduroys and a patterned gray shirt over a new black t-shirt. He has a Joseph Fiennes face, one that's supposed to look interesting and sharp, but just comes across as self-involved. He's leaning forward, hissing just loud enough for her to hear whatever terrible things he's saying. I know they're terrible things because of the stricken look on her face. Her blouse tonight is pale pink and makes her look washed out. A big red stain covers the front. Mister Covert Whiskey appears to have flung her glass of cabernet at her chest. At least it's not blood.

I clear my throat and raise my voice a little. "Excuse me, Miss?"

She's wearing her usual helpless look.

And yet Mister Covert Whiskey doesn't show up at just anybody's door. No matter what I do, it's not going to change anything. She has to do it herself. I'm not saying it's her fault. I'm saying the only thing these three men have in common is her.

Then Mister Covert Whiskey Number Three turns, spots me, and gestures a *come here,* and I startle at the familiarity of it.

I go over. Miss Foodie Cabernet is eating beef tartare and pimento cheese toasts. Mister Covert Whiskey ordered the grilled hangar steak, which we put back onto the menu after Lavinia insisted. The fava beans and trumpet mushrooms have been pushed to the side of his plate.

Again.

I sway on my feet.

It's the guy. The same guy.

The same guy all three times.

Hopping from body to body.

Following her.

And I let him.

"Bring me the check," Mister Covert Whiskey says. Then, to her, "I tried being gentle with you. I tried treating you like an equal. *I did everything you wanted.* Now we're doing things *my* way. And you're going to pay for everything I've ever done for you."

"Would you like a box?" I ask, interrupting.

"We're good," Mister Whiskey says.

I wait until the lady answers. She says in a voice quavering with nerves, "Yes, a box, please."

"Bring the check," Mister Covert Whiskey says.

I bring the box, then say, "Right, the check," before he can growl at me to bring it.

I wait until she has her leftovers packed up. On her plate is a red, juicy circle from the tartare.

I bring the check. I lay it on the table in front of the woman.

Mister Covert Whiskey says, "What the fuck? I'm paying."

"Who pays is up to the lady," I say. Miss Foodie Cabernet looks up at me. She looks at the check. The total has been zeroed out—comped. She's not getting it. I pick up her plate, dip a finger in the meat-juice from the tartare, and run it across the front of the check.

"Just who do you think you are?" Mister Covert Whiskey says.

I don't take my eyes off Miss Foodie Cabernet. She chews on the inside of her cheek, then slides the bill over to Mister Covert Whiskey.

He pays.

"There's no hunting at Lavinia's Tragic & Magic," I say to Mister Covert. "Rule number one. Not here... not within ten blocks... and *never* anyone you met here. And you've met her here, not once, but three times."

That's when I smile, stop being the forgettable bartender, and start becoming someone worth noticing.

Mister Covert Whiskey's eyes widen. Then he sprints for the door. Too late.

* * *

So it's 10 p.m. again, and the foodies are going home for the night. They come, they eat all the things I can't eat anymore—the glassy fried pork rinds with black garlic spread, the cured trout on rye, the duck confit with za'atar. They drink their hipster cocktails and lovingly crafted beers, they take their haunted eyes and they go home again. We love foodies, hipsters, and casual partiers here at Lavinia's. Bring on the boys' nights out, the bacchanals, the christenings, the funerals— the daytime people pay for everything else.

But soon the only people left will be my people, the creatures of the night. Some of them, sure, are vampires and werewolves, but that's not the important part. The important part is that every single one of them understands the sacrament we are performing tonight.

We lock the doors, and the night people move downstairs, to the pit in front of the stage.

The menu downstairs tonight is something special.

Oak-roasted, dry-aged meat with Gruyère bread pudding, roasted root vegetables with rosemary, whipped potatoes, bitter greens with sour orange dressing. Lavinia approved the menu.

But the real treat is in a flask filled with a demon's body-hopping soul. It smells like lemon verbena and tobacco leaves, musk and cheap whiskey.

Tables are pushed together. Old friends slip in through the

back doors of the stage, trailing smoke. Feather boas... silver combat boots... eye makeup sharp enough to slice... leather jackets... teeth.

I pour the soul into cut-crystal cordial glasses, just enough in each to sting the tongue. Miss Foodie Cabernet, the guest of honor, raises her glass for the toast along with the rest of us. She's shaking, but not because of the company.

I ponder the perfect thing to say.

Marisco, dressed in a tuxedo jacket over fishnets, clears their throat. I nod at them.

They raise their glass and say, with a slight stutter, "May each and every one of us give the Devil his due."

The rules are no killing or hunting until you get ten blocks away from Lavinia's Tragic & Magic Brewpub, and *never* anyone you met here. No politics. No running someone else's life for them; saying *should* three times can get you booted for the night, as in, "Let me tell you what you *should* do." And everybody—*everybody*—gets a chance to be heard.

Simple things. The basics. I try to keep things civil. Civility is in short supply these days, even among the night people.

We drink.

About the Author

DeAnna Knippling is a professional freelance writer, ghostwriter, and editor. She writes across many genres, but has a soft spot for all things crime, horror, and gothic. Her latest book is The Knight of Shattered Dreams, an Alice in Wonderland retelling; coming soon is The House Without A Summer, a novel of cosmic, gothic horror set in 1816. You can find her at www.WonderlandPress.com, or follow her on Twitter: @dknippling or Instagram: @deanna.knippling.

FIELD TRIP

J. L. Knight

A nd if you look to your left, you will see the field where the battle occurred."

Mrs. Hamilton's sixth-grade class shuffled to a stop and gazed dutifully across the empty field. The guide's words droned in the late autumn sun like a sleepy bumblebee among the weeds. A red-tailed hawk circled overhead.

Calvin watched the hawk until it dipped out of sight. He began idly digging the toe of his sneaker into the dirt at the edge of the trail.

"...a turning point of the war. We must never forget the brave sacrifice these thousands of men and women..."

A gleam of white from the dust captured Calvin's attention. He bent down to examine it more closely.

"...last ditch effort. An uprising of citizens armed only with whatever weapons they could scavenge..."

Calvin picked up a stick and scraped at the hard, dry dirt. The outline of eye sockets and a nose hole emerged from the ground.

"...gave their lives to save our country..."

Calvin barely heard the guide's voice. He used the stick to loosen the packed earth from the skull's empty eyes, the gaping jaws. He wasn't quite ready to share his discovery with anyone. Once he told, it would no longer be his. It would be gathered by the historical committee on the Great War and labeled and placed on a shelf somewhere. For now, it was his own private knowledge, his secret. He stuck his fingers in between the yawning jaws to scoop out the dirt he had loosened.

The jaws snapped shut like a bear trap. Calvin gasped loudly and snatched back his hand. A few kids turned and looked at him with mild curiosity. He stood up quickly, stuffing his hands in his pockets. They turned back to the guide and his tired lecture.

"Thanks to their heroic deeds on this battlefield a hundred years ago, today we are free from the Zombie scourge. But we must remain ever vigilant, to ensure that such horrors never happen again. Our next stop on the tour is the Excavation Center, where we will learn how artifacts are safely collected from the battle site."

The class trudged off behind the guide, feet crunching on the dry leaves. Calvin kept his hands shoved deep in his pockets. A trickle of blood ran from his fingers. He tried to ignore the growing tingling sensation creeping up his arm.

The red-tailed hawk was back. It gave a thin, lonely screech as it circled high in the crisp blue sky.

About the Author

J.L. Knight lives in Lexington, Kentucky with her husband and two teenage children. Her stories have been published in numerous indie anthologies and magazines. By day, she works for a non-profit bookstore serving the Lexington Public Library system. By night, she writes things that make some people look at her funny.

THE BUGS COME OUT AT NIGHT

Mike Sullivan

Eight-year-old Bradley Donner couldn't sit still any longer. She bounded out of the yellow VW Bug before the puttering of its little engine stopped. *Finally!* she thought. *That ride was forever!* Road trips didn't usually bother her, but this had been her first long drive in Samm's car. The old Beetle might look cool, but it was not very comfortable. Bumpity, bump bump bump.

"Hold on there, Brad," Samm called out. "We gotta wait for Mom and Dad."

"I know, but I gotta pee!"

"They'll be here in a minute." Samm extended her long legs from the driver's seat and stood.

"You're so tall," Bradley said. "Isn't it hard sitting in this tiny car?"

Samm closed the door firmly. "It's not bad." She put her hands on her hips and arched her back. "I do get a little stiff on these long drives, but I love my car. When you get a car someday, you'll know what I mean."

Watching Samm stretch, Bradley wondered, not for the first time, if they were truly sisters. With her tall frame and dark hair, Samm didn't look like anyone else in the family. Dad often joked that he had found Samm in a basket on their doorstep. Bradley knew that wasn't true, but... Bradley had Mom's thin, blonde hair, a round, pudgy face like Dad, and she suspected that she'd never be as tall as Samm.

"What do you think of the house?" Samm asked.

Bradley turned to look at the place that was to be home for the next few days. Dad had called it a cabin, but it didn't look like any cabin she had ever seen. It certainly wasn't made of logs. She wasn't sure what she had been expecting, but the last few miles had been on a dirt road, and then that had turned into a glorified path, so she figured they would find a tiny log cabin up here in the mountains. But, nope, no logs. Just a house.

"I like it," she said.

Samm frowned. "I don't know. Reminds me of the Witch's cottage in Hansel and Gretel."

Bradley smirked, shook her head. Why was Samm always so negative? *Witch's cottage? It's just a house.* It had a front door, a back door (*probably*), two floors, and—she counted—five windows. At least five that she could see from this angle. One window, way up near the roof, was a circle. Bradley thought that was kind of cool. The wood was painted brown and the trim was red. There was no driveway, just a couple of gravelly ruts gouged into what passed for the front lawn. The surrounding trees were almost close enough to reach from inside, as if someone had chiseled out just enough of the forest to comfortably contain the little house.

Bradley ran around to the back.

"Hey, don't disappear!" Samm yelled.

"I won't!"

The backyard was also tiny. There was a small deck off the back with a picnic table and a grill. Three beach chairs sat open on the grass. Bradley noticed that there was no propane tank near the grill. *Cool,* she thought, *it must be that other kind.* She'd never seen one before, but a boy at school had said that hamburgers cooked on that kind tasted better. Her stomach rumbled. *Mmmmm, hamburgers.*

She took a few steps toward the trees beyond the backyard but stopped just at the edge of the grass. The rumble in her belly turned into a weird, little flutter. The woods were dark, the trees were tall. The sunlight that managed to get through them had to battle its way to the ground. She had thought it might be a fun area to explore, but now she wasn't so sure. A wispy breeze caused a few hairs to cross her face. It felt like a tickle from a spider's web.

Bradley began to walk backwards, away from the woods. For some reason she didn't want to turn her back to the dark trees. Another step and she heard a dull crunch under her foot. She looked down to see a dead bird. Or what remained of a dead bird—bones, some gray feathers, and a tiny skull. Something hungry had picked it clean.

"Bradley!" Samm's voice distracted her from the bird and the woods. "They're here!"

A mosquito buzzed Bradley's ear. She waved it away, but it landed on her arm. She smacked it and flicked it away.

"Ugh," she said. "Bugs."

* * *

Dan pulled the Explorer in behind Samm's VW. *Wow,* he thought, *her car actually made it.* He'd half expected to find the yellow Bug broken down somewhere between home and here. But the Bug was resilient.

"The girls beat us," Rosalie said from the back seat. The front seat was empty. She had claimed carsickness halfway into the trip and had insisted on lying in the back with her sleep mask. Which of course he had to dig out of her luggage. Which of course took about forty minutes to find among the four full bags she had packed for a three-day getaway. Which of course meant that Samm and Bradley had arrived first.

"What do you think of the cabin?" Dan asked, straining to see it through the filthy windshield.

He turned on the windshield wipers to clean off the dust, dead bugs and grime that had accumulated during the drive, but he had used up the last of the wiper fluid about an hour ago, so they just made the filth worse. *Hey, dummy,* he thought to himself. *Just get out of the car.*

A strong feeling of relief overcame him as he got out of the SUV. He had been worried, based on the too-good-to-be-true price, that they would find a decrepit shack with a leaky roof and a dirt floor. *God, wouldn't Rosalie have loved that?* But from here, the cabin actually looked nice. Quaint, even. Noise certainly wouldn't be a problem. She wouldn't have that to complain about. They hadn't passed another house for miles. The rental agency had said there were no neighbors. No phone. No cell signal. No wireless. For the next three days, it was just the four of them. Family time. For better or worse.

"Can you feel the moisture in the air?" Rosalie asked, her blue, padded sleep mask still covering her eyes. "I bet the place is full of black mold."

Not even out of the car and she's already bitching. Dan took in a deep breath. *What was that line from Seinfeld? Serenity now.* He was determined to make sure his family had a fun weekend. Even if it killed him.

"C'mon, Rose. Don't be so negative. It looks nice."

Bradley came sprinting from the back of the house as if she were being chased by a mountain lion.

"Dad! Let's go inside! I gotta peeee!"

"Ugh, honestly, Bradley. Must you be so crude?" Rosalie said. She had removed the sleep mask and was finally extracting herself from the SUV.

Dan clapped his hands together once and grinned. "Okay, okay. Let's go in."

He rummaged through his pocket and came out with an old, rusty key on a ring with a neon blue fob in the shape of a house. Printed upon it was *McCormick Realty and Rentals* in bold, yet faded, black type.

"Jeez, look at the size of this keychain. It was digging into my leg the whole ride."

Dan slipped the key into the doorknob. It stuck for a beat. He wiggled it, feeling Rosalie's eyes on his neck. *If they gave me the wrong key...,* he thought, just before the key turned and the door opened.

* * *

Bradley burst through the front door and immediately galloped up the wooden steps just to the right of the entrance that led to the loft. Her clomping feet echoed through the house. She didn't need to pee as badly as she had let on. First things first. She had read the description on the rental website and knew that the loft held three beds, and she wanted to make sure she got first choice. She pushed the door open and leapt on the closest. *Nope,* she thought, *not this one. Too close to the door. First victim if a serial killer breaks in!* The second choice was next to the window. *Good escape route,* she thought as she fell onto the mattress. *Ooh. Nice and soft.*

"This one's mine!" she called out.

No one answered her. She could hear her parents downstairs talking low and then a door was closed. Samm was probably walking around outside. Right next to her bed was the cool round window. It was very dirty. Bradley got up on her knees, wiped a clean spot in the middle of the glass and peered outside. Not the best view. Below, she could see the parked cars and other than that? Trees, trees, and more trees. Movement caught her eye, and she glanced to her left to see a ladybug making its way down the side of the curved window frame.

"Hi there, little guy."

The blood-red back of the insect stood out bright against the yellowed wood. She put her finger just ahead of the bug's path, and it climbed on without a pause. Its little legs tickled her skin. She giggled. Ladybugs were cute. She brought her hand up close to her eyes to get a good look. The bug stopped, and Bradley felt its teeny-tiny eyes upon her.

"Don't worry. I'm not gonna hurt you. Here, I'll put you back."

She lowered her hand to the windowsill and waited as the ladybug climbed off of her finger.

"On your way now," she said. "I gotta go pee."

* * *

Samm was outside, but she wasn't walking. She was sitting on one of the beach chairs looking at the small deck that was attached to the rear of the house. There was a charcoal grill and a picnic table for outdoor dining, but she doubted they would be eating out here. Mom hated mosquitoes, and Samm figured the ones around here were monstrous. Just another thing Dad hadn't thought about. That was his biggest problem, always acting before really thinking things through. *Family time? Good idea. Weekend in the mountains in the middle of nowhere with no internet and no cable? Bad idea.*

A small breeze delivered the scents and sounds of the forest. Samm closed her eyes and focused her ears. She was so used to urban living that the silence that surrounded her was virtually alien. But, it wasn't really silent, was it? Sure, there were no car horns, loud music, or random voices, but she could hear the sing-song of birds, the branches of the trees swaying in the wind, and small animals (*squirrels?*) scurrying among the dried leaves that covered the forest floor. Maybe this weekend wouldn't be *that* bad.

Samm wasn't stupid. She knew that things were not going well between Mom and Dad. They were putting less and less effort into hiding their fights and arguments, but that didn't really matter anyway because their facial expressions revealed all. Dad tried to wear a mask, but Mom was an open book of resentment and anger. This weekend getaway was not going to help. She figured her parents would be split by October. Which would mean a weird and awkward holiday season. She really felt bad for her sister. She'd be off to college in a year, but Bradley still had a lot of growing up to do. *Hopefully Dad's insurance covers therapy.*

She took her phone from her pocket and checked the screen. Maybe the realtor had been wrong and there was some faint wireless or 3G signal she could pick up. Nope. Nothing.

"Awesome," she said to herself. *Well,* she thought, *might as well go inside and try to make it as painless as possible. At least for Bradley.* She stood and walked toward the sliding glass door that led into the kitchen. *On a list from one to fun, this weekend's gonna be a zero.*

A mosquito buzzed in her ear, and she absentmindedly waved her hand to shoo it away.

* * *

Dan walked into the kitchen just as Samm came in. He smiled at his oldest daughter. "What do you think, Sammy?" he asked.

"Awesome, Dad. Good find." She gave him a weak thumb's up.

Dan nodded. "Yeah," he said. *It was a good find.* "I knew you and Brad would love it. Hopefully your mother likes it too."

He examined the small kitchen. It was split down the middle by a tiled breakfast bar that extended from the rear wall. On one side was the fridge, sink, cabinets, and drawers. *No dishwasher.* He tested the hot and cold taps.

On the other side, directly in front of the glass doors, sat a wooden kitchen table and four non-matching chairs, each painted a different color—red, green, yellow, and blue. Dan figured the entire place was furnished with things bought at yard sales and flea markets or taken from somebody's curb on trash day.

Samm sat down in the blue chair. "You know Mom. Not the biggest fan of the outdoors. But she'll come around. It's only for the weekend."

"I hope so," he said, leaning on the breakfast bar. "There's something else I read online that I knew you'd find interesting."

"Oh, yeah? What's that?"

Dan went over and sat next to Samm and looked this way and that. "Well, supposedly, we are in the middle of the Blackburn Triangle," he said in a low, conspiratorial voice.

Samm gave him a blank look. "The what?"

"It's like the Bermuda Triangle. Lot of weird things have happened around these parts. Like, there was an Indian village—"

"Native American, Dad. Not Indian."

"Sorry. A *Native American* village that simply disappeared. Well, the people in the village disappeared. And, there have been several other mysterious disappearances over the last hundred years or so. People would go hiking up on the trails and never come back. As recently as ten years ago some college boys, here for winter break, up and vanished. Never to be seen again."

She gave him the cold, hard stare she had inherited from her Mother. "So, you're saying you brought your family to stay in a house built on a cursed Native American burial ground?"

Was that true? He had never thought about it that way. "Uh, well, no…"

Her eyes brightened, and she grinned. "I'm just kidding. Cool story, but I wouldn't bring it up around Bradley. Or Mom, for that matter."

Dan nodded. "Good idea."

His oldest child had always enjoyed macabre myths and legends, but Bradley didn't like ghost stories, monster movies, or anything remotely scary. Of course, all the spooky stuff he had read about this area of Vermont was hogwash, but still, he wondered—regardless of folklore—*had* it been a mistake to come here?

When the idea to take Rosalie and the girls away for a long weekend had popped into his head, he had immediately Googled rental homes. His first instinct had been the Cape, but the costs for Cape Cod rentals were frightening. Plus, he didn't want everyone splitting up on a beach or something. He wanted them to be almost *forced* to spend time together. *No, he decided, it wasn't a mistake.* This place was perfect. They could hike in the woods, drive the SUV along the mountain roads, or just sit around and play Parcheesi or Chinese Checkers, like he and Rosalie used to do with Samm when she was a toddler.

He smiled at the memory. "Do you remember playing Chinese Checkers when you were little?"

"Oh sure. I remember. That was B.B."

B.B. *Before Bradley.* Samm's recurring tease towards her sister. The implication being that life was better before Bradley was born. Completely unfair and Samm knew that, she just said it to be funny, but it was not entirely untrue. Indeed, life *had* been better then, but the fact that things were worse now had absolutely nothing to do with Bradley. In fact, when Rosalie had told him, years after they had given up trying, that she was pregnant again, he had naively hoped that a new baby would solve all their problems. But no matter how much love existed between Dan and the girls, and Rosalie and the girls, there was less and less between Rosalie and Dan. Would things be any different when they returned home on Monday night? Probably not.

"Well, maybe we can play again. With Bradley. Or another game. There's supposed to be a bunch of board games around here somewhere."

"Can we eat first? I'm starving."

"I'm starving too!" Bradley announced as she slid into the kitchen on her stocking feet.

Dan clapped his hands together once. "Okay then," he said. "Your Mom's resting. Why don't we unload the cars? Bring in our stuff and the groceries, and then I'll cook us up some grub. How's that sound?"

Bradley scrunched up her nose. "I don't want grubs. Aren't they bugs?"

Dan laughed.

Samm smiled. "Grub is just a nickname for food. We're not gonna eat bugs. Not tonight anyway, right Dad?"

"Nope, no bugs tonight."

Bradley bent down and scooped something from the floor under the table. "Dad, what's this?"

She was holding an old piece of lined notebook paper. It had been folded and unfolded so many times that the creases had torn in a couple of spots, and there was an old, brown coffee stain in the shape of a bumblebee with a missing wing.

Dan pulled out his reading glasses from his shirt pocket and took the paper from Bradley. "Where'd you find this?"

"Under the table here. Maybe it fell or blew off when the door opened?"

It was a note. The writing was a faded, but still legible old school cursive with large round letters.

DEAR RENTERS, it read. PLEASE TREAT THIS HOME AS IF IT WERE YOUR OWN. KEEP ALL SMOKING OUTSIDE. SORRY, BUT NO DISHWASHER OR LAUNDRY. PLEASE CLEAN UP ANY FOOD WASTE (ANTS!) AND KEEP TRASH CANS INDOORS (RACCOONS!) ALSO, PLAN YOUR ACTIVITIES SO YOU ARE NOT OUTSIDE AFTER SUNSET. THE BUGS COME OUT AT NIGHT.

* * *

"The bugs come out at night? What do you think that means, Samm?"

"Not sure."

"I picked the bed near the window."

"Okay."

"If there's a fire I can get out first."

"Good to know."

"I found a ladybug."

"Cool."

The girls sat the kitchen table. Bradley had demanded the green chair because green was her favorite color (this week). Crumbs, crumpled up napkins, and other remains of a meal were spread out in front of them. After carrying all the luggage inside, Dad declared himself too tired to cook, so dinner had consisted of tuna fish sandwiches, Fritos, and lemonade.

Rosalie was cleaning up. She took the last few paper plates and plastic cups from the table. "It means the mosquitoes here are a menace and we could all catch malaria," she said as she walked into the kitchen and shoved the trash down into the bag that Dan held open.

"Easy, Rosalie," he said.

Samm knew that tone from her mother. She wanted to pick a fight. She looked at Dad, trying to will her thoughts into his head. *Don't take the bait, Dad!*

"What's ma-lar-eee-ya?" Bradley asked.

"It's nothing, honey," Dan said.

Rosalie snatched the last of the dinner refuse from the table. "It's a disease spread by mosquitoes. Easily prevented by simply avoiding places with lots of mosquitoes."

"But mosquitoes are everywhere," Bradley said, with worry in her tiny voice.

Dan tied up the trash bag and stepped over to Bradley. He gave the back of her neck a little squeeze. "Don't worry, Brad. You're not going to get malaria. We've got plenty of bug spray."

"Bug spray," Rosalie muttered under her breath.

Uh, oh, thought Samm.

Dan looked toward Rosalie. "What are you doing? Why? Do you want her to spend the entire weekend under the bed?"

Her spine straightened and Rosalie's eyes locked in on Dan.

Here we go. Samm reached toward her sister, ready to take Bradley upstairs once the yelling began.

Rosalie opened her mouth to speak, but a loud, high-pitched

bark cut her off before she could begin. The sharp sound startled all of them. Dan looked from Rosalie to Samm and then back. Bradley leapt from her chair.

Dan and Samm spoke at the same time, their words overlapping.

Dan: "What the hell?"

Samm: "Was that a dog?"

Another bark.

"It is a dog!"

Samm turned to see Bradley at the sliding glass door, hopping from one foot to the other and punching her pointer finger excitedly against the glass. Thump, thump, thump.

"Do you see him?" She turned and looked at Samm, her eyes wide. "Do you see him?"

Samm and Dan approached the glass. She saw the dog just as it barked again.

"He wants to come in!" Bradley was practically jumping from her clothes.

"No way," Rosalie said.

Samm knew that dogs ranked near the top on her mother's long *Things-I-Can't-Stand* list. Right up there with mosquitoes, winter, and Democrats. Where had the animal come from? There weren't any homes nearby. *It must be lost.*

It was getting dark outside. Dan leaned his forehead against the door and put his hands up against his eyes in an effort to see better. His breath fogged up the glass. "I don't see a collar."

Bradley looked from Dan to Samm. "He must be lost." Then, before anyone could respond, she slid the glass door open and stepped out onto the deck.

Dan quickly followed. "Hold on there, squirt. Not so fast." He held Bradley by the shoulder and kept her close to him.

Samm found the switch for the lone outdoor light and flicked it on. It popped and buzzed a couple of times before finally staying lit. Then she, too, stepped out to get a closer look at this mysterious hound. It sat on its haunches just at the spot where the grass ended and the woods began. She couldn't tell the breed. *Probably just a mutt,* she thought. Panting, with a long pink tongue hanging from one side of its mouth, he (*she?*) didn't look vicious or mean. She blinked as some kind of gnat flew in front of her face.

Bradley tried to get away, but Dan held on to her. "Can't we bring him in, Dad? Pleeeeease?"

"Sorry, honey. I know he looks okay, but you never know with strange animals. I'm sure he has a home. He'll go back there eventually."

"He doesn't have a home. I know it. There's no other houses around here!"

Dan waved his hand in front of his face and forcibly spit air. "Uckth. A bug flew in my mouth. There has to be, Brad. If he was a stray he'd be much thinner."

Samm agreed with her dad. Maybe there were other rentals nearby, and they just hadn't noticed. Or a campground? Was there an area around for campers or tents? She took a step forward and scanned above the tree-line for smoke from a campfire.

The leftover oranges and purples from the sunset were rapidly fading into the slate gray of night, and stars were just becoming visible. But, Samm saw no smoke. Something big flew just over her head, skimming her hair, causing her to duck. What was that? She looked up and saw the largest moth she had ever seen flapping about the light fixture. It was the size of a large butterfly, but it had the ugly, white, papery wings of a moth.

"Dad, look at that."

As she stared at the moth a few of its brothers and sisters flew into and around the light. Samm looked over to see that Dan and Bradley were also swatting away flying insects. Mosquitoes, sensing a good meal, came swarming from all sides.

The dog barked again.

Rosalie stepped outside and grabbed Bradley's hand, pulling her in.

"Everybody inside before you get rabies *and* malaria."

* * *

That night, Samm woke up to use the bathroom. After, as she slowly ascended the stairs, the barking began again. She stopped halfway up and listened. The sound was faint, further away, but it was the same bark. She was sure of it. The dog began barking again and again and again, over and over. A few years before, when Bradley was a baby, their neighbor—Mr. Royce—brought home a new dog for his kids. For some reason they named him Howard. Less than a week later, Mom had filed a complaint with the police because of the incessant noise. The Royce kids would leave Howard chained outside for hours, and he would bark and snarl and whine until they finally let him in. This dog was making the same angry sounds as Howard. *What the hell could it be barking at?* Finally, as abruptly as it began, the barking stopped. She couldn't be sure, but Samm thought the last thing she heard had been not a bark, but a yelp of pain. Samm hoped Bradley hadn't heard that final sound.

Until recently, Bradley had slept like the dead. Now, her sleep was restless, and she sometimes woke up several times during the night. When Mom and Dad's arguing got especially loud, Bradley would wander into Samm's room and crawl into her bed.

I'd better check on her. She climbed one more step then stopped. The quiet that immediately followed the long string of barks was eerie. Samm thought of that dumb line from a thousand movies, *It's quiet. Too quiet.* But right now, that line made sense. It took a moment, but then she realized what she was reacting to—no crickets. Odd. Maybe it was too cold? She was no expert, but for some reason the crickets were quiet.

Still, she felt.... unsettled. She climbed two more steps and stopped again, one hand on the railing. Now she felt like she was being watched. Impossible. *There's no one around for miles.* Regardless, she had the queasy sensation of eyes upon her. *Should I look around the house?* From her perspective, she could see the den and, beyond that, into the kitchen. Her eyes were adjusted enough to the dark that she was fairly confident there were no villains lurking about. Maybe the deeper shadows hid a knife-wielding maniac ready to butcher them all, but probably not. *You're being silly. There's nobody here.* She still had that weird pitter-patter in her belly. She took a deep breath and quickly sprinted up the remaining stairs and ran into the bedroom.

She immediately felt stupid. *Oh yeah, I'm ready to live alone,* she thought, as she quietly closed the door. Her fingers explored the knob, looking for a lock, but not finding one. Then she saw Bradley, up on her knees, looking out of the window next to her bed.

"Brad?" she whispered.

Samm approached her sister slowly. She reached out and gently touched Bradley's shoulder.

She didn't turn, but she spoke. Samm recognized the tone of voice. Bradley was basically asleep, but something had woken her and caused her to look out of the window. Had she heard the dog?

"Samm, the trees," she said, her voice slow.

Then she turned to look at Samm.

"There's monsters in the trees. With shiny eyes."

* * *

The next morning Dan sat on the back deck, a mug of hot, fresh, black coffee in his hand, and watched the sun rise. He had set his alarm for 5 a.m., but he hadn't expected that he would actually get up at that ungodly hour. Dan Donner was many things, but an early riser he was not. An old joke came to mind: *I hate how funerals are always at 9 or 10 a.m.—I'm not really a mourning person.*

He had been as surprised as anyone when the alarm had gone off and, instead of punching the snooze button, he had opened his eyes, swung his legs from the bed, and stood to greet the day. Now, as he watched the brilliant colors of daybreak settle into their final cerulean hues, Dan wondered if he could make this a habit. Not rising with the sun every day, of course, but if he could manage to wake just one hour earlier, he would have time to eat a real, halfway-nutritious breakfast instead of wolfing down a bacon, egg, and cheese sandwich, glazed donut, and coffee from Dunkies every day. His arteries would thank him, that was for sure. Not to mention his waistline.

Ah, who am I kidding? He knew that would never happen. If Rosalie had another hour of his time, she would only fill it with more grief and aggravation.

He took one last sip, tipped the coffee mug upside-down, and absently watched the last few drips slip from the ceramic and blow away. *What the heck was up with Rosalie last night?* Not just last night. Rosalie had been miserable to live with for months. It hadn't always been this way—there used to be happiness in their home. Sometimes he wondered if there had been one moment, one event, one decision that he could pinpoint and mark as the true beginning of the end. If he could travel backward in time, he would only need to go to that one specific moment to course correct. If only it was that simple. He knew it could never be narrowed down to the consequence of just one decision. The all-too-common refrain. Too many unspoken words, false promises, and destructive indifference until any chance of lasting happiness had moldered like a forgotten jack-o'-lantern after Halloween.

Feeling the last remnants of the predawn chill, Dan finally accepted that this weekend was not going to fix anything with Rosalie. But that didn't mean that the girls couldn't have fun. They deserved some fun.

* * *

Up in the loft, Bradley was awake. She lay face down with her head and arms dangling from the foot of the bed, her fingertips just brushing against the floor.

"What are we gonna do today?"

"I dunno," Samm mumbled from the other bed, her voice muffled by the thick comforter that covered her face.

"I hope it's a nice day. What do you think?"

"God, Bradley. How do I know? Is the sun even up? Go back to sleep."

Bradley flopped herself over and observed the upside-down room. "Do you think the dog's okay?"

Samm's answer was something between a groan and a cough.

"Huh?" Bradley asked.

"He's fine! Let me sleep!"

Blood was rushing to her head, so Bradley sat up. She scooted over to the window and rested her chin on the sill. The woods looked the same as yesterday. Was the ladybug still here? She didn't see it. *Ladybugs can fly,* she thought. *It could be anywhere. Maybe it has a family somewhere.*

"Samm?"

No response.

"Samm?"

Nothing.

"Samm?"

"Arghh!" Samm threw the comforter off and violently pivoted over onto her back. "What?!"

Still gazing out the window, Bradley softly asked, "Do you think Mom and Dad are getting die-vorced?"

* * *

Samm stared up at the dirty ceiling. Dusty gray cobwebs stretched out in the corners, and here and there brown stains that looked like ink blots dotted the plaster. *Fuck, why do I have to deal with this?*

"You mean divorced?" She punched the *dee* sound.

"Yeah."

Samm sat up and massaged her face. She blinked a few times, rubbed her eyes with her knuckles, and popped her jaw.

"Why would you think that?"

"Because they fight."

"Well, everybody fights sometimes."

"But Mom and Dad fight a lot. And that means they will get, umm, dee-vorced."

"Did someone tell you that?"

"Yeah. A boy at school. Jeffrey Weinstock."

Note to self: give Jeffrey Weinstock a smack. "Boys are dumb, Brad. Don't listen to them. Ever. You'll live a much happier life."

That generated a little smile. Samm watched as Bradley slowly traced her finger down the window glass. *Should I tell her the truth?* she wondered. *Not right now, that's for sure.* Mom and Dad should have been the ones to talk to her about the D-word. They were the adults, after all. *Then they'd better start acting like adults. I'm the older sister. I'm supposed to tease her and tickle her. Teach her about makeup and music. Help her with homework and how to deal with asshole teachers. Maybe some advice about boyfriends.* Though really, Samm was the one who could have used some help in that department. Regardless, the end of the family unit was definitely *not* a topic for big sister.

* * *

Bradley thought Samm was fibbing about the dee-vorce, but she wasn't angry. Fibbing was different from lying, and she knew her sister wouldn't lie. Maybe she didn't really know the answer. *Maybe thinking about it makes her sad the way it makes me sad.* She tried not to allow those thoughts into her head. Seemed easy enough, but sometimes she couldn't help it. Even when she pushed the thoughts away, they still came back. Just like the weeds Dad was always pulling from their lawn at home.

Samm finally got up. "Want to stretch with me?"

"Sure!"

Bradley hopped off her bed and stood next to Samm and copied her morning stretch routine. Hands reach to the sky, fingers wide, then bend at the waist and touch the floor. Make sure your back is straight and stick your bum out!

"Don't forget to breathe."

Bradley realized she was holding her breath. *Oops.* In through the nose, out through the mouth. After three repetitions she stopped and plopped herself down on the floor.

"Whew. I'm pooped."

"Pooped?" Samm laughed. "You only did, like, two."

"I did three!"

"Oh. That's different, then."

Samm spread her legs wide and, with her hands on her hips, bent backwards at the waist revealing the small tattoo near her belly button. She had only recently shown it to Bradley and made her promise not to tell anyone. She agreed. It made her feel special to be part of Samm's secret. Not even Mom and Dad knew about the tattoo.

"What's that thing called again?"

"A scarab."

"Looks like a beetle."

"It's a *kind* of beetle. It's a symbol from ancient Egypt. It means renewal."

"Does it hurt?"

"It did when I got it. Not anymore."

Bradley lifted up her pajama top and looked at her own belly. "I want one."

"Gotta wait until you're eighteen."

"Bummer." A thought abruptly popped into Bradley's head. "But you're seventeen."

Samm winked, smiled, and put her finger to her lips. Bradley giggled.

"Hey girls!" Dad's voice called from downstairs. "Who wants pancakes?!"

Bradley leapt to her feet as if she had been poked in the butt with a sharp stick. *Pancakes!*

"I do!"

* * *

Dan was sweating like a pig. After breakfast they had decided to attack one of the hiking paths nearby. Dan had found a map in a kitchen drawer that illustrated the various trails and their levels of difficulty. He knew Samm could handle any of them, but Bradley—and likely Rosalie—would whine if it became too difficult. And he was not in any kind of shape for the harder climbs, so they chose the easiest and shortest.

Right now, he was convinced that taking the shortest and easiest trail might have been the best decision he had ever made. *God, it's hot,* he thought, wiping his forearm across his forehead. His calves were sore, and the backpack slung full of water bottles and snacks was getting heavier by the minute. They had been out for less than an hour. *It's gonna be a long day.*

They had found the beginning of the trail in the woods just behind the cabin, but it quickly opened up to a wide, grassy climb up several small inclines. The drawing on the map looked as if a yellowish-green river of grass had snaked down the mountain long ago, pushing the trees to either side as it descended.

"You should have brought a hat, Dan."

Rosalie walked next to him. She had packed several hats, and her choice for the hike was spectacular: white, extremely wide-brimmed, with a hot-pink band that matched the frames of the brilliant sunglasses perfectly perched upon the bridge of her aquiline nose.

"I know, Rosalie."

"Why didn't you?"

"I guess I didn't think to."

"Well, next time, think ahead."

"I'll try."

"You don't want to get skin cancer, do you?"

Skin cancer? Who cares about skin cancer? I'm going to have a heart attack right here on this mountain anyway. "No, I certainly don't want skin cancer."

Dan stopped next to a large boulder that jutted out of the ground. He dropped the backpack and took a long swallow from his water bottle. *The heat!* Rosalie came toward him. It appeared that she was going to say something when the lower half of her face abruptly puckered like she had just tasted something sour, and she reversed two big steps.

"I'm going to walk with the girls, Dan. You're starting to stink."

She turned and called out, "Samantha? Bradley? Hold up there and wait for me."

She adjusted her sunglasses and made her way up the trail. Dan watched her go. He had always thought her gait was odd. She walked as if she had a cigarette in her hand even though she had never been a smoker. He didn't really blame her for moving upwind. His head and face were dripping, and his sweat-saturated Boston University T-shirt hewed uncomfortably to his torso. He suspected he was pretty rank.

* * *

Samm heard her mother's voice calling to them.

"Hold up there, Squirt. Mom's coming."

Bradley was crossing the top of a fallen tree trunk like a

balance-beam, her arms spread out wide. She stopped and bent forward on her left foot, stretching her right leg straight out behind her.

"Hey, Samm! Lookitmee!"

"I'm watching. Be careful."

"I am."

Samm noticed Bradley's supporting leg tremble. The log rotated slightly. She tensed, ready to catch her sister should she fall, but Bradley felt the movement and leapt from the trunk—landing as graceful as a gazelle, with her hands up high and grin a mile wide.

"Ta-daa!"

Samm clapped. "Well done."

Bradley took a gymnastics class at the Y, and she did well, but Samm thought that dancing might be a better fit. Lower chance of horrible injury. She took two waters from her backpack and handed one to the tiny gymnast. They both sat in the grass and waited for their Mom.

"Why is Mom coming with us?" Bradley asked.

"I dunno."

"Did they get in a fight?"

Samm removed the BU baseball cap she was wearing and pushed her bangs back from her face. She replaced the cap and thought, *Probably*, but she said, "Nah. I bet Dad's just slowing her down. She wants to be with us cool kids."

That seemed to placate Bradley, because she didn't pursue the topic. There was a honking sound above, and Samm looked up to see a flock of geese soar past in an elongated "V" shape. *Is it called a flock of geese? Or something else?* She'd read somewhere that a group of crows was called a murder of crows. That's a weird one. She ran her fingers through the grass. It was dry and prickly. *I wonder when it rained last,* she thought. *Not gonna rain today.* There wasn't a cloud in the sky. For the first time since they had arrived, she felt calm. Relaxed. She yawned. *I could lay back right here and fall asleep.*

Bradley abruptly sprang up and announced, "I'm gonna walk in the woods."

"Mom will be here in a minute. Then we can go on."

"I'll be right back."

She ran off into the trees.

* * *

"Don't go far!" Samm called out as Bradley crossed into the woods.

"I won't!" Bradley called back.

It was cooler in the shade of the forest. *Is this a forest?* As she meandered between the tall tree trunks, Bradley wondered about the difference between the woods and a forest. Maybe the words are cinnamons. Her teacher, Mrs. Flaherty, had been teaching Bradley's class about cinnamons—different words that mean the same thing—and anti-mins—words that are opposites. *What would be the opposite of forest?* she wondered. *A desert*, she decided.

She could still see Samm back through the treeline, sitting in the sun, running her hands through the grass. Bradley walked a few steps further into the woods, stepping over tree roots and rocks. She had been bored just sitting and waiting for Mom. She was also worried that when Mom got there, she would have her just-had-a-fight-with-Dad face on. Bradley did not like that face. She kicked at a stone and watched as it rolled through brown pine needles.

"I wish she'd go away," she said aloud.

She stopped. *What was that?* Did she really wish her Mom would go away? In her head she was thinking she wanted that *face* to go away. Not Mom. Sure, it seemed that Mom was mad a lot, and she said mean things sometimes, but she was still… Mom.

A breeze curved around the trees and blew back her hair. She smelled pine trees. Just like Christmas time. Mom always made such wonderful Christmas cookies. Bradley always helped. They would roll the dough flat and use plastic cookie cutters to create Santa and Mrs. Claus shapes. Then they would sprinkle red and green sugar on top of each cookie before the tray went into the oven. Oh, there was nothing better than warm Christmas cookies right out of the oven! If Mom and Dad got dee-vorced, would there still be Christmas cookies?

Tears formed and spilled and she turned in a circle, wanting to run to her Mom, but she had gone too far into the woods. Which way was the trail? How do I get back?

Confusion. Fright. Panic. *I'm lost!*

She was crying harder now, sobbing. She wanted to yell for Mom, but she couldn't catch her breath. She chose a direction and ran.

* * *

Samm cupped her hands around her mouth. "Yo! Bradster! Come back, Mom's here!" she yelled into the woods. *Don't leave me alone with her,* she added silently. A few awkward minutes passed. Samm saw Rosalie look at her wrist twice as if she were wearing a watch.

"You've got to talk to her, Mom," Samm said to her mother. Rosalie lowered her sunglasses a bit and peered down at Samm over the lenses.

"About?" she asked.

Laying in the grass, using the backpack as a pillow, Samm was able to look up at Rosalie without squinting, because her ridiculous hat blocked the sun.

"About everything." Samm stood up and brushed grass and grit from her rear end. "She's not dumb, Mom. She sees what's going on with you and Dad. She asked *me* if you guys are getting a divorce."

Rosalie said nothing. She pushed her glasses up with one finger and looked off into the distance. Samm shook her head in disbelief. *God, she can be so... so frustrating!* She opened her mouth to speak, but was cut off by an ear-piercing shriek.

"Aaaaiiiiiieeeeeeeeeee!"

Bradley!

"Mommmmmmmyyy!"

Samm dropped her water bottle and she and Rosalie sprinted into the woods.

* * *

The first scream woke Dan up. His eyes snapped open.

Whatwasthat?

He remembered sitting on the ground, his back against the large rock, after Rosalie left to join the girls. *I'll just rest here for a minute.* He must have dozed off.

The sound was distant and unclear, but the primal, protective-parent area of his brain—the part that was always connected to his kids—knew it had been a yell or a scream. He sat forward. *Was that Bradley?*

Then: "Mommmmmmmmyyy!"

It was! He leapt to his feet and ran.

How far ahead were they? Horrible images flashed through his head. Broken ankle. Cracked skull. Snakebite! Are there poisonous snakes in Vermont? There must be. Why hadn't he checked Google for *that* instead of stupid ghost stories! *I knew this was a bad idea. No cell phones? Idiot! How can I call an ambulance? Police? Help?*

Dan ran. He ran as fast as he could up the grassy hill, breathing heavy, the heat forgotten, ignoring the pain in his calves, the cramp in his side. His little girl needed him!

A thought: No more screams. Why? Was she unconscious? Or worse? He pictured Bradley in a ditch with two broken legs, surrounded by hundreds of venomous rattlesnakes. He could hear the noise, all of them rattling at the same time, like radio static turned up to eleven.

Where was Rosalie? Samm? Had they heard Bradley yell? Maybe they were hurt, too. Why wasn't Bradley yelling anymore? Where were they?

Then he saw them. Coming out of the woods. Bradley walked next to Rosalie, practically attached to her hip. No broken legs. No snakes. But her little face was beet red, and her eyes were wet with tears. Samm was a few steps behind. She looked upset as well. Rosalie just looked angry.

Dan stopped and bent at the waist, hands on his knees. He was dizzy, he couldn't get a decent breath, and his heart was beating hard enough to crack a rib. There was also a strong possibility that he might throw up.

He stood up straight and began walking in a small circle,

holding his side, and getting his breathing under control.

"You…. You okay, huh-honey?" he was able to ask between breaths.

Bradley nodded.

Rosalie said, "She's fine. Had a fright, that's all."

Dan looked at his wife with confusion. "A fright?" Then, lower, "It wasn't a snake was it?"

"What? No. Samm will show you." She walked past him, Bradley still clinging to her. "We're going back to the cabin."

He watched them go, then looked back at Samm.

Samm said, "This way," and she turned and walked back into the woods. Dan followed.

* * *

"What happened?"

Samm heard the question. She toyed with the idea of ignoring it, but instead she said, "It's easier to show you."

She stopped in the woods, a short way past the tree line, to make sure Dan was still with her.

"You alright, Dad?"

"Yeah. Why?"

"You don't look so good."

"Thanks for noticing. I did run all the way up here you know. It's hot. I'm old."

"Well, at least it's a little cooler under the trees. Come on."

She led him into the woods. They walked in silence. Their feet crunched on dead leaves and pine needles. A squirrel darted along a branch above them and vaulted from one tree to another.

Samm knew that she would never forget the look on her sister's face when she and Rosalie had finally reached her. Sadness, fear, disbelief and shock—it was the sudden and immediate end to childhood innocence. What should occur gradually over time had, instead, been thrust upon her sister in an instant. The true understanding that the world is cold and unfair.

When they got to a small clearing in the woods, Samm stopped and turned to Dan.

"Over there," she said, pointing.

Dan looked toward the clearing then back at Samm.

"You'll see it," she said.

He took a few steps forward. Samm waited until she heard him mutter, "Oh, dammit," under his breath, then she joined him.

It looked just as horrible the second time. The dog lay on its side. There was a large, gaping cavity in its midsection; strewn about the carcass were pieces of fur, chunks of flesh and bloody organs. One of the hind legs and the tail had been ripped or bitten off completely and were nowhere to be found. The jaw was wide open and the tongue—which had several harsh tears and rips in it as well—lolled out onto the ground. The eyes were gone. The sockets were just bloody craters.

Dan wiped both hands down his face. "It's the same dog from last night?"

Samm said nothing. She wasn't sure if he was asking her or making a statement to himself. It didn't matter anyway. If it was a question—the answer was right there on the ground.

* * *

The ladybug was back. It was sitting *(Or was it standing? Do bugs sit?)* on the windowsill when Bradley returned to the loft, as if it had been waiting for her. There were probably a lot of ladybugs around, but she just knew that this was her friend from the other day. It was the same vibrant shade of red and, although she hadn't actually counted them the last time, she was sure it had the same number of black spots.

The little bug climbed onto her finger again. She watched as its tiny legs carried it over her knuckle and down toward the back of her hand. It tickled.

Bradley did not want to think about the dog, but she couldn't help it. Part of her was angry at Dad. If he had allowed her to bring the poor guy inside, he would still be alive. But, part of her sort of understood why he had said no.

I bet he wanted to bring the dog in, she thought, *but Mom would have freaked.* Was that true? Was it really Mom's fault? She remembered what she had said earlier, in the woods, about Mom. Why was she having so many angry ideas about Mom? She recalled the words she had spoken out loud earlier, in the woods. *I wish she'd go away.* Those feelings of guilt and sadness came tumbling back again and got all mixed up with her grief about the dog. Why couldn't she just push all these sad thoughts away? *Is this what it's like to be a grown-up? Just going from one sad thought to the next? Then being a grown-up stinks.*

The ladybug was moving toward her thumb. Bradley slowly rotated her hand, making sure the ladybug didn't fall. It kept moving up and over between her thumb and pointer-finger until her hand was flat again, with her palm facing up. The tickle was more intense on that part of her hand, and for a brief moment she did forget about the dog, her Mom, and being sad.

* * *

Samm came up the steps to the loft and slowly opened the door, not sure what to expect. She saw Bradley sitting crosswise on the bed, with her back against the wall, her right hand held open in front of her. She was staring intently at something in her flattened palm, something Samm couldn't see. Sunlight spilled into the room from the round window behind Bradley, enveloping her in its golden rays.

Samm was struck by how pretty her sister was and, for a brief moment, she saw the grown woman Bradley would become. Adult Bradley was just as beautiful; she had the same flaxen hair and pale blue eyes, but Samm saw sorrow in those eyes. A pain so great she nearly fell to her knees.

Adult Bradley turned her head and looked at Samm. Her mouth moved, but there was no sound. Then she faded away and it was just Bradley again.

"What are you staring at?" she asked. "Samm?"

Samm blinked. *Wow, what was that?* She shook her head and ran both hands across her face. "Nothing. Just zoned out for a second."

She tossed her ball cap onto her bed and sat next to Bradley. "What's'at you got there?"

Bradley looked down at her hand. "A ladybug."

At that point, the ladybug spread its wings and took flight. The girls followed it with their eyes until it disappeared somewhere in the far shadows of the room. Bradley let her arm drop into her lap.

Samm asked, "You alright?"

Bradley shrugged.

"Do you…"

"I don't wanna talk about it."

"Okay."

They sat together in silence. There was no activity downstairs. When she and Dad had returned to the cabin, he'd plopped himself down on one of the deck chairs—she figured he was still there—and Mom had to be lying down in the master bedroom. It was probably a good thing that they were separated. Samm knew a fight was imminent. She could sense it the same way a dog senses a change in the weather. There was an emotional static in the air. A storm was coming, a different kind of storm, but a storm nonetheless.

"Well," she said and clapped her hands once. "I don't know about you, but I'm wiped. A nap sounds good. Whattaya think?"

Bradley nodded.

"Great." Samm stood and took a step toward the other bed.

"Samm…?" Bradley asked in a tiny voice.

Samm turned.

"Will you lay here with me?"

"Sure."

* * *

Dan slid the deck door open, entered the kitchen, slowly closed the door, and leaned back against the glass. He wasn't sure what to do. Everything had come unraveled. All his plans, all his hopes. He knew Rosalie was pissed and was avoiding him. Samm seemed angry, too. Maybe they had a right to be mad. And Bradley? Did she blame him? What should he say? He felt terrible. Knowing the dog was dead was bad enough, but the *way* it had died… horrible. Why did Bradley have to be the one to discover the remains? It wasn't fair.

He should have brought the dog inside. If he had only done that then everything would be fine. *But, would it really?*

He needed something to do besides feel sorry for himself, so he went to the fridge and fumbled about looking for salad fixings. *I know we brought a bunch of veggies,* he thought as he shoved aside a bottle of Coke and a gallon of milk and rummaged through the plastic drawers. He finally found them, still in the plastic supermarket bag, on the bottom shelf, shoved way in the back.

It's not my fault the fucking dog died!

He emptied the shopping bag onto the counter. A head of lettuce rolled out followed by a package of shredded carrots, three tomatoes, an onion, and a green pepper. Dan looked at the produce. *Not much of a salad,* he thought. *Not much of a Dad, either.*

Was that his fault? *No. I'm trying my best.* Oh, but Rosalie hated that word, didn't she? He heard her voice in his head saying, *You need to stop trying and start doing.* Doing? *I did something. I brought us up here.* He knew what she'd say to that. *And how's that going so far? Hmm? Black mold. Malaria. Dead dogs.*

He ripped open the lettuce, slammed it into the sink, and turned on the cold faucet. While the water ran, he tore through the cabinets until he found a large, plastic bowl. Then he turned off the water and began ripping the lettuce into pieces and dropping them into the bowl.

Rosalie would complain that he had only bought iceberg lettuce. *It's basically just water, you know. You should have bought the mixed greens.* Well, she could have done the shopping, right? Oh no, she might have seen someone she knew. How embarrassing. *Oh, hi there! Oh, you heard about that did you? Well, only temporary. You know how it is.*

Like he had control over the *economy.* Or had any influence on decisions his *bosses* made. He was just a tiny cog in a giant, corporate machine. He was lucky to still have a job, for fuck's sake!

Finished with the lettuce, he scooped up the tomatoes and washed them under cold water. He ripped open the drawers. *Where are the goddamn knives?* Of course, they were in the last drawer he opened. He grabbed a cutting knife entirely too big for the job. The remaining silverware clanged as he shoved the drawer closed.

What was he supposed to do? Quit? Walk out in protest? Sure, it had been years since his last review, and maybe he should have spoken up. But, he figured they'd notice his dedication eventually and reward him. *Squeaky wheel gets the grease, Dan!* Not always, Rosalie. Sometimes the squeaky wheel gets fired.

He began chopping the tomatoes. Not into slices, Bradley didn't like the slices, she liked wedges. God forbid she try something a little different. The knife wasn't very sharp. He had to press down and pull to get it to cut properly. It made a dull thunk each time it hit the counter. *How was I supposed to know the dog would be eaten for crying out loud?*

Chop, chop, chop.

Now, the whole weekend is ruined because of that stupid mutt.

Chop, chop.

Might as well go home right now.

Cho— Slice!

"Oww!"

Lost in his thoughts, his fingers has gotten too close to the knife and he sliced right down his thumb.

Goddamn—stupid!

Blood dripped onto the counter and the tomato. He went to the sink and put his hand under the cold water watching the blood go down the drain.

"Perfect," he said to the empty room.

* * *

At dinner, it was decided to scrap the original itinerary and leave first thing in the morning. Samm could tell Dad was disappointed, but he agreed it was probably for the best. Rosalie, however, wasn't content with the decision. She strongly suggested that they leave right after dinner, but Dad didn't think it was safe to drive down the mountain roads in the dark. There were no streetlights.

While she and Dad were debating the pros and cons of leaving at night, Bradley whispered to Samm, "What about the bugs? The bugs that come out at night?"

Samm had no answer for that.

Dinner was grilled cheese (Bradley's favorite) and salad (minus the bloody tomato). Bradley was not herself at all. Samm had been elected chef and she had prepared the sandwiches exactly the way Bradley liked it—one piece of cheese, no crusts, cut diagonally. Bradley dutifully cleared her plate, but she barely said a word during the entire meal. Samm wondered if this kind of reaction was normal.

Dad had barely touched his food. Samm watched as he distractedly pushed the lettuce about his plate. He put his fork down and lifted the bandage on his thumb to inspect the wound.

"Does it hurt, Dad?" she asked.

"Kills."

Rosalie finished chewing and said, "You probably need stitches. It's a deep cut."

"I don't need stitches."

In her mind, Samm pictured a pot of water on a stove. And someone had just turned on the burner.

"The trash can in the bathroom is full of bloody paper-towels," she said, trying to release some tension. "Whoever cleans up this place after we leave will think we murdered someone."

"That's not funny, Samantha," Rosalie said. She plunged her fork into a piece of tomato. "Anyway," she began.

The pot of water in Samm's mind was bubbling heavily.

Rosalie held the fork, sallow red tomato juice dripping, over the plate. "If we leave tonight, we can get to the emergency room and have a *doctor* decide if you need stitches." She chomped the tomato from the fork.

The lid on the pot started banging.

"Dammit, Rosalie."

The water boiled over.

Dad slapped his non-injured hand on the table. Samm saw Bradley jump. "You just can't let it go, can you?"

"Let what go, Dan?"

Dad sat straighter in his chair and inhaled deeply through his nose, his mouth a thin black slit. He stared down at the table until, finally, he said, "God forbid I make a correct decision around here. I told you why it's a bad idea to drive down the mountain at night. There's no lights. It's a dirt path, for Christ's sake. And Samm's car could easily hit something and break down. Then what? How much would that cost to get a tow truck to bring her silly car home?"

Rosalie glared at Dad. "Maybe we shouldn't have come up here, then."

Dad slapped both hands down on the table, and Samm saw his eyes light up in pain. She looked at Bradley and saw terror in her eyes.

"Maybe so. But we can't change that, can we? Can't change the past, Rosalie. No matter how bad *you* want to. Or how many times you bring it up. We're here. I don't like it any more than you do. Do you think I want to spend another night with you?"

There it is. Samm stood and grasped Bradley's hand. "Come on, Brad. Let's go upstairs."

* * *

Bradley took her big sister's hand and walked with her. They left the kitchen area and climbed the stairs to the loft, but she didn't think they would be far enough away. Even with the door closed, they'd still be able to hear Mom and Dad fighting. Why did they have to fight so much?

She remembered how happy and excited she had been yesterday when she had run up these stairs. Now, she hated them. She hated the stairs, the house, and the mountain. She just wanted to be home, in her own bed, in her own room. She wanted everyone to be happy and not fighting.

They lay down on Samm's bed. Bradley folded her hands over her belly and looked up at the ceiling.

"It'll be okay, Squirt," Samm said, patting her on the leg.

No, it won't, she thought. Samm wasn't lying, but she wasn't fibbing this time, either. She was doing something else. Once, another time when her parents were yelling at each other, Bradley heard Mom say, "Stop just telling me what I want to hear!" That's what Samm was doing. *Telling me what I want to hear.* She knew it wasn't true. It wasn't going to be okay.

Bradley wasn't mad at Samm. *She's just trying to make me feel better.* In all the world, Bradley knew that her sister was the only person who would always be there to make her feel better. She was sure that when they did get home tomorrow, everything in her life was going to be very different. *At least Samm will be there.*

* * *

For a few minutes it seemed as if the fight had ended, but Samm knew that they were simply between rounds. As soon as Mom and Dad figured the kids were out of earshot, they'd start right up again. She was right.

Dad was first this time: "If you're so goddamned miserable why don't you leave now. Go! I don't care!"

Mom: "You don't think I will? Coming up here at the last minute was a dumb idea in the first place!"

Dad: "Well, you didn't even try to come up with a better one."

Mom: "I told you I'm done trying. You've had your chance. Too many of them. You know what? I am gonna leave. I'm going home tonight, and I'm packing your shit up. Or I'm throwing it out! You bring the girls home tomorrow and then you leave."

Stomping footsteps into the master bedroom. Samm heard the sound of one of the kitchen chairs dragged and then the unmistakable sigh as Dad fell into the seat.

Dad: "Rosalie, I swear to God, if you—"

Footsteps again, this time from the bedroom back to the kitchen.

Mom: "What? Go ahead. What are you gonna say?"

A pause. Then—

Dad: "Nothing."

Mom: "Thought so."

The front door pulled open and slammed shut.

Bradley sat up. "She can't leave at night."

Samm moved across the room and looked out of the round window. Bradley quickly joined her. "It's night, Samm. The bugs come out at night."

Samm looked down at her sister for a moment. Then she looked back out of the window. She saw her mother storm across the lawn, her travel bag hung from one shoulder, toward the parked cars. Although from this angle she couldn't see her mom's face, Samm knew exactly the expression upon it. She'd seen it a thousand times. She also knew that Mom would be muttering under her breath. She could almost hear it.

The girls watched as Rosalie went directly to the Explorer and tried to open the driver's side door. It must have been locked because she went around the front and tried the passenger door. Also locked. She waved her hand a couple of times to shoo away mosquitoes. The back doors were locked too. Rosalie rummaged violently through her purse. She obviously did not have the keys. She kicked the Ford in frustration. She turned back toward the house. Samm wondered what she'd do next. Rosalie waved her hands in front of her face again. It seemed that the mosquitoes were even worse than the night before.

A giant moth alighted on the window directly in front of Samm and fluttered its wide white wings. She jerked back involuntarily. She could hear the *flup-flup-flup* sound of the wings.

Bradley slapped her palm on the glass. "Go away!"

The moth flew away, and Samm looked back down at Rosalie. She was waving her arms like a crazy person; bugs—mosquitoes, moths, gnats—surrounded her. Samm had never seen so many insects at one time. It was unreal.

"Samm?" Bradley asked. "What's happening?"

Samm couldn't answer. She had no words. She couldn't look away from what she was seeing. Rosalie was slapping herself in the head, on her arms, her chest, trying to get rid of the bugs. No matter how many she slapped away, more kept appearing. Where were they coming from?

Bradley grabbed Samm's shoulder and shook it. "Why doesn't she come back *inside?*"

Maybe Rosalie heard her, or maybe she had the same thought, whatever the reason she took a step toward the house. More bugs descended upon her. There were so many black things swirling about—it looked like Samm's mom was wearing a black cloak. She was waving her purse around like a baseball bat in a vain attempt to drive the invading insects away. Samm got a brief glimpse of her face. It was completely covered with black bugs. Her eyes were closed. She took another couple of steps, but in the wrong direction. She was heading *away* from the house.

Finally, Samm snapped out of her paralysis. She fumbled at the window, trying to find the release. Once she found it, she shoved the window open.

"Mom! No! The other way!"

Bradley thrust her head next to Samm's. "Mommy! Come inside!"

Still more bugs came, seemingly from everywhere. Mom fell to her knees. Samm leapt off the bed and jumped down the stairs.

"Dad!" she yelled as she got to the front door.

He came out of the kitchen. He looked like he had been crying. "What?"

"Mom needs help!"

Samm yanked the front door open. What she saw froze her in her tracks.

Mom hadn't made it any closer. She was on her hands and knees near the tree line. There was no part of her not covered with bugs. She convulsed, completely enshrouded by a shimmering, throbbing dark mass of what looked to Samm like chunky peanut-butter, only black. Flying insects surrounded her, darting towards and away from the other bugs, the ones that were feeding. Samm realized—that's what they were doing. The bugs were eating her.

Rosalie was still trying to wave the bugs away, but her movements were much smaller and weaker. She pushed both hands down into the dirt and opened her mouth. Samm thought she was going to scream, but instead she vomited. Chunks of bugs, nasty black goo, blood and bile spewed from her mouth and splashed onto the ground.

Then she screamed.

* * *

"Oh my God!" Dan yelled. He grabbed Samm by the shoulders and pushed her back in the house. "Stay inside!" Then he ran out to Rosalie, slamming the door behind him.

The bugs were everywhere. It was like running through a fog of needles. He could feel them hitting his face and head as he ran.

In seconds, his hands and arms were covered, like he was wearing black gloves up to his biceps. Mosquitoes, gnats, and other tiny flying pests surrounded him. They flew into his mouth, his nose. He felt them in his ears. He could hear the buzzing of their tiny wings. He stopped and waved his arms as much as he could, but it changed nothing.

There were too many. Just too many.

He felt a tickling on his ankles and looked down. Thousands of ants were emerging from the dirt and crawling up onto his legs. He swatted some off, but still more appeared. The ground looked like it was exhaling insects. Ants and crickets and beetles. Long, worm-like centipedes.

A strange sensation pierced his left hand. He looked and saw that the bugs had burrowed *into* his hand through the open wound in his thumb. He could feel them crawling and squirming *inside* him. He could see the bulges in his skin as they wriggled through his wrist and up his arm.

A wave of flying bugs hit him from behind, strong enough to knock him over. He fell and rolled onto his back. He opened his mouth to yell. *Girls! Stay inside!* Before he could speak, a piston of flying insects rammed itself down his throat. He gagged and choked, breath cut off by the bugs invading his lungs.

Insects crawling all over his face, his scalp, into his ears, up his nose and down his throat, Dan flipped onto his belly and attempted to crawl back towards the cabin, to his daughters, but the bugs, the bugs were too much. He rolled over and looked up at the house. A whirlwind of flying insects surrounded it, like a black tornado just spinning around the cabin. It was the last thing he saw as the bugs began to eat his eyes.

* * *

WhatdoIdoWhatdoIdoWhatdoIdo?

Samm opened then immediately slammed the front door. There was nothing she could do for her parents. *Don't freak out.*

Stay calm. Think. Could the bugs get in here? No idea. The note! The note said get inside by nightfall. Was that enough? Was simply being inside the house really enough protection? *How is that possible? Had this happened before? Did someone know this would happen?*

"Saammmmmm!"

Bradley! Had she seen everything? *Oh my God.* She was at the top of the steps. Samm twisted the deadbolt on the front door—*Why bother? Would a locked door keep the insects out?*—and darted up the steps two at a time. She grabbed her sister and hugged her close. Bradley clung to her.

"Are you hurt?"

Bradley shook her head. Samm spun her around, looking all over for insects of any kind.

"The bugs," Bradley said. "The bugs got Mom and Dad."

"I know." Samm spun Bradley back around to face her. She combed her fingers through Bradley's hair, making sure there were no nasty things crawling around her scalp.

"Will the bugs eat us, too?"

Samm looked her sister in the eye. "No."

She walked Bradley down to the kitchen and had her sit at the table. She checked the sliding doors and the kitchen window to make sure they were closed tight. She did the same in the master bedroom and the den.

She sat with Bradley at the table. Her hands were shaking, and she was exhausted.

"Don't worry, Brad. We just have to wait until tomorrow. Once the sun comes up, we'll leave and go to the, I don't know, the police?"

Bradley nodded, but Samm wasn't sure if she believed her. Samm wasn't sure if she believed herself either.

* * *

Bradley knew she was dreaming. She just knew it. Because there was no way Mom and Dad were gone. (She didn't want to use that awful d-word that rhymes with red.) That kind of thing simply didn't happen. So, even though everything seemed real—

the things she touched, the things she heard, the things she saw—it was a dream. Not like the dreams she usually had. Those were usually colorful and fun. This was a nightmare. A horrible nightmare, but very soon, she would wake up.

Where would she wake up? *Am I really even in Vermont?* How long was this dream? Did she dream this whole trip? *Am I going to wake up at home? In my own bed? In my own room?* The more she thought about it, the more she was sure that a person could have a dream like this. A dream that lasted a few days. Of course it was possible. Had to be. Because what she saw outside? *That* was *im*possible. Bugs can't do that. No way.

She thought about the little ladybug. It was probably upstairs right now looking for her. A cute little, red ladybug would never bite. *I don't even think they have teeth*, she thought. Anyway, bugs eat leaves and grass. She thought she had seen something on TV once that said bugs eat grass. Well, she knew they didn't eat people. Especially Mommies and Daddies. Nosireebob.

Next to her Samm was resting in the blue chair, with her head in her arms. *Was Samm dreaming inside of my dream? That would be weird.* Bradley looked out of the glass doors at the spot where the dog had been sitting. It made her happy to know that, since this was all a dream, the dog wasn't dea—gone. She folded her hands in front of her. *I just need to wait until I wake up.* She could hear Samm's sleepy breaths beside her.

She felt something on her hand. She looked down. The ladybug. It had flown downstairs and found her.

A large *thunk* startled her, and she jerked in the chair. The ladybug flew away. A huge beetle, the size of a pigeon, had hit the door. It was walking up the glass. Bradley could see its belly. Another bug landed on the door with a *thunk*. This one was different. It looked like a giant mosquito. She could see more insects flying in the yard now. Also, there was a new sound outside. It was a strange mix of buzzing and humming. And it was getting louder.

Even though it was a dream, Bradley was scared. Her heart was beating like crazy. The sound was getting so loud it hurt her ears. More and more bugs were flying around outside. It was hard to see the trees. Some hit the windows and bounced off and some stuck, walking up and down, their wings flapping.

She reached over and shook Samm's arm until her sister snapped her head up.

"I'm here! What's up?" Samm looked about with a confused look.

Bradley calmly pointed out the window. "The dream's getting worse."

* * *

Can't believe I fell asleep! Samm woke up foggy, but the sight outside the glass doors slapped her right back to reality.

Outside, the air was so thick with flying insects she couldn't see the yard anymore. *Where can they all be coming from?* was her first thought. Then: *Can they get in?* It didn't look like it. She didn't see anything flying about in the house. *Not yet anyway.*

What about Bradley? Samm looked down at her sister. She seemed unusually calm. What was it she had said? Something about a dream.

"Brad, don't worry. They can't get in. We're safe as long as we stay inside."

Bradley wouldn't look at her. She remained focused on the bugs outside. "I know. It's only a bad dream anyway."

"It is?"

"Yes. It has to be."

"Umm, right. Okay, but I still want to check all the windows and doors. Would that be okay with you? Can you sit right here while I do that?"

Samm waited as Bradley thought this over. Finally, she said, "Yes. I'll wait."

"Good." Samm stood up and kissed Bradley on top of her head.

"Samm?"

"Yeah?"

"You should start upstairs. The window by my bed. It's open."

* * *

"Oh, shit!"

Samm leapt up, sprinted from the kitchen area, and scrambled up the stairs to the loft. She stopped at the closed door, grabbed the knob with one hand, and put her other hand up against the door as if feeling for heat during a housefire. She leaned in. There was a strange sibilation coming from the other room. She looked down at her feet. A chain of big, black carpenter ants was marching out from under the door. They began crawling over Samm's sneakers and up her legs. She slapped at them, kicked and stomped on the floor.

Still looking down at the ants, Samm turned the knob and opened the door.

* * *

Boom! Boom! Boom! The bugs outside started slamming into the glass harder and harder.

Bradley screamed.

Bigger and bigger bugs were bashing against the glass door.

Upstairs, Samm yelled. "No. No. NO!"

There was a loud crash from the loft and Samm cried out in pain.

Bradley turned in her chair.

Bugs spewed from the loft. Hundreds. Thousands. Flying down the stairs. Scuttling down the railings. Bradley could hear their legs, their wings, their teeth. The noise was so loud.

Samm jumped down the stairs—bursting through all the bugs. She lost her balance and slammed into the front door and fell to her knees, got up quickly, limped to Bradley and grabbed her arm.

"Come on!"

The bugs were everywhere.

Samm dragged Bradley into the bathroom and slammed the door. She grabbed a towel and stuffed it in the crack between the floor and the door. Then she picked up Bradley and dropped her in the tub, covering her with her body.

Bradley grabbed her sister. Held onto her so tight. She wanted this dream to stop. She wanted the noise to stop. For everything to stop. She screamed with all her might:

"MAKEITSTOP!MAKEITSTOP!MAKEITSTOP!MAKEI TSTOP!MAKEITSTOP!"

* * *

The mud-spattered Ford F-150 rolled through the early morning sunshine, passing the Explorer and VW Bug. The old pickup slowed to a stop, and the engine quit with a brutal shudder. The magnetic sign on the driver's side—*McCormick Realty & Rentals: Over 150 Years of Service!*—slipped down as Gerri McCormick pushed the door open and slowly climbed from the cab. She was pushing sixty years old and disliked climbing in and out of the big truck, but nothing else was as reliable when it came to traversing these dirt roads. You never knew what kind of terrain you'd be dealing with going up the mountain. *Can't believe that little Bug actually made it up here.* After snapping on a pair of latex gloves and making sure she had all the correct paperwork and a pen, she slammed the heavy door shut and straightened the McCormick Realty sign. *Well, let's get this over with.*

The front of the house looked good. No broken windows or missing shingles. She clicked her pen (also printed with the *McCormick Realty & Rentals* logo—there was still a box of two hundred pens in her office) and quickly scribbled a notation on the exit questionnaire. There had been a string of renters in the nineties that had smashed the glass and caused other kinds of cosmetic damage. But nothing of that sort had occurred since she had switched the marketing strategy back to focus on families instead of young, rowdy college kids. The most damage in recent memory was the fire of '02. She would never forget the stench. Horrid. *What were those people thinking?* The fire had only succeeded in burning enough of the house that rebuilding was the only option. That hadn't been cheap.

She checked underneath the renter's vehicles. Clear. All car doors were locked. She peered through the windows to check the ignitions for keys. She saw none. She checked the proper boxes on her forms. The yellowed grass was disturbed in a few areas, but she didn't see any detritus. It was rare to find that kind of evidence in the front, but she always checked. Better safe than sorry.

As she was finishing her inspection of the front, she heard the other trucks approaching. The big white service van was first, driven by Carl, her oldest boy. The flatbed tow truck followed with the new guy at the wheel. *What's his name? Steve? No, Scott.* He was Carl's wife's cousin, so Gerri figured he came from trustworthy folk, but she made a mental note to keep quiet about the finer details of the rental business for now. She knew Carl would do the same.

The side door of the van slid open with an unpleasant screech and Carl popped his head out, waiting for instructions.

Gerri waved her arm in the general direction of the house. "All right, then, don't just stare at me like you've never done this before. Give the inside a look-see and then start cleanin' up."

"Yes, ma'am." Carl jumped down from the van and went toward the front door.

"Don' touch anything in there without gloves!"

"Yes, ma'am," Carl said, pulling on the extra-large latex gloves she had to order special, just for him.

Steve—Scott!—had pulled the flatbed to the opposite side of the yard. Its engine grumbled like a black bear.

"You too, Stee—, er, Scott. We need both these vehicles outta here. Chop, chop."

As the boys began the grunt work, Gerri steeled herself for the backyard. The backyard was always the worst.

* * *

She noticed the holes in the roof immediately. Three round punctures, each the size of a manhole cover. There were also several long gouges that had scraped off some roofing tiles. The holes would need to be repaired, but it didn't look like the entire roof would need to be replaced. That was good news. Money was tight. She jotted down the pertinent information on the forms.

Gerri always worried about the deck, but this time it was clean. The heaviest clean-ups were generally on or around the deck. It made sense. Renters always wanted to eat outdoors. They lost track of time. The sun went down…

She turned and looked around the grass at the tree line. That was another popular area. They often tried to run. *Yep, I knew it.* Something was fluttering in the breeze near the woods. It was a tangle of thin, blond hair caught in the tall grass. *The little girl.* She recalled a blonde youngster when the family had picked up the house key at her office. The girl was probably eight or ten years old. Gerri removed a large ziplock storage bag from her coat pocket. Her knees popped as she squatted down to retrieve the hairs.

Sometimes Gerri felt small pangs of guilt when she saw this kind of chaff. She was a mother after all, and it could sting to consider what happened here during the Annual, but she was generally well-practiced at keeping those thoughts at bay. She had to be. Yet, today, the image of the little blonde girl stuck with her. She ran her fingers through the grass, making sure she hadn't missed anything, then she stood and took one step closer to the woods.

She stared off into the trees, unconsciously clicking the pen in her right hand. The tinny *click-click-click* of the pen seemed very loud because there were no other sounds. No birds tweeting or animals scurrying about. It was always this way directly after the Annual. The animals and birds would come back in a few days. They always did.

* * *

It was stuffy inside the house. Gerri closed the sliding glass door behind her. Carl was just getting into his plastic hazmat suit. A six-gallon metal backpack power sprayer sat on the floor. Next to it lay the coiled hose and long, brass wand with adjustable spray tip. Top of the line equipment.

"There was one in the bathroom, Ma. Already bagged and tagged." She handed him the baggie with the blonde hairs.

"Really? Inside?" she asked.

Carl folded the baggie and placed it in his pocket.

"Yeah. The screen had been knocked out in the loft window."

"Hmm." Gerri made another note on the forms. *How'd I miss that?* It was unusual to find a renter indoors.

Carl pulled the hood tight and held up his gas mask.

"You better get outside."

"In a minute."

The image of the little girl flashed through her head again. *Am I getting too old for this work?* Compartmentalizing her emotions had never been this difficult. She understood the necessity for the Annual. Although she had only been a child, Gerri could still remember what had happened the year the town had taken a chance and let the Annual date come and go without an observance. Today, everyone who had been a part of that fateful decision was long gone, but there were still a few who remembered what had followed. For Gerri, the most vivid memories were auditory. The buzzing. And screaming.

The Annual had never been skipped again. *It's only once a year,* Gerri told herself every time. *That's not so bad, is it? In the grand scheme of things? One family a year.* At least she gave them a warning. Deep down she knew it wasn't enough, but it helped her sleep at night. Most nights.

Gerri centered the note on the kitchen table. She placed the saltshaker on top of it so it wouldn't blow away.

About the Author

Mike Sullivan has always loved telling stories. He started writing short scripts for a film class and turned that love of film into a profession. After years of editing documentary films, reading works of others, and raising a family, Mike started writing stories. They were dark and twisted, luckily his wife and daughter found them entertaining. His menagerie of dogs and cats were much more severe critics. When Mike isn't writing or working or editing films, he is chasing down the plot for his next new story. Find Mike online at www.sullivanedit.com.

IF YOU LIKED...

If you liked *Stories We Tell After Midnight, Volume 2,* you might also enjoy:

Stories We Tell After Midnight, Volume 1
Coppice & Brake